Further from the the Madding Crowd

by

Nick Thorne

THE CHOIR PRESS

First published in the United Kingdom in 2024 by
The Choir Press

ISBN 978-1-78963-458-7

To Helen, Adam and Jessica

Part One

Chapter One

'Crikey Moses!' exclaimed Joshua Latham, as the sheep wandered aimlessly across the road in front of his car. He stabbed the brake pedal and spun the wheel right then left, the car's ABS preventing a potentially catastrophic skid on the wet road. He glanced at the sat nav. It showed just under ten miles to reach Bramton. Light snow flitted in the headlights and a thin covering had started to cover the verges. It was the first such fall of the winter and, not for the first time, the local gritting teams had been caught unawares.

Joshua looked at the clock on the dashboard. Six-thirty. But it had been dark for seemingly ages. Within a few more miles the snow started to cover the road, the car tracks compressing the snow to ice. This bit of civilisation was slowly succumbing. He badly wanted to make Bramton before the weather completely closed in, and he drove on with a light touch on the pedals and steering. The road was edged with unforgiving drystone walls. The last thing he needed right now was an accident in his car.

His car. OK, it was a company car, but Joshua thought of it as his own, and took pride in it. He thought of Holroyd. His boss would do his absolute crust if another car in the fleet, especially a new one like this one, got damaged.

At last he started the long descent into Bramton. He could see the glimmer of street lighting ahead. The sat nav indicating he was closing in on The Crown Hotel where he'd booked his reservation. Holroyd having pulled rank and pinched his original reservation at The Oakland, Joshua had had to scout around for an alternative, and that hadn't been easy. Bramton, despite its ambitions as a tourist destination, and pretensions as a conference centre and all-round thriving community, clearly wasn't over endowed with hotels. Joshua had almost had to resort to an Airbnb.

The snow in the town was lighter but was still settling on the roads and pavements. Before long, a sign over the front of a large imposing building was just visible through the snow. The feeble light cast on it by one strip light, others around it having apparently failed, announced "The Crown". The rest of the large stone building, stretched to three full floors, and what looked like a fourth floor peeking out of some dormer windows in the roof, was all in darkness. The place did not look particularly inviting, and Joshua even wondered if it was actually open. He could just make out a sign indicating a car park around the back of the building and he drove off in that direction. Rounding the building, he descended a short slope and pulled up in front of a low, stone wall. He had arrived, safe at last, the anticipated three-hour drive from Bristol having been stretched to a fraught four-and-a-half-hour one by the deteriorating weather.

He checked the booking on his phone. Yep. The place is right. It was the right date. Joshua turned the engine off. Then there was a crunch, and the air bags detonated. He hadn't heard the approach of the car behind, the snow seeming to deaden all sound. He'd barely registered its headlights before it shunted into the back of his own. There was a sickening noise of crumpling metal and the tinkling of broken glass.

'Jesus Christ!' he shouted out loud. He quickly got out of his car and surveyed the scene. His car had been rammed from the rear by another vehicle, and shunted forwards into the wall. The incoming vehicle that had caused the damage still lay behind Joshua's car, mute but for the quiet hiss of escaping steam. 'Jesus Christ!' he said again, mainly as a reflex, whilst he assessed the situation and otherwise lost for words.

'What the bloody hell do you think you're doing?' was the best he could muster, the comment directed as much at the newly arrived car as the occupant.

'Oh, God! I'm ever so sorry. What a mess! Your car... Are you OK?'

The well-modulated tones came from of a woman emerging from the other car. Whether she had heard his oath or not, she obviously felt some considerable guilt at having used Joshua's rather large and expensive car as a buffer. She gushed her explanation.

'It was icy on the slope down to the car park. I just touched the brakes and slid. I am dreadfully sorry. I hope I haven't done too much damage.'

For reasons Joshua was later not able to be totally sure about, he paused for breath. He had been about to launch into a tirade against the other driver when he suddenly stopped himself. The driver had made what was tantamount to an admission of guilt, even if the circumstances of the accident hadn't made it obvious. She was clearly, profusely apologetic, which mollified Joshua somewhat. Of greater subtlety perhaps was the fact that the other driver was a woman. Joshua was old school. Feminism had largely passed him by. He knew he couldn't speak to a woman in these circumstances, the way he might do with, for example, a burly male lorry driver. He couldn't help it. And this woman was no ordinary woman. Joshua was struck by the fact that she was clearly quite attractive. Not that Joshua knew much about fashion, but he thought she could even be catwalk material. In the dim lighting that illuminated the crash scene, Joshua looked at her fresh face and reckoned she must be around mid- twenties, with long, dark, slightly wavy hair. In this light he couldn't be sure of the exact colour. Her cheeks were dimpled, and her eyes sparkled. She was wearing a tight-fitting, dark roll neck sweater, and jeans tucked into her knee-length, tan leather boots. Joshua's mouth opened and closed, then opened again.

'It's OK,' he heard himself say. 'Are you OK?'

'Yes, I'm fine. Gosh! I really do seem to have made a bit of a mess. What are we going to do? Are you staying at the hotel?'

'Yes,' said Joshua. 'At least I hope I am. I've only just got here myself. The place looks closed.'

There was a short, awkward silence as the two surveyed the scene. Joshua finally said, 'Perhaps we should try to reverse your car up a bit. It might need a bit of a push to get it going over the icy bit.' The exercise seemed a little futile as Joshua suspected his car wouldn't be driveable. He just wanted to see the extent of the damage, such as was possible in the evening gloom.

'I'll just see if there's someone inside who can help,' said the woman. 'I'll be back in a minute.'

Joshua shrugged and looked on sceptically as the woman disappeared around the side of the hotel. He had been quite prepared to give the car a push himself. He looked at his own poor car. Three weeks he'd had the thing! Holroyd would go into orbit. His boss's new policy of self-insurance for the company fleet, designed to cut costs, was now looking decidedly misguided. The nearside headlight had smashed, and the whole front wing, no match for the local gritstone, had been pushed back onto the wheel. The rear of the car didn't look too bad. Some of the taillights had broken, but Joshua knew that tomorrow's daylight would reveal more bodywork damage. The damage to the front of the woman's car looked worse. With the age of the vehicle, probably a write off, he thought to himself.

Joshua sighed. This whole job was going wrong. Bramton wasn't even his area, but in a small firm, you had to be flexible. With Peter Kelly off sick – a suspected heart attack they said – Joshua had been 'volunteered'. There was young Meredith, of course. He'd be OK in a support role, but too inexperienced to take on a job like Walklate's. So Holroyd had picked him. Joshua hadn't minded too much at first. He had no particular ties and quite enjoyed the variety. But then had come Friday's call. Holroyd, no less, was coming himself. Just for the presentation, he'd told Joshua, to give the thing more "presence". Joshua knew from that moment that Holroyd's involvement would be far more than that though. The bloody man would take over. If Holroyd wanted to run the damned assignment himself, then why did he rope Joshua into it in the first place? Didn't he trust him? Admittedly the Walklate consultancy was potentially lucrative. A lot hinged on tomorrow's presentations, but surely there was no need for this kind of heavy-handed approach? Consultancy always came in fits and starts. It was the nature of the beast. And to cap it all, Holroyd had then pinched Joshua's reservation, the last room available at the clearly more prestigious Oakland Hotel.

Joshua ruefully reflected. First the Walklate job, Holroyd's last-minute decision to muscle in on it, even his modest expectations of The Crown appearing optimistic and now, the tin hat on it all, his brand new car was damaged. If ever a job had disaster written all over it, this was the one.

'Crikey, Tara, what have you done?'

It was a woman's voice, but clearly not one from the same school as the first. Joshua spun round to see two figures approach. The leather-booted driver of the hatchback was now accompanied by a slightly shorter, stockier woman wearing a dress of an indeterminate dark colour, an apron, and incongruously, carpet slippers.

'Oh, you must be Mr. Latham,' said the carpet slippers, and without waiting for confirmation, 'We've got you booked in for tonight. Terrible weather, isn't it? Winter's come early. This is a right mess, isn't it?'

The questions came one after another, without pause for an answer. Joshua felt resigned.

'Yes, I'm Mr. Latham. It's OK. I'm sure we can sort this out,' and without waiting for further comment, he turned to the woman called Tara, and said, 'Your car doesn't look too bad,' by which he meant it was still driveable, at least until the engine, deprived off its coolant, seized. 'If you could just try reversing yours up a bit.'

Tara got into her car without a word and started the engine. She engaged reverse, but initially there was no movement. The front wheels spun on the thin layer of snow. Tara revved even harder. The car didn't move. The snow under the wheels packed down.

'No, no,' shouted Joshua. 'Easy does it.'

Tara wound down her car window, and Joshua said to her, 'There's a patch of ice under the wheels, and I think the bumpers are locked together somehow. Just rev the engine slowly and go easy on the clutch.'

After a couple more fruitless efforts and much wheel spin, Joshua offered to have a go. They swapped places, Joshua spinning the wheels while Tara took her turn at looking on helplessly.

'Give it a push!' shouted Joshua.

Tara leaned over precariously between the two locked vehicles, and with clear distaste etched on her face, put her hands on the grime-encrusted bonnet of her car.

At that moment, the air was treated to an electronic rendition of Mozart's 40th. Tara heard Joshua say, 'You must be bloody joking!' The ring tone continued as he tried again to separate the two cars. Suddenly, with a jolt and a cracking sound, the two bumpers separated. More glass fell. Joshua reversed the battered hatchback up the driveway and parked it on more level ground. His phone stopped ringing.

'That should do for now,' said Joshua, getting out of the car. 'Let's go inside, and we can sort out the details. We can inspect the damage better in the morning.'

'I take it, you're staying here too?' he continued, as he collected a bag from the back seat of his car.

'Yes,' said Tara. 'You could say that.'

'Looks a bit run down, doesn't it?' said Joshua, looking at the imposing stone walls of the striking building. Large old-fashioned sash windows, all in darkness, lent an air of sadness to the place. 'I hope it's more inviting inside.'

Joshua pushed open the large front door of the hotel, and the three of them went inside. The reception as such was really just a hallway. A table lamp on a sideboard was the only illumination. Old pictures, all unremarkable, decorated the cream walls. A door marked "Private" opened, and the carpet slipper-clad proprietor joined them in the hallway cum reception. Now divested of her apron she delivered another high-speed volley of non-sequiturs.

'Right, Mr. Latham. Number 5, on the first floor. Just up the stairs, second door on the right. When you've a minute, could you sign the book please? Bathroom's opposite. I've put the gas fire on.'

Joshua felt the need to interrupt the flow before he drowned. 'Thank you,' he said. 'Is it possible to get something to eat?'

He could feel himself anticipating the answer with the question barely out of his mouth. Looking around, the frosted glass door marked "Dining Room" showed an ominous darkness beyond. This really wasn't going to plan. The next barrage confirmed his prognosis.

'Ooh, I'm sorry, we don't do meals on Sunday nights. Never have, really. My name's Rose by the way. You could try the chippy on the Market Square. I think he'll be open in an hour or so. Or there's an Indian on Silver Street. Ring the bell if you need anything. I've left your key in your room. There's a front door key on it too, but I put the bolt across about 11.30. If you're after that, you'll have to ring the bell… the one on the outside, that is. Oh, and breakfast's 7.30 to 8.30.'

There was a slight, but discernible pause for breath as Rose turned to Tara.

'Now Tara, do you want a hand unloading that car? Have you sorted it? I've made up the bed in number 12. Do you remember that one? I hope it's big enough for all your stuff. It's the one Mr. Douglas always used for situations like this.'

'Rose!' Tara interrupted. A faint, benign smile crossed Tara's lips. 'Rose, I'm sure 12 will be fine. I'll leave the unpacking for a bit. I've got some details to exchange with Mr. Latham. Now, what I could really die for is a nice cup of tea. Any chance? And I'm sure Mr. Latham would like one too.'

Rose agreed and sped back towards the door marked "Private".

Joshua noted the adroitness with which Tara had dealt with the verbal whirlwind. This Tara had obviously stayed here before. She must be some sort of regular. Each to their own he supposed. He remembered describing the place to her as a bit run down and felt a slight sense of guilt. Perhaps he'd maligned one of her favourite haunts. At least it was cheap, he thought, as he spied the tariffs. Holroyd would be pleased at that at least.

'I'm Tara Beaumont-Smith, by the way,' said Tara. Joshua introduced himself, somewhat academically, and they shook hands.

'Sorry we had to bump into one another quite so spectacularly,' said Joshua. He cleared his throat. 'I think perhaps we need to exchange some insurance details.'

For the second time in ten minutes, Mozart's 40th issued forth from Joshua's inside jacket pocket. 'Excuse me a minute. I'd better just take this call.' He fumbled in his pocket for his phone. He looked at the display and frowned. Joshua stabbed a finger at the phone.

'Joshua Latham,' he said.

'Latham! Where the hell have you been? I've been trying to get hold of you for ages.'

'Sorry Stuart, the signal over the tops was pretty poor—'

'Well never mind that now,' Holroyd interrupted. 'Where are you now?'

'I'm just checking in at the hotel,' said Joshua.

'Good,' said Holroyd. 'You obviously got in somewhere.'

'Yeah. The Crown, in Bramton,' said Joshua, with the slightly deflating feeling that Stuart Holroyd didn't really care.

'Right. Anyway, come over and join Meredith and me for dinner. I want to run through the programme for tomorrow. We're at The Oakland. You know where that is?'

'Yes,' said Joshua. Career prospects prevented him adding, 'Only too well, matey. It was originally my hotel booking, don't forget. I did it online. You took it over when you invited yourself on this escapade. Now instead, I'm having to make do in this place.'

'Good. See you in ten minutes.' Holroyd's voice snapped Joshua out of his brief reverie. Before he could say, 'Make it fifteen,' Holroyd had hung up.

'Goodbye,' said Joshua to the dialling tone. Even if he'd had the time to tell Holroyd about his car, he'd decided that now was not the moment. Holroyd always tended to be a bit abrupt. Except in front of clients, of course. It was as if he saved all his tact, patience and diplomacy for when he was in front of a customer. All well and good, but behind the scenes, Joshua knew the signs. At times like these, just agree with the man.

At that moment, Rose returned with a tray of tea. 'I'll just pop it in the front lounge, Tara,' she said. As Rose left, Tara and Joshua sat in the lounge.

'I'm really so sorry, Mr. Latham,' said Tara again, 'I've really caused you a lot of bother, haven't I?'

'It's Joshua, by the way. Don't worry about it. These things happen,' he said. 'I've got to go out shortly, but I'm sure I'll get hold of a taxi.'

In better lighting, he was once more struck by her looks. He almost had to will himself to look away to ensure he didn't stare. He felt self-conscious, almost embarrassed. What was happening to him? Was the young woman aware of his awkwardness? If she was, she didn't show it. Perhaps she was used to leaving a trail of wide-eyed, gauche-looking stares. It really had been a long time since a woman had had this effect on him.

'Now then,' said Tara, 'what do we have to do?'

'Just swap names, addresses, insurers, and any details of the cars, should be enough.'

As they exchanged details, Joshua asked, 'Are you stopping long?'

'Hopefully,' said Tara.

'Well, I hope they put the bloody heating on for us. It's freezing in here.'

Tara made no comment.

'Thanks,' said Joshua as Tara handed him her insurance certificate. 'Now then, what's your home address?'

'It's The Crown Hotel, Bramton, I suppose,' said Tara.

'What?' said Joshua, taken aback. 'You actually live here?'

'Well, yes,' said Tara. 'As a matter of fact, I own it.'

Chapter Two

'Well, where in God's name is he?' Theodore Walklate's stentorian voice bounced off the wainscoting. He paced the dining room of his house, Fallowfield Grange. A modest stone construction, built towards the end of the nineteenth century, the house was far too big for Theodore, who lived alone. He nonetheless enjoyed the atmosphere, the rural location, and the air of an old-style country squire that it instilled within him. With a cook cum housekeeper, a gardener to tend the couple of acres of ground surrounding the property, and regular visits from the cleaning lady, it was home. Set well back from the road, and some seven miles outside Bramton, Fallowfield Grange afforded Theodore the privacy and solitude that enabled him to think. Comfortable in his own company, the house was the antithesis of the hurly-burly of his daily working life, an ideal foil: a retreat. Normally only family, perhaps occasionally, the upper echelons of Walklate & Co, and very close friends were treated to a glimpse of this private abode. Tonight, Theodore was entertaining family. At least he liked to call it entertaining. The family thought it more duty. It was, in truth, a meeting, conveniently coinciding with dinner, at which they could discuss the state of the business.

He walked back and forth. He was not used to being kept waiting. He didn't like to be kept waiting, but he had in fact, grown used to it, particularly when it came to his nephew.

The dining room had a log fire burning in the large stone fireplace. The room felt alternately warm in the direct line of sight of the fire, and cold in the draughts induced by it. There was a rather ageing central heating system in Fallowfield Grange, but it was expensive to run, and Theodore rather preferred the ambience of the open fire. He'd lived at the house for over ten years now, and not only tolerated its foibles, the cast iron radiators and clanking pipework, the creaky floorboards, the heavy oak doors, the ever so slightly fusty smell of the place, but had grown positively fond of them. Up a grand wooden staircase, there were five bedrooms, and two bathrooms, all sadly underutilised.

'He won't be long,' said Marjorie Forsythe. As Andrew Forsythe's mother, and Theodore's sister, she often found herself arbitrating between the two men who, in her eyes at least, ran Walklate & Co. 'It's frightful weather out there, in case you hadn't noticed. Now just be patient. He won't be long, I'm sure.'

She wasn't sure at all. She knew her son better than anyone, and punctuality was not his strongest point. Frequently they would have family summit meetings, and frequently they would get off to a bad start as a result of Andrew being late. He seemed to be devoid, not so much of a sense of urgency, but of a complete concept of time. And such meetings were getting a bit more regular over the last six months. Gone now was the proud boast that Walklate's had made a profit every year since it had been started forty years earlier by old George Walklate.

Profitability was not a boast shouted from the rooftops, as Walklate's, like a lot of family businesses, kept their finances as private as possible. There were statutory declarations of course, but these were invariably ancient history by the time that they were published. They could also be sufficiently clouded by a good accountant such to make it difficult to establish exact performance. So Walklate's had marched on, year after year, making money, every year… until last year.

The sound of the front door of the house opening and closing could be heard, followed by a muffled, 'Hello.'

'In here, darling,' shouted Marjorie, and Andrew joined them in the dining room.

'There you are,' said Theodore, ostentatiously looking at his watch. A more junior member of the firm would have felt a far more fierce blast from the Managing Director. But Andrew, not only with family connections, but family connections actually in the same room, felt only the sarcastic aside. Theodore was a big man, over six feet tall, and broad shouldered, clean shaven with a slightly ruddy complexion that betrayed his love of both the outdoors and of fine wines. His hair was luxuriant but almost completely grey now, cut short, but with sideburns a little too long for the current fashion. Not that Theodore concerned himself much with fashion. Comfortable in practical clothes rather than fashionable ones, he was frequently to be seen, as now, in a dark brown single-breasted tweed jacket, white shirt with a brown woollen tie and similar-coloured trousers. He stood in front of the fireplace, back straight, his whole stance and facial appearance confirming the way most would describe the man: dignified. He looked at his nephew.

'Sorry, I'm late,' said Andrew. 'Terrible weather outside. It's just starting to snow again.'

Andrew, not as tall as his uncle, but certainly as wide, had a fresh face and dark, straight hair, cut short. Some of the shorter hairs near the crown of his head stuck up in the air like mini antennae. If asked he would attribute this unkempt state of his locks to the current easterly Force 5. The truth, however, was that his hair was almost always like this, even in dead calm conditions. His appearance was that of an overgrown schoolboy. Under a red woollen pullover he wore a check shirt, intentionally open at the neck, and accidentally at the waist – a common configuration for him. The buttons in between strained under the weight of enclosed stomach. Andrew had a genial manner, was always eager to please, and hated to cause offence, not that he was always aware of how others viewed him. He noted Theodore's flushed appearance. His uncle was clearly vexed.

'I'll tell Janice to bring the soup in,' Theodore said to Andrew, and left the room, banging the door closed behind him. Janice Hartle was the cook at Fallowfield Grange, and had worked miracles with good food and late arriving guests ever since Theodore had first moved in.

Theodore's voice bawled from the hall, 'Help yourself to a sherry from the side. And offer your mother a top up, too.'

Andrew did as he was bid, giving his mother an affectionate peck on the cheek as he topped up her sherry glass.

'Looks like I've done it again,' whispered Andrew to his mother.

'Oh, don't worry about him,' replied his mother. 'I swear he's getting more irritable the older he gets. And he'll be 49 next month. Just try to be agreeable, but make sure he doesn't get these consultant types to plonk the blame on your sales people.'

Marjorie had always been protective of her son. It was more her guidance, coupled with an enthusiasm that eclipsed his own, that had got Andrew through university. She had then engineered, bullied and cajoled Andrew, Theodore and anyone else who dared to stand in the way, to get Andrew his job at Walklate's. She was a big, buxom woman, with a will to match. Time had been kinder to her than to her brother. She retained much of her natural auburn hair colour, this factor alone, contrasting with Theodore's greyness, making her appear at least ten years younger than her brother. Her face was beginning to show wrinkles, but kindly ones, spreading as laughter lines from the corners of her eyes, rather than worry ones across her brow. She could be matronly, stern even, but in family related matters, always with the best of intentions. Andrew never questioned her counsel, indeed seemed rather happy that she forged his career, acting as coach and mentor.

Theodore returned and played host throughout the meal, with Janice rushing in with each course. The conversation was dominated by the prospect of the forthcoming management consultants. Theodore, his sister and his nephew were the "family board", really a board within a board, the "inner sanctum" amongst Walklate's' decision makers. Their policy on this potentially controversial issue needed to be uniform. They had to present a united front before the rest of the company's executive.

'So who is it tomorrow then?' asked Andrew, as he tucked into his roast pheasant.

'It's three chaps from Ellis, Nash and Holroyd,' explained Theodore with more patience than he really felt. 'They've submitted the most competitive quotation so far,' he went on. 'Certainly a damn sight cheaper than the one from Beaufort Proudman International. One of them's a partner in the concern, Stuart Holroyd. I've met him before. Seemed a good chap. On the ball. Seems to know what he's about.'

'I thought you'd found somebody even cheaper,' said Marjorie, ever mindful of expenses.

'Well yes, there were a couple actually, but they were only really one-man bands. If we're going to do this exercise, we may as well do it properly,' replied Theodore. He knew full well that Marjorie, backed by Andrew, had forced the issue, and had asked for consultants to be brought in. Theodore considered the suggestion an implied criticism of his management of the company, but he and the rest of the board had been unable to suggest any other course of action to stem the continuing losses. There was a part of Theodore that wanted the exercise to be expensive, and not particularly cost effective, just so that he could claim a moral victory over Marjorie. 'I told you it was a waste of money,' he would like to be able to say.

'You're not thinking of changing your mind, are you Marjorie?' asked Theodore.

'No, certainly not,' she replied quickly. 'I think it essential. The business clearly isn't being managed properly; or else we wouldn't be losing money. An outsider will give a fresh view on things. An open mind. That's what's required. If you and the board consider this Ellis lot right for the job, then so be it. You have talked it over with the rest of the board, haven't you? Finance and Technical need to be onboard.'

'Yes,' replied Theodore, 'I've told Bill, of course, and Jas and Alastair. They're OK about it, and, subject to tomorrow's presentation being half decent, are happy to go with Ellis, Nash and Holroyd. I haven't told anybody else.'

Theodore emphasised his words and looked pointedly at Andrew. Andrew, blissfully unaware of the implication that he might inadvertently have blathered news of the consultancy to others, stuffed in another mouthful of the succulent roast pheasant.

Andrew then let out a stifled shriek. With Theodore and Marjorie looking on, he proceeded to take a piece of shot from his mouth and put it on the side of his plate.

'One of yours, eh, Uncle?' said Andrew. 'One of the hazards, as they say… When did you shoot this one?'

'A while ago. It's been in the freezer. I don't know,' replied Theodore impatiently. He enjoyed shooting game birds, as well as eating the produce. Andrew merely enjoyed eating the produce.

'I haven't had time to go shooting for ages,' said Theodore, slightly irritated at the distraction. 'As I was saying, you haven't told anybody else about the consultancy, have you Andrew?'

'No, no, no. Wouldn't dream of it. Wouldn't want the troops to get wind of it, eh?'

'It's not just a question of that,' explained Theodore. 'The shop floor can get hold of quite enough rumours as it is, without us fuelling the situation. I'm keen that we have the thing all signed up and the plan agreed before we tell the employees. I don't want to go off half-cocked. It'll be unsettling I'm sure, and they'll be suspicious. There may even be some casualties.'

'You mean redundancies,' Marjorie interrupted. 'Do you think so?'

'Very likely, I'd have thought,' said Theodore. 'Savings will have to come from somewhere. We can only afford to keep the best, those most competent at their jobs.'

This latter comment was again accompanied by a glance at Andrew. Andrew, as before, was oblivious to all but the next savoury morsel of game bird. He looked up, somewhat startled, by his mother's next interjection.

'Look Theo! I've had enough of this. You are forever goading Andrew, and criticising sales. He's done a fine job so far. If there's a problem anywhere, it's late deliveries. It's hardly surprising that sales are down when we've had so many complaints. The factory must do better. That's where the problem is!'

'Spare me the bloody hearts and flowers, Marjorie,' Theodore came back, his temper rising. 'That's a completely different issue. And how would you know that it's all down to the factory? You couldn't even find your way around the factory these days, let alone comment on its performance!'

Marjorie, realising that this comment was in fact dangerously close to the truth, changed tack. 'You're just trying to prejudge the situation. You're going to try and condition these consultants to blame sales and leave the factory alone. Well, it just won't do!'

'I am doing no such thing,' said Theodore, almost shouting now. 'If we're going to have this pantomime, then it's going to be full and frank, right across the company. No stone unturned.'

'This pantomime, as you call it, is going to cost the best part of £300,000 if that quotation you showed me is correct,' said Marjorie. 'And for that I expect nothing less than a full review right across the firm, including the factory.'

The delivery of these last three words she drew out for emphasis and pointed at Theodore with her knife. Battle lines were being clearly demarcated.

The argument raged for the rest of the main course, Janice choosing a relative lull to retrieve the plates. Her intervention cooled the arguments. Theodore realised full well that Janice could probably hear every word they said, but he still didn't like to exhibit family arguments in front of the staff. Marjorie lit up a cigarette. She knew it annoyed Theodore, particularly in his house, but like all siblings they seemed to show affection for each other by such baiting tactics.

By the time coffee was served, they'd agreed to a truce.

'I know you didn't want this exercise, Theo,' said Marjorie. 'I know you think it's a criticism of the way you've run the business, but really… And I know it's expensive, but it's for the best.'

Marjorie frequently called her brother "Theo". Theodore's parents had always insisted on the full rendition, but Marjorie liked to rebel. As in many family firms, names were a curious issue. Formality and status normally always prevailed. When Theodore had joined the company, however, "Mr. Walklate" had had to be substituted by "Mr. Theodore" and "Mr. George" in order to distinguish son from father. When the old man had died, custom had reverted for all but the longer standing employees. Only the most senior employees ever called the Managing Director merely "Theodore", and then only in private. Besides Marjorie, there was probably only the Production Director, Bill Hunter, who could get away with simply "Theo".

'Yes,' replied Theodore in a measured tone, 'but we all have to realise that the exercise will only be worth it if we agree with the findings and implement them. Whatever they are, and whoever they concern. This exercise is likely to be very far-reaching. Walklate's could be fundamentally changed by it all.'

He refrained from looking at Andrew this time. He knew he

had made his case, and further pointed comment would only serve to rile his sister even more. In spite of their regular squabbles, there remained a deep-seated mutual loyalty to one another that is normally only found within family.

Theodore knew that he couldn't win the argument at this stage. The whole purpose of the meal had been to bring the matters into the open. Each family member had had a chance to air their views, and had agreed in principle that their public face (that presented to the rest of the board, the management and the employees), was absolutely as one, in support of the consultancy exercise. Much as he would like the consultants to give the company a clean bill of health, he knew they wouldn't. Theodore was, if anything, a reflective man, a deep thinker. He knew full well that Marjorie was right, the business was in trouble. Any petty victory over who was "right" would be a purely Pyrrhic – nothing compared to the sanctity of the business itself. It was their business, and they had to pull together to ensure its success.

With the meal finished, Andrew and Marjorie left. Theodore got up and looked into the log fire, sipped a brandy, and reflected on his circumstances. He felt he had no choice but to go along with the whole exercise. It clearly implied a criticism of the way he'd run the business. This was indicated by the very nature of inviting outsiders to come in and hopefully sort things out. What else could he have done? If he'd been prouder, dug his heels in, and insisted on running it all his way, perhaps the business would continue to decline. For the first time in his life, he found himself lacking a little self-confidence. It was a totally alien concept to him, and it disturbed him. He had devoted his life to the business, and it had all gone so well until the last twelve months. The success of the company had seemingly given him all the satisfaction, the lifestyle and the fulfilment that he cherished. And now it was ebbing away, and he appeared helpless to stop the process. Had he made a wrong choice in life? Should he have sold out the business years ago, and done something else? Less involved, he may even have met the right woman, and got married and had children. This final thought made him feel unutterably lonely, again an almost unprecedented emotion. He envied Marjorie's family life. Even Andrew! Andrew was married, had a young wife, and surely it wouldn't be long before they had children? Whilst he suffered Andrew's corporate incompetence, he didn't despise the boy. Andrew was too easy-going to evoke that strong an emotion. And now Theodore Walklate, alone with his thoughts, even found himself envious of Andrew's lifestyle, the support he enjoyed from his mother, and would doubtless get from his wife. Theodore, by contrast, had no one. He'd never needed anyone. He'd never lacked the confidence to go through life on his own, as had seemed his destiny. Not until now. He felt old as he stared into the embers of the log fire, lost in his innermost thoughts, private, as always. For the first time in his life, he felt a twinge of regret.

Chapter Three

'The Oakland please,' said Joshua to the taxi driver, as he climbed into the large, ageing Ford.

The driver was also large, with a round smiling face. He was a talkative sort, much to Joshua's annoyance, and immediately gave Joshua his views on that conversational faithful, the weather.

'They say it only rains in Bramton for nine months of the year. The rest of the time it snows!'

'Really,' said Joshua tolerantly. Why did he have to land such a loquacious chauffeur when he craved just a few minutes' quiet contemplation? It surely couldn't be more than a couple of miles to The Oakland? His mind was still grappling with the news that Tara had imparted. She owned the place! He struggled slightly to come to terms with such a young woman owning a hotel. Granted it wasn't exactly the Ritz, but even the building alone, Joshua reckoned, would be worth a lot of money. Joshua was a materialistic man, given to envy, and was generally impressed by wealth. He replayed their conversation in his mind. He recognised his initial stumbling for words had been in part due to his being distracted by her looks. He cringed when he remembered calling the hotel "a bit run down". He'd effectively called her hotel a bit of a dump. His room had turned out to be actually quite pleasant. Basic, but clean and functional, and he was sure that with the gas fire on, it would eventually warm sufficient for his breath not to form condensation.

Tara intrigued him. It was nothing more, he tried convincing himself. But a further, more relaxed and wide-ranging conversation with her would be pleasant, he thought. Infinitely more pleasant, he reflected, than his current prospect, that of dull functional conversation with the taxi driver, followed closely by an even worse and more functional one with Holroyd.

'Pardon?' said Joshua, aware that the taxi driver had been speaking and that, in his reverie, he hadn't heard a word.

'I was just saying, are you stopping long in Bramton?'

'Not sure at the moment,' said Joshua. 'Maybe just a couple of days, maybe a bit longer. It depends. By the way, I'll need a lift back tonight. Probably about ten o'clock at a guess. Will you be free?'

'Yeah, sure. Me or one of the others. Give us a ring. Here, take a card.'

The man handed Joshua a dog-eared card giving the phone number, and emblazoned with all the services offered by A1 Taxis, including airport runs, wedding limos, and minibuses and the like. Joshua couldn't help but notice the driver smoking a cigarette in defiance of the notice in the man's own taxi. The driver's window was open a crack, just wide enough to draw most of the smoke out of the vehicle and enable the smoker to flick the ash out, too. Joshua thought about complaining but kept silent. He didn't want to make a fuss and would need the service again later.

'Bob Lumsden's the name. Tell you what. I'll pop by around about ten unless you ring otherwise. OK?'

'Fine,' said Joshua.

'It's only sensible these days, innit? Drink driving, I mean. It's only right you let us do the driving. Allows you to have a drop of pop, don't it?'

'Yes,' said Joshua, not at all sure that he wanted "a drop of pop". He enjoyed a drink but recognised it as a social function. His impending evening with Holroyd didn't fall into this category. It would be business, and with Holroyd holding court, discussion would likely be one way. And then there was his car. He would have to pick his moment to tell Holroyd, and he knew that the news wouldn't go down well.

'Oh, I'll need a lift in the morning too.'

'Blimey! You are going to have some pop!'

'No, no. I've got a problem with my car.'

'Now don't tell me. It's your motor around the back of The Crown. That BMW. The one that's been twatted both ends.'

'Yeah.'

'How did that happen? Bet you're chuffed. New as well, innit?'

Joshua was sitting in the back of the car, and Lumsden had to crane slightly forward, and talk to Joshua's reflection in his rearview mirror.

'Yes. Anyway, I'll need a lift in the morning, probably about 8:30. Will that be OK?' Joshua was eager to get off the subject of his car.

'No problem, chief. I'll be there. Where will you be going?'

'Only to Walklate's.'

Joshua had thought he ought to ask Stuart Holroyd for a lift, but he didn't want to be seen relying on his boss.

'That's not far from The Crown. You could walk in less than ten minutes,' said Lumsden, failing to realise the potential folly of talking himself out of business.

'I know,' replied Joshua, who didn't in fact know, but merely suspected the proximity of Walklate's. 'But I've got a lot of stuff to carry.'

'About that car of yours. I know a man who could help if you need a hire car for a day or two,' said Lumsden, ever helpful.

Joshua assured him that, as it was a new vehicle, he'd got a warranty from the manufacturer that covered breakdown and if necessary, a replacement vehicle. He'd already phoned them, and hopefully it would all be sorted sometime tomorrow, so no thank you, he didn't need any help.

'Here you go, sir,' said Lumsden, as they pulled off the road and into a wide driveway. A brightly lit sign proclaimed The Oakland Hotel, part of the Travelite Group, 50 bedrooms, all en-suite, bar, conference facilities, and the unsurpassed grandeur and delectable French cuisine of La Cigale restaurant.

'I'll see you about 10 o'clock, then chief,' said Lumsden as he pulled up at the front door. 'We can confirm tomorrow's pick up then. Cash or card, sir?'

'Er, cash,' said Joshua. 'How much?'

'Eight quid, fifty,' replied Lumsden.

Joshua handed him a ten-pound note, told him to keep the change, and asked for a receipt.

'Certainly sir. How many would you like?' and before Joshua could answer, Lumsden handed him five blank receipts.

'Here you go. Should help you with your expenses,' said Lumsden with a wink. Joshua got out and shut the car door and watched as the taxi quickly drove off into the night.

'Good evening, sir. Welcome to The Oakland Hotel. My name is Jane. How may I help you?'

Joshua had only just entered the hotel lobby, through the two sets of automatic doors, and found himself standing by the reception desk. The reception was large, bright, and airy. The floor was tiled so that footfalls would have echoed but for the walls being covered in a thick blue tufted wallpaper that looked for all the world like carpet. In between metal and glass display stands exhibiting silk ties, cuff links, watches, cameras and other indispensable items for the well-heeled traveller, was the reception desk, and behind the reception desk, was Jane.

A mature blonde woman with a ready smile, Jane looked bright and efficient in her corporate maroon uniform. When Joshua enquired of his companions, Jane was about to reply, when a male voice called from the office behind her.

'Ah, you must be Mr. Latham.' The voice belonged to a young, dark-haired man, who emerged from the office. He pointedly ushered Jane aside.

'I'll see to this, Jane. Right this way, sir.'

Joshua followed the man into the bar where he met up with Stuart Holroyd and Martin Meredith. After the three colleagues had reacquainted themselves with one another, they ordered drinks and perused the menu. After a brief dig at Joshua's tardiness, Holroyd launched straight into the programme for the next day. He was a tall man, of large build, with a thinning crop of hair, originally fair in colour, but now largely grey. He spoke in a brusque manner with a northern accent. Between large mouthfuls of beer, he stressed the importance of the presentation to Walklate's, who was going to say what, and in what order.

'You've brought the projector and all the other stuff, haven't you?' Holroyd enquired of Joshua. Joshua assured his boss that he'd brought *all* his 'stuff'. In fact, Joshua had all the modern conveniences and paraphernalia for as slick a presentation as you could wish for. He only just managed to contain his rising sense frustration. Provided Walklate's had mains electricity, he'd be able to make a good presentation of Ellis, Nash & Holroyd.

Meredith, a more sensitive man than their boss, was wise to Joshua's rising indignity, and whilst Holroyd disappeared to the toilet, he said to Joshua, 'Don't let him get to you. He's dead nervous about this job. He talked of nothing else the whole drive. I think winning the Walklate's job is more important than we think.'

Joshua heeded the younger man's words. Martin was only 27, which was young in this game, and had been with the company barely two years, having trained in finance. He had a full head of dark hair, which he wore short, and with hair gel that gave it that "fresh out of the shower" look. He appeared sophisticated beyond his years, and the irony of the younger man giving him advice disconcerted Joshua, all the more so as he suspected it was good advice.

'We know you could have handled the job, but the guy's under some pressure. Cut him some slack,' continued Martin. 'Say, how's the new motor?'

'Well, it was fine until tonight,' said Joshua. 'Look, I've had a bit of prang in it this evening. Not my fault, mind. Nothing too serious, but it's not driveable.'

'Shit,' was Meredith's sole exclamation.

'Do me a favour, will you? Just don't bring the subject up tonight. I don't want to mention it to Holroyd until he's in a more relaxed mood, if you know what I mean. He can get a bit funny about these things.'

'Sure.'

Holroyd returned, the three men finished their beers, ordered their meal and were shown into the restaurant. For a supposedly full hotel, the restaurant was far from busy, with only half a dozen or so other diners. Joshua wondered whether the haute cuisine came with suitably haute prices.

Throughout the meal Holroyd gave the background on Walklate & Co.

'They make electric motors and bits for the auto and white goods industries. Family business, of course. Thirty-two million turnover. Always profitable – until last year. Cash rich. They're now losing money pretty consistently and running round like bloody headless chickens. Have you read the brief?'

Joshua and Martin assured Holroyd that they had and waited for the pep talk to continue.

'You know the score. Massage their egos. They've had to swallow a lot of pride to consider the likes of us. Easy on the criticisms, especially the family members on the board. There's a nephew, Andrew, who's a bit wet apparently. Only there because of his mother or whoever. Wait until we've got the job before we get involved in issues like that. Play up to the old man, Theodore, and keep an eye on a guy called Bill Hunter.'

'Why?' asked Joshua.

'He's the Production Director. Haven't you read the brief?'

'Yes, but…' countered Joshua, but Holroyd cut across him.

'Also covers a bit of the Technical Department. He's not family, but I think Theodore Walklate's grooming him as his replacement. The old man's a bachelor. No son and heir. Marjorie, that's Andrew's mother… Are you following this, Latham?'

Joshua looked up from his steak. 'Yeah, sure.'

'Good. It's important. Marjorie'll want the business to go to Andrew when Theodore retires. There'll be a power struggle sooner or later.'

'Problem with that?' asked Martin.

'Yeah,' said Holroyd. 'Andrew's a useless prat. At least that's the impression I got reading between the lines when I met old man Walklate. He'll ruin it all in a generation.'

As their conversation proceeded, Joshua noted a change in Meredith since he'd last seen him. Martin had always been a bright guy, and obviously harboured some ambitions to get on in the firm. But in the six months or so since they'd last met Joshua detected a shift. His younger colleague had seemingly become more of a "yes man" and was clearly out to impress Holroyd with frequent use of modern management speak. Talk of "a deep dive" and "taking things to another level of granularity" made Joshua's stomach turn.

As the three men ate their meal and prepared for the next day's work, they were the subject of passing conversation between Jane and The Oakland's Assistant Manager, Bradley King.

'Quiet, isn't it?' said Jane. 'Them three are the last we've got booked in the restaurant, and it's only nine o'clock.'

'Yeah,' replied Bradley. He was standing behind the reception desk, alongside Jane. To a hotel guest he would appear to be studying some essential hotel correspondence that lay hidden behind the raised front of the desk. A rear view, however, would show his study to be focused on the sports section of a newspaper. Without looking up, he said, 'Our beloved Gallic chef looks like having an early night. Bless his little profiteroles.'

'Oh, you do tease him.'

'I know, but he deserves it, and he takes it all in good heart. There's nobody I'd like to have breathe garlic over me than dear Didier.'

'Gillman always has Sunday evenings off, doesn't he?' said Jane, changing the subject. She was referring to Jeremy Gillman, Manager of The Oakland.

'Yeah,' said Bradley again, still engrossed in the racing form for the week ahead. ''Cause it's always quiet. And when it's quiet, he knows there's less chance for me to make a balls of things.'

Jane laughed. Bradley had a casual charm about him that steered a delicate course between being offensive and endearingly cheeky. He always seemed able to deliver a sentence which, from the lips of others, would seem coarse, or cheap, or just downright rude. But from Bradley, it seemed always to carry a tone of benign teasing. He was a confident man, good at his job. He would frequently bounce between being self-assured to the point of cockiness at one extreme, and self-deprecating at the other. This latter mode was only a foil – any modesty implied being quite false. He could make such jibes at his own expense, but he defied others to do so. He knew his talents and either by exercising them, or more often by use of devastating wit, he defied others to make mock. He was one of life's natural charmers, capable of defusing seemingly any situation by a sharp riposte or teasing vocal barb.

'I bet you didn't come to work on that bike of yours, did you?' Jane asked.

'No. Thought about it,' replied Bradley, 'but when I saw the weather, I thought I'd let the train take the strain.'

Bradley lived in a flat in Chapel Harrington, a village about eight miles north of Bramton. He rented the flat, although he told most people that he owned it. His normal mode of transport to work was his beloved motorcycle. Having had a motorcycle of one sort or another since the age when the law said he could ride one, and his mother said he couldn't, he had proven to be an accomplished rider. He had, much to the surprise of anyone who'd seen him ride, or heard his tales of death-defying stunts, avoided serious accident or injury. Every couple of years, he exchanged his machine for a bigger, better, newer and more powerful motorcycle. From very modest beginnings, the current two-wheeled incarnation of his dreams was a bright yellow superbike from Honda. Only in the severest weather conditions, as now, did Bradley forsake the motorcycle for something more sensible.

'Ah, so there is some limit to your daring-do on that bike,' said Jane. 'I remember the day you first arrived. Poor old Brian thought we were being taken over by Hell's Angels!'

'Less of the 'old' if you don't mind.'

Jane and Bradley looked up to see Brian Mellor, the barman, sauntering over to join them, his area being almost as quiet as the restaurant. Jane was keen to talk but noted Bradley's reluctance to participate. She changed tack. 'Now then, when are you going to make an honest woman of young Sally?'

Ignoring the question, Bradley turned to Brian and said, 'Do me a favour, Brian. Tell Didier he can wrap up after sweets on table 9.'

When Brian was out of earshot he turned back to Jane and said in mock horror, 'Now, don't you start. You sound more like my mother every day! I'll marry Sally in my own good time, and not before. Why should I be miserable like all the other married blokes?'

Bradley had only been at The Oakland for six months, following its acquisition by the Travelite Group. His relative popularity amongst the staff of The Oakland varied typically with each individual's age and gender. His good looks and charm made him a firm favourite with the women, although this affection for him tended to tail off with their age. The more mature women, such as Jane, clearly saw Bradley's attractions, but tended to be more worldly wise to his ways and were less easily taken in by his offhand jocularity. Bradley's general repartee made him readily acceptable to the men with whom he worked, but again, what was refreshing and dynamic to youth came over as bizarre and slightly threatening to the older employees. Chief amongst this latter group was of course Jeremy Gillman. Bradley King saw the Manager as a staid time-server, now well out of his depth. Bradley couldn't quite understand why head office hadn't given Gillman what he wanted, that is, early retirement. Bradley assumed that they wanted him to prove himself first as Assistant Manager. He guessed he'd have to bide his time, keep out of any trouble, and the top job would be given to him in due course. Gillman, predictably, had taken a more or less instant dislike to Bradley King. It wasn't that he was a threat to Gillman's job, after all he'd wanted a successor, and sooner rather than later. Gillman's dislike stemmed more from style.

Bradley's arrival had been nothing if not unconventional. The Oakland staff, Gillman not the least amongst them, had expected their new Assistant Manager to be like a younger clone of Gillman. The shock of the motorcycle alone almost registered on the Richter scale. This was quiet old Bramton. The hotel had undergone considerable modernisation, (some of the older hands called it 'sanitisation'), under the stewardship of Travelite. The changes were mainly to bring the décor into line with the corporate style, but the physical changes to the building were nothing compared to the change in management style brought about by Bradley King. With scant respect for Gillman, and under the direction of Head Office, Bradley employed Frenchman Didier Merle as head chef and established the new Cigale restaurant. He set about a series of briefing seminars for the hotel staff which he always began with a few quips, such as, 'I'll start off with third biggest lie in the English language. "I'm from head office and I'm here to help you".'

After a silent pause he would continue, 'In case you're wondering, the first biggest lie is, "The cheque's in the post",' a comment that normally brought a snigger from the audience.

And finally he'd say, 'And the second is, "I'll still respect you in the morning",' which invariably drew a bigger laugh from the younger members of the audience.

He'd gone on to explain about "customer focus" and "delighting the customer". Gillman had groaned inwardly. The elder stalwarts amongst the staff had politely nodded. The rest had accepted the message with some enthusiasm, and the younger women, failing to see past the dark eyes and handsome features, had thought it all manna from Heaven.

Chief amongst those almost swooning on the front row of the seminars were some of the hotel's housekeepers, or chambermaids as Gillman, not quite on message, still referred to them. The front runners amongst this group vying for Bradley's attention were Sally Jones, closely followed by Nicole Greenfield. Each 21 years old and friends as well as work colleagues, they soon became fierce rivals for the affections of the hotel's new Assistant Manager.

Bradley revelled in his new position, both at work and socially. He could have the pick of the single women at the hotel, and his scruples would not have prevented him from sampling some of the married ones either. He had to be discreet, of course. He now had a position of responsibility. He did not want to be seen to abuse his power, and any overt relationship conducted with a member of staff could, if handled badly, undermine his authority and credibility.

'So, has Sally got another job yet?' asked Jane. 'I could never understand why she had to finish really.'

'Well, just imagine,' said Bradley, judiciously addressing the second comment without answering the first. 'What if it ever came to a question of discipline? I'm not saying it would, but just think if I had to reprimand some of the housekeepers for something.'

'Anne Barrowclough'd do that,' said Jane. 'She's Head of Housekeeping.'

'Hardly,' said Bradley. 'Anne Barrowclough couldn't deliver a reprimand if her life depended on it. It'd be down to me. And if Sally still worked here, I'd be open to all sorts of accusations that I favoured her, and let her off lightly, and so on. There would be a conflict of interest. No, it's for the best really.'

So serious could these situations become, that Travelite even had a "code of conduct" covering relationships between staff members, not that this was known by the likes of Jane Hope.

Bradley and Sally's relationship had therefore started clandestinely. Sally had then wanted to get engaged and was prepared, slightly to Bradley's surprise, to give up her job at The Oakland to avoid what she thought was the hideous interference of company policy. Although her job was hardly a career one, the fact that she was prepared to pack it in and take her chances elsewhere, had made an impression on Bradley. Sally's commitment to the relationship was clearly greater than Bradley's.

In a boyishly naïve way Bradley had thought getting engaged would somehow decrease the pressure on him to proceed to marriage. He'd soon found that he had badly miscalculated. Sally saw the engagement for what it really should be, a commitment to marriage.

'Has she moved in with you yet?' said Jane, ever probing for gossip.

'No,' said Bradley. 'The flat's too small.'

'Oh come on,' said Jane. 'It'd be real cosy.'

Bradley realised how thin his excuses had been. It was bad enough listening to this sort of teasing from Sally. The last thing he needed was similar digs from Jane Hope.

He folded his newspaper, having finally concluded his scan of the racing pages, and moved off to the kitchen before Jane could ask any more questions. Sally had found some part-time work as a cashier at the local supermarket. Bradley felt awkward about this. He held great store by image. He'd always thought that when he settled down, it would be to some gorgeous-looking stockbroker or lawyer, someone with beauty and brains combined, and a "power" job earning pots of money. Sally was certainly a looker. A natural blonde, with a shapely figure, long legs and a penchant for short skirts, she was, he felt, clearly the pick of his present social circle. But brains? She was intelligent but she'd wasted her school days worse than he had. She'd never have a "power" job as long as she had breath in her body. Had he compromised his ideals? He had been prepared to help her better herself, but going from housekeeper to supermarket cashier was not an auspicious start. Whilst he was sure that Jane, in a small community like Bramton, would soon find out that Sally was ringing up groceries, he didn't want to be the one to tell her. As he entered the kitchen, he thought perhaps he could tell them she was doing evening classes in something? He shrugged to himself. He'd think of something. He always did.

Chapter Four

After their dinner, the taxi driver, Lumsden, had appeared with remarkable alacrity. Joshua had left Holroyd and Meredith in the restaurant, and as he had walked into the reception area he had found Lumsden deep in conversation with Jane, the receptionist. She burst out laughing at something Lumsden had obviously said, before seeing Joshua and quickly reverting to a more demure stance.

Lumsden dropped Joshua at the front of The Crown rather than risk the slope down to the car park. A thin layer of snow completely covered the ground. The sky had cleared, and underfoot it was becoming crisp in the lowering temperatures.

As Joshua approached the glazed front door of the hotel, he stopped. He saw Tara inside standing in the hall. She was leaning over the sideboard in the reception area, looking at herself in a mirror on the wall. It wasn't the studied look of a woman concerned over a particular aspect of her make-up. It seemed to Joshua more like an altogether more thorough examination than that. As Joshua stood outside in the freezing temperatures he watched, fascinated by Tara's vanity. She'd changed her clothes from earlier. She was still wearing her sweater, but she'd changed from her jeans into a shortish skirt. Both skirt and sweater, Joshua noted critically, were a flatteringly tight fit.

Joshua pushed open the front door. Tara quickly looked round and said, 'Hi. You're back early. I thought you'd be out 'til late.'

'No. I just had a few things to fix up with my colleagues over dinner.'

The two stood in the hallway facing each other. There was a slightly awkward silence before Tara said, 'Look. I really would like to apologise for the accident earlier on.'

'Oh that's OK. Really.'

'No. We were a bit rushed earlier on and well, I know my insurance company wouldn't want me to say this, but it really was my fault. I came down the driveway too quickly for the conditions. I'd just like to say sorry properly. I feel awful about it. Your car's new, isn't it?'

'Yeah,' said Joshua ruefully. He then said something he'd never said before in his life. 'But it's only a company car.' This girl could be really disarming. 'Yours might be a write off, I'd guess.'

'Well if it is, too bad. It doesn't owe me anything, and it was pretty much on its last legs. Look, rather than talk here in the hall, how about we go into the bar, and I buy you a drink?'

Suddenly whatever vestiges of tiredness had crept up on Joshua at The Oakland seemed to vanish.

'You've got a bar?' he said.

'Yes,' she said with a friendly, mocking smile. 'I know the hotel's a bit "run down", but we do have a bar!'

Joshua didn't know quite what to say before Tara, still smiling, continued sarcastically, 'And we've turned on the "bloody heating!"'

She laughed, and he couldn't help but smile.

'Hey look, I'm sorry, but the place did look a bit like it was closed.'

'I'm only joking. You're right, it did look a bit in the dark. Come on. The bar's this way.'

He followed her into the bar, which turned out to be a fairly cosy little room next to the lounge. In it there were a few tables and chairs, a small TV, a flame effect gas fire, and in the corner, a small bar. They were the only ones in there, although Rose soon emerged from another door that apparently linked to the kitchen.

'Oh, is that you, Mr. Latham? You're the last in. Would you like a drink? I'll just drop the latch on the front door.' And without waiting for any answers, she headed off to the front door. Tara looked at him and smiled.

'Don't worry. You'll soon get used to her. Now what would you like to drink? It's my treat.'

Joshua ordered a wine, opting for a bottle rather than a glass on the strict proviso that Tara shared it with him. And so as soon as Rose returned from her locking up round, she was duly despatched to the cellar to retrieve a bottle of Beaujolais. Once uncorked and poured, Joshua offered a glass to Rose.

'Well, just a small one then. I don't usually,' she said.

'Go on, Rose. You haven't got anything else to do tonight, surely,' said Tara, pulling up a chair for Rose to join them.

'Just for a while then, but I have got to get some bacon out of the freezer for breakfast.'

'Tell me something, Rose,' said Joshua. 'Is there anything around here that you don't do?'

Joshua had meant the question partly in jest, but Rose looked pensive. 'Well, since Mr. Douglas has gone – he was Tara's father, you know. He used to own the place. Died about six weeks ago. Heart attack. Just like that!' She clicked her fingers in the air.

'I'm sorry to hear that,' said Joshua. He looked across at Tara, who was looking suitably subdued at the mention of her father.

'Well,' Rose continued, 'me and him, we used to do pretty well most of it really. There's young Fraser. You'll meet him tomorrow. He does the waiting in the dining room. Just breakfasts and dinners, mind. We don't do lunches. Or Sunday dinners. And then there's Joanna. She helps me do the beds. Well, she does most of them, and the hoovering. And I do the cooking and seeing to the guests.'

Joshua took a large mouthful of wine. There seemed to be no stopping Rose now that she was in full flow.

'Anyway. Mr. Douglas, he used to see to the guests, the money and stuff, and do all the odd jobs about the place. Fraser, bless 'im Tara, he's been doing a bit of painting, just to keep the place looking nice. Oh Tara, it is good to see you again. It must be three years since you've been here. I'm so glad you decided to come to live up here. Me and Fraser, and Joanna was obviously wondering what was going to happen. That lawyer feller, doing your father's will, he just told us to carry on, and that you'd decide what'd happen up here. Well, it's up to you of course, but, well, we all thought we'd all be down the road, you know, out of work, and that you'd want the place closed and sold. Ever so glad you decided to come. I'm sure we can make a good go of it. What do you reckon?'

There were only ever so slight, almost imperceptible, breaks in Rose's speech, barely long enough for her to draw breath.

'Don't you worry, Rose,' said Tara, 'I'm sure it's going to be just fine.'

'Yes, I suspect you're right. Anyway,' Rose drained her wineglass and continued, 'I must get that bacon out, and then I'm off to bed. Don't you worry about breakfasts, Tara. Me and Fraser have got a good routine. You have yourself a lie in.'

'Have you far to go?' asked Joshua.

Rose laughed. 'Oh, I should say about fifty feet, what say you, Tara?' Cackling away to herself, Rose ambled out of the room.

'She lives in,' explained Tara. 'She's got a room up on the top floor.'

Joshua topped up their glasses, and Tara continued, 'She's been here for years, ever since she left school, even before my father bought the place.'

'When was that?'

'I guess it must have been twelve years ago. My mother and father split up at the time. We used to live in the Lake District.'

'Where exactly?' Joshua asked, genuinely interested.

'It was in Keswick. They ran a small guesthouse. But they never got on. They were always having a row about almost anything, it seemed. I let it all wash over me. I never thought they really meant anything by it. Then one day, Daddy just got up and left. I was dumbstruck. My mother was very bitter. I stayed with her. I guess I must have been about thirteen at the time.

'Father came here and bought this place. They were obviously growing further apart, but I think this was the final straw. He was always more ambitious. There had always been quite a bit of money in the family, and he was keen to see it put to good use. Mother just wanted a quiet life.'

'It must have been difficult for you.'

'Oh, I suppose, in a way. But I shouldn't get too sympathetic really, if I were you. He wasn't a particularly likeable man, if I'm honest. I know that must sound awful. I was sent off to private school as a boarder. It was only in Yorkshire, but I didn't go home except in the holidays. I was well off out of it for the most part. I used to visit Bramton occasionally, but he never made me feel very welcome. Gradually, I came less and less. Like Rose said, I bet it's three years since I've last been here.'

'Where's your mother now?' asked Joshua.

'She died a few years ago, when I was eighteen. I was pretty independent. And impulsive. I'd just left school. I was quite prepared to make my own way in life. The place in Keswick was sold. I got some money from mother's estate, and I just took off. I travelled a bit, mainly around Europe, and I went over to the States a couple of times. I'm afraid I've blown most of it.'

'What sort of work do you do?'

'A bit of this and that, really. I guess I drifted a bit. I was a nanny for a while, but it was awful. And I taught English as a foreign language in various places in Europe. Anyway, when Daddy died I had to come here to sort out the will and things. I'd got no ties and was only renting a pretty dreadful place near Madrid. So I thought, it's time for a change. I obviously know a bit about running these sorts of places from what I've picked up from my parents.'

She drained her glass, and Joshua refilled it.

'And what about you, Joshua? What brings you to sunny Bramton?'

It was the first time he'd heard her say his first name, and he had to concede to himself that it sounded rather nice. Whether it was the warmth of the room, or the excellence of the Beaujolais, which was slipping down well, he couldn't be sure, but he acknowledged to himself that he was enjoying this little tête-à-tête.

'Business,' he said. 'I work for a firm of management consultants.'

'Hmm,' said Tara. 'Sounds very important. Who've you come to see in Bramton?'

'Walklate's,' replied Joshua. 'Although that's pretty hush-hush at the moment.' He went on to describe the Bramton company and some of the things he was hoping to do to help them return to profitability. As he dropped into consultant mode, he couldn't be sure if Tara was taking it all in or just appearing to listen to him out of politeness.

'How can you do all these things?' Tara asked eventually. 'What makes you know more about motors or whatever it is you said they make, than they do themselves?'

'Ah, that's just the point. We don't, but we don't really need to. There are a number of golden rules to running a business, whatever it makes or does. Walklate's'll doubtless have all the expertise on how to make their stuff. It's management expertise that we'll bring to the party. Take this place, for instance. It wouldn't take a good consultant long to work out what you do well, what you do badly, and make some improvements. It could be marketing, cost control, cash flow, health and safety stuff. I could have a field day here.'

'I'm sure you could, but I'm also sure I couldn't afford you,' said Tara.

Joshua hadn't intended his comment to be a proposal in any way, but he soon realised that even if he had, Tara was almost certainly right. Ellis, Nash and Holroyd didn't give their expertise away for nothing.

'Yeah,' he said.

'What made you choose to stop at The Crown?' asked Tara, genuinely curious. She eyed him more closely. She reckoned him to be about mid-thirties. His hair was slightly wavy, brown in colour but showing the odd few flecks of grey. He had a moustache, also going grey. Tara thought he had an attractive face, especially his eyes. They were a liquid dark brown, almost feminine in appearance, with dark eyebrows. He was of fairly slim build, slightly athletic. Tara guessed management consultancy to be pretty sedentary. He must work out or do some form of exercise, she thought.

As Joshua explained about Holroyd's intervention, and The Oakland, somewhat surprisingly, being full, the conversation flowed easily. Tara in turn voiced some of her hopes and ambitions for The Crown. She acknowledged Joshua's earlier point. The hotel didn't look inviting, and it lacked some of the facilities that people had come to expect these days.

'Trouble is,' said Tara, 'it's all going to take money. I mean, to do the place up a bit. I went through some of the books with Rose this evening. It's pretty grim really. I know it's a quiet time of year, but as you've found out, other places manage to keep busy. I'd rather thought that the business was more successful than it obviously has been.' Tara momentarily looked downcast.

'Still,' she continued, 'I'm sure I'll manage somehow. How long are staying?'

'It depends on tomorrow really,' replied Joshua. 'If it goes well, I may be here for the week. If not, I could be checking out tomorrow.'

After the wine, Joshua treated himself to a large brandy. When they'd covered the Bramton weather and the benefits of modern braking systems on cars, Tara asked the question that Joshua was hoping for.

'Tell me, are you married?'

'No,' replied Joshua. 'I used to be. Divorced now. We married early, and after a few years realised we just weren't really suited. Daft really. The split was fairly amicable, I suppose. No kids fortunately.'

Tara stifled a yawn with some difficulty. 'I'm sorry, I am interested, but I'm so tired. I'm going to have to go to bed.'

Joshua was tired too, but he'd so enjoyed the exclusive company of this particular woman that he wished it could go on longer. As they stood up, Joshua suddenly became aware that he'd had more to drink than he'd had for a long time. As they left the bar, Tara turned off the lights. They climbed the stairs together, and as Joshua struggled with the key to his room, he turned to Tara and said, 'Tara. I'd really like to thank you for a very pleasant evening.' He swayed ever so slightly on his feet. His brain, suitably dulled with alcohol, was hastily analysing what Tara's reaction would be if he just leant forward and kissed her.

Tara looked him in the eye. 'Joshua. I've really enjoyed it too. Goodnight.'

And with that she'd gone.

'Too slow by half, you daft bugger,' Joshua berated himself when safely inside his room. Even in his youth he'd never been totally confident with women. His greatest successes had always been when he'd done something spontaneous. Anything he tried premeditated usually turned into gawkish embarrassment. Acting on the spur of the moment had always been best policy for him, and this time he'd missed his chance. Maybe he was out of practice, he thought. He just remembered to set his alarm before he collapsed onto the bed. Still, he consoled himself, with a bit of luck, the firm should get the Walklate's job, and so there ought to be more opportunities to try his luck. A smile settled on his face as the tiredness and alcohol took him off to sleep.

Chapter Five

Less than twenty-four hours later, Joshua stood downcast in the reception of The Crown. He was just in time to see his damaged car being loaded onto a trailer. Rose came out to see him when he'd rung the bell.

'I'll be checking out, Rose. If you could let me have the bill, please.'

'Certainly Mr. Latham. By the way, the man's just come for your car. And he's delivered a replacement one for you.'

She handed Joshua the keys to the complimentary replacement car. Joshua went upstairs to collect his other luggage. When he returned to the hall, Rose gave him a hastily handwritten bill. Tara then came into the hall.

'Hi,' she said. 'Leaving so soon?'

'Yes,' said Joshua slightly distractedly.

'Bad news then, I take it,' said Tara, 'you didn't get the job up at Walklate's.'

'Well, we don't know for sure,' said Joshua, handing Rose his credit card. 'We should know by the end of the week, but…' His sentence drifted off. He was thinking of Holroyd's defeatism, and the stinging rebuke he'd just received. Joshua hadn't thought the presentation had gone too badly. Holroyd clearly thought otherwise. He'd expected a positive decision there and then. Instead they'd been 'fobbed off', as Holroyd put it, with Walklate's deferring their decision. And Holroyd had blamed Joshua.

'Are you OK?' asked Tara.

'Yeah, sure. It's just been a tough morning. Anyway, it doesn't look good. Never mind. There'll be others. I'd better be off. Thanks again for last night.' He reflected how much his mood had swung in the intervening hours, and the fact that now he'd quite likely not see Tara again.

'Good luck with the hotel,' he said.

'Thanks,' said Tara smiling. 'Well, Joshua, whenever you're next in Bramton, you've got to stay with us, you know!'

'Yeah, sure,' he smiled. 'You never know.' He shut the door behind him on his way out.

During the long drive back south, he reflected on the day. It had all started badly. For some unknown reason his taxi had turned up late. Holroyd and Martin Meredith had been waiting in the car park at Walklate's. Holroyd had been red-faced, and had spluttered his indignation. Further condemnation had been heaped on Joshua as he'd explained why he needed a taxi. Holroyd's face had turned from red to a shade of mid-purple. Before he'd been able to say anything more, they'd all been ushered into the Walklate's boardroom. After introductions the consultants had been shown around the works prior to giving their presentation.

The radio in the car muted and Joshua's mobile rang. He glanced from the road ahead to the caller ID displayed, and his heart sank. He pressed the "OK" button.

'Hello Stuart,' he said, trying not to sound too resigned.

'Latham,' barked Holroyd, 'don't forget those references for Theodore Walklate. I promised him them for this afternoon, without fail.'

'Stuart, I've done it. I emailed them through before I left Bramton.'

'Good,' Holroyd said begrudgingly. 'And I hope you phoned each of 'em first. You know, these referees. Softened 'em up a bit.'

'Yes of course I did,' said Joshua, feeling patronised. He could imagine Meredith in Holroyd's car with him, smirking at Joshua's discomfort.

There was an awkward silence. Both men felt the need to finish the acrimonious exchanges they'd had as they'd left Walklate's.

'I think we're still in with a chance,' said Joshua with perhaps more optimism than he felt.

'I'm not so sure,' countered Holroyd. 'What the fuck did you say that bit about "abilities" and "the right people in the right positions" for? And all the time looking at Andrew bloody Forsythe!'

'Stuart – I wasn't.'

'You bloody well were! I think Andrew's probably too dim to realise it, but I'm sure the others did. Especially that Bill Hunter – shrewd cookie he is. Very quietly spoken for a big man. Sounded almost sinister to me. Knew his stuff mind – all the figures at his fingertips. Confident.'

'Did he say anything to indicate the problems with the business?'

'No,' replied Holroyd. 'Just the usual crap about us consultants borrowing his watch, telling him the time, then walking off with his watch. I wouldn't want to get on the wrong side of him. What was the bloke who showed you round like?'

'Scott Sanders? He was pretty good. He's the Production Manager. Reports to Bill Hunter. Young. Talkative. I liked him.'

'Any clues on the business?'

'Yeah. There was the usual stuff about wanting more capital spend than the family are prepared to pay. They're overstaffed on the shop floor, and there's a least one layer of supervision that can come out.'

Holroyd grunted an acknowledgement. 'We'd have to tread carefully on that. You know how funny family businesses can be when it comes to shedding labour.'

After a further pause, Joshua spoke again. 'And he was pretty open about the sales and marketing side too. He pretty much confirmed your view, that Andrew's the weak link and get this: Scott's had previous experience in sales.'

Holroyd mumbled something that Joshua lost as he drove under a bridge on the motorway.

'So, we can do 'em a job if we can only land the contract,' said Holroyd. 'I'll ring Walklate later in the week and offer him a further discount.'

Joshua was stunned. 'A further discount? After what you gave them this morning we'll soon be doing the job at cost.'

'Well how the hell else are we going to get the business? Latham, you and young Meredith have just got to realise we are *desperate* for this job. Walklate's aren't the only company in the shit, you know. Ellis, Nash and Holroyd need the cashflow. Got that?'

Joshua was getting the message and said so, but Holroyd laboured on. 'So, now you've given 'em the references, just leave all the contact with me. I don't want you going in with your bloody size tens again. Do you hear?'

Joshua thought of cutting the call, turning the phone off and pretending he was out of signal.

'Yeah. Sure,' he said.

There was a further awkward silence. Joshua could sense Holroyd quietly fuming. Finally Holroyd said ominously, 'I'll be in touch with you.'

Joshua drove on, enjoying the silence.

***

'Mrs. Barrowclough, have you seen Mr. King lately?' The question came from Jeremy Gillman. He was standing beside Jane Hope in the reception of The Oakland, just as Anne Barrowclough was passing.

'No, Mr. Gillman. I haven't seen him for the last hour or so. If I see him, I'll tell him you want him, shall I?' Anne Barrowclough, as Head of Housekeeping, was one of Gillman's longer-standing employees at the hotel, her employment dating back before the advent of Travelite. She was a mature woman, with long, straight, dark hair, now turning to grey. She wore it tied back, giving her face a slightly gaunt, severe look.

'And Mrs. Barrowclough,' continued Gillman, 'I've been meaning to have a word with you about that young Nicole Greenfield.'

'Oh, Mr. Gillman? Something wrong?'

'Jewellery.'

Gillman said the word as if it alone ought to be sufficient to convey his meaning. Anne Barrowclough looked suitably blank.

'I don't like those coloured streaks in her hair. And she's sprouting earrings and the like. Every time I see her, I swear there's more. Then last Thursday I noticed…' The ageing Gillman struggled to publicly describe the physique of a young girl. 'I noticed she'd got one in her, you know,' he said, pointing to his midriff. 'You know. Her belly button.'

'I see,' said Anne Barrowclough, not really seeing what her employer was really getting at.

'If she'd been wearing her regulation blouse, it wouldn't have been visible. As it was, she was wearing some short thing. Far too short as it happens, and you could see her stomach. It's a wonder she doesn't catch cold.'

'I see,' repeated Anne. 'I'll tell her to wear her proper uniform in future.'

'It's more than that. You can warn her against all those damn earrings too. I don't mind one or two, but the number she's got. It's not on. It doesn't look appropriate in front of the guests. You of all people Mrs. Barrowclough, know my standards. We're on public view. We have to be presentable. It's not as though she's hidden away in the kitchen or something. She regularly must come into contact with the guests. If we don't put a stop to it, she'll be having nose rings, tattoos and all sorts. She must frighten the living daylights out of some of the older guests as it is.'

'I'll see her right away, Mr. Gillman. She'll be up in one of the rooms right now.'

Jane Hope buried her head in the cashbook to avoid eye contact with Anne Barrowclough. They found it difficult to take Gillman seriously sometimes. As longstanding employees, both Jane and Anne had grown fond of the old man, and his traditional values. In many ways they respected him all the more for them, but they did find his manner comical whenever he was faced with anything modern or, dare to mention the word, fashionable. If they'd looked at each other at that moment, they'd probably not have been able to suppress a snigger.

Anne took the lift to the third floor, in search of her charge, in order to deliver the rebuke over the wearing of excessive jewellery and non-regulation uniform. Firstly, she looked in all the rooms with open doors. They were either empty or had some of her other "girls", as she liked to call them, working in them. When asked, none of them had seen Nicole recently. She started knocking on the closed doors. Some had guests still in and she moved on. The others she opened with her passkey, and these too proved empty. She was just about to search the last room on the floor, number 312, when her mobile pinged. She looked at the message. It asked her to go to the side door of the hotel. She suspected it would be the laundry man. She hesitated. Surely he could wait a few minutes while she continued to look for the errant Nicole?

Unbeknown to Anne Barrowclough, the mobile's tone had also alerted the occupants of room 312.

'Oh Bradley,' groaned Nicole. Bradley moved his lips over hers, and silenced her with a prolonged, passionate, open-mouthed kiss. She responded, holding him close to her. She placed one of her hands behind his head and ran her fingers through his hair. She placed her other hand on his bottom and hugged his body against hers. She could feel him becoming aroused. They were standing, of a fashion, locked in this embrace in the middle of room 312.

'Oh Bradley,' she gasped, 'you did lock the door, didn't you?'

'Yes, yes,' he assured her impatiently. As they both knew, there were people out there with passkeys. He knew, however, that this particular room had already been made up, and nobody was due to check into it until that night. It was still only eleven o'clock in the morning, so he figured that their chances of being discovered were minimal.

The chance of discovery, albeit slight, added to the excitement for him. The woman in his arms, not being his fiancée, seemed to stimulate him further. Sally had been working evening shifts at the supermarket for the last fortnight, and she was finishing too late to visit Bradley. The last weekend had also been a bit of a wash out, with Sally constantly carping on about fixing a date for the wedding, and suggesting that they look around a few estate agents for somewhere suitable where they could live together. Bradley had got sick of it, and on the Saturday night, had got on his motorcycle and ridden with a fury into Manchester to meet friends. He hadn't got back until the small hours of Sunday morning, by which time Sally had returned to her bedsit in Bramton. Sunday, as has been described, saw Bradley at work. Bradley King, as a young virile male, with an urge he regularly needed to satisfy, and few scruples to keep him in check, was now at his most susceptible. He was predisposed to exploit almost any opportunity.

And along had come Nicole on the Monday morning. She had once again been wearing the cropped top that Gillman had found so irritating, and a short skirt, split several inches up one thigh. Bradley had been aware of Nicole's attention since his first day at The Oakland. They had frequently flirted together. During their conversations, he'd always been left with the impression, correct as it happened, that Nicole was looking for lust rather than love: sex rather than a lasting relationship. But he had always preferred Sally to Nicole. He thought her shapelier, and generally prettier. But Nicole had represented the here and now, and Bradley had found himself unable to resist.

He'd bumped into her in the corridor on the first floor, earlier in the morning.

'My! Who is this gorgeous wanton I see before me?' he'd said jokingly with his usual well-developed sense of irony. 'And what's this I see?' he'd continued, as he'd put his hand out to her bare midriff. He'd touched the little gold stud in her belly and let his hand dwell over her skin for a few seconds.

Nicole had giggled. 'That's my little jewel. Do you like it?'

'I do indeed. Got any more like that?' he'd asked with a grin.

'Wouldn't you like to know!'

Bradley had then quickly looked up and down the corridor, and seeing no one else about, had looked straight into Nicole's eyes. He'd then said, in little more than a whisper that had really conveyed the seriousness of his intent, 'As a matter of fact, I would.'

Nicole's smile had turned to a look of surprise.

He'd put his hand back over her stomach as he'd continued to look into her eyes. She hadn't moved. He'd inched closer, and after a further momentary hesitation, he'd kissed her. As he'd expected, she'd returned his kiss. The sound of the lift had made them break apart, but before the lift doors had opened, Bradley had had just time to say, 'I'll find us a room. I'll check the register, and let you know the number. It'll be about eleven o'clock.'

And now here they were, locked in room 312, unaware that both their respective bosses were looking for them. Bradley's hand again took advantage of Nicole's skimpy blouse and the exposed flesh of her middle. He caressed her bare stomach, and slowly moved his hand upwards, pushing her blouse up, all the time kissing her mouth, ears and neck. Her breath came in short gasps. With practised ease, he reached round, unclasped her bra with one hand, and clamped the other firmly over her right breast. She moved her hand down to the front of his trousers and began unbuttoning the waistband.

At that moment they heard the mobile outside. Its sound in such close proximity froze them to the spot. For several seconds they stood, locked in their embrace. They stared at the door to the room, daring it not to open. Bradley was quickly calculating the options. Who was it out there? A guest? Maybe Barrowclough. What would she want in this room? Probably nothing. She'll go away. He didn't want to spoil things just as they were getting interesting. Christ! He was sweating now. He could see his career flash before him if things went badly here. After all the supposedly high moral standards he'd exhibited over his engagement to Sally, what would this look like? Caught, almost literally, with his trousers down. The scandal would rock the hotel. He'd be looking at a transfer to another hotel at best; dismissal at worse. Being here with Nicole was very enjoyable, very exciting, no question. But it really was playing with fire. He hesitated a moment longer. He agonised. Nicole, her breasts still bared, looked from the door to Bradley. She was waiting for his lead. What to do?

'Quick,' he said. 'Cover yourself up!'

No sooner had he said the words, than they heard a knock on the door and Anne Barraclough's voice say, 'Housekeeping.' This was quickly followed by the sound of a key card unlocking the door. They were both suddenly galvanised. They stood apart. Nicole yanked her top down, leaving her bra still undone. Bradley quickly refastened his trousers. He smoothed a hand over his hair. The two leapt further apart as the door opened, almost as if distance between them were proportional to innocence.

Anne Barrowclough stood in the doorway.

Chapter Six

Theodore Walklate was doing his daily tour of the factory when he came upon Bill Hunter.

'Everything OK, Bill?'

'Not too bad, Theo. We're going to be a bit tight on the delivery this week for Pradit Electronics. We've been let down by the supplier of castings. They only came in yesterday.'

The assembly shop where they stood was not particularly noisy compared to some of the other areas of the works, and it was possible to carry on a conversation without raising one's voice. Theodore looked around him to make sure that nobody could overhear him.

'Tell me, Bill, any leaks on the consultancy yet?'

Bill lowered his normally quiet voice until it was barely above a whisper. 'No. Not heard a thing. References OK?'

'Fine.'

'Marjorie OK with it?'

'Seems so.' Theodore regarded his Production Director. 'You look surprised.'

'A bit. I was sure that Joshua guy was having a go at Andrew.'

'Well, if he was, and you know my views on that one, it was certainly lost on Marjorie. She described him as very down-to-earth. It might be nothing, mind. They were only here for a couple of hours.'

'Have you given them the go ahead yet?' asked Bill.

'Not yet. I promised them an answer by Friday.'

'Leave it 'til Monday,' said Bill. 'Make 'em sweat. You never know. You might be able to squeeze the price a bit more. They could still start the following week.'

Theodore regarded Bill with a sly grin before the two parted. Within half an hour, Theodore's relative levity was quickly dispelled.

First to take the shine off his day was Norman Crabtree, the toolroom foreman. Norman was a large man in his mid-forties. His company issue smock coat, its royal blue colour indicating his status as a foreman and seemingly always splashed in the oil and grease of his trade, covered his bulky frame. His hair was as black as his steel-toe-capped boots and cut short. It was normally liberally coated in a popular make of hair oil. Norman had learnt recently that such hair treatment was once again fashionable, his patronage of the stuff of course, dating back from its popularity the first time around. Theodore had chanced upon him in the company car park. Norman had been making his way to the "smoker's hut" – a steel and Perspex affair – the sole refuge on site where smokers could indulge their habit.

Theodore had a high regard for Norman Crabtree. The man could do his job well, and he exercised at least some control over some of Walklate's more challenging employees. He had an encyclopaedic knowledge of the products and processes and, often of particular value to Theodore, Norman, as Bramton born and bred, had an extensive knowledge of the goings-on of most of the firm's employees.

'How are the lads these days?' Theodore had asked. By "lads" in this context, Theodore meant Norman's toolroom operators. By the nature of their jobs, they were amongst the brightest of the factory hourly paid employees. They were also the most vocal and would always be in the vanguard of any industrial relations issue. They all belonged to a union, but not a particularly strong one. Theodore had long since regarded the feelings of the toolroom operators as a barometer of the factory as a whole, hence his question to Norman.

'Oh, you know,' Norman had said, 'a bit nervy, what with the company not doing so well, like.'

The reply had been pretty much as Theodore had expected. Nonetheless he'd looked around to make sure that nobody else was within the considerable range of Norman's sonorous voice. They were alone in the car park.

'I think some of 'em are thinking they'll be down the road shortly,' Norman had continued, alluding to the possibility of redundancies.

'Oh, I would hope not,' Theodore had countered. 'What's making them think like that?'

'Well, obviously we've been struggling a bit lately. Looks like it'll be going on for a bit yet. Then there was them suits around the place on Monday. Consultants or something.'

Theodore had been stunned. Walklate's frequently had "suits" being given escorted tours of the works. More often than not these were customers. Occasionally some were suppliers, and even more occasionally, local dignitaries, but never consultants. Such visitors invariably incited passing comment from the employees. The fact that Norman had referred to them as consultants could not be coincidence. There must have been a leak. Theodore was dismayed, but not entirely surprised at the senior management's inability to keep anything confidential. Theodore had pleaded for Norman to keep the matter to himself. He could trust to Norman's confidentiality he was sure, but from what he'd heard, the damage appeared done. He'd tried to assure Norman that redundancies were unlikely, and Norman had nodded politely, clearly unconvinced.

Theodore had continued his tour, somewhat disturbed, wondering which of his team had been indiscreet. Out of respect for Norman, he had not embarrassed the man by asking him to identify the source of his information. On this occasion, Norman would in fact have happily told his boss, but Norman thought he looked harassed enough as it was without knowing he'd been told about the consultants by a local taxi driver.

Theodore brooded. He finished his tour of the factory with a quick once-over of the welfare and canteen block. By the time he reached his office he was positively fuming.

'Shirley!' he bellowed, almost rending his office door from its hinges.

Shirley Hays, a mature woman with grey hair and half-moon spectacles, leapt up from an enormous array of paperwork that covered her desk in the adjoining office. She appeared in Theodore's office in an instant with notepad in hand.

'Morning Mr. Walklate,' she said.

Theodore ignored the courtesy. 'Get hold of Stan Whitmore in maintenance. Tell him I want the gent's factory toilet walls repainted.'

'Yes, Mr. Walklate.' Shirley hovered to see if there were any more instructions forthcoming.

'Now!' shouted Theodore.

'Of course, Mr. Walklate.' Shirley turned to go.

'I want it doing this morning – without fail!' Theodore continued to his PA as she retreated. Shirley made her way to the door separating her office from her boss's. She'd half opened the door when Theodore spoke again, this time slightly less abruptly.

'Next,' he said, 'if Stuart Holroyd phones either today or tomorrow wanting an answer on the consultancy contract, just stonewall him, OK?'

Good as she was, Shirley knew perfectly how to protect her boss's privacy when he requested it. She made a note on her pad.

'Tell him I'm not available. But promise I'll get back to him by Monday at the latest.'

Shirley tentatively returned to her own office, and Theodore slumped heavily into his chair behind his large mahogany desk. Why oh why did people in his employ insist on writing on the bloody walls? Graffiti seemed almost an occupational irritant in running a significant-sized factory, but Theodore wondered why he let it bother him so much. As the boss, he expected to be the regular subject matter of the frenzied scribblers. Why did he get so angry about it? *He* knew he wasn't a homosexual. He was also not homophobic. He had the intelligence and sufficient liberalism to accept differing sexuality in others. He was, he felt, up to speed on such matters. He thought the cheap comments by the more primitive mindset of some of his employees struck a particularly personal note, mocking his bachelor status. Whilst he wasn't exactly proud of being a bachelor – he would have married but for the right woman and opportunity – he disliked being teased about it. Only the previous Sunday night his regrets about having a single life had surfaced. He got up and paced the office.

Theodore Walklate was intellectually streets ahead of the Neanderthal who had written on the toilet walls. He struggled to comprehend the mentality of someone who automatically associated being a bachelor at the age of 48 with being homosexual. And even if it were true, then so what? The graffiti was more an indictment of the primitive shop floor view on sexuality, than anything else, but the hurt remained all the same. This was how some people viewed him. They would taunt him with it, at the same time accepting the employment and wages that he gave, and he didn't like it.

He stormed through to Shirley's office. She looked up, startled. Theodore hesitated and realised that he shouldn't take his feelings out on Shirley.

'Shirley,' he said quietly. 'Would you fix me up a cup of coffee, please?'

Shirley assented and got up from behind her desk. Theodore then made to return to his office when he noticed the piles of correspondence on Shirley's desk. 'What are you doing?' he asked.

'The invitations for the Christmas party,' she said. 'It's only seven weeks away. That pile is the employees and their spouses,' she said pointing. 'Those are the local suppliers, and these ones are your other local contacts. I was going to get you to sign them all later today. I've made a few alterations to the lists from last year, especially the suppliers one and some of the local people. I checked it all with Mr. Hunter, and he said it was fine.'

Theodore silently praised Shirley. She had initiative. "Gumption" as George Walklate had always called it. She'd worked for Theodore for over ten years now and had gumption in armfuls. An older woman, married with grown up children, she was always immaculately turned out, wearing smart but sensible clothes, and a modicum of make-up.

The Walklate's Christmas party generally took the form of a sit-down meal, with a disco to follow. The function was normally free for employees, but spouses had to pay a notional charge. Attendance each year was patchy. Some employees would go because they couldn't resist a cheap night out. Others wouldn't go because they resented having to pay for their husbands or wives.

Theodore hated Christmas. On a personal level, he had no family close enough to make it a special occasion. Marjorie or Andrew would normally invite him over for lunch on Christmas day, but he always felt that they did so only out of duty. At work, the festive season represented nothing but hassle. There were production schedules to change, maintenance jobs to arrange, suppliers to sort out, shifts to alter, security issues during the shutdown to address, and by no means least, customers to service. These would invariably want something delivered on Christmas Eve, or between Christmas and New Year, and special arrangements would be required. And on top of all the upheaval came the social functions, the factory Christmas party being but one. Customers were wined and dined separately at private functions. Theodore always thought it far too risky inviting a customer to the factory party. Every year there was always somebody who would have too much to drink and end up making an embarrassing spectacle of themselves. This sort of boorish behaviour Theodore thought bad enough, but in front of a customer, it would be commercial suicide. Above all else Theodore abhorred the materialism and ingratitude that had come to represent Christmas at work. Led inevitably by the toolroom operators, enquiries came in to management as soon as October about an early finish on the last working day before the holidays. As if the holidays themselves were not sufficient, the employees always wanted to slope off to the pub at lunchtime on the last day. Theodore didn't object in principle, but he was paying them for a full day's work, and he resented the way they all thought the early finish their right rather than an additional gift from the employer. And who ever thanked him for it? Nobody. He only ever really wanted a little expression of gratitude, but each year he was disappointed.

With little seasonal cheer, Theodore was grateful to Shirley for her organisational abilities. She booked the function room, and the DJ, organised the guest lists, seating plan, and so on. This left Theodore little to do but sign the invitations, which he always preferred to do individually, by hand. He would then just have to turn up on the night and make some form of rallying speech to the assembled masses, before sloping off as early as he decently could.

'Oakland again this year, I suppose,' he asked.

'Yes,' said Shirley. She was sure Theodore had remembered anyway, it having been booked a full twelve months previously. There was in fact little choice in the Bramton area that could accommodate the expected 180 Christmas revellers.

'I've done you a summary sheet of all the names of the guests for you to check before you sign the invitations,' said Shirley, handing him three sheets of paper. Theodore turned to the list of guests being invited from outside the company.

'Hmm,' he mused. 'Looks alright.' He actually felt that the list seemed to grow longer every year. This year he thought he was looking at a Who's Who of Bramton, but he declined to say anything for fear of enhancing his already scrooge-like reputation.

'Who's this T. Beaumont-Smith?' he asked. 'Shouldn't that be D. Beaumont-Smith?'

'No, no,' said Shirley looking over the top of her spectacles. 'Douglas Beaumont-Smith died a while back. T. Beaumont-Smith's his daughter. She's just moved into The Crown this week.'

Theodore vaguely remembered that Walklate's had housed some overseas students at The Crown once some years ago. Seemingly ever since, Walklate's had stood the proprietor a free meal every Christmas. *Goodness me*, thought Theodore to himself. *Now he's bequeathed the ruddy benefit to his daughter. Where will it end?*

'Shall I scrub that one off the list?' asked Shirley, seeing Theodore's brow furrow with consternation.

Theodore thought for a moment. He was tempted to make the economy. On a whim he then thought that the cost of one meal wasn't going to make much impression on the current financial situation, and striking the name off would only serve to show him as parsimonious, which he didn't like the idea of.

Finally he said, 'No. Let the invitation stand.'

★★★

Bradley had his back half turned from Anne as she stood in the doorway of room 312. Nicole was facing him, her arms folded tightly across her chest. She was in full view of the Head of Housekeeping. Bradley spoke first.

'No Nicole, this room looks fine to me.' He made a sweep of the room with his arm. 'I can't think what there is to complain about.'

Looking around at Anne Barrowclough, he said, 'Morning Anne. I was just explaining to Nicole we'd had a complaint about this room. Some stains on the carpets apparently. All seems to be fine though. Anyway, must dash.'

He made his way to the door.

'Mr. King,' said Anne. She didn't feel happy with this modern management credo of first names. Bradley pulled up short of leaving the room, turned and fixed Anne with a smile.

Anne looked at him. She wasn't fooled. She knew what she'd seen. This pair was clearly up to something they shouldn't. They looked guilty. Their faces were flushed. Bradley's hair, normally well groomed, was obviously ruffled. They'd been in each other's arms, she was sure. They'd been kissing, she guessed. How far would they have gone? She knew Nicole had a certain reputation, and she thought she knew Bradley's type.

She was at a loss as to what to say. She was not an erudite woman and she struggled to find the words to describe her shock and dismay. She felt their behaviour cheap, disloyal, faithless and unprofessional. She wanted to shout at them, especially Bradley. She could forgive Nicole, who was still a young girl and single, but Bradley was older and engaged to be married. He should know better. His was the abuse of power. She continued to look at Bradley King, what little respect she'd had for him, now all gone.

'Yes, Anne?' Bradley prompted.

What could she say? What in fact had she actually seen? She couldn't accuse them of anything. It would be her word against theirs. She could prove nothing. All that would follow would be rumour. As the perpetrator of such stories she would be cast as a gossip, a bitter, catty middle-aged woman. She'd been in the hotel trade for nearly twenty years. She'd seen it happen to others. She looked down at the floor and back up to Bradley King. She hated him now. Any lingering professional respect had vaporised in a second. His disloyalty to Sally choked her. But, as she looked at his smiling handsome face she realised that she was no match for him. She resented his superior wits and intelligence.

She stammered, 'Er, Mr. Gillman's looking for you,' she said, now hating herself. She cursed her weakness. She felt deflated. The moment to make a stand against his behaviour had gone in a moment.

Bradley fished his mobile out of his pocket and held it so that only he could see the screen.

'That's funny,' he said. 'There's no message on my phone.' He quickly put it back in his pocket before Anne could see it. He didn't want her to see that there was no message on it for the simple reason that it was turned off.

'Is he down in reception?'

'Yes.'

'I'll go and see what he wants.' And he left.

Anne let the door close behind her and turned to face Nicole. She felt far stronger dealing with her subordinate.

'What the bloody hell do you think you're up to?' she shouted. 'You were having it away with him in here, weren't you?'

'I weren't!' exclaimed Nicole with as much indignity as she could muster.

'Don't give me that,' retorted Anne. 'Just look at you.'

'I ain't done nothing!'

'The bloody door was locked!'

'It closed behind us.'

'Nicole, don't treat me like a bloody idiot. I didn't come down with yesterday's rain. I can see the signs. I know bloody well what you were up to and don't try and deny it.'

But deny it she did.

'We weren't doing nothing, honest,' Nicole pleaded in her broad Derbyshire accent. She stood with her arms firmly crossed over her chest, her shoulders hunched. A student of body language would probably interpret the posture as one of defiance. Anne, no such student, subconsciously put this interpretation on Nicole's stance. Unbeknown to Anne of course was the true reason for Nicole's pose, which was that her bra was still unfastened. Any other posture and the unfettered nature of Nicole's not inconsiderable bosom would have been obvious to her accuser. Anne, denied this damning evidence, could see no admission coming. She changed tack.

'Look at you. That's not a company issue blouse, is it?'

'But they're so boring.'

'I don't care. And those earrings…'

Anne may well have been in the hotel trade for nigh on twenty years, the last ten in a minor supervisory role, but she would never progress further for the simple expedient that nobody had ever told her that she had to own the orders that she gave out. Simply relaying the boss's words made one a messenger not a manager. She failed again.

'Gillman says one pair of earrings only, and you've got to wear your regulation skirt and blouse. OK?'

'Do I have to?' said Nicole, her face sullen.

'Yes, Nicole, you do. You're here to work, not go clubbing.'

The two continued to face each other.

'Nicole,' Anne continued, quieter now, a friend. 'Don't do it. Please. I know you think I'm an old frump but take my word for it. I've seen it happen before. It's not worth it. Think of Sally. She's your friend, isn't she? Don't mess with Bradley King.'

Nicole remained silent, her face set. Anne knew the conversation had run its course. She consoled herself. At least she'd tried. She opened the door. Nicole stalked out, arms still resolutely folded.

For what remained of the morning and for the whole of the afternoon, both Bradley and Nicole were on tenterhooks. What exactly had Anne Barrowclough seen? Would she say anything to Gillman? Would she start a rumour around the hotel? Bradley left the hotel shortly after lunch, returning around four o'clock for his evening stint. As he acknowledged each person that he saw on his return he half expected some comment or cheap aside that would confirm that his behaviour of the morning was being talked about. As each greeting passed without adverse comment he became more relaxed, confident that Barrowclough hadn't seen anything that mattered, and that she was not about to spread any gossip.

'Bon jour, mon ami!' Bradley almost shouted at Didier Merle as he strode into the kitchen and put his arm around the French chef. 'Comment ça va?' he continued in a deliberately heavy English accent.

'Bien, Monsieur,' replied Didier, 'et vous?'

'Absolutely chipper, my fine friend,' said Bradley, having almost exhausted his entire French vocabulary. He released Didier to allow the chef to change into his work clothes, the chef, like Bradley, having only just come back on shift. Didier was a short, stocky man in his early thirties. His hair was light brown, short and straight. He had a moustache that he wore long and droopy. He was a chauvinistic man, proud of all things French, especially, predictably, food and wine. He was moody and ran a disciplined kitchen. He didn't normally tolerate any messing about in his domain and was not slow to shout and scream at his commis chef or the waiters if he felt they were not doing their jobs properly. Bradley was the only exception. Didier would put up with Bradley's sometimes boisterous ways as it was Bradley who had given him the job. Recently married to an English girl, Didier and his wife had decided they would like to live in England for now. Jobs were not easy to come by even for a qualified and experienced chef. He had started to despair and had considered moving back to France rather than take up work outside his trade. Then along had come Bradley King. Didier couldn't be sure how Bradley had found him. The job in question had not been advertised. He didn't care, however. He was just grateful for the work and putting up with Bradley's gentle teasing was a small price to pay.

At that moment, Nicole walked into the kitchen. She was wearing her coat, and was heading for the rear exit of the hotel, her day's work having finished. The kitchen was far too populated for Bradley to exchange anything with her other than a knowing look, and a quick, 'OK?'

'Yeah, fine,' replied Nicole with a smile. She too had become more relieved as the afternoon had worn on, comfortable now in the knowledge that no gossip had spread. She made her way to the back door, where she stopped and turned. She looked at Bradley and, across the ever-increasing melee of the kitchen, he looked back at her. He drew his hand across his forehead and shook it once in a mime of wiping sweat from his brow. Nicole grinned, turned and walked out of the door.

A little later Bradley's mobile went off, showing a message from Sally. She was apparently in reception. At the time he was in a small office on the first floor looking at the diary of forthcoming events booked in the function room. In his typically cavalier style, he ignored the message until another one arrived, this time from Jane Hope, asking him to go to reception. He reluctantly got up and made his way to reception.

Once there, his heart skipped a beat as he saw his fiancée, Sally talking in hushed whispers to Jane Hope. Bradley sauntered up with a look of calm casualness. Having gone through the rest of the day without any gossip arising, he was now plunged back into nervousness. *It would be just typical of that bitch, Barrowclough*, thought Bradley to himself, *to keep quiet all day, then phone up Sally and spill the beans to her. Maximise the damage. Well tough shit, lady. You saw nothing, and whatever you've said about me, I'll deny it.*

'Hello, sweetheart,' he said leaning forward to give Sally a kiss.

'Hi,' she said with a smile.

'I thought you were working tonight?' he said, knowing full well that she was doing evening shifts at the supermarket. It was part of the shop's campaign of late opening in the run up to Christmas.

'I am,' replied Sally. 'I'm just on my way there now.'

Sally looked down at the floor, obviously wanting to say more but for some reason reluctant.

'I just thought since I hadn't seen you for a few days,' she said, 'I'd just pop by and say hello.'

'Great,' said Bradley with a touch more enthusiasm than he felt.

'Can we step outside for a second?' said Sally in a quiet voice. She looked at Jane, who was busying herself behind the reception desk. It was obvious that Sally wanted to say something private. Alarm bells started ringing again in Bradley's head. *So, maybe she doesn't want a scene, but there's something coming that I'm not sure I'm going to like*, thought Bradley.

Bradley agreed, and taking Sally by the arm, the couple walked outside.

'What's up?' asked Bradley, hoping that this wasn't going to take long. Although not exactly freezing, it was cold standing outside in the open porch of the hotel.

'Well,' said Sally hesitantly. She looked at the floor, then back up at Bradley's eyes, desperately trying to anticipate his reaction. 'I've got some news.'

Chapter Seven

Joshua was driving along the motorway, heading north again, a smile on his face. He'd been right and Holroyd had been wrong. They'd landed the Walklate's job after all. It had been on the Monday lunchtime, a week after their initial visit, when Holroyd had called Joshua to tell him the news. He'd been less than gracious when he'd phoned.

'I'm still convinced they weren't going for it,' Holroyd had said, 'but I swung it when I offered them another two percent off for payment in 14 days rather than net monthly.'

Now that had been generous. Such credit terms were well outside the norm for Ellis, Nash and Holroyd. Combined with the extra discount, it once again exhibited a desire to win the job that smacked of desperation. Margins were tight already, Joshua knew, but now it looked like the job would be done at cost.

'Get in your car and get up to Bramton right away. We're starting tomorrow,' Holroyd had said. 'Meredith's on his way there now. He'll work with you as we agreed.'

Joshua had noted the subtlety. Martin Meredith was now on the project working *with* Joshua rather *for* Joshua.

'You two'll have to fix yourselves up with somewhere to stay. I'll be coming down for a few hours tomorrow, just to kick it off.' Joshua had felt able to contain his welcome for Holroyd at this point.

And then had come the lecture.

'And remember, Latham. I want no foul ups on this job. It's tight on time and budget, and it's going to have to run on rails. Got that?' Holroyd hadn't waited for an answer. 'With these margins it's important we get our invoices in weekly. Understand? We need the cash flow.'

Joshua thought he'd managed to assure the man. Holroyd had

rung off with typical abruptness. Joshua had then thrown some clothes into a suitcase and, along with his work paraphernalia, put it all in his car. It was still the replacement hire car, his own being in the repair shop for at least another week.

Whilst battling with the traffic on the motorway he tapped out the number for The Crown Hotel from the phone's memory. When Rose Whitworth answered, he asked if he could speak to Tara.

'Hi,' he said when he heard her voice. 'Good news. I promised I'd stay at The Crown the next time I was in Bramton. And I always keep my word! Now, don't tell me you're booked up.'

'For when?' asked Tara.

'Tonight. I'm on my way now. We got the job at Walklate's after all. We're starting tomorrow.'

'Oh, that's super,' said Tara. 'We'll look forward to seeing you.'

'You've got a room spare, I take it?'

'Well, we've actually got about twelve spare tonight,' said Tara, who then giggled at her own sarcasm. 'We're almost empty. You can take your pick!'

Listening to that giggle made Joshua smile with anticipation.

'That's good,' he said. 'Now tell me. Would you do me a favour?'

'Sure.'

'Will you let me take you out to dinner tonight?'

Tara hesitated. Joshua filled the space in the conversation.

'I feel like a celebration, what with getting the contract. Just somewhere local. My treat. What do you say?'

Tara felt that she could hardly refuse. It would seem churlish, and she had enjoyed Joshua's company the previous week.

'OK,' she said, 'I will. Thank you. Where do you want to go?'

'You know Bramton better than me. Any suggestions?'

'How about The Oakland? They have a new French restaurant.'

'No,' said Joshua quickly. He guessed Martin Meredith would probably be staying there. Joshua wouldn't want the quiet soiree he'd got planned spoilt by bumping into his colleague. He couldn't give this reason, so instead he said, 'I was there the other week. It's a bit nouvelle cuisine. You know what I mean?' He let his humour and engineering functionality dominate his culinary appreciation and added, 'You get a plate the size of a small dustbin lid. They put a child's portion of meat on it, and one new potato and three runner beans. All arranged very artistically, mind.'

Tara couldn't help but laugh.

'And then when it comes to the bill,' Joshua continued, 'they just hold you upside down by the ankles and shake until they've got all your money!'

'OK, OK, I get the impression you weren't impressed. Where do you suggest?' she said.

'There's that pub on the road between Macclesfield and Bramton. You know, right up in the hills. I noticed they had a restaurant.' Joshua was sure it was remote enough for his intentions. 'It's called The Staging Post, or something.'

'Oh, that's a long way out,' said Tara, 'and if you want to have a drink too, you won't want to have to drive. Just a minute. I'll ask Rose.'

Joshua could vaguely hear her conversation with Rose before Tara returned to the phone.

'Rose says there's a new Italian restaurant opened in town, La Scala or something. She's heard it's very good and it's within walking distance.'

'Is it open on a Monday night?' asked Joshua, barely able to keep his voice serious.

'Now, now,' said Tara, recognising his teasing. 'It's only Sunday when Bramton goes to sleep. I'll book a table, shall I?'

'Yes, please. Say about eight o'clock?'

'Fine. I'll look forward to it.'

After saying goodbye, Joshua's smile grew even broader. 'You old smoothie,' he said to himself. He'd always found himself relatively shy with women. He'd been nervous about making the call to Tara, but he needn't have worried. He'd forgotten how easy he found her to talk to.

As he basked in his new-found confidence his phone rang. It was Martin Meredith.

'Hi, Joshua, I take it you're on your way to Bramton?' said Martin.

'Yeah,' he replied. 'So we got the job after all.'

Martin made no comment on this, instead asking, 'I was booking in at The Oakland. Do you want me to make you a reservation there too?'

'No. It's OK, thanks. I've already made a booking elsewhere.'

When he didn't elaborate, Martin, out of curiosity, had to ask where Joshua was staying. When Joshua told him it was The Crown Martin quickly came back with, 'But I thought you said it was a dump?'

'Oh, it wasn't so bad really when you got inside. And they're very friendly people,' said Joshua. 'More my sort of place really.'

Martin was not convinced, but he let it pass. 'Anyway,' he said, 'are we meeting up for dinner tonight?'

'Er, sorry Martin, but I've got an alternative arrangement tonight. Somebody I've got to meet. I'll catch up with you tomorrow. What time do you want to meet in the morning?'

These consultancy exercises often started out in a standard pattern, so Joshua's absence at dinner Meredith found socially curious rather than functionally problematic. The two continued to talk on the phone for a few more minutes. They made their arrangements to meet the next day, and what the timetable was going to look like. After the phone call, Meredith thought his colleague's replies stranger still. He wondered what Latham was up to. *Probably a job interview*, thought Meredith to himself. *Lining himself up with another job. With Holroyd on his case just lately, I wouldn't blame him.*

★★★

Joshua and Tara walked along the street, making their way back from La Scala towards The Crown. Joshua had been nervous to start with, but a bottle and a half of a very acceptable Chianti, and Tara's relaxed company, had transformed him. Never one for a Tinder account, he couldn't remember how many years it had been since he'd actually asked a woman out for a date. He'd never consciously given up on romance, but one failed marriage and five years of bachelor lifestyle, without even a hint of romance had made him think it all a thing of the past. To his surprise, he now felt like a teenager again.

Tara was wearing a long, dark blue coat, the collar turned up against the cold evening air. Underneath, she wore a black trouser suit, and a silver blouse, open at the neck. A black choker, studded discreetly with several small gems, and some silver pendant earrings, completed the image. She wore her hair up, but with several locks purposefully dangling by her ears. Joshua thought that she looked absolutely beautiful, and he'd said as much.

By contrast, Joshua had been self-conscious about his clothes, and had felt vaguely ill at ease until the wine had had its effect. As they walked, he caught the occasional waft of Tara's perfume. He tried to commit the smell to memory, for future reference.

Rose had been right. The restaurant had been good. Joshua and Tara had eaten their way through most of a four-course meal and had conversed freely. Joshua had talked about the sudden about turn in winning the assignment at Walklate's, and what work was involved in the programme. Tara had then explained more of her intentions for The Crown. Still unsure how to fund the work, she'd spoken of the need for more en-suite bathrooms, a new boiler and extending the central heating to more of the rooms. Joshua had been so full of enthusiasm and many bright ideas to make the hotel business succeed that Tara had almost wished she'd been taking notes.

They walked the dimly lit streets of Bramton in silence for a few minutes.

'Who's the man in charge at Walklate's?' asked Tara, as Joshua swayed slightly as he walked next to her.

'A guy called Theodore Walklate. He's the son of the founder,' replied Joshua.

'I don't think I've ever met him, but I seem to recall Daddy mention him before now. What's he like?'

'Bit strange really. He must be late forties or early fifties. My boss described him to me as a bit of a country squire type, which seems about right. Lives in some draughty old manor up in the hills somewhere. In with the huntin', shootin', fishin' set. He's quite an authoritarian figure, I suppose. Very driven, if you know what I mean. Seems to live for the company pretty much.'

'Is he married?'

'I don't think so. Bachelor, I believe.'

'And you're going to turn them around in twelve weeks?' said Tara sceptically.

'Sure. There'll be follow up visits every few months for a while after that, depending on how it all goes, but twelve weeks should be more than enough time to crack the job.'

They took a short cut walking through the public gardens. Joshua knew that they'd not far to go before reaching The Crown, and he felt his nervousness return. He struggled for conversation. He was enjoying the companionship and wanted to prolong the moment. As they walked along Joshua wondered frantically what to do next. He wanted to show some indication of the ever-increasing attraction that he felt for Tara. Should he put his arm around her? No, too familiar. Should he link arms with her? He'd had a few drinks, certainly more than Tara, and he didn't want her to think he needed physical support! Hold her hand? In his indecision, he did nothing other than walk next to her, weaving steadily under the effects of the wine and the cold night air.

'I see you've got the light over the front sign fixed,' he said. 'First impressions and all that. It counts for a lot.'

'Yes, that was Fraser. I'm glad he doesn't just stick to being a waiter. I'd probably have had to call out an electrician otherwise.'

'He must have been the guy I met earlier when I checked in. Tallish, thin with fair hair.'

'Yes, that's him,' said Tara. 'He doesn't say a lot, but when he does, you can't miss the accent. And that every other sentence is about his beloved Celtic.'

'Ah, he's a bhoy, then,' said Joshua.

'No,' said Tara looking slightly puzzled. 'He must be about thirty at a guess.'

'No. He's a bhoy.' Joshua spelt the word. 'It's what they call themselves up there, the Celtic supporters.'

Tara was intrigued. 'I hadn't got you down as a closet football fan.'

'I'm not really,' said Joshua, not quite truthfully. He assumed, using a classic masculine stereotype, that Tara would not be interested in football. Joshua returned to the conversation about the hotel.

'You want to target potential guests, you know. I guess you get a lot of outdoor types, especially in the summer. Your website could do with a revamp. Buy some walking magazines. Take out a few adverts. You could try students. Is there a local college?'

The Crown came into view. Without waiting for an answer, Joshua carried on. 'Perhaps foreign exchange students. You could target local businesses. You could offer facilities for training courses. Use the dining room. Shift the furniture around, get a projector or big flat screen TV for presentations, a flip chart, white board and Bob's your uncle, five hundred quid the day!'

Tara laughed, 'You make it all sound so easy. I'm half expecting you to bill me for all this advice, Mr. Management Consultant.'

'No, the simple pleasure of being here with you is more than adequate payment,' he said. Without considerably more than his fair share of the Chianti, he would have cringed at such a corny line, but under the influence of the alcohol he thought it sounded just fine.

Tara remained silent.

'Have you had much chance to go walking around here?' Joshua asked as he tripped on a raised paving stone. 'I used to do a bit of walking. I bet you did too up in The Lakes.'

'Yes,' said Tara, 'but nothing recently. I didn't do anything too adventurous even back in those days. It was mainly walking the dog. It got me out of the house.'

'We'll have to have a walk around here together sometime. I was thinking of staying over for some of the weekends during the project. What do you say?'

'Yes,' replied Tara, 'I'd like that.'

The closer they got to The Crown, the more Joshua felt the need to make a move, to do something. If he did nothing, they would soon be back at the hotel. Rose would be there. The evening would effectively be over, and the opportunity gone. There were only fifty yards to go. His heartbeat quickened. Their pace was quite swift along the dimly lit streets. They were nearly home. They were almost on the doorstep of the hotel now.

'Look,' he said pointing at the starry sky. 'You can see Orion.'

They stopped and Tara gazed in the direction in which he

was pointing. Brilliant! He'd at least bought himself some more time. The male mind, a device that so often functions best when it's processing only one line of thought at a time, on this occasion, had to juggle two. Joshua struggled to dredge back a fifteen-year-old astronomy lesson and, at the same time, control his mounting self-consciousness and tell the attractive woman next to him just what he thought of her.

'Where?' said Tara. She knew enough to know he was referring to a constellation, but not enough to know which. 'Which one?'

The street lighting was poor and with the sky clear, it enabled the constellation of Orion, The Hunter, to be seen just above the horizon.

'There,' he said, continuing to point. 'Where you see those three stars close together. That's his belt. And the reddish bright one up and to the left, that's his shoulder, and the other bright one down to the right, that's his ankle. Those in between are his sword.'

'My, if it's not football, or management consultancy, it's astronomy. I'm impressed,' Tara said with a characteristic smile, still not sure that she was looking in the right direction.

Joshua turned to her.

'Tara?' he said tentatively. 'I've had a really terrific evening.' He reached out and held her arm, firmly though not tightly. He leant towards her, aiming to plant a kiss on her lips. Tara quickly saw her view of the distant constellation eclipsed by Joshua's face. She immediately stepped back a pace and said firmly, 'No!'

'Please,' Joshua said. 'Just a kiss?'

He looked intently, imploringly, into her eyes.

Tara hesitated. She too had enjoyed the evening. She really had. She had said as much and had thanked Joshua for it. She was always conscious of the attention she received from men though, and, for the most part, was flattered by it. Tara drank in the compliments and used them to fuel her self-esteem. But rarely, and certainly not in recent months, had she wanted more. Joshua, she knew, was genuine, and as he looked at her with his deep brown eyes and a pleading, almost doleful expression, she almost said yes. But she dwelt a little longer. She was unsure where it all might lead. Her life had undergone quite an upheaval recently, and she didn't feel the need to do anything hasty or complicate matters further at the moment.

She said, 'No.'

'Please,' Joshua repeated. Whilst women need to feel cherished, and Tara was no different in this respect, men need to be needed. Rejection comes hard.

'No,' she said again. 'I don't think it would be a good idea.'

'Why not?' he said, his expression becoming mournful now. 'You've enjoyed the evening, haven't you?'

'Yes, I have,' she said, 'but that doesn't mean we have to finish it like this.'

'But why not? Please.' He was pleading now, and becoming desperate, realising that his romantic evening was ending other than as he had planned.

'Because I don't want to,' said Tara slowly, with the tone of an exasperated parent to a child.

He should have left it there. In the cold light of the following morning, he recognised that he should have accepted Tara's decision at this point. If he'd swallowed his hurt pride, accepted the firm but polite rebuff, he could easily have salvaged the situation, and gone on, over subsequent days and weeks, to try again. As it was, the Chianti said try again now. He maintained his grip on her arm. Still it was firm, still it was without threat. He leaned towards her.

'No!' said Tara again, almost shouting. She easily broke from his grip and took a further step backwards. 'Just because you take me out to dinner, doesn't mean I have to kiss you.'

Joshua was now truly crestfallen and looked away. 'I'm sorry,' he mumbled. 'I didn't mean any harm.'

'You're drunk, that's all.'

Tara intended her comment to be a casual throwaway line, a simple and harmless explanation of a misunderstanding. But Joshua was stung by the criticism almost as much as he had been by the rebuff. To be merry, he thought, seemed socially quite appealing. To be drunk, painted him as some sort of inadequate loner, and he didn't like the image.

'Oh bloody hell,' he said. 'I'm sorry.'

Just then the front door of the hotel opened, and Rose stuck her head out.

'Oh, it's you, Tara,' she said, seeing Joshua and Tara facing each other several steps apart. 'I thought I heard somebody shouting. Everything alright?'

'Yes, thank you, Rose. We'll be in, in a minute,' said Tara with a finality that made Rose immediately go back inside.

'I'm sorry,' said Joshua again, not realising how pathetic he now sounded. He was filled with remorse and embarrassment. 'I'll check out in the morning.'

'Oh, come on, Joshua,' said Tara, 'whatever for? There's no need to overreact.'

Tara actually saw the whole end to the evening as slightly comical. Boys would always be boys. She was sure that she wouldn't feel the slightest embarrassment over the close of the evening. She hadn't been offended. Why, she wondered, couldn't he just accept the setback for what it was? Why make it into some "all or nothing" drama? She thought Joshua a vulnerable, overgrown schoolboy, and any incipient affection for him now turned to sympathy. She didn't want him to martyr himself over a fleeting episode that, as far as she was concerned, was of no lasting consequence. But he wouldn't listen.

'No,' he said, looking at the ground, inconsolable. 'It'll be for the best.' Joshua, in contrast to Tara, thought the whole thing far from trivial. It served to confirm his poor understanding of women. His fragile confidence that had so flourished during the evening, was once again in pieces. He felt his world was coming to an end, and Orion's sword about to fall on his head. He couldn't face the embarrassment of seeing Tara the next day, and he repeated his assertion that he ought to find somewhere else to stay. Tara felt unable to reason with him further, so convinced did he seem about his intention to leave. After quietly thanking him again for the evening, she said goodnight, turned and went into the hotel, leaving Joshua alone on the doorstep.

And so, in the morning, for the second time in as many weeks, Joshua left The Crown with a heavy heart, checking out before breakfast was served.

Part Two

Chapter Eight

'So you made it in the end,' said Scott Sanders, Walklate's Production Manager, as Joshua took his seat beside him. 'I thought you said you weren't going to make it.'

'No, I wasn't,' said Joshua sheepishly, 'but I suddenly found a few things changed in my diary.' He didn't want to concede to Scott that he was only attending Walklate's Christmas party by compulsion. 'They're bloody customers, for God's sake, and you're going!' had been Holroyd's exact words.

'Well, it's good to see you,' said Scott before introducing Joshua to his wife and the other employees and their partners seated at the table. Joshua felt some relief. His conversation with Shirley Hays over the seating plan had avoided the worst embarrassment he might otherwise have felt. He made only polite conversation with his fellow guests as he nervously scanned the room. Then he saw her. She was unmistakable. She hadn't seen him.

Without there being a specific "top table", there was always one where the family sat, along with the board, which thus became one by default. This table also accommodated most of Walklate's guests and it was this one that contained Tara Beaumont-Smith, Martin Meredith and Stuart Holroyd.

Tara had been, almost from the moment that she'd walked into The Oakland's largest function room, receiving a lot of attention. She was dressed in a full-length designer evening gown of a pale blue, silk finish material. It was backless with a halter neck, split to mid-thigh, and suitably contoured. Tara, with her hair up and with minimal make up, save for eye shadow almost exactly matching the colour of her dress, looked stunning. From the moment she arrived until the time she left, almost all the eyes in the room glanced at her at some time or another. Seeing the lengthening line of guests, mainly male, it had to be said, queuing up to talk to Tara throughout the evening, an outside observer would not have realised that she'd turned up to the party barely knowing anyone else there.

Joshua, still smarting over their Italian soiree, was happy to keep his head down. He thought she looked exquisite, albeit now seemingly totally out of his league. Once he'd moved out of The Crown after that fateful evening, Joshua had thrown himself into the Walklate's project with great energy and tried, with some success, to put his embarrassment behind him. Joshua didn't want to erase his whole memory of his evening out with Tara exactly, more expunge the last five minutes of it. He'd not seen Tara since, and felt unsure what to expect when, and if, he eventually did meet her again. He had more or less accepted his place amongst the ranks of also-rans, but he had to acknowledge odd twinges of jealousy at every man that came up to her and chatted or made her laugh or smile. He promised himself that he'd leave as soon as he decently could.

'So how do you think the project's going?'

Joshua, distracted, glanced back at Scott. 'Oh, fine. It's been tough so far, and I think we'd all like to have seen a bit more effect on the bottom line, but that'll come.'

It was a diplomatic answer. Walklate's were still losing money each month, and the board, particularly the family, were getting distinctly anxious. The consultancy project was now about six weeks old, although to the management of the company, the time felt more like six months. Staid and steady shop floor supervision had had their views challenged. Taken aback by the high work ethic shown by Martin and particularly Joshua, the foremen and chargehands within the factory had had to rethink many of their strategies, plans and methods. The changes brought about during the many long days left a number of them quite unnerved. Others were even disconsolate, as their true capabilities had been exposed by changes in work practices. The traditionalists within Walklate's, unhappy with modern management techniques, could often be found huddled together, wishing it could all be like it was in "the good old days", and wondering how long it would be before they got demoted or made redundant.

The evening was obviously a busy one for The Oakland. Extra temporary staff had been recruited to help with all the Christmas functions, the Walklate's party being by far the biggest of these. Bradley King had been the driving force behind the enrolment and had taken a particular interest in the training of the new recruits. Frustrating, therefore, for Jeremy Gillman, that this was also the evening when, for the first time, Bradley King was off sick.

'Any news from King?' Gillman had curtly asked Jane Hope every half hour as the evening wore on, and the hotel staff rushed and sweated their way through the huge logistical exercise of serving hot roast turkey meals to one hundred and eighty guests. Bradley King did phone eventually, but spoke only to Jane on reception.

'I think Mr. Gillman would like a word with you,' she'd said.

'Tell him I'm too ill to answer the phone, and just need to rest up,' he'd replied, before quickly hanging up.

'What's the matter with him?' Gillman had asked, insisting that Jane kept trying to get Bradley back on the phone.

'Keep trying his mobile. And try young Sally's place,' he'd said, red-faced. 'Tonight of all nights!'

'He said he was too ill to answer the phone again, and he was going to switch it off,' Jane had said. 'I think he said he'd got a migraine,' Jane had added after unsuccessfully trying to call Bradley back. His mobile went unanswered. Jane had then tried Sally's bedsit in Bramton but was told by one of the other tenants that Sally was out working. Jane had eventually given up. Bradley, knowing that it was the hotel phoning, seemed to be ignoring them. He'd made one brief call to explain his absence, and that would have to be enough.

The evening wore on. Coffee was served and Theodore prepared to speak. Tara, sitting at the top table between Stuart Holroyd and Bill Hunter, watched her host as he shifted uncomfortably in his seat. She'd been introduced to Theodore Walklate upon her arrival. It had been the first time she'd met the man. He'd been polite but curt, almost dismissive, and had quickly moved on. She thought he'd obviously got a lot of people to see, to circulate amongst, and that he couldn't afford much time with any one individual. Throughout the meal, and indeed for the rest of the evening, she noticed, however, that Theodore Walklate didn't circulate amongst the diners. She thought he struck a rather lonely figure and seemed distracted and disinterested in the function or the guests. He ate his meal in a desultory manner, and seemed only to be involved in either small talk or conversations about the business.

Among growing mumbles of impatience amongst the partygoers, Theodore Walklate eventually rose to his feet. Ideally a speaker should start only when he has the full attention of his audience. On this occasion, as in every previous year, this was not possible, and Theodore launched into his address when the masses were at their quietest rather than totally silent. Theodore gratefully borrowed the DJ's microphone, so he could at least assure himself of being heard over the discontent of his audience.

'Ladies and gentlemen,' he started. 'I promise not to keep you for long.'

'Good!' A shout from the toolroom table. Drunken laughter and embarrassed tittering.

'But I always like to take this opportunity,' Theodore continued blithely, 'to express thanks on behalf of the family and the board…'

'That's enough!' Maintenance now taking their lead, as ever, from the toolroom employees. More sniggers. Bill Hunter glared at the perpetrators. Marjorie looked stonily at the nearest wall. Why did her brother persist with this farce every year? Before this year's event she'd even ventured to suggest that Theodore say nothing at all. But the same feelings about ingratitude that made Theodore hate the modern incarnation of Christmas, drove him on. He was determined not to descend to the same level of materialism and greed as the majority of his employees seemed to exhibit. He was going to say "thank you" to all his people for their hard work throughout the year, whether they particularly wanted to hear it or not.

'To you all, for all your efforts and the hard work you've put in throughout the year.'

'Mine's a pint then!' The toolroom again, early drinks giving them the courage to shout out at the boss in a manner that they'd never otherwise dream of doing. This comment, like the others, unfunny when sober, but under the influence of alcohol, seemingly hilarious. Theodore went on to thank, amidst more polite murmuring, all those involved in organising the evening. Over an ever-increasing babble he spoke briefly about the present state of the business before drawing to some kind of finish.

'And lastly this year, I'd like to thank some of the guests who've been able to join us here this evening.'

Theodore then began to list the names. When he announced Tara Beaumont-Smith, there was a wolf whistle from one of the tables, followed by a ripple of laughter and a few cheers. Joshua shook his head in disbelief, but when he looked at Tara, he saw that she was laughing. Then came his turn.

'And three guests from Ellis, Nash and Holroyd.'

The boos, jeers and catcalls drowned out the names. Marjorie, if it were possible, looked even more embarrassed. Bill Hunter was expressionless. Stuart Holroyd put on an air being greatly amused by it all, and Meredith, being Meredith, followed suit. Joshua put on a brave face and grinned. He'd expected nothing less. Theodore, seemingly totally oblivious to the reaction, carried on as if nothing had been said.

'I'm sure, with their help, we can look forward to a happy and prosperous New Year.'

'Whoever's left!' The toolroom wag again. Ironic cheers.

'Which just leaves me to wish you all, again on behalf of the family and the board, a very merry Christmas. Thank you.'

Theodore sat down to ribald cheers, jeers, and sporadic applause. The microphone was quickly taken back by the DJ, the volume turned up and, as The Oakland staff cleared the tables, the music and dancing began. This signalled the change in atmosphere of the evening. Quickly dispelled was the slightly stuffy dining ambience, replaced by an altogether more raucous, musical one. After ten minutes or so, Marjorie, as she did every year at this time, made her excuses and left. This started the exodus of other board members, and shortly, of Theodore himself. Before he left, he looked once more around the room. The lights had been dimmed. Unseen, his eyes rested upon Tara.

Contrary to Tara's impression, Theodore had in fact taken good note of her, and after their introduction, had surreptitiously glanced in her direction a number of times, acknowledging to himself her good looks. He had expected an older woman to be in charge of The Crown, and he'd been intrigued by her youth as much as anything. An enquiry of Norman Crabtree over pre-dinner drinks had established her as just twenty-five years old.

Generally, women were somewhat of a mystery to Theodore. He'd gone to an all-boys public school. He'd followed this up with three years at Cambridge University, attending one of the last colleges to remain all male. Male undergraduates at the university had still outnumbered female ones by a large ratio. To make this gender perspective even more skewed, he'd read Engineering, a subject that at the time was, and still largely remains, heavily male-dominated. Socially, he'd tried rowing, but wasn't into the drinking culture that seemed to go with it. Team sports were not his thing, and he became socially quite reclusive. The dearth of women in his academic and social circle at university had been exacerbated by the nature and circumstances of the few women that he did encounter. Numerically in the minority, the women undergraduates, Theodore found, tended to be academically brighter and more driven than many of their male counterparts. Their studies came first, their social life a distant second. He also found the relative rarity of female company made them all the more selective. The young Theodore, slightly gauche and awkward, never stood much of a chance at getting a girlfriend whilst at university, a fate that he had quickly accepted. For Theodore Walklate, the entire educational experience had been staid and abstemious. Consequently, difficult though it may seem to modern generations, he had achieved the grand age of twenty-one, and had remained a virgin.

After graduating, Theodore had plunged himself into the commerce of the family firm. As the son of the founder, at a stroke he was considered, as much by the women employees as by Theodore himself, to be socially above his immediate colleagues. Outside of work he remained a poor social mixer. The years went by, and his single ways became more entrenched. And so here he was, having just turned forty-nine, a bachelor, not by conscious choice and planning, but by circumstances and simple drift. He had grown older with little or no experience of purely social interaction with women, family aside. He could command his cook, Mrs. Hartle, he could order his PA, Shirley Hays, without a moment's self-consciousness, treating women in a work context almost as honorary men. But put in a social context and he was lost, emotionally stunted, not knowing what to say or do. He was, perhaps predictably, old fashioned in such matters. He was always very polite to women, of course. Feminism had largely passed him by, always letting 'ladies go first', and opening doors for them, etc. He recognised feminine beauty, of course, but viewed it as some sort of slightly abstract concept, something at a distance. And the greater the beauty, the more remote and abstract the woman seemed to be to Theodore. Someone as eye-catching as Tara he looked upon in much the same way as another may look upon a grand panorama, or fine painting; worthy in itself, a provider of momentary spiritual uplift, but ultimately not necessarily an end in itself. So deep had his feelings been buried and for so long, he remained, at least unconsciously, largely untouched by the likes of Tara Beaumont-Smith. For him, she represented the unattainable.

For Tara, this sort of attitude to women was not something she could ever have guessed at, let alone understood. Indeed, she had never knowingly met a man quite like Theodore Walklate before. She interpreted his apparent indifference to her initially as preoccupation, then, after his speech, perhaps as something more intriguing. His reaction was not rudeness, she was sure. It appeared as disinterest, not something Tara normally encountered. To a woman of Tara's looks, and with the vanity that her looks had instilled in her over the years, disinterest, as a male reaction, was almost inconceivable to her. Theodore left the party before Tara had the chance to thank him for the evening or speak to him further. For her, his mystery had to remain.

Tara made her way out to the hotel reception, and asked Jane Hope to book a taxi. She turned back and walked towards the function room when, outside the cloakrooms, she bumped, almost literally, into Joshua. He had his jacket on and was clearly heading purposefully towards the hotel lifts.

'Hi,' Tara said with a smile.

'Hi,' said Joshua, altogether more hesitatingly.

'Leaving already?' she said.

'Well, yes,' replied Joshua. 'I've had a long day, and, well, you know how it is.'

'I was just coming to find you. You weren't going to go without at least coming over to say hello, were you?'

'Well, er, no.' Joshua spoke quietly, his eyes looking everywhere but directly at Tara. 'But you looked sort of busy.' He recognised the pathetic evasiveness in his own words and cringed at what it must have sounded like to Tara.

'And you haven't been to see us at The Crown lately,' said Tara. She recognised his embarrassment, and without malice, knew that her presence probably exacerbated the situation. As before, she felt some sympathy for Joshua, and not a little exasperation. She thought he surely must have reconciled his feelings and pulled himself together by now.

'Er, no,' said Joshua, 'I haven't had the time. It's been very hectic at Walklate's these past few weeks. Even some shift working. I've not really had a second.'

Some of the other diners, one looking particularly the worse for wear, staggered past them towards the toilets. Instinctively, Tara and Joshua moved together to a more secluded corner of the hotel lobby.

'So, how's it going?' asked Tara.

'OK,' said Joshua, then quickly adding, 'Well, no, it's not actually. It's been pretty tough, and frankly there's not a lot to show for it at the moment. My boss is giving me some grief. Wants results a bit quicker, you know. Everyone's desperately looking for the bottom line to improve. It's all part of the game really. And what about you? How's the hotel trade?'

'It's pretty tough at the moment too,' said Tara with a shrug. 'We'll actually close for a few weeks over Christmas and New Year. It's not really our busy time, so Rose tells me, and it'll give us a chance to do some more decorating and a few jobs.'

There was a pause, before Tara said, 'We bought some flat screen TVs and kettles for the bedrooms. Like you said. And some of those special low energy bulbs.'

'Oh, good,' said Joshua, without sounding especially enthusiastic, but managing a smile, nonetheless.

'How's your car? Did you get it fixed?' she said.

'Yeah, fine,' he said. 'Good as new. What about yours?'

'It was a write off, I'm afraid. I've bought another one. Still pretty old, but it gets me around.'

There was another silence. Tara was getting slightly frustrated at having to make most of the running in the conversation.

'Look,' she said, 'I still want us to be friends, you know. Our evening out the other week. It was fine. I enjoyed it. OK?'

'You did?' Joshua said tentatively. 'I'm just sorry about how it ended.'

'Yes, I did enjoy it,' said Tara emphatically, 'and as for the ending, I wasn't bothered by it then and I'm not bothered by it now.' She was smiling now, her tone almost motherly. She touched his arm. 'For goodness' sake, don't get so screwed up about it. It really didn't matter. Just forget about it. OK?'

Joshua brightened almost visibly and looked straight at Tara.

'I like your dress,' he said. 'You look terrific.'

'Thank you.'

'It was a bit embarrassing earlier, you know, for you I mean, during the speech.'

Tara laughed. 'No. Certainly not for me. I think it was for poor Mr. Walklate. They certainly gave him a hard time. I'm not sure why he bothers.'

'Pride, I think,' said Joshua, 'and stubbornness.'

'He's a bit of a funny guy, isn't he?' said Tara, still grappling with her first impressions of the head of Walklate and Co.

'Oh, he's OK, when you get to know him.' Joshua, having now worked with the man, knew him from the business perspective, a view that reinforced Theodore's dignity, integrity and sharp commercial acumen. Joshua could not appreciate Tara's altogether more mystifying perspective of the man.

'Your taxi's here, madam.' It was Jane Hope, interrupting their conversation.

'Thank you,' said Tara. She looked at Joshua. He looked at her.

'Well, if I don't see you again before Christmas,' he said, 'you have a good one, and all the best for the New Year.'

Joshua then had a wild, fleeting thought. With Christmas in the air, and the party mood now prevalent, he thought he might risk once again asking Tara for a kiss. The brief chat with her had exorcised his earlier gloom. He felt much happier, and the busy Oakland foyer gave an air of mutual security. As ever, Joshua hesitated, and once again he misjudged the moment. He was happy to be friends with Tara, and philosophical about the fact that nothing more would ever likely develop. Having restored his relationship with her to this more comfortable equilibrium, he was disinclined or too timid to risk another upset.

'And Merry Christmas to you too,' she said, 'and don't forget to drop by and see us some time.'

'I promise.'

And with that she went into the cloakrooms, emerging a minute later with her coat. Joshua, standing by the lifts, watched from across the hotel lobby as she went out through the automatic doors, and got into the waiting taxi. He recognised Lumsden's vehicle. Was he the only taxi driver in Bramton? His car was now resplendent with a small, illuminated plastic Christmas tree on the dashboard. Joshua couldn't help but smile. It was partly due to the suitability of the tacky Christmas decoration to the taxi driver, but mainly due to the way the evening had gone. Having almost dreaded the occasion beforehand, he felt it had ended up on a bit of a high. Tara wanted to be friends. Joshua thought he understood this now. She's a beautiful girl. She knows it. She's vain. She enjoys the attention she inevitably gets. But that didn't mean she wanted romance everywhere she looked. He always knew he'd have a soft spot, an affection for her, but he felt more comfortable now with this feeling, rather than anything more. He was plain old Joshua Latham again, boring management consultant maybe, destined never to be a success with glamorous women, but at least he had her friendship. He felt safely back on the ground.

Chapter Nine

'What do you mean by this "cracking bird"?' asked Didier Merle in his heavily accented English. He was in conversation with Brian Mellor and Bradley King. The three of them were standing in the reception area of The Oakland Hotel. The time was shortly after lunch on the second Friday of the New Year. What few luncheon guests that there had been had drifted away, and activity at the hotel was entering one of its regular daily lulls. Didier had changed out of his work clothes and was waiting to be picked up by his wife. Brian Mellor, having washed the glasses in the bar, and changed a barrel, was about to close up and leave too. Bradley was doing a short relief stint behind reception. The impromptu conference between the three had occurred for no better reason than some last-minute considerations of the afternoon's racing card. Discussion had then lurched from "fine filly" to more graphic descriptions of the human female form. Brian had remembered the glamorous girl in the pale blue evening gown from a few weeks before at the Walklate's Christmas party. She was someone both he and Didier had remarked upon at the time, and Brian was using her as an example to explain some words and phrases of the English language that, for some reason, the French educational system, and Didier's English wife, had deemed unnecessary.

'You missed her, didn't you, chief?' said Brian, taking familiarity with management a step further than even the latest business texts suggested. 'Off sick or something?'

'Yes,' said Bradley, looking up from a large pile of invoices that he was working through. 'Although I've heard so bloody much about her, I feel as though I was there.'

'Anyway Didier,' Brian continued with his language class, 'she was what you'd call a "cracking bird". It just means really good-looking.'

From previous lessons, Didier was acutely aware that learning vernacular words and phrases in a foreign language was a tricky business. Done badly, it simply ridicules the speaker, and embarrasses others. The actual words themselves are easy to learn and can be picked up in the environment of a hotel kitchen as easily as a child learns swear words on their first day in the school playground. The difficult bit is not the words, but the context in which they are employed. When do you use which words, and in front of which people? The best advice to all novice language students is to avoid such words altogether. But Didier was a more accomplished student than his heavy accent may have initially portrayed. Whilst his pronunciation may not have been good, his vocabulary was quite extensive and, thanks to the ever-helpful staff at The Oakland, he was now tentatively moving into the minefield of swearing and other ribaldry in a foreign language. Brian Mellor he'd found a good tutor in these matters, and Brian was conscious of the question of context.

'It's not a really bad phrase,' he explained helpfully, 'but you'd use it really only in male company, certainly not in front of your mother! And never in front of the woman concerned either. Some might like it, but it's a bit rough really. Best left amongst the blokes, that one.'

'Come on, you pair,' said Bradley, 'the lesson's over for today. Haven't you got homes to go to? You're making the place look untidy.'

They took the hint. Brian returned to close up the bar, and Didier sauntered outside to wait for his wife. At that moment Joshua Latham and Martin Meredith walked through the front door.

'Good afternoon, gentlemen,' said Bradley. 'We don't normally see you here at this time of day.'

'No,' said Joshua, 'but we just need somewhere quiet to work on something for a few hours. Any chance of one of the small conference rooms for bit?'

Both Joshua and Martin were obviously regulars at The Oakland, having been staying Monday to Friday most weeks, Christmas aside, for the last eight weeks or so.

'I'm sure we can fix you up with something. We're not very

full at the moment. Have you already checked out today?' asked Bradley.

'Yes,' said Joshua. 'Can you hold over any charge to next week's account?'

'Oh, I'm sure we can come to some arrangement,' said Bradley, tapping away at a computer keyboard.

'Pot of tea wouldn't go amiss either,' said Martin.

'Room 100,' said Bradley, handing Joshua a key, 'It's kitted out as a breakout room to one of the main conference rooms. It's on the first floor, and I'll have pot of tea sent up. There's no charge. Have this one on me.'

'That's very kind of you,' said Joshua. Turning to Martin, 'Heard from Holroyd lately?'

As the two men made their way to the lifts, Martin, evading the question, said, 'Were you expecting to?'

'Yes,' said Joshua, in a slightly pensive tone. 'I emailed Holroyd an update on the project last Friday, and I raised a few questions. I need some answers quickly. Mainly about the sales side of things at Walklate's, as we've talked about. I remember at the outset Holroyd was a bit nervy about that side of things. I want to make sure our approach is correct.'

The lift doors opened, and the two men got in. Joshua carried on, 'Only I've not heard back from him. I've tried to phone him about four times this week, and left messages, but I've had no reply.'

'Did you try his office number?' asked Martin.

'Yep. Same result,' said Joshua. 'I even tried him at home last night, but I just got his wife. She said he was out. I've left message after message. It's almost as if he's avoiding me.'

The lift doors opened, and the two men got out and made their way towards room 100.

'That's funny,' said Martin, 'only I've spoken to him maybe a couple of times this week. He even said he was going to try and make it over this week sometime.'

'Well,' said Joshua, 'he's fast running out of time. If he doesn't call this afternoon, I'll try him at home again this evening.'

Joshua opened the door, and the two men entered the room. They worked for perhaps twenty minutes, with their laptops open, and a dozen sheets of paper spread about the floor. They were still on their first cups of tea when the phone rang. Joshua picked it up.

'Latham,' he said.

'Ah, Mr. Latham.' It was Bradley King. 'I have a visitor for you. Shall I send him up?'

'Who is it?' asked Joshua.

There was a pause before Bradley came back on the phone. 'It's a Mr. Holroyd.'

Joshua was surprised and couldn't quite conceal the fact.

'Er, well, send him up,' he said.

Joshua hung up the phone, looked at Martin Meredith, and said, 'It's Holroyd. What the hell's he doing here?'

'Well, he did say he would try to make it over this week,' said Martin.

'Yeah,' said Joshua, 'but Friday afternoon?'

In a short while there was a knock on the door. Joshua opened it, and in walked Stuart Holroyd.

'So this is where you two are hiding,' he said. Joshua was instantly alerted to the fact that Holroyd's tone was actually quite relaxed. It was uncharacteristic. He had said the words almost as a bit of friendly banter rather than his more usual hectoring inquisitorial style.

'Hello, Stuart,' said Joshua. 'We were just working on a revision to the production scheduling system. We thought we'd work at the hotel. You know how it is. It's easier to think away from the hurly-burly of the factory site.'

'Sure, sure,' said Holroyd, still amiable.

There was a silence. Joshua was about to describe his fruitless attempts throughout the week to contact the senior man, but Holroyd spoke first.

'Martin,' he said, 'I've got a private matter that I need to talk to Joshua about.'

Joshua noted the use of his Christian name. Again, it seemed oddly out of place compared to the usual barking of the word, "Latham". Joshua felt his stomach tighten. Deep within his mind, a suspicion stirred.

'If you wouldn't mind waiting downstairs for a bit,' Holroyd continued to Meredith. 'This shouldn't take too long.'

Martin made a brief acknowledgement of the other two men and left the room. As the door closed Holroyd sat down.

'Joshua,' Holroyd started, 'there's no easy way to say this, so I'll come straight to the point.' Joshua's stomach now churned. He started to get a sinking feeling. He took a deep breath and put his hand up and stroked his chin.

'As you know,' continued Holroyd, 'trading within the consultancy has been pretty tough of late. Like any business, and some would say of course, that as a management consultancy, we should know about these things probably better than most, but, as I was saying, like any business during these times, we have to consider our costs.'

Joshua was ahead of Holroyd now. As his boss uttered each word, Joshua metaphorically sank lower. He'd guessed by now. He'd seen this type of thing before. He knew what was coming now but he wasn't going to say anything. He didn't want to make Holroyd's job any easier for him.

'Along with my partners in the business,' Holroyd, looking suitably sombre, carried on with his well-rehearsed homily, 'I have conducted a lengthy review of our cost base, and our immediate market needs.'

Christ! thought Joshua, *I thought you said you'd get straight to the point.*

'After very careful consideration,' Holroyd spoke slowly, his enunciation far better than his normal accent allowed, 'we have decided that we can dispense with your services.'

There was a silence. Joshua ran a hand through his hair and wiped it over his face. He exhaled.

'So that's it,' said Joshua. 'I'm finished. Redundant.'

He let the final word hang in the air for a few seconds, before saying, 'When?'

'Well, obviously it's difficult, being in the middle of an exercise at the moment.'

'Too fucking right, it's difficult!' Joshua could contain himself no longer, and he banged his fist down on the table next to him. 'I've worked my bollocks off for the last two months. This is a difficult job. And this is the thanks I get!'

'Joshua, Joshua,' Holroyd kept his cool, 'I know you're upset. It's only natural.'

'Why me?' Joshua stood up and started to pace the room. 'What about Meredith? Is he going too? He's not been with the firm as long as me.'

'We've done a complete review of all the staff.'

'Stuart, I asked you a fucking question. Is Meredith going?'

'Well, no—'

'How's that fair?' Joshua interrupted, shouting.

'Joshua, you know how these things work. We have to consider everybody, and lots of factors, not just length of service.'

'Is there anybody else going, or is it just me?'

'Well, at the moment, it's just you.'

'Just as I thought,' said Joshua, 'you've just got it in for me. That's it really, isn't it? All this cost-cutting crap. It's all bullshit.'

'No, Joshua, that's not true.'

'It all falls into place now. You've known about this for a while, haven't you? You've been avoiding me, haven't you?'

'No, Joshua. I got your messages. It's just been very hectic at the moment.'

'When do I finish?' asked Joshua.

'All things considered, Joshua,' said Holroyd, 'I thought under the circumstances you perhaps ought to finish today.'

'Fair enough,' said Joshua, tight-lipped. Once again, he had anticipated this, but the shock was no less palpable. They both knew full well that it would be unreasonable at the best of times, to work in front of a client whilst under notice. For a consultancy firm under the present circumstances, it would be potential commercial suicide.

'There's a package, of course.' Holroyd was conscious of losing control of the meeting, and desperately wanted to keep the agenda on track.

'I should bloody well think there is,' said Joshua, glaring at his executioner. 'OK, so let's cut to the meat of it. How much do I get?'

He could sense Holroyd breathing easier now.

'I've got a settlement agreement here,' said Holroyd. 'I'm sure you're familiar with them.'

'Yeah,' said Joshua, 'I've heard of 'em. Just some legal nicety you want me to put my name to. I sign away all my statutory rights in exchange for an enhanced severance payment.'

'Yes, that's about it,' said Holroyd.

'Well, there'd better be enough noughts on the end of the cheque, pal, because you're driving a coach and horses through my employment rights.'

'Calm down, Joshua, please,' said Holroyd. Joshua still couldn't get used to this politeness coming from his boss. 'Let's go through it, clause by clause.'

Joshua slumped in his chair. He was calmer now, brooding, berating himself for not having seen this coming earlier. As they went through the legal document, Joshua could tell that it had been well thought out. It proposed a payment that covered his pay to the end of the month, his pay in lieu of notice, and a compensation payment to cover his redundancy entitlement. It even covered an agreed form of words that could be used by either party as a reference for a future employer. There was then an additional compensation payment for the loss of his company car and fuel. He sighed inwardly at the thought of his car going. His car! He knew immediately that he was going to find the return to private motoring hard going. It was a practicality like this that struck him the most. What was he going to do? He glanced at the total compensation figure. Very clever. He knew it was pitched at just enough to make it not worth his while taking the firm to an Employment Tribunal.

'We'll let you keep the car for the duration of your notice period,' Holroyd explained, 'but there'll be no fuel. You can return the vehicle to the Bristol office before your official notice period is up. That's mentioned here. Again, we'd appreciate it if you could drop your laptop and mobile in at the office sometime on Monday, and any other files that you may have.'

'Who's going to carry on with the Walklate job?' Joshua asked. His voice was mechanical. The question was academic to him now. He'd even guessed the answer before he'd formed the words, but with a perverse masochistic sentiment he asked anyway.

'Well, it'll be Meredith for the moment.'

'Pah!' Joshua spat the word out. 'For pity's sake, Stuart, he's a bloody kid. He can't handle it.'

'Oh, I think you underestimate the man,' said Holroyd. 'Besides which, I intend to spend a bit more time on the job too.'

There was a silence. It lasted over a minute. Joshua stared at the floor.

'I'm sorry,' said Holroyd, and for once Joshua actually believed him. There was a further pause before Holroyd added, 'For your own sake, you should run a copy of the settlement agreement past a solicitor first. We'll pay the fee for that. Just bung it in on a claim form. There's no big rush, say end of next week?' Holroyd handed Joshua two copies of the legal agreement.

'Sure,' said Joshua quietly.

'We'll transfer your money then.'

There was a yet another pause, and Holroyd said, the worst of the meeting over, 'You're taking it harder than I thought.'

'I am?' said Joshua. 'What did you expect? I'm hardly going to bloody joke about it, am I?'

'No, of course not, but I thought you knew, had some inkling that it was coming.'

'No, 'fraid not,' said Joshua bitterly. 'Call me Mr. Thicko, but I was too wrapped up in this bloody caper to notice.'

'We even thought you'd got another job lined up,' said Holroyd.

'What? How the hell did you come by that idea?'

'Oh, it doesn't matter,' said Holroyd, quickly wanting to back off the topic. What Meredith had told him had either been wide of the mark, or the new job Joshua was lining up hadn't come off. 'Let's just say it was a hunch.'

There was a further awkward silence.

'Well, I guess that just about wraps it up,' said Holroyd as he stood up. He was now anxious to get away.

'Christ!' said Joshua, 'I thought things were bad, but I never thought we'd reached this stage. Why, Stuart, why?'

'Like I said, it's costs. Obviously, your severance pay will cause a bit of drain on cash for the firm in the short term, but we have to take the longer view. It's been really tough. Obviously worse than you'd realised. We have to make these decisions to make sure we survive. You know that.'

He paused before adding, 'Are you going to be OK driving home?' Holroyd continued to confound Joshua with his consideration.

'Yeah,' said Joshua, 'I'll be fine. Don't you worry about me.'

'Good,' said Holroyd. He held out his hand. Joshua stared at it for a second, and then put out his own, and they shook hands.

Holroyd walked to the door of the room and opened it. As he stood on the threshold, he turned and said, 'Thanks for everything, Joshua.'

'And thank you,' said Joshua with a bitter sarcasm. Holroyd turned and left.

Joshua walked over to the window of the room and looked out. The rain that had been falling all day had now stopped. There were breaks in the cloud, and some weak, wintry sunshine threatened to break through. All of a sudden he hated the place, and wanted to be away. He started to pack his things together. He looked at his watch. Barely a quarter of an hour had passed since Holroyd had first entered the room. Fifteen minutes for the roof to fall in on his world.

Chapter Ten

Bradley watched the comings and goings of the three consultants with increasing curiosity. Soon after the man Holroyd had arrived and gone upstairs, Meredith had come back to the hotel foyer and, with hands in his pockets, appeared just to be killing time. A quarter of an hour later, Holroyd returned and engaged Meredith in an obviously serious conversation, their faces cast with stony expressions. A few minutes after that, Joshua Latham came down to reception complete with his briefcase and laptop. He walked over to Bradley at the reception desk.

'My colleague has some stuff in the room still. He'll need this,' said Joshua as he handed Bradley the room key. 'There's been a change of plan. Please cancel my booking for next week.'

Bradley thought Mr. Latham looked unduly sullen, and he also noted that Latham, as he turned and left, made no acknowledgement of his colleagues. Shortly afterwards the two remaining consultants cleared room 100 and, looking more grave than sullen, left the hotel. Bradley rang housekeeping and asked them to check the room over. No sooner had he put the phone down, than Sally walked through the front door. Inwardly, Bradley groaned.

'Hello sweetheart,' he said, mustering as much enthusiasm as he could manage.

'Hi,' said Sally. She leant over the reception desk, and they kissed. The kiss was perfunctory. An observer of this scene would be forgiven for thinking that this was due to the public arena in which it was being enacted. But the two participants knew only too well that there was a deeper reason for this frostiness. A rift had developed between the couple, based upon their disparate views on their impending nuptials and the bombshell that Sally had dropped before Christmas, that of the future of their unborn child.

'And to what do we owe this unexpected visit?' asked Bradley with just a hint of sarcasm.

'Bradley. We need to talk.'

'Yes, but I'm a tad busy just now.'

'You can't be. It's gone half past two. You're due a few hours off.'

This was, alas for Bradley, all true. Jeremy Gillman had promised him that whilst Jane Hope, the normal reception cover, was having the afternoon off, they would cover the front desk between the two of them. By a previous arrangement Gillman was due to take over between two-thirty and four-thirty. Bradley recalled that he had told Sally of this arrangement. He felt cornered. A distasteful discussion with his fiancée was now inescapable. The subject was likely to back him further into a corner, forcing the issues. He'd thought through the argument for some time now, and he knew that what was to follow was not going to be pretty.

'Right,' he said, 'I'll try and find Gillman.'

Bradley's last hope, that Gillman would be somehow untraceable, failed immediately. The hotel manager was in the first floor office and promised to come down to reception in a minute.

'Where shall we go?' Bradley asked Sally.

She shrugged and then suggested, 'Let's go into town. I've got the car outside. We can find a pub or something.'

Gillman duly arrived, and Bradley and Sally set off in search of a suitably quiet and secluded pub. Their journey was short and silent. The first public house they came to, The Red Lion, dutifully advertised "all day opening", and Sally pulled into the car park. Once inside they ordered drinks at the bar. Bradley and Sally were the only ones in there, with the exception of one old man sitting on a stool at the bar, and a couple of younger men playing a gaming machine. Bradley was relieved at least to know they wouldn't have too big an audience.

'What would you like?' Bradley asked, having ordered a pint of bitter for himself.

'I'll have a mineral water, please.'

It was a statement, Bradley knew. Sally had always enjoyed a drink. Her favourite tipple was vodka and tonic, which she would normally despatch in copious volume when in the right mood. She'd always been more sensible when driving. On such occasions she would limit herself to no more than two alcoholic drinks. Since her pregnancy had first been suspected, however, she'd reverted strictly to non-alcoholic drinks at all times. Rightly or wrongly, Bradley thought she was taking medical advice just a little too seriously. He'd previously tried to tempt her with lager, or even a shandy, but no, Sally was adamant: no alcohol. Bradley half suspected it was her way of constantly reminding him of her condition and the decisions that lay ahead. He ordered her drink and when served, they found a seat in the far corner of the room.

'Well,' said Bradley mischievously, 'what do you want to talk about?'

Sally was not taken in. 'You know bloody well. I must be in my sixteenth week by now. The doctor's asking why I haven't been to see the midwife yet. People are going to start noticing soon.'

She put her hand over her stomach. 'We can't keep it a secret forever.'

'So?' said Bradley in a sullen voice. 'Let's bloody tell everybody.'

'Bradley!' They'd been down this road before. Over the previous few weeks Bradley's attitude to impending fatherhood had become crystal clear to her. He didn't want the child. They'd argued over the matter. Recriminations had been flung back and forth over how they'd got into this predicament, but as the foetus grew the pointlessness of these arguments became obvious. They had become belligerents. Bradley had then put forward a suggestion about which he'd been almost fearful, but to him it provided the neatest solution. He'd suggested to Sally that she have an abortion.

She'd gone ballistic at the very idea. She'd actually slapped his face. Whilst not being a particularly religious girl, she clearly felt that she had a higher moral standard than Bradley. She'd been genuinely incensed at the very suggestion, and Bradley had backed off the idea quickly. He had hoped in the intervening weeks that Sally's conviction over the matter might have eased. It hadn't. She was going to have this baby come what may.

What Sally really wanted was for the two of them to get married, and preferably before the baby was born. She wasn't particularly bothered by the ceremony itself. She had been to enough weddings to realise that the ceremony, and the day itself, is often as much a show for the relatives than for the enjoyment of the couple getting wed. With no immediate family to impress, Sally would have been quite happy to slope off to a quiet registry office to do the deed. She simply wanted to cement the relationship. She dreaded the prospect of Bradley leaving her, of being an unmarried, single parent. The financial penalties of such a situation were actually quite well countered by the government of the day, and the social stigma attached to being a single parent had largely vanished. But in spite of this, being an unmarried mother did not conform to Sally's views and outlook on life. Overly conventional for one her age maybe, but her mind was set. She didn't just want to move in with Bradley, she wanted to be married, and the child brought up in a traditional family environment. Although she never said so in so few words, she was now hoping to use the expected child as leverage to get Bradley to commit. It was not a strategy without some risk.

'Look,' she said, 'I know you're not sure about being a dad but, well, it's too late to change now. Just accept it. I just want us to do the decent thing and get married.'

Bradley was silent. He looked at Sally. He could tell that she was getting emotional. The strain of the last few weeks showed.

'Please, Bradley, say we'll get married. We've been engaged a long time now. Let's just do it. Let's just go away, in secret, and do it. What do you say?'

She was pleading now, and her voice betrayed her desperation. Bradley thought for a moment longer, then said, in a cold and quiet voice, 'Sally. There's something that we're going to have to face here, and it's not going to be easy.'

Sally immediately showed alarm at these words. She searched his face, her expression imploring him to get his words out more quickly. She was desperate for his views.

'I've been thinking very seriously about this for the last few weeks, and…'

He hesitated. This lack of spontaneity was most unusual for Bradley King. Sally recognised this and became even more anxious.

'You're not going to like this,' he carried on, 'but the long and the short of it is, I don't want to get married at all.'

She was horrified, but still she hadn't seen the full trauma. Tears welled up in her eyes.

'Oh, but Bradley, why ever not? I don't want us to just live together. You do love me, don't you?'

His initial silence conveyed more than his words that followed.

'Well, that's just it. I've found out that I'm not sure I do really.'

She tried to stifle a cry but succeeded only in drawing the attention of the old man at the bar. Tears started to run down her cheeks.

'Please don't say that, Bradley. You know it's not true. Please say it's not true. Please!'

She was getting hysterical now, and Bradley was conscious of the barman's sideways glances at them. Bradley wanted to finish the conversation as soon as he decently could and leave the place.

'I'm afraid it's true. We're just not suited,' he said.

'Oh, but we are,' Sally exclaimed, her rising anger momentarily bettering her tears.

'We're not!' Bradley felt the need to raise his voice to counter Sally's denials. 'I think we should split.'

The two were silent for a minute, both thinking furiously. Sally had always been a slightly insecure girl without a highly developed sense of self-esteem. Her relationship with a man as handsome as Bradley King had been she felt, the highlight of her life. She loved him very deeply. She had frequently found herself marvelling at the fact that he had chosen her, never quite believing her luck. Moments of self-doubt would often raise themselves in her mind, and she would sometimes grow suspicious of Bradley. She was only too well aware of his charm and wit. These were, after all, some of his major attractions, but these same facets also fuelled her suspicions. She never openly acknowledged, even to herself, the full extent of how popular Bradley was, or could be, with other women, but subconsciously the feeling was always there. As she sat here in the bar of The Red Lion, the air tinged with the smell of stale beer, she could feel her confidence plumbing new depths. Her suspicions, never previously voiced, now surfaced.

'You're seeing someone else.'

It was both statement and question. She was not at all sure of the validity of the statement or the pertinence of the question. She had no concrete proof that he was being unfaithful to her. It was merely her self-doubt that was making her words anything other than an outright question.

'What?' Bradley professed innocence. In fact, he was caught slightly off guard by this direction of the conversation. The discussion was turning out as unpleasantly as he'd thought, but not in quite the way he'd anticipated.

'You have got to be joking,' he said. 'What the hell gives you that idea?'

'Where were you that last Friday before Christmas?'

Bradley feigned puzzlement and pretended that he couldn't remember. She jogged his memory.

'You know. It was the night of that big Christmas party at the hotel, and you were off sick.'

'So?' Bradley was concerned. What did Sally know? What was she getting at? He was relying on his usual calm exterior to carry off a show of surprise.

'I rang the hotel from work. You weren't there. Jane said you'd got a headache.'

Bradley could feel himself sliding into a pit of deceit. But Sally was no police interrogation expert. Bradley volunteered nothing, and waited for Sally to fill in some gaps until she'd said all she knew.

'So?' he repeated.

'You didn't answer your mobile. You weren't at the flat either,' said Sally.

He hadn't been. She obviously knew this. How did she know? Had she phoned the landline? He might have just ignored the phone ringing. Sally had spoken with some conviction.

'You came round?' he said.

'Yes. After work. I was worried. It's not like you to be ill and off work. But you weren't there.'

Bradley was thinking fast. She'd got a key to his flat. She could have waited all night.

'I waited 'til gone midnight,' Sally continued, 'then I went home.'

Bradley thought it curious that she hadn't waited until he'd got home, but this was not the time for that line of enquiry. Sally, at the time, had thought of staying, but for the first occasion in their relationship, she had discovered Bradley lying, and her conscience was troubled. This previously unforeseen dishonesty of his had shaken her. What had he been doing? Would he tell her where he'd been that evening? It was these thoughts that had raised in her mind the possibility of Bradley being unfaithful. She'd not been able to trust herself to a confrontation there and then. Perhaps there was an innocent explanation of where he'd gone that evening. She'd returned to her bedsit hoping that the succeeding days would see a full explanation surface.

But no such explanation had occurred. The fateful Friday evening was never mentioned. Sally had even ventured some oblique questions on the issue but got nowhere. Her doubts grew and her suspicions festered unhealthily. She became trapped. The longer she left the subject, the deeper became her unease. But similarly, the longer she left it, the more scheming she felt herself being, and such a characteristic was unnatural to her. If she had doubts, why wait two weeks to ask about them? On such lack of trust, compounded by lack of communication, relationships founder. She'd spent a miserable Christmas, uncertain as to her future, physically and emotionally. She waited here now, silent tears drying on her cheeks, to hear Bradley's explanation.

'Look,' he said, 'things are happening at the hotel. There are changes afoot. It's top secret for now. I had to go and meet some guys from head office.'

'At bloody midnight?'

'It was in the regional offices. It went on late.'

'How come Gillman didn't know?'

'You know as well as I do, he's retiring soon. Another few months and he'll be gone. They're lining me up to take over. No one up there knows, not even Gillman. You mustn't say anything.'

Sally knew, from her days at The Oakland, as did the rest of the hotel staff, that Gillman would retire sometime later in the year. They all also suspected that Bradley would be lined up to take over. In her naivety, Sally thought that such changes might well be guarded in secrecy. Bradley had successfully woven this little snippet of truth and plausibility into his story, and by this tactic alone, Sally felt a sense of rising frustration. She couldn't easily check his story. The secrecy made any enquiries she might make at The Oakland quite worthless. She didn't know anyone from the regional office or head office to even ask to verify his version of events. Bradley's tale had a hint of truth about it. It might be the truth. And at the same time, it didn't allay her fears and suspicions. It might be completely untrue. She retreated.

'You could have told me,' she said.

'I know, I'm sorry, but it really is secret. I just don't want it to get out.'

Bradley paused for a moment. This whole conversation was taking a lot longer than he'd thought. He wanted to get it over with.

'Anyway,' he continued, 'it still doesn't alter the fact that we're just not suited to each other.'

'Oh, Bradley, but we are.' Sally again could not stop tears welling up. Their discussion, destined to be fraught, was turning into a disaster. Bradley's continued lack of enthusiasm for parenting had not altogether surprised her. Whilst her ultimate goal was to marry, as the conversation had gone on, she'd recognised the need for progressively lesser ambitions. She would have settled for living with him, then for merely continuing their relationship. The ultimate catastrophe was now unfolding before her. Bradley appeared not just to be running from his parental responsibilities, but he seemed to be curtailing their whole alliance.

'We are not. Look at how we're always arguing these days,' he said. 'It just wouldn't work. Just because we've made a mistake with the kid, doesn't mean we have to make another, and bugger up the rest of our lives together. We should split. I just don't love you.'

This was more brutal than he'd intended. No matter how much he'd rehearsed his arguments, his frustrations were now getting the better of him. He'd meant to finish with "I just don't love you anymore". His omission of the last word conveyed to Sally a really deflating sense of worthlessness, of her having been used, and not cared for, right from the start of the relationship.

Sally attempted to wipe away her tears. She was now feeling angry. Not only was she not likely to get married, but the whole relationship was now foundering. Bradley sat stony faced. Between sobs, Sally wailed, 'But what am I going to do about the kid?'

'Well, since you won't have an abortion, you're going to have to have the bloody thing, aren't you?'

'But how will I manage? Oh, Bradley, I need you.'

'Well, you should have thought about that before,' he said, as he stood up.

'Oh, Bradley, don't go, please.'

He drained his beer in long, gulping mouthfuls, and slammed the glass back on the table with an air of definitive finality.

'I'm off,' he said. 'We're finished. We've said all there is to say on the matter.'

'Bradley, how will I manage? You've got to help me.'

'You'll find a way. I suppose with the Child Support Agency these days, you'll try and get the shirt off my back!' And with that he stormed off out of the pub.

'Don't leave me!' she shouted at his back as he made his way through the door. Her anger finally then came to the fore, and as the door swung closed, she yelled, 'You bastard!'

It was only when Bradley was outside that he realised that it was a good two-mile walk back to The Oakland on the outskirts of the town. He hadn't brought a coat. Fortunately, the rain had stopped, the cloud cover was broken, and there was the occasional burst of weak sunshine. There was a bitingly cold wind though. He cursed under his breath, turned up the collar of his jacket, and strode purposefully along the road towards The Oakland. He felt truly rotten but couldn't deny himself a sense of relief.

Meanwhile, back in The Red Lion, Sally cried in her solitude for a good five minutes. The barman, whether through embarrassment, tact or the need to perform some duty elsewhere, was nowhere to be seen. The two younger men playing on the gaming machine had left sometime earlier, leaving the old man at the bar, nursing an almost empty glass of beer, as the only other occupant of the room. In truth the old man had made his final pint last as long as possible so that he could witness the best entertainment that he'd had at The Red Lion in a good while.

Pulling a tissue from her handbag, Sally dried her eyes as much as she could. She got out a small make-up bag, and briefly checked her face. She took a deep breath. Her hopes had been dashed. Any notion of using the baby to get Bradley to get married had spectacularly failed. She'd been left literally holding the baby. She now felt totally alone, stuck with the one prospect, that of single parenthood, that she'd dreaded. She knew that she and Bradley had not been getting on well recently, but she'd always thought it a passing phase. He was, she'd assured herself, simply getting used to the idea of added responsibilities. It had never really occurred to her that he would actually run away from those responsibilities. And in her troubled and distorted imagination she remembered his parting words. He'd said that he'd never loved her! What was she going to do? She was totally at a loss, totally miserable.

She stood and walked over to the bar. There was a small hand bell resting on the counter. She picked it up and gave it a ring. The old man at the bar looked across at her with curiosity. The barman soon returned from a back room.

'Yes, love?' he said.

'Large vodka and tonic, please,' said Sally.

Chapter Eleven

As Joshua drove, his mind was full of jumbled thoughts and unanswered questions. He was not fully concentrating on the road. He selected his route between Bramton and the southbound motorway almost by instinct, ignoring the sat nav. He was angry. Why was it necessary to have any redundancies? How come he'd never anticipated the situation? Why him? Why was he made redundant rather than say, Martin Meredith? Joshua was more experienced than the younger man was. The decision just didn't make sense. In spite of it being obvious that it was Holroyd's decision, Joshua even found himself focusing his anger on Meredith. He felt the younger man had not only influenced Holroyd against him, but Joshua felt resentment at his former colleague usurping his position on the Walklate job.

Why had the situation come to redundancies at all? As a business consultant he advised other companies how to run businesses themselves, and yet, apparently, the company he worked for were making a huge mess of their own enterprise. Joshua just couldn't see where it had all gone wrong. Ellis, Nash and Holroyd were having a thin time of things, it was true, but nothing that they hadn't lived through before. Across the country he could think of at least half a dozen current contracts beside the Walklate job. Surely that was enough business to keep the company afloat? Maybe the margins were tight? Although Walklate's was probably one of their bigger contracts currently, it had been won at little more than cost price. Holroyd had wanted it so badly. Walklate's had driven a hard bargain, and Holroyd had given discount after discount. Joshua recalled the final discount given and thought of Holroyd's words.

'It's important we get our invoices in weekly. Understand? We need the cash flow.'

Cash flow. The firm needed the cash flow. Of course! It was cash flow. How many times had Joshua said to a client, 'Make cash or die today, make profit or die tomorrow, make product or die eventually.' It was standard rote to help get over to business people that it was cash that mattered most. It wasn't lack of profitability that brought most companies down, it was lack of cash.

Joshua berated himself. He knew what to do now, and he cursed at not having thought of it before. He hadn't been paying much attention to the passing scenery. He vaguely recalled the rolling moorland on either side of the road, its covering of heather now a brown matting over the ground. In places deep water-filled channels cut the surface and exposed the peat soil underneath. This blackness contrasted sharply with light patches of snow. What had fallen as rain all morning in Bramton, had done so as sleet and snow at this altitude. As he peered into the distance, he saw a large stone building. He recognised it as The Staging Post public house. Set high in the hills, the building stood sentry at a col, guarding this key access route to the Peak District. With its lonely vantage point, the pub, claiming to be one of the highest in the country, marked a bleak spot. As it came into view, Joshua knew though that it would be ideal for his purposes. He was sure to get a strong signal on his mobile from there. He turned into the pub's car park and came to a halt, overlooking a tremendous panorama. The weather was clear now, but very cold in the late afternoon sunshine.

Joshua grabbed his mobile from its cradle. Within a couple of minutes, searching on the internet he had listed all Holroyd's directorships. 'Bingo!' said Joshua to himself. *The bastards are all in it, he thought.* He then made four phone calls.

For the first he heard a ringing tone, followed by the familiar voice of one of his now erstwhile work colleagues, 'Hello. I'm sorry no one can come to the phone right now, but if you've a message for anyone in the Kelly family, please—' The voice was cut short with a click, and the same voice then continued, 'Hello?'

'Peter? It's Joshua, Joshua Latham.'

'Joshua! How are you?'

'I'm fine,' said Joshua, but then realised that that was far from true, and he added, 'Well, I'm not really, but I'll come onto that. More to the point, how are you?'

'Oh, terrific now, all things considered. I've been out of hospital for about a month now following my bypass surgery. Still need plenty of rest, but if I'm honest, I haven't felt this good for years. It's done me no end of good. It's just a pity I had to have a heart attack to bring it all about.'

'That's good to hear,' said Joshua.

'I got your card, by the way. Thanks very much. When you're off work for a while, it's nice for people to keep in touch. Now what's troubling you?'

'I've been made redundant, Peter.'

There was a silence at the other end, and Joshua hoped he hadn't caused another coronary problem by breaking the news so quickly. He was relieved to hear Peter Kelly's voice again.

'What? I can't believe it. You of all people. When was this?'

'This afternoon. I'm in the middle of quite a big project too,' said Joshua.

'I know,' said Peter. 'It was going to one of mine, wasn't it? Walklate and Co?'

'That's the one. Anyway, I'm only halfway through, and I've been finished. Holroyd came over from Manchester, and that's that.'

'Well, I am sorry Joshua, I really am. Like I say, I just can't understand it. I know the firm's been off the boil for a bit, and I always thought there might be a few redundancies, but never you. I thought I'd go before you. Have they looked after you?'

'Yes. I can't complain. I've got a settlement agreement to sign. I'll run it past a solicitor, but I can tell, without being generous, it's more than I'd get at tribunal. Holroyd's pitched it just right. I'm stuffed, basically.'

'Any thoughts on what you're going to do?'

'Not yet. I'm afraid I'm still a bit shocked by it all. I haven't a clue what I'll do.'

There was a short pause before Joshua continued, 'Tell me, Peter, have you ever heard of an outfit called Adventure Venture?'

'Yes. Why?'

'Well, I hadn't. Least not until today. What do you know about them?'

'Same as everybody else, I guess. I thought everybody in the firm had heard about 'em.'

'Apparently not,' said Joshua ruefully. 'So tell me about them.'

'Oh, there's not a lot to tell really. It was originally Ken Ellis's idea, I think, but he persuaded the other two to join him. The consultancy business was doing very nicely, thank you, at the time, but it was never going to make them millionaires. So, they set up this investment management company. I'm not sure what the form is, but I gather they try to get funding for various projects. The big idea was the leisure industry. Ken was all fired up about it. "Going to be the real growth area," I remember him telling me. The intention was that they were going to put money into theme parks, you know, with all these big rides and stuff.'

'Where does the money come from?' asked Joshua.

'I'm not totally sure how it was all meant to work. Obviously they try to tap up any financial institution that'll give them money, but they have to make a contribution themselves, of course. I understand Holroyd went into it with quite a big wedge. Served him right, if you asked me, couldn't have happened to a nicer bloke. Ha!'

'What happened?' asked Joshua.

'Oh, of course, you hadn't heard of them. Well anyway, they handed over a large amount of capital to some new development company, somewhere down south. I can't remember where. They'd got a leasehold on some ground, and they'd got their planning. In turn, they ordered a load of equipment, you know, these big fairground type rides, from an American supplier. The supplier went tits up, I'm afraid. Some sort of litigation in the States. It pulled the whole company down. There was a bit about it in the FT at the time. Of course, the theme park developers then went the same way, and Adventure Venture or whatever they're called, lost their money. It could have been big profit, but it's also big risk.'

'When was this, Peter?' asked Joshua.

'Oh, I'd say about three months ago. Why?'

'It's just a hunch, really. Holroyd's been making a lot of noise lately about cash flow. We always used to have fairly healthy reserves, and never used to worry too much. I was going to phone Richard Denning.'

'Hmm, I know what you're getting at. I suppose you could ring him. As the financial controller of E, N and H, if anybody would know, he would.'

There was a silence, before Peter Kelly continued, 'You know, Joshua, it's not illegal. It's their company. If Stuart Holroyd wants to draw money out of one company and put it into another, there's a thousand ways to do it. They're directors of both companies. They're perfectly entitled, and there's damn all you can do about it.'

'I know, Peter, I know,' said Joshua, suddenly feeling resigned, 'but I just wanted to know, that's all. I just wanted to know what they hell they were up to, because it's me who's had to pay a price. I guess I'm just angry, that's all.'

'That's understandable. Get it out of your system, and the sooner the better. What they've done may not be fair, but that's the way it goes. I've been made redundant before. You have to put the bitterness behind you. It won't do you any good. Look forward. It's the only way.'

'Thanks, Peter. Look, I've got to go. Thanks for the chat, and you look after yourself now, d'you hear?'

'I will. And you stay in touch.'

Joshua hung up. He then phoned Richard Denning, the financial controller for Ellis, Nash and Holroyd. At first Richard was apologetic. He was, Joshua felt, genuinely sorry to hear of Joshua's departure. Initially cagey, he did eventually confirm that the cash reserves of the management consultancy had been raided to prop up the failing investment management company. Things were indeed desperate, and more redundancies were possible. Joshua hung up. He now knew the facts, at least in as much detail as he needed. It still didn't answer the question as to why it was him rather than anybody else who was made redundant first, but he put that down to personalities. Holroyd hadn't really liked Joshua from the first time he'd met him, and the feeling was mutual.

'Put it behind you, Josh, mate,' he said to himself, 'just like Peter told you to.' And already he began to feel a little better.

His third phone call was to a solicitor he knew in the Bristol area. Being an old friend, and recognising Joshua's plight, the solicitor agreed to see him that evening to run through the settlement agreement.

His final phone call was to The Crown Hotel. In a more balanced frame of mind, he would have visited to say goodbye in person. Other than Tara, he hardly knew the staff that well. But he'd promised to stay in touch with Tara. After much ebb and flow in their short acquaintance, and particularly after their discussion at the Walklate's Christmas party, he felt that they had a more mature understanding of one another. Although Joshua felt that he may come back to this part of the country only rarely now, Tara was someone he felt he wanted to stay in contact with.

After a few rings, the phone was picked up. It was Tara. She sounded genuinely pleased to hear from him.

'Happy New Year, if it's not too late,' she said.

'And to you,' Joshua said, not quite matching her enthusiasm.

'And how is it the frantic world of business?' said Tara. 'You can't have many more weeks left at Walklate's. You must come to see us before you finish the job.'

'Well, that's a bit of problem really,' he replied. Her voice alone had cheered his spirits. As he spoke, he mentally tossed around the idea of turning around and driving back into Bramton to say goodbye properly. Practicalities prevailed. It was getting dark, and he'd a long way to drive.

'I've finished already, as it happens.'

'What? That was quick,' she interrupted.

'Well, the job's not finished. It's just me. I've been made redundant.'

'What! From Ellis, Nash and Thingy bob? Can they do that?' she said.

'Yes, they can, and they did. Thingy bob came to see me this afternoon.'

'Oh, Joshua, I am sorry to hear that. What are you going to do?' He was touched by the sincerity in her voice.

'I really don't know. I haven't really had time to think about it.'

'I don't know what to say,' Tara said.

'Well, there's nothing really to say. I was just ringing up to say cheerio really.'

'Where are you now?' she asked.

'I'm part way home,' he said. He didn't want to elaborate. If he told what tiny part of the journey home he'd actually covered, he knew she might persuade him to return, and he felt such a prospect might somehow prolong the agony of leaving.

'You'll come back this way sometime?' She sounded genuinely concerned.

'I very much doubt it. I'll probably initially look for work in the south somewhere. But you never know.'

There was a silence.

'Well, I guess it's goodbye then,' he said, then added with forced enthusiasm, 'now, you get that hotel sorted!'

'I will. And if you ever come to Bramton again, you'll want to stay at The Crown rather than that artificial monstrosity up the road!'

'You bet!' he managed.

After a pause, Tara said, 'Joshua, thanks for all the advice. I mean it. Do stay in touch, won't you?'

'Sure. Look, I've got to go.'

There was a final agonised pause. To both parties it signified a genuine regret at what appeared to be a final parting. They said their goodbyes and hung up. Joshua cradled his mobile for a few minutes and stared out at the gathering gloom of the hillside, before throwing the phone onto the passenger seat of his car. He started the engine. He pulled out of the car park and headed towards the motorway. A magnificent sunset was in prospect, and he felt it prophetic.

★★★

Sally sat disconsolately on the end of her bed. She'd left The Red Lion after her drink and returned to her bedsit. She'd lain on the bed for several hours and cried again. After a while she'd got up.

The vodka she'd had at the pub had reawakened in her a taste that she'd forgotten these last few months. She'd rummaged around in her cupboards and got out a brand-new bottle of vodka. It had been a Christmas present from Nicole Greenfield, and but for Sally's present condition, she would have thoroughly appreciated it. She'd been tempted before to open it, but her resolve over no alcohol during pregnancy had so far held. Her genuine belief in the medical dangers of alcohol on her unborn child, combined with a reluctance to open a new bottle, had kept her strong. But now things had changed. In her distress at The Red Lion, for a reason that she was no longer sure of, she'd had a drink. The first mouthful had broken the spell, and fatally wounded her resolve. It had tasted good, and once back at her bedsit, she'd found it comparatively easy to open the new bottle and pour herself a generous measure. She'd no tonic, but a raid on the communal fridge had turned up a half carton of orange juice, which she'd found a more than adequate substitute for her favourite mixer. After a couple of drinks her judgement became impaired, and a third one, masked by an excess of orange juice, was the largest measure so far.

Alcohol doesn't create opinions. By reducing inhibitions, it emphasises feelings and emotions already held. As Sally drank, her feelings of anger developed. Her ire, directed towards Bradley King, became more acute and turned to bitter loathing. She'd make him pay. She'd make him suffer. Her feelings towards her unborn child changed too. She still loved it, but it was hers now, not theirs. She also persuaded herself that she'd over-played the medical concerns, and that an occasional small tipple wouldn't harm the foetus.

Sally sat on her bed, pale-faced, her mouth tightly clamped, and her head in her hands. She may not have wanted to be a single parent, but if that was to be her fate, she'd accept it. She'd make the best of it. She felt a grim determination. She'd make a success of her life, and a success of her child's life, without Bradley King. She reflected on the irony of her recent life. Instead of being at its most enjoyable as it should have been, it had been thoroughly miserable, filled with self-doubts and worries. She resolved to enjoy herself.

This resolve lasted whilst she fixed herself a sandwich, and poured what she promised herself was an absolutely final tot of vodka. The alcohol continued to amplify her feelings. Her emotions were understandably jumbled. The vodka now flowed over another vein of misery, and her mood darkened accordingly. Finishing her sandwich and her drink, she put the vodka bottle down on the floor, and sighed deeply. She stared around the room. The accommodation was small even by the modest standards of a bedsit. She had a solitary room on the top floor of a three storey Victorian mid-terrace house. The ceiling of her room sloped on one side reflecting the profile of the roof above. The angled ceiling was relieved by a small dormer window, which now showed nothing but a dark clear sky. A sofa-bed, almost permanently set as the latter rather than the former, a wardrobe, a table, chair and a small cupboard were the only items of furniture. In addition to the communal kitchen, where each tenant seemed to raid each other's supplies, there was a communal bathroom. The décor throughout was drab and old, the carpets threadbare and the curtains grubby. As she took in her surroundings, she felt depressed and imprisoned. How could she make a success of her own life, let alone that of her child, from such dispiriting beginnings? She needed to get out of this place. She needed to better herself, work more hours at the supermarket, get a better job, earn more money, and get somewhere better to live. Her despondency retreated a little. Her fresh resolve made her impatient. As she sat looking around the room, she felt a sense of claustrophobia. She wanted a break, some relief. She felt an urgent need to get out, even if only for a few hours.

But where could she go? The time was now well past dusk. There was no prospect of relief for her at work, as she was on early shifts at the supermarket this week. She didn't want to go out alone. Who could she go to see? She looked at the bottle of vodka again and knew instantly. She got up and, grabbed her handbag. She rummaged for her mobile. She dialled the number for Nicole Greenfield.

'Hello?' Sally recognised Nicole's mother's voice.

'Hello, Mrs. Greenfield. It's Sally here. Sally Jones.'

'Oh, hello Sally. How are you?' The question was purely rhetorical. 'Did you want to speak to Nicole?'

'Yes, please Mrs. Greenfield. Is she there?'

'Let me see. She was just on her way out. I'll see if I can catch her.'

With this, she put the phone down, and Sally could hear Nicole's mother shout out. After perhaps a minute Nicole came on the phone.

'Hello stranger,' Nicole said. 'How the bloody hell are you?' Her friendly voice lifted Sally in an instant.

'Oh, I'm OK. I was just wondering what you were doing tonight, but you're obviously off out.'

'Yeah. We're off to Congreave tonight. Just a pub crawl, really.'

'Wow!' said Sally. 'That's a fair trek for a drink.'

'Yeah,' replied Nicole, 'but there's this new night-club there, you know, "Secrets" it's called. It's really good, apparently.'

'Who's going?' asked Sally.

'There's me and Jacky, and Carol, and even Alina and Jana from work said they'd come,' said Nicole, reeling off the names of mutual friends and some of The Oakland Hotel's more humble employees, all of whom were still well known to Sally. 'Why? Do you want to come too?'

'Well,' Sally said hesitatingly. She desperately wanted company, and a girl's night out sounded an enticing prospect, but there were practical problems. Congreave was some miles away, and she'd had a drink already.

'How are you getting there?' she asked.

'We're all going in Carol's car. In fact, she's waiting for me outside right now. We've got a car full already I'm afraid, but you could meet us over there. We're starting at the Swan.'

Sally looked at her watch and was surprised to see that it was already half past seven.

'Nah,' said Sally, 'I've got no money.' This was true as a generalisation, but not specific to the moment. Friday was payday. She was just using it as an excuse.

'Come on,' encouraged Nicole. 'Don't be miserable. I'll buy you a drink.'

Sally hesitated further. She was mainly concerned about the amount she'd drunk already. Their social group actually had quite a responsible attitude towards drink driving, but Sally would be ashamed to admit to Nicole that, at this early hour of the evening, she was already likely to be unfit to drive. She weighed up the situation. She didn't feel drunk, and she had had something to eat. The road to Congreave was a remote one. The chances of being stopped by the police, particularly early in the evening, were very slight. And, if she drank only soft drinks, she'd be sober enough to drive home, and she wouldn't have to spend a fortune.

'I bet boring Bradley's working tonight, isn't he?' laughed Nicole. 'Why don't you come out and have some fun?' The irony of what Nicole had just said was lost on both girls, but the comment hit the spot, nonetheless. The mention of Bradley galvanised Sally and brought to the fore her reason for the call.

'Yeah, he is,' said Sally. 'I've got something to tell you.'

'What?' said Nicole, before adding, 'You'd better be quick about it. You're keeping my drinking mates waiting!'

'OK,' said Sally, 'I'll tell you later. I'll see you in the Swan. Give me half an hour. I'm not changed or anything.' It was an impossible time scale, but grateful for the impromptu invitation, Sally didn't want to keep her friends waiting any longer.

'OK,' said Nicole. 'We'll see you there. Gotta go!' And with the sound of a car horn tooting in the background, Nicole said a hasty goodbye and hung up.

Sally looked through her party clothes and selected a ridiculously short red dress. Once she'd put it on, she instinctively knew that it was a slightly tighter fit than when she'd previously worn it, but she convinced herself that no one else would notice. She hastily put on some tights, shoes and some make-up, grabbed her coat and handbag, and dashed out to her car.

The road out of Bramton was initially the same one that Joshua had taken earlier in the day, but after a steady climb uphill, the route forked. Joshua's path had been right towards The Staging Post and beyond. Sally's went left. The road gained more height and undulated its way across the heather moorland towards Congreave. The evening was cold, and a strong wind buffeted Sally's little hatchback car. The sky was dark and moonless. Rocky outcrops, some natural features, some relics of old quarry workings, loomed out of the darkness on either side of the road. Anxious not to keep her friends waiting, she drove perhaps a little too fast. But the road was straight, and the conditions dry. She was keen for company. She felt an old chapter in her life now closed, and a new one beginning. She had things to tell them.

A sheep crossed the road in front of her. If the dumb animal had been facing her, then she may have seen its eyes reflecting the headlights of her car, but unfortunately it had its back to her when it chose just that moment to start out for the grass on the other side. She saw it late.

Sally let out a shriek. She instinctively swerved and braked to avoid the animal. In spite of the dry road, these actions induced a skid. The front wheel hit something, and the steering wheel yanked itself round in her hands. Sally's shriek turned into a full-blooded scream. The car leapt into the air.

Chapter Twelve

'*Try it again, Frank. The signal may be better here.*'

'*Hello Control. This is unit Sierra Tango 5812.*'

Frank waited a few moments and repeated his message.

'*Hello Control. This is unit Sierra Tango 5812.*'

'*Hi Frank. Receiving you loud and clear. What's the status on the reported RTC?*'

'*We're at the scene. We've located one vehicle. It's gone off the A54, west bound, just after Norton Farm. The grid reference is Sierra Kilo zero zero six six niner four. I say again, Sierra Kilo zero zero six six niner four. It appears only one vehicle involved.*'

'*Understood. Do you have casualties?*'

'*That's affirmative. Cat one. There appears to be a lone female driver. The police are working on the ID. They've got the index number, so that should help.*'

'*What's the status on the casualty?*'

'*We're not going to arrive with this one, I'm afraid. It's difficult right now. The weather's closing in. It's blowing an absolute hooley up here, and starting to snow again. They're going to need some heavy haulage or a crane in here too. We're going to have a conflab with the others, but I think may have to stand down, and try a recovery at first light.*'

'*OK. Understood. Sorry Frank. It sounds pretty grim. Give us an update when you know what's happening for sure.*'

'*Will do. Speak later.*'

★★★

Gillman looked up from the diary and considered his Assistant Manager. Gillman was sensitive enough to know that something troubled the younger man, but their relationship, strained as it perpetually seemed to be, prevented him from asking intrusive questions. The two were in the first-floor office of The Oakland. The Saturday lunchtime rush had been and gone.

'Do you want a hand with those invoices?' asked Gillman. He made the offer more out of a need to make conversation, than any real desire for the administrative chore of vetting suppliers' invoices and approving them for payment.

'No, no, I'll see to them,' said Bradley.

'I see in the middle of next month,' said Gillman after a further pause, 'that we're hosting the Peak District Hoteliers' Association meeting.'

'What's that?' said Bradley, between mouthfuls of chips, taken from the kitchen. The meal constituted his lunch. He continued to initial the invoices as he ate.

'Oh, it's just some jamboree held amongst the hotel owners and managers, guesthouses and the like in Bramton and nearby. It's just a talking shop really. I think it may have been the tourist board who first set it up. Either them or the council. They hold meetings twice a year or so, mainly just to moan about the rates.'

Gillman was about to really expound his full invective for what he considered to be an organisation that, whilst not totally worthless, certainly seemed that way to the management of a hotel like The Oakland. As the biggest, most expensive hotel in town, and part of a national chain, they had little to gain, and potentially a lot to lose by any "co-operation" with other hotels. Having previously attended the regular meetings of the group and found them to be an almost complete waste of time, he was keen to avoid any future gatherings. Before colouring Bradley King's view too much though, Gillman had an idea.

'I suppose the meetings are of some value,' he said, hoping Bradley wouldn't pick up on his apparent about face. 'Good PR for us.'

Gillman knew he had to be careful. Bandying about terms like "PR" was not exactly stock Gillman vocabulary, and it might make Bradley suspicious.

'It's probably good experience for you to attend this one, particularly since I'll have retired before the one after.'

Bradley acknowledged the suggestion without commitment.

'I see it's on the 15th,' continued Gillman. 'That's a Sunday. My night off. You'll be on though, won't you?'

'Yeah, I expect so,' said Bradley. 'You carry on. Since it's here at The Oakland, I'm sure I'll manage.'

Gillman, satisfied that his little dodge had worked, said, 'It's starts at seven-thirty in the evening. Shouldn't last more than an hour and a half or so.'

'Good,' said Bradley out aloud, before thinking to himself, *It'd better not.* He had plans for later on that particular Sunday evening.

At that moment, the phone rang. Gillman answered it, and after a few grunts, hung up. He then said to Bradley, 'Somebody in reception. Wants to see you personally.' He didn't elaborate.

Bradley finished his chips and made his way to reception where he was confronted by a police officer.

'Mr. King?' he said.

'Yes.'

'My name's PC Pemberton. Is there somewhere we could have a private word?'

A number of thoughts ran through Bradley's mind, none of which happened to be even close to the real reason for a visit from the police.

'Sure,' said Bradley. 'Follow me.'

He led the police officer up to the first-floor office, where after a brief introduction to Gillman, Bradley asked Gillman if he would excuse them. When they were alone, PC Pemberton spoke.

'You are Bradley King of Flat 2, Birch Court, Chapel Harrington?'

'Yes,' said Bradley, getting more than a little nervous. 'What's the problem?'

'Am I right in thinking you are engaged to a Miss Sally Jones?'

'Yes,' said Bradley, leaving aside the police officer's use of the present tense.

'I'm afraid, Mr. King,' continued the police officer, looking suitably grave, 'I've some bad news for you. Your fiancée has been killed in a car accident.'

The words hit Bradley as if they were a physical entity. He sat down and stared up at the police officer. His mind raced through disbelief, denial, agony, regret and back again.

'What? When?' he said, after a short period.

'Yesterday evening. I'm sorry. It must come as a terrible shock to you.'

'God! How did it happen?'

'We're not totally sure. She was driving along the Bramton to Congreave road. She obviously lost control and left the road. There doesn't appear to be any other vehicle involved. Some woman in a following car reported it. It took us some time to find the vehicle.'

'Did she…' Bradley broke off, and put his head in his hands. 'Did she die straight away?'

'Again, we can't be sure. There appear to be multiple injuries.' Pemberton was careful not to be too graphic about the accident, the inordinate time it had taken them to actually locate the vehicle, and the astonishing place in which it had finally come to rest. The woman who had reported the accident had given them only sketchy details. She'd clearly seen something, but in her nervousness, she couldn't pinpoint the exact spot. The police had spent over an hour to even find the crash site. They had cruised up and down the road three times, peering into the dark moorland, straining to see signs of the car. And even when they had eventually found it, they had shaken their heads in disbelief. Recovery of both body and vehicle had been major operations. But Pemberton recognised a pattern familiar to a lot of bereaved people he'd had to deal with over the years, that of wanting to know facts, certainties, and detail, as if somehow, the more information known, the nearer the bereaved may be to explanation, reasons and cause.

'We think she died pretty well straight away,' Pemberton continued. From what the paramedics had said to him, he was sure death must have been instantaneous.

'Was she alone in the car?'

'Yes.'

Bradley was now utterly mortified. After finishing their relationship the previous day, he'd felt awful. In spite of a certain relief at bringing the whole festering situation out into open discussion, the conclusion had left him empty. He'd thought a lot during his trek back to The Oakland. Whilst he may have escaped marriage, there was no way, in this modern age, whereby he could truly escape all his future responsibilities as a parent. During this introspection he felt he might, in time, be prepared to have settled down with Sally, but the thought of a child would have restricted his lifestyle more than he felt he could bear. Why wouldn't she have an abortion? Had he been too hasty? Could he have persuaded her eventually to have a termination?

In his mind, he'd replayed their last conversation, and he'd regretted his final brutality. It had been too harsh. His words had conveyed a feeling of never having loved Sally. As he'd walked up the road in the cold afternoon sunshine, he'd realised that that wasn't true. He had really loved Sally like no girl he'd ever previously known, even in spite of her pregnancy. He thought he still loved her. By the time he'd reached The Oakland, he was mentally halfway to a reconciliation.

But now she was gone. Any change of heart now was too late. In spite of their separation being but hours old, it was totally permanent. Bradley then began to wonder whether Sally had told anybody else of their split. Even if she had, he could possibly still deny it, pretending to the outside world that they were together right up to the moment of her untimely death. Even in this early grieving, Bradley's conscience allowed him to reflect momentarily on such martyrdom. He rather thought it suited him. How much better this, than onlookers knowing that he'd dumped her only hours before she'd died?

The convenience of avoiding an unwanted parenthood by the death of the expectant mother was far too high a price, even for someone of Bradley King's cynical worldliness. He had been deprived of his first true love by brutal tragedy, and however he related it to the world at large hereafter, he alone would know the shabby treatment he'd meted out in her final hours. He tried to remember their happier times together. He tried to put out of his mind some of the more recent routine drudgery. He recognised now that no matter what he did, he could never revert back to the happier times. The utter finality of death is obvious, but in his relatively young life, it was something that Bradley had never really dwelt upon. Sally was emotionally the closest person he'd ever known die. Her death now changed his view of life.

Bradley thought of Sally, his Sally, bruised and broken, lying in the mangled wreckage of her car. He thought of the injustice of him on his motorcycle, the way he rode it sometimes, having in the past escaped death by inches. Whereas now, sensible Sally, driving her steady little car, had contrived to kill herself. Such irony was so unfair. He desperately hoped that their final argument had not contributed, even indirectly, to the accident. He pictured her alone up on the cold, dark, windswept moor, bleeding, dying, alone. The image was too tragic for him, too graphic, and it broke him. He let out a sob, and then wept uncontrollably. This was not the way he'd intended things.

PC Pemberton put a comforting hand on the shoulder of the younger man.

'It's tough, I know. It's always hard when somebody dies, but when it's a loved one, it's even harder.'

No matter how many times Pemberton had to break this sort of bad news, he'd never get used to it. His words seemed woefully inadequate. It was at times like these when he thought policing was a shitty job. The younger the victims, the greater the waste of life, and the harder he felt the situation himself. This was a tough one.

After some minutes, Bradley composed himself.

'What happens now?' he said.

'Well,' said Pemberton, 'there'll be an inquest. It's pretty routine when there's been an accident like this.'

Bradley's brain tried to unscramble itself.

'Officer…'

'Ken.'

'Ken. Will there be some sort of medical examination?'

'It's up to the coroner, but he'll almost certainly order a post-mortem.'

'It's just…' Bradley hesitated.

'Yes?' the police officer prompted.

'Well, it's just that… Sally was pregnant.'

Pemberton expressed his further sympathy before Bradley continued, 'It's just that we'd not told anybody. It was kind of a secret, and…'

'I see,' said Pemberton.

'Will the post-mortem find out?'

'I can't say for sure. Probably.'

'Only, in a way, I'd rather it didn't come out.' Bradley couldn't be sure of his exact reasoning for this. He was still wondering whether Sally had told anyone of their break-up. If she had, and news then broke of the pregnancy, he would be considered not as some dignified, tragic martyr, but rather some heartless, callous brute, deserting his bride-to-be in her hour of need. He really thought it would be better if neither news of the break-up nor the pregnancy got into the public domain.

'It'll depend on the coroner, whether he feels he should find it as a fact,' explained the police officer.

After further consoling words, Pemberton came to the final difficult bit of the conversation.

'We understand that Miss Jones didn't have any surviving relatives. Is that right?'

'Yeah,' said Bradley. 'Her folks died quite a while ago. She'd no brothers or sisters.'

'It's just that, well, we're pretty sure of her identity from her car, her handbag and stuff, but we'd still like a positive ID from you, if you wouldn't mind.'

Bradley said he wouldn't mind. He'd already steeled himself against the gore that his imagination had conjured, and he couldn't believe that reality would be worse. He felt a comfort too, at the prospect of one last look at Sally and the opportunity to say goodbye to her.

Chapter Thirteen

'It's not happening for us, is it?' said Theodore. 'I can't believe we're going to let them get away with this.'

'No,' said Bill Hunter.

'What was the problem this morning?' asked Theodore.

'Oh, it was nothing really,' said Bill. 'Just Stan Whitmore getting a bit excited. He had a bit of a toe-to-toe with the consultant guy, Meredith. Stan was just getting a bit aerated about the way Meredith was going about the new planned maintenance system.'

'Well, it didn't sound like "nothing" from what I've heard,' said Theodore, ever thankful for Norman Crabtree's tip-off.

'Yes, well, I believe Stan did threaten to lamp him at one stage, but that's just Stan. Fortunately, Scott was on hand to smooth the thing over.'

Theodore couldn't help but smile to himself at Bill's choice of words. He admired Bill's quiet calculating manner, but he also respected the way he related to the employees on the shop floor. This was no better illustrated than in his use of certain phrases, the like of which Theodore could never hope to deliver with any credibility.

'If it's not one thing, it's another,' said Theodore. 'And as for them removing Latham off the job, it just smacks of bloody crass amateurism. Like I said, I just can't believe we're going to just lie down and let them do it to us.'

The two men were in Theodore's office, talking over a mid-morning coffee. Theodore had called Bill in to discuss the morning's incident in the maintenance department, along with the ever more pressing question of the consultancy as a whole. It had been nearly two weeks since Theodore had had his disturbing Monday morning meeting with Stuart Holroyd.

Holroyd had phoned Theodore Walklate over the previous weekend and insisted on seeing him first thing on the Monday morning. The meeting, when it arrived, had proven short and to the point. There had been a change of personnel. Ellis, Nash and Holroyd were "releasing" Joshua Latham, and Martin Meredith would be taking over the lead role for the balance of the exercise. Holroyd had been profusely apologetic over the change but had assured Theodore of his own, personal, continued support for the project, and emphasised his confidence in Meredith. Theodore had not been convinced. As well as thinking the change, coming as it did, part way through the exercise, was amateurish, he got the distinct impression from Holroyd that he wasn't getting the full picture. Theodore Walklate distrusted Holroyd. He felt the man was hiding something.

The consultancy exercise was not going as well as it might. Nobody expected miracles overnight, but improvement in performance was disappointingly slow. As the weekly charges from the outside help mounted, the pressure to see some benefit grew. A new weekly reporting system, installed by Joshua, was giving a pretty accurate picture of current factory performance, well before the traditional month end accounts came out. But all it was also showing to Theodore and Bill right now was that, even before January finally drew to a close, Walklate's likely financial performance for the month was not good.

'Have you seen the latest figures, Bill?' asked Theodore. 'We're still not going to make any bloody money.'

'Yes,' said Bill gloomily. 'Did Holroyd ever say what Latham was going off to do?'

'No, he didn't. He just said he was being "released". I pressed him on the matter, but he just clammed up. I'm sure he was trying to hide something.'

'He was much better than Meredith, wasn't he? Latham, I mean,' said Bill.

'Yes,' said Theodore. 'He was good, really. Very personable. I got some good feedback on him. Meredith's not in the same league. And as for bloody Holroyd, he promised to spend more time here. And what's happened? It's been nearly two weeks and we've seen him, what, twice? It's just not good enough!'

Theodore was winding himself up with ever increasing indignity.

'That bloody clown's bleeding us white, sending his invoices in every week, and we're getting nothing to show for it. The bottom line's no bloody better.'

'You might just rattle his cage a bit,' suggested Bill.

'What are you thinking of?'

'Well,' said Bill, 'we did write into the contract the fact that we can cancel the thing at a week's notice. We could threaten him with that. Or maybe just suspend the whole thing for a week or two. Make him sweat a bit.'

Bill had intended merely a little sabre rattling, but Theodore was already advancing the idea. He was wary about taking any major steps without consulting the rest of the board, particularly Marjorie Forsythe, but he felt an opportunity arising. He sat forward in his chair and flicked a switch on the intercom on his desk.

'Shirley?'

'Yes, Mr. Walklate.'

'Get me Stuart Holroyd on the phone, will you?'

He flicked the switch back and eased back in his chair.

Bill eyed his boss carefully, both men thinking deeply.

'You said you thought Holroyd was holding back something on Latham,' said Bill. 'You don't suppose he left to go and work for a rival set up, you know, another consultancy firm?'

'Hmm,' mused Theodore, his earlier idea advancing still further.

The phone rang and Theodore picked it up.

'Hello.'

'Mr. Holroyd on line one, Mr. Walklate,' said Shirley.

'Thank you,' said Theodore, 'and one more thing, Shirley.'

'Yes, Mr. Walklate.'

'Do a bit of detective work for me, will you? Find me Joshua Latham's home phone number. His mobile seems to be no longer in service. And Shirley, this is very important, you are not to speak to anyone at Ellis, Nash and Holroyd in order to get it. OK?'

'Yes, Mr. Walklate.' Shirley was curious, but now was not the time to ask questions. She set to the task straight away.

Theodore pressed the button next to the flashing light on his telephone console.

'Holroyd!' he barked.

'Theodore,' Holroyd answered back in a pale imitation of camaraderie. Holroyd had tried to ingratiate himself before by insisting on using first names. Theodore had resisted all attempts so far and was not about to weaken.

'We're not happy,' said Theodore. 'In fact, we're bloody upset. We're past halfway in the exercise, and whilst we recognise the effort going in, we're not getting the results out. We're in for another poor month in January.'

Holroyd leapt in.

'Theodore, I'm really surprised and sorry to hear that. What—'

'Never mind being sorry. And what about this business with Latham going? He was your best man on the job.'

This was actually news to Holroyd. Holroyd, when he'd told Theodore Walklate of Joshua's departure, had detected a certain disappointment. He'd recognised that the senior man at Walklate's had a certain respect for Joshua, but nothing quite as succinct as what he'd just heard.

'This Meredith chap,' Theodore continued, 'I'm afraid he's just not up to scratch. I appreciate there are sometimes some difficult issues to deal with, but he's like a bull in a china shop. No inter-personal skills.'

Holroyd tried to protest but couldn't interrupt Theodore's flow.

'Only this morning we had an incident, badly upsetting my maintenance foreman.'

Holroyd would have understood Bill Hunter's description of the incident somewhat faster, but he was getting the message anyway.

'He's very confrontational,' continued Theodore. 'I'm afraid this whole thing's not working out. We're paying a lot of money each week, and we're seeing damn all in return on the bottom line.'

'Theo,' said Holroyd. Big mistake. Far too familiar. 'I really am sorry. I'm sure we can work something out. Perhaps if I had a word with Martin. I could be over there this afternoon.' There was a slightly nervous edge to Holroyd's voice that Theodore recognised from before.

'Don't bother,' said Theodore. 'I'm suspending the contract immediately, and I'm going to convene a board meeting to discuss the matter. We'll decide then whether or not to cancel the whole contract.'

Theodore could feel the effect of his words as Holroyd's tone changed from edginess to near panic.

'No! Please. Don't do that. I'm sure that won't be necessary.' Holroyd was now sinking. He was mentally cursing Meredith. He'd listened to his young protégé too much. Obviously he'd misread the signs. Walklate's wanted Latham to do the job, not Meredith. His little economy, to ease the financial pressures on his own firm, had backfired. He may have made a reduction in employee costs, but he was about to lose a big slice of cash flow as a consequence. He was desperate to retrieve the situation. He even briefly considered re-employing Joshua Latham, but before the thought fully crystallised, he scanned his desk. His eyes rested on the signed copy of Joshua's settlement agreement. The severance payment had already been sent. He cursed his own precipitate judgement and the administrative alacrity with which his company had carried out the execution.

'I'll come over,' said Holroyd. 'We can discuss it.'

'Forget it, Holroyd,' said Theodore. 'I'll let you know the outcome of our meeting.' He hung up the phone and smiled across at Bill Hunter.

'This is the best I've felt for months!' Theodore said. He flicked the intercom again.

'Shirley. Any luck with that phone number?'

'Not yet, Mr. Walklate.'

'Where have you tried?'

'Er, online directory enquiries, Mr. Walklate, but we can't be sure of his exact home address, and there are 63 Lathams in the Bristol area as a whole. I've also tried The Oakland Hotel where he stayed, but they won't tell me. They say it's confidential information. They can't divulge private details about their guests.'

'Who did you speak to at The Oakland?'

'Mr. Gillman, the manager,' said Shirley, before adding, a little plaintively, 'sorry.'

'No, no, that's alright,' said Theodore. He knew Shirley well enough. She could be distinctly authoritarian when she wanted to be, and she'd gone straight for the top man at the hotel. Theodore felt even his added weight and gravitas couldn't elicit the information from that source any more successfully. He thought for a moment, the intercom line still open.

'Did he ever stay anywhere else?' asked Theodore. 'Only I seem to remember him saying he stopped elsewhere early on in the exercise.'

'Now you come to mention it, Mr. Walklate,' said Shirley, 'I think you're right. It was The Crown, I believe. I'll try them straight away.'

'No,' said Theodore quickly, 'I'll pop round and see them.'

He knew the hotel was but a short distance away. He felt visiting in person would be the surest way to get Latham's home phone number. Should he not be able to persuade, cajole or simply browbeat the hotel management into giving him Latham's details, he thought he might even distract attention easily enough for a surreptitious scan of the hotel's register.

Theodore closed the intercom line and smiled across at Bill Hunter. His plan was taking shape.

'I think we'll do more than rattle Holroyd's bloody cage,' he said, before standing up and adding, 'I've just got to pop out for half an hour or so.'

The weather being unseasonably mild, Theodore Walklate decided to walk the short distance to The Crown. As he approached the stone façade of the hotel, he observed a workman up a ladder, painting some of the window frames. He exchanged greetings with the man before entering the building. Inside he at once saw a young, blonde girl, painfully thin in Theodore's view.

'Morning,' he said. 'My name's Walklate. I'd like to speak to the manager, please.'

The girl looked overawed and in a nervous, almost squeaky voice said, 'I'll just go and find her for you.'

The girl went through a door marked "Private", and Theodore looked around the hall. He noticed the register lying closed on a sideboard that served as the reception desk. He looked quickly up at the door through which the girl had gone, and back to the register. He heard voices and footsteps and quickly dispelled any notion of helping himself to a look at the register. The door opened and an attractive-looking, dark-haired woman, whose face he vaguely remembered from somewhere, came through, followed by the mousy little blonde girl.

'Hello Mr. Walklate, I'm Tara Beaumont Smith,' said Tara, holding out her hand. 'It's nice to see you again.'

'Oh, er, yes,' said Theodore, his brain, quite happy to store obscure motor brush housing designs, sales turnover figures, production outputs, etc., now struggled.

'Thank you, Joanna,' Tara said, addressing the young girl. 'You can get on with mopping the kitchen floor again now.'

The girl turned to go but before she left, Tara added, 'And you'd better ask Fraser if he'd like a cup of coffee. He's outside, up the ladder.'

The girl made a squeak of acknowledgement. Tara turned back to Theodore Walklate. She thought he looked slightly confused.

'We met at the Christmas party,' she said. 'I never did get to thank you for the invitation. I had an absolutely super time.'

'Oh, yes, of course,' said Theodore, his mind suitably jogged. He now recalled Tara. He even managed to conjure up an image of the dress she'd worn that night, although the possibility of making any comment on it never occurred to him, either then or now.

'How can I help you?' said Tara, in the most practised version of what she thought was her business voice. She remembered Joshua's advice and recognised the potential importance of a man like Theodore Walklate to the future of her hotel business. She hadn't a clue why he'd called at The Crown, but she wasn't about to let the opportunity pass. She simply had to make a sales pitch of some sort.

'Information, really,' said Theodore. 'I understand that you had a Mr. Latham, Joshua Latham, staying here once.'

'Yes,' said Tara warily. 'He stopped a couple of times.'

'He did some work for us recently, and I need to contact him urgently. He's changed his mobile number, so I'm after his home phone number, or his address if you have it.'

'Well,' said Tara hesitatingly, 'I suppose so.'

'Oh, it's perfectly alright. I know you hotel types don't like to divulge information about your guests, but I can assure you that it's all perfectly legitimate.'

'I'm sure,' said Tara, which was true, but she was curious. 'I thought he'd been made redundant.'

'Er, well, yes,' said Theodore, not absolutely sure of the exact circumstances of Joshua's departure from Ellis, Nash and Holroyd. He was not to know that Tara had already made up her mind to give him Joshua's details. Not only was she predisposed to help Mr. Walklate in any reasonable way possible, but also she felt sure that the Walklate's interest could only be beneficial to Joshua. Without prompting, Theodore gave further, unnecessary, explanation.

'He certainly left their employment fairly suddenly,' he said. 'It's just that I'd like to talk to him. I may have a little business proposition for him.'

'Of course, Mr. Walklate.'

Tara opened the hotel register and soon found Joshua's details. She copied them onto a sheet of notepaper and handed it to Theodore. She hoped he'd be impressed with such efficiency and co-operation. She thought she'd then try hospitality.

'Would you like a cup of coffee, Mr. Walklate, whilst you're here?'

'No, thank you,' he replied quickly, in a very matter of fact tone. No reason for refusal was forthcoming, so Tara tried a different tack.

'I know you must be busy, but I understand that your company occasionally used to put people up here when my father ran the place. I was just wondering, whilst you're here, whether you'd like to have a quick look around the hotel? In case you thought of using the facilities again in the future.'

Theodore looked around the room rather than directly at Tara. She wondered at first if he'd actually heard her. She felt the need to fill the silence.

'We're actually closed at the moment. Things are pretty quiet just now, but we're taking the opportunity to make some improvements. We're doing a bit of painting and decorating.' Her voice started to trail off, as she felt herself rambling slightly.

'Some other time, perhaps,' he said. 'I do remember your father, come to think of it. Died a while back, didn't he?'

'Yes,' said Tara, getting somewhat exasperated. 'He did.'

'Hmm,' Theodore mused. 'Well, as I say, some other time maybe. Thanks very much for the information. Good day to you.'

Tara said goodbye and shook her head in disbelief. Her first meaningful conversation, assuming their dialogue actually qualified as such, had simply confirmed her impressions of the man. She thought him a rather peculiar, cold man. He came across to her as very direct, almost abrupt, and unemotional. She remembered Joshua being complimentary about Walklate's business skills which, from what she knew, she accepted without question. But from a personal view, the man behind the business seemed to her oddly awkward, almost socially unaware. She wondered what the man underneath was really like.

★★★

Outwardly, Bradley's mourning was brief. All those who thought that they knew the man, felt that this was in character. A naturally witty, jocular person, Bradley threw himself into the work of the hotel and this had a cathartic effect. He could still make people smile. He could still get employees to carry out their duties by kindly coercion rather than by diktat. Despite his obvious and profound grief, he continued his job at The Oakland with a lot of his old style. The other staff were not overly surprised at Bradley's power of recovery. It would have seemed out of character for him to be seen brooding for long. Some even thought he cut a rather noble figure, bearing his private anguish with dignity whilst projecting an affable exterior.

The brevity of his public grief, however, didn't mask the depth of his torment to those closest to him. Gillman was sympathetic to a much greater degree than Bradley had expected. The concern of the older man quite touched him.

Gillman became almost fatherly, and very understanding and considerate. He allowed Bradley all the time off that he required to enable him to carry out numerous sorry, difficult, but necessary official duties. Bradley, previously quite disparaging of the top man at the hotel, developed a new-found respect for Gillman.

Bradley had a long chat with Nicole Greenfield. The young Assistant Housekeeper had come in on the Saturday morning following her night out in Congreave with the other girls from the hotel. The new night-club had been as good as they'd hoped, and Nicole had been more than a little hung over. With puffy eyes and a thumping head, she'd gone about her duties as a pained automaton. It was only in the afternoon, her recovery almost complete, just before she was about to leave, when she'd heard the news. Between the girls the night before, they'd been disappointed at Sally's non-appearance. Some, Nicole not amongst them, had been sarcastically scathing about their absent brethren, saying that Sally was under Bradley's thumb. Nicole, having spoken to Sally on the phone, had been certain that she'd turn up, and had been confident that there must be a more serious reason for Sally's absence. But they'd waited at the Swan for nearly two hours. Sally hadn't shown, and there had been no answer from her mobile, so in the end the girls had moved on. Nicole had resolved to ring her friend the next day, or even visit her. That Saturday afternoon, when she learnt the true reason for Sally's absence, she felt positively sick. It was a hammer blow, a tragedy the likes of which she'd never known before in her young life.

It had been some days later when she and Bradley had talked. It had been a touching conversation, devoid of the sexual frisson of their earlier encounters. Their earlier intimacies made Bradley trust Nicole with a deeper insight into his true feelings. Nicole, in turn, recognised Bradley's genuine and deep-seated love of Sally, and she now felt her earlier overtures to him somewhat cheap. They consoled each other in their respective loss, and their friendship became truly platonic.

Even Anne Barrowclough, who more than most knew Bradley's less desirable track record, treated the Assistant Manager with a becoming dignity. The men at the hotel, particularly Didier Merle and Brian Mellor, to whom Bradley was closest, communicated their condolences more quietly. A knowing look, a hand on the shoulder, conveyed more amongst the male society during these dark times, than any words.

Bradley had been greatly helped in his mourning, and the sympathy offered by his colleagues made more heartfelt, by the official public pronouncements following the accident. There had been an inquest into Sally's death. The local newspaper had reported the accident. The thoroughness of the former was contrasted by the superficial sensationalism of the latter. Following the accident, the tabloid *Bramton Chronicle* duly made a front-page splash of the "horror death crash". The follow-up article the week after relegated the findings of the inquest to a small paragraph near the bottom of page five. The car accident had occurred over the county boundary and came under the Cheshire district. The inquest had been held in Warrington. This was sufficiently far removed to ensure that the *Chronicle* simply gleaned its information from a phone call to a sister publication. The inquest returned a verdict of accidental death. The post-mortem found that the deceased driver had been over twice the legal limit for blood alcohol. It also revealed the pregnancy of the deceased. The coroner duly recorded this as fact, but the reporter on the *Bramton Chronicle* somehow lost this little snippet. To Bradley's eternal gratitude, the knowledge of Sally's pregnancy never properly entered the wider public domain.

Bradley had attended the inquest. He was astonished as the reports from the emergency services revealed the full facts of Sally's final moments. The fact that the driver was over the legal limit for alcohol was viewed with some surprise by all who knew Sally. Most thought of her as a sensible girl, who simply didn't do silly things like drink driving. But in the light of the scientific evidence, they all accepted that this must be the true cause of the accident. Nobody but Bradley ever looked for anything deeper. He apparently was the only person in Bramton to know of Sally's pregnancy and the strength of her abstinence. That she was drunk, let alone drunk whilst driving, he found disturbing. In the darkest corner of his conscience, he wondered if their final argument had driven her to drink, and whether, indirectly, he had contributed to her death.

Would the accident have happened even if Sally had been sober? The skid marks on the road clearly indicated her loss of control of the vehicle for whatever reason. Her car had hit a storm drain at the road edge. At a speed estimated to be around that of the national limit, the vehicle had clearly bounced up into the air, and projected over the adjacent drystone wall. The car had then glissaded over the narrow, waterlogged and steeply sloping field beside the road, and had tipped over the face of some old quarry workings. Bradley had learnt a hard lesson regarding the local geology and geography. The gritstone that formed the landscape of the hills that surrounded Bramton to the south, had provided man for many years with a workable material. Like most others now, the quarry near Norton's Farm had long since been exhausted. A fence had been erected to protect livestock from the old quarry edge. Totally inadequate for anything more substantial, it had collapsed on impact by the car.

Bradley had sat impassioned, listening to the evidence given by the emergency services. Initially incredulous at the final resting place of Sally's car, he had later visited the site. His pilgrimage showed just why, especially in the dark, it had taken so long to find the vehicle, and why, once found, the emergency services had even included the local mountain rescue team in the recovery operation.

Following the inquest, the funeral was as emotionally charged as such events ever can be. Given Sally's lack of surviving relatives, the turnout, consisting of friends and work colleagues, past and present, was impressive. During the service, many cried openly. At one point one of the younger, more impressionable girls from The Oakland, let out a plaintive wail. At this moment Bradley did question in his own mind, why people put themselves through the trauma of a funeral service. After further thought he concluded that, even for non-religious people, the service did offer an opportunity to formally say goodbye to the departed. Bradley certainly found the funeral a line drawn, underscoring a completed chapter in his life. Afterwards, recent though his pain still was, he felt able to look forward. He was emotionally scarred, both from Sally's love, as well as her death, but at least he felt able to face the future, once again, on his own. He became mentally tougher, colder. Ironically, in spite of this hardening of spirit, he also became emotionally more temperamental.

Bereavement begets introspection. As January turned into February, Bradley reflected on what a hard winter it had been, at least for him emotionally. He'd known people die before, but nobody as close to him as Sally had been. Both his parents were still alive, his siblings, and even his grandparents. Death of a close personal friend or relative was something he'd previously only read or heard about involving other people. Bradley knew that death was an everyday occurrence, but subconsciously, he'd always felt it somehow only ever involved other, more detached people. Sally's death had smashed a fist clean through this benign self-deception. During the weeks following, Bradley matured. For the first time in his life, he really understood and appreciated the transience of life, and the finality of death. His personality was too well developed to fundamentally change, but the events of the winter made him grow up.

His final duty had been to clear out Sally's personal effects from her bedsit. There was no will. The winding up of Sally's bank account, a building society savings account and her employment details, would all have to wait for the legal process to grind inexorably to a conclusion. But in the meantime, an impatient landlord had insisted that Bradley clear out Sally's belongings from her room. Bradley gave all her clothes to a local charity shop. Her remaining artefacts came to an astonishingly small amount. After throwing away some magazines and some other worthless trinkets, and clearing out her stuff in the communal kitchen, he'd been left with barely enough to fill a large shoe box. In a poignant gesture, he gave the girls at the hotel the pick of the surplus make-up, perfume and jewellery. Overwhelmed by the sheer pathos represented by such remnant trivia that was all that remained of his Sally, he cried for the last time. He had felt an almost overwhelming desire to rid himself of all her possessions. It had been an action, a futile one as he had quickly realised, to try to expunge her from his memory. He did not feel the need for any mementoes. But he had soon realised that he would never forget her. She'd meant too much to him for that. Only at the last had he relented, making a solitary gesture. He had looked long and hard at Sally's engagement ring. It was a slim gold band complete with a single imitation gem. It had little intrinsic value, but in sentiment, it spoke volumes to Bradley. He resolved to keep the engagement ring as his lone physical keepsake, quietly slipping it into his pocket.

Chapter Fourteen

'So, will you do it?' asked Theodore Walklate of Joshua Latham. The two men, along with Bill Hunter, were in the dining room of Fallowfield Grange, having just finished another exquisite concoction prepared by Janice Hurtle. Theodore poured each of his two guests another large measure of brandy whilst he waited, quietly confident, for Joshua's response.

'Well, Theodore,' said Joshua, now having been included amongst the privileged elite, allowed, at least in private, to call his host by his first name. 'In the present circumstances, it's an offer I can't refuse.'

Joshua had driven up that afternoon following the phone call from Theodore inviting him to dinner. Theodore had said that he wanted to discuss a certain proposition with him. Intrigued, Joshua had made a few phone calls, and had correctly anticipated the subject matter to be discussed. Joshua had been unable to resist a smile on learning of the suspension of Ellis, Nash and Holroyd, and he revelled in Theodore's description of Stuart Holroyd's resultant apoplexy. Holroyd, despite instruction to the contrary, had come over to Bramton. Utterly desperate, he'd pleaded to have a meeting with Theodore Walklate. Theodore had refused, claiming to be busy. Joshua allowed himself a little schadenfreude as he enjoyed the discomfort of his former boss. Uncharitable maybe, but the comeuppance, particularly as it related so closely to one involving Joshua's own recent demise, was especially sweet. After his abortive attempt to meet the top man at Walklate's, Holroyd had driven home disconsolate, to await the outcome of the forthcoming meeting of the Walklate board.

Aside from some initial reservations from Marjorie, Theodore's impulsive decision to suspend the contract had met with general approval. At first, Marjorie had suspected Theodore of some subterfuge, and had tried to fathom out his motives. The consultants had thus far given the sales function a pretty wide berth. Compared to the other departments, her son Andrew had been largely spared serious interrogation. When she had attended the hastily convened board meeting, however, and learned of Theodore's alternative, she had felt more relaxed. Initial consensus at the meeting agreed that the consultancy exercise had been expensive, and whilst promising much, had thus far delivered little financial reward. There had been a suggestion that the exercise be formally terminated, simply paying up outstanding expenses. Jasminder Kaur, the Finance Director, had argued against such a move, saying that they would probably be denying themselves the full benefits of the project. Having come as far as they had with the exercise, there was a distinct feeling that there couldn't be much more corporate pain to endure before its conclusion, and that substantial improvements were "only just around the corner". The management team had been reluctant to start again with another consultant. Opinion had been voiced saying that the suspension itself may have delivered sufficient shock, and that Ellis, Nash and Holroyd, if allowed, would recommence the exercise with more concentrated minds. It had been at this point that Theodore had tabled his proposal. He had suggested that they formally cut all links with Holroyd and his company, and approach Joshua Latham privately. His intention was that Walklate's should offer Joshua a contract to continue the exercise. The plan was very attractive. It ensured continuity of the project through to its rightful conclusion. It addressed the vexed question of personalities, Joshua being seen universally amongst the Walklate's staff as the best, most personable and experienced of the outsiders. And Theodore had then carried the day when he had pointed out that, in all reasonableness, they would likely get Joshua Latham for less money!

'What if the guy's got another job already?' Jasminder Kaur had asked.

Theodore had been able to deliver a very satisfactory response.

'He hasn't,' he'd said. 'I checked with him. Whatever Holroyd's told us about Latham being "released", he's actually been made redundant. As we speak, he's out of work. I think, since we all seem agreed, I would like this meeting to sanction an approach directly to Mr. Latham by Bill Hunter and myself, with a view to offering him the balance of the contract. Any objections?'

There had not been a murmur. And so Theodore had phoned and invited Joshua to come up to Bramton and have dinner at Fallowfield Grange. During the drive, Joshua had reflected on how all his northbound journeys seemed so optimistic, in sharp contrast to those undertaken in the other direction. He'd set off in good heart and was at least halfway before he'd realised that he'd not booked any hotel accommodation. He was still using his old company car, it being contractually his for at least another three weeks, but he'd had to give his old company mobile phone back. He'd bought a new one privately and thought of making a call to make a reservation, but he'd known that the hotel where he really wanted to stay would not be full. He decided he'd just turn up and surprise the management.

Tara had been duly surprised and pleased to see Joshua. Rose had immediately gone into a flap, saying that the hotel was in fact, shut. Tara had patiently assured her number two that opening the hotel for their surprise guest simply meant making up a bed, turning some heating on, and moving some of the paint pots and dust sheets. The next problem for Rose, that of no dinner being prepared, had been solved by Joshua himself, when he'd announced his dinner appointment at Fallowfield. He'd barely had ten minutes to change before he'd had to go out again.

'I'll happily accept your offer,' said Joshua. 'When do you want me to start?' He knew that Theodore Walklate had shrewdly screwed the fee for the remaining work as low as possible. In the short interval since his redundancy though, Joshua had made little headway in searching for alternative employment, and here, almost literally on a plate, was an offer of work, albeit only on a temporary basis. Other prospects had looked slim. He was disinclined to argue over the price.

He had vaguely thought of becoming self-employed, working as a management consultant, but he'd been slightly overawed, knowing that building up his own client base would take time. Touting for new business, even cold calls, was a necessary part of the job, and one that Joshua always felt the least confident about. He was not naturally gregarious, and always preferred to leave the task of gaining new business to others within the organisation. His forte he felt, was the project work itself. The risk in becoming self-employed was that of exhausting his redundancy money before much new business came in. The proposition from Walklate's now bolstered Joshua's confidence.

'Shall we say Monday?' suggested Theodore.

'That sounds fine,' said Joshua, and they shook hands on the deal.

'You feel confident about the restrictive covenant in your old contract?' asked Bill Hunter, ever pragmatic.

'Yes,' said Joshua. 'It's been superseded by my settlement agreement. I'm in the clear.'

'Good,' said Bill.

'No,' continued Joshua, 'I'm afraid Holroyd may not like me working for you, but legally, there's damn all he can do about it.'

'And even if Holroyd did cut up a bit rough,' said Theodore, 'we'd stick by you, rest assured.'

Joshua couldn't be sure just how far Theodore Walklate would support him under such circumstances, but he was nonetheless grateful for the sentiment.

The remaining conversation centred on specific areas to be addressed during the rest of the project, particularly sales.

'Quite candidly, gentlemen,' said Joshua, 'we recognised a few problems with the set up in sales and maybe even with the people involved. We'd tossed around a few possible solutions, but frankly we…' Joshua hesitated, 'well, it was Holroyd really, he told me to back off. He said I should leave the sales side until near the end of the project.'

'What were you thinking of?' asked Bill.

Over a further cup of coffee, Joshua outlined what he had originally intended for the structure of the sales and marketing set up at Walklate's.

'I'd always intended to spend some time out on the road with Andrew,' concluded Joshua, 'just to see the lie of the land, but I thought the plan, if instigated sensitively, would work.'

'Sure, sure,' said Theodore, nodding vigorously. 'It sounds very good to me. Just make sure you don't wait too long. If it all proves feasible, I'd like you to implement the plan before you finish.'

The conversation came to a natural conclusion and after liqueurs, Bill and Joshua made to leave.

'I take it you came by taxi too?' said Bill Hunter. 'We can share one on the way back if you like.'

Joshua agreed, Theodore telephoned to book the taxi, and the men filled their remaining time with small talk.

'Done much shooting recently?' asked Bill of Theodore.

'No,' said the older man with a slightly doleful expression. 'It's not the season. I haven't been for ages now. I've still got my guns, but I'm afraid, with the state of the firm lately, I've not really had the time, even down at the range. These days I seem to spend more and more time in the office.'

He avoided adding that his extra time at work seemed to go in inverse proportion to the performance of the company.

'You never got another dog either, did you, Theo?' asked Bill.

'No,' said Theodore, before explaining for Joshua's benefit, 'My gun dog died about eighteen months ago. It was a Labrador. Lovely dog. I'd had him since he was a puppy. I was going to get another, but with one thing and another, I never seemed to find the time. I never thought it fair to have a dog, only to keep it cooped up in the house most of the time.'

For the first time Joshua could remember, he thought he detected a small spark of emotional attachment within Theodore Walklate. The distinguished grey-haired man, his eyes rheumy, looked pensive. He clearly had fond memories of his dog, doubtless a faithful companion, retrieving his master's kills. It was a side to Theodore Walklate that Joshua hadn't seen before. The doorbell rang and interrupted the reverie. Bill and Joshua put on their coats. Joshua thanked his host for the meal and the forthcoming business and went out to the waiting taxi.

'Evening, Bill,' said the driver.

'Hello, Bob,' replied Bill. 'How are you?'

'Good, thanks. I know you, don't I?' said the driver to Joshua, as he and Bill got in the car.

'Yeah,' said Joshua, recognising Bob Lumsden. 'You must be the only taxi driver in town. Whenever I need a taxi, it always seems to be you.' Joshua was smiling as he spoke the words.

'Nah,' laughed Lumsden. 'But I am the best! Where to first, gents?'

They decided to drop Bill Hunter off first. Once reminded of the address, Lumsden set off confidently. Joshua suspected that he'd done the journey a few times before. The taxi took a number of narrow lanes and turns, before reaching the small village of Boarheadclough.

'Put it on the account,' said Bill Hunter to Lumsden as he got out of the car. He leant back in and shook hands with Joshua. 'See you Monday.'

From Boarheadclough, Lumsden drove up a short hill to a "T" junction with a major road.

'I'm glad you know where you're going,' said Joshua, 'because you've lost me!'

'This is the main Congreave to Bramton road now,' said Bob, ever chatty. 'Oakland is it, chief?'

'No. The Crown, please.'

'Bad smash 'ere the other week,' the driver said, 'about half a mile up 'ere, on the right. Girl got killed.'

'That's bad news,' said Joshua. 'Local girl?'

'Yeah. Bramton. Pissed up, mind. But even so, kind o' tragic. Nobody else involved. Young, she was, too.'

In a short distance, Lumsden pointed out the exact spot where the accident had occurred, expressing, not for the first time, his amazement over the circumstances of the crash and the final resting place of the vehicle. Joshua peered into the passing gloom and tried to imagine the scene.

'How the bloody hell she managed it, I'll never know,' continued Lumsden. 'She was engaged to a bloke who works at The Oakland. You might know him. Oh, what's 'is name? King. Bradley King. That's it. Do you know 'im?'

'Yes, I do actually,' said Joshua. 'He's the Assistant Manager. Seemed quite a reasonable bloke to me. Not that I know him that well.'

'Hmm,' mused Lumsden. 'I'm not so sure about that. When I said, "engaged" I meant, they were, but I understood they'd split up. On the day she was killed too.'

'Oh,' said Joshua, genuinely curious, 'how on earth do you know that?'

'One of the lads on the rank told me. He picked up a fare from The Red Lion, late lunchtime that day. This old boy then told 'im how he'd seen these two, you know, King and his missus, having a right ding-dong. A real 'umdinger apparently. At each other's throats, apparently. Reckoned it was better than the telly. Anyway, the long and the short of it was that he chucked 'er.'

'That's sad,' said Joshua trying not to be too judgmental. Lumsden cut rudely across this sentiment.

'Bastard!' said Lumsden.

'Beg pardon?'

'Bit of a bastard. No pun intended.'

'Who?' asked Joshua.

'Bradley King. Bit of a bastard, if you ask me.'

Joshua wasn't at all sure he was actually asking, but he had a sneaky feeling that the garrulous driver was going to give him the benefit of some further juicy titbit.

'His girlfriend, fiancée or whatever she was,' continued Lumsden, 'she was up the duff. According to this bloke anyway. That's what they were arguing about.'

'Pardon?' said Joshua, unfamiliar with the vernacular.

'She was pregnant. At the time he chucked 'er. And then she got 'erself killed. Poor lass. Fancy dumping 'er at a time like that!'

Joshua was genuinely quite shocked at this bit of gossip. Whether it was true or not, it certainly conjured up a hideous scenario. Still trying not to judge people that he didn't know well, Joshua thought the whole episode could only reflect badly on the young Assistant Manager of The Oakland. Either Lumsden was right in his prognosis of the man, or the girl must have done something truly awful to merit such treatment. Joshua shrugged. As the car descended the long hill into Bramton, Joshua turned and looked back at the moorland now towering over them. He spent the rest of the journey in silence.

Chapter Fifteen

———

'Looking for something?' asked Tara. She'd come into the kitchen of The Crown to find Rose rummaging around in a briefcase containing some of the hotel's records.

'Yeah,' said Rose distractedly, without looking up. 'I'm looking for Fraser's home address.'

'Why?' said Tara.

'Well,' said Rose, 'I've got something to send him.'

'Rose?' said Tara with a quizzical incline of her head. 'It's finally happened, hasn't it?'

'Uh?' said Rose, looking up. 'What's happened?'

'You've gone completely loopy,' said Tara laughing. 'You are looking for Fraser's address, so that you can post him something?' Her words rang with mocking incredulity.

'You'll be seeing him in another hour or so,' Tara continued. 'He'll be here, serving dinners.' A sudden rush of three unexpected guests over the weekend, all hardy outdoor walking types, had forced the postponement of some of the more ambitious decorating in the hotel's public areas. Fraser had consequently gone home to change with the intention of returning later, to his more usual role of waiting at tables.

'Ah!' said Rose sheepishly, instantly seeing that her explanation had been less than full and satisfactory. 'Well, you see, it's got to be posted, as he mustn't know who it's from.'

'You're posting it. And he mustn't know who it's from? You're not making any sense.'

'It's a Valentine card,' said Rose sheepishly.

Tara couldn't contain her amusement and let out giggle. 'What! You're sending a Valentine to Fraser?'

'Oh, it's only a joke. I don't really fancy him. It's just a bit of a laugh.'

'Rose,' said Tara, 'I look upon you in a new light. Come on, I'll find his address for you, if you let me see the card.'

Rose agreed, and Tara took over the searching duties, quickly locating her employee's address. As she passed it to Rose, Tara looked at the romantic missive.

'You've got two cards here,' said Tara.

'Oh, I know,' said Rose, 'but I haven't thought what to do with the other one, yet.'

'So you, Rose Whitworth, are now a serial romantic. Not content with stirring the passion of our dear Scottish waiter and part-time handyman, you're going to inflict your affection on some other poor unsuspecting man. You are incorrigible!'

'Give over,' said Rose, sharing her employer's mirth with an embarrassed laugh of her own. 'I've decided to send that one to Fraser,' she said, pointing.

Tara looked at the card. It was a comic one, with a suitably rude ditty inside. Rose had signed it with a simple question mark and a series of crosses.

'Oh, I do like a bit of romance,' said Rose as she transcribed Fraser's address to the envelope.

'I thought you said you didn't fancy him?' said Tara.

'I don't!' protested Rose. 'He's ugly, always talking football, and when he gets excited, you can't hardly tell what he's saying.'

'How old is he?' asked Tara.

'About thirty, I think,' replied Rose.

'So he could be your toy-boy, then,' said Tara, smiling. Rose was sitting at the big kitchen table, sealing down the envelope.

'Now, now,' said Rose with simulated indignity, 'I'm not that much older than him!'

Tara pulled up a stool, sat down next to Rose, and continued her playful baiting.

'And does he still live at home with his mother?' It was a question to which Tara already knew the answer.

'So what if he does?' Rose tried to feign indifference. Rose looked across at Tara, and the instant their eyes met, they both burst out laughing.

'So you do fancy him!' said Tara, thoroughly enjoying teasing her assistant.

'I do not!' said Rose, but with slightly less conviction than earlier. 'It's just that, well, I like to receive Valentines, and I figure if you don't send 'em, you'll likely not receive any. You'd like to receive a card on Valentine's Day, wouldn't you?'

Tara could feel their conversation being turned.

'I suppose so,' she said, 'I'm not sure.'

'Well,' said Rose, 'maybe when you're as pretty as you are, you don't have to send any. Just sit back and wait for the postman. But when you're a plain Jane like me, you got to work at it.'

'So,' said Tara, 'who's the lucky recipient of this other card?'

The two women looked at the second Valentine card. Unlike the first, this one was a seriously romantic one. On the cover, under the words, "On Valentine's Day", was a watercolour depicting red roses in a vase, and the inside contained a short verse, which Tara read aloud. It said:

Come live with me, and be my love,
And we will some new pleasures prove,
Of golden sands, and crystal brooks,
With silken lines, and silver hooks.
                              (John Donne)

'Bit serious, isn't it?' said Tara.

'Well, they hadn't got much choice in the shop,' said Rose. 'I wasn't sure which one would be suitable, so I bought both. I was in a hurry.'

Tara laughed again. She really thought the whole idea of Rose sending out Valentine cards to be hilarious.

'Rose,' she said, 'you're *always* in a hurry. Well, I think you chose the right one to send to Fraser. I think this one's a mite too intellectual for him. Come on then, so who's it going to be? Whose heart are you going break next?'

'I don't know,' continued Rose, 'I shall save it for next year probably, unless you want to send it?'

'Me!'

'Yes, go on.' Rose was determined to enjoy her turn to tease. 'You must fancy someone.'

'Not really,' said Tara.

Rose was not to be put off so easily. 'What about that Joshua bloke, the one who took you to that Italian place that time. Here earlier this week. You soon opened up the place for ' im, didn't you?'

'Hmm,' Tara mused, 'he's alright.'

'I thought he was quite a dish. You said so too I seem to remember. Just your type an' all. And you were getting on so well,' said Rose.

'Rose! Stop it! You'll have me marrying him, next. Besides, he'll be here again Sunday afternoon. He's working in Bramton again. If I send it to his home address, it'll probably not get there until Monday.'

'Go on with you. Today's Friday. Tomorrow's Valentine's Day. First class post ought to do it.'

'No,' said Tara firmly.

The two women sat in silence for a few seconds, delighting in acting like a couple of carefree schoolgirls.

'Oh,' said Rose, 'there must be someone's heart you want to melt. Someone who'd be a challenge, even for you.'

After further brief thought, Rose said, 'What about that old frosty bloke? You know, the one you told me about at that Christmas party.'

'You mean Mr. Walklate?' said Tara, with rising scepticism.

'Yeah. He came here the other day for something. You said he was a bachelor.'

'But he's old enough to be my father!' said Tara with a shriek. 'I couldn't send it to him!'

'Well, you were the one going on about toy-boys,' said Rose. 'He could be your sugar daddy. He's quite good looking for his age. And he must have pots of money.'

There was a short silence.

'Go on,' egged Rose.

Tara could feel her resolve weakening. It was true. Theodore Walklate maybe wasn't her type at all, but he certainly represented a challenge. Rose's description of frosty had been apt. Tara recalled how she'd been intrigued by the man's seeming indifference to her at the Christmas party. Tara had a feeling of being set up by the mischievous Rose, but her impulsive tendencies took over.

'Oh, give it here, then!' Tara said, and the two girls, for that is what they'd become again, fell about in fits of conspiratorial giggles.

Rose handed Tara the ballpoint pen she'd been using.

'No, no,' said Tara. 'This calls for my fountain pen.'

Tara got up and fetched her handbag from some coat pegs by the back door of the kitchen. She sat back down, and after a brief root around the contents of her bag, came out with her best writing implement.

'Right,' she said, 'what shall I put?'

After a moment she began writing inside the card. Careful to use only capital letters, she wrote very neatly, the words, "From a secret admirer" under the printed verse.

'There!' she said. 'That ought to mystify him. Now what's his address?'

A quick consultation online initially proved fruitless.

'He'll be ex-directory, I bet,' said Rose. 'Send it to his work.'

Tara agreed. The internet now gave the full postal address of Walklate and Co, and she duly addressed the envelope, again being sure to use capitals throughout. Before sealing the envelope, Tara hesitated. Rose looked at her. Tara dived back into her handbag.

'Now what are you doing?' asked Rose.

'We'll just give him a dose of something exotic,' said Tara, pulling out of her handbag a small bottle of perfume. As Tara put a tiny dab of the scented oil on the inside flap of the envelope, the two couldn't resist another fit of giggles.

'Oh,' said Rose, 'that's that expensive stuff too, innit?'

'It's "Lovely",' said Tara.

'Hmm, it is, isn't it,' said Rose slowly, savouring the smell, 'but I don't think it'd suit me.'

'No,' said Tara. 'That's the name. It's called "Lovely".

Tara put her card in its now lightly scented, pale blue envelope and sealed it.

The door from the hall opened, and in walked Joanna Pierce.

'Hello, Jo,' said Rose. 'You finished now?'

'Yeah,' said Joanna in her customary quiet voice. 'I'll be getting off now, then.'

'Is it that time already?' said Rose, looking at her watch before continuing, 'right, my girl, well, you'd best be off then.'

Rose now got up and looked out of the window. 'I should make haste too. It's just starting to rain out there.'

Joanna put on her coat, and was about to go out of the back door of the kitchen, when Rose said, 'Joanna, can you just nip to the Post Office for us please, on your way home?'

Without waiting for a response, Rose went to her handbag, and produced a book of stamps. She stuck one on each of the two recently sealed envelopes, and with a wink at Tara, Rose said, 'There you go, Jo. Can you put them in the box at the main Post Office? They must be delivered on time. They're very important, particularly this here one from Tara.'

Rose demonstrably waved the pale blue envelope. 'So you make sure you put them in the main Post Office, OK?'

Tara could see that Rose was struggling to keep a straight face.

'It's not far out of your way, is it?' said Rose.

It wasn't, and Joanna quietly assented to the task, said goodbye, and left. As Tara watched her young employee leave, she got up to shut the back door properly. Recent rain had made it damp, and it had warped slightly. It now required a hefty slam to close effectively, something that seemed quite beyond the elfin Joanna Pierce. As Tara opened the door in preparation to give it the desired slam, her eye caught some movement in the small yard immediately outside the kitchen. She had to look twice to be sure but there was no mistake. With the door still ajar, she turned to Rose, who now had her hands in the kitchen sink, peeling potatoes.

'Rose?' said Tara.

'Yes,' said Rose, without looking up.

'Rose. There's a small black Labrador out here.'

'Oh, is there?' said Rose in surprise.

'Rose,' said Tara patiently, 'don't act so surprised. It appears to be eating some of our left-over beef, and it's eating it off one of our hotel plates.'

Rose was silent.

'Have you put this food out for it?' Tara asked.

'Well, yes,' said Rose, 'it was only a few scraps. We were going to chuck 'em out anyway. And it's not an "it", it's a "she".'

'Rose,' said Tara dryly, still looking quizzically at her assistant. 'I feel the second Rose Whitworth surprise of the day coming on. This dog, it's not the first time she's been here, is it?'

'Er, well, no, not exactly,' said Rose.

'How long have you been feeding this animal, Rose?'

'Oh,' said Rose, 'I can't just remember—'

'Rose!' Tara's voice was raised ever so slightly, but at the same time, a sly turning up of the corners of her mouth betrayed her lack of any real severity.

'About five weeks,' said Rose, looking down at the floor.

'Five weeks!'

'Yes, well,' said Rose, resuming her normal vocal skills. 'It was just after Christmas, and she were ever so thin. I reckon she was one of them unwanted Christmas presents, you know. She's only young. Probably got slung out by Boxing Day. She just turned up one day. I had to feed 'er. She just keeps coming back. I call her Bess.'

'Rose,' said Tara, noting that their new, non-paying guest now had a name, 'what's the health officer going to say if he ever comes round to inspect the place? We can't have dog bowls full of half-eaten scraps lying all over the floor, and where's she going to do her business? Who's going to take her for walkies?'

'Oh, I'll do that. I'll take her for walks in the park, and in the woods. And she always eats all her food. And she doesn't come in the kitchen. I only feed 'er in the back yard, and she only sleeps in the laundry.'

'She sleeps in the laundry room!'

The laundry room consisted of a large, detached stone building occupying a good half of the back yard of The Crown. It housed a large, industrial-sized washing machine, and an equally large tumble drier, both machines designed to cope with laundering all the hotel bedding and towels. What room that was left in the outbuilding was almost all taken up with a couple of freezers that housed the provisions for the hotel.

'Well,' continued Rose, 'it's been so cold lately. I bought her a basket off the market, earlier on in the week. It was only cheap. I paid for it myself.'

Tara sighed. For the second time in half an hour, she could

feel herself losing control of the situation, largely, if not exclusively, at the behest of her so-called assistant.

'Go on,' said Rose, 'you know you like dogs. You said so yourself. You told me all about the one you had as a kid, and how you enjoyed taking it for walks and stuff. She won't be any trouble. Please say we can keep her.'

Tara knew the truth of all that Rose had just said. Tara had always liked dogs. It had only been her itinerant lifestyle of the last few years that had made keeping such a pet impractical. Now that she was settled in Bramton that difficulty was removed. Rose had argued a good case and was clearly prepared to do the lion's share of looking after the animal. Tara looked out at the dog. Having demolished the last of the food, and dutifully licked the plate clean, Bess looked up at Tara expectantly, wagging her tail excitedly. The dog's eyes were large, staring, pleading. Never one to ponder long over a decision, Tara relented.

'Alright then,' she said, 'but she's your responsibility, Rose. She only sleeps in the laundry room, and you keep her out of the kitchen and all the public areas of the hotel. In fact, keep her out of the main hotel building altogether. Do you hear?'

'Yes, of course,' said Rose. 'Oh, thank you.'

Rose put down her potato peeler, shook the excess water off her hands, and made to go out to greet her newly legitimised pet. As she passed Tara standing by the kitchen door, Rose put her wet hands up to Tara's cheeks and gave them a playful pinch.

'You won't regret it, you'll see,' said Rose.

Tara, smiling now, wiped her cheeks with her hands, sighed again, and shook her head.

Meanwhile, as Tara and Rose were discussing canine practicalities, Joanna made her way home. The rain, that had started as she'd left the hotel, now turned into a steady downpour. Her hair, face and coat soon became sodden. As she trudged on through the ever-increasing puddles on the pavement, she became aware of a large car slowly pulling up beside her. She stopped and turned to the vehicle. It was a taxi. The nearside front window of the car glided downwards.

'It's young Joanna Pierce, isn't it? Do you want a lift?' It was the affable Bob Lumsden.

Joanna leaned in through the window.

'Hello, Mr. Lumsden,' she said, relieved to see a face she recognised. 'I'm afraid I've not got much money on me at the moment.'

'Oh, I didn't mean for a fare,' he said. 'Hop in, or you'll drown in this weather.'

Joanna opened the car door and got in. The car was warm and dry, and Bob Lumsden immediately closed the window with the press of a button, and turned the blower up to full, to keep the windscreen clear.

'Nah,' he said smiling. 'Only being charitable. I couldn't see a young lass getting soaked, even if it does do me out of a fare. You on your way home? You still live up Parkside?'

'Yes,' said Joanna meekly. 'Are you sure it's not out of your way?'

'No problem. I was on my way back to the rank, anyway. I used to go to school with your mum, you know. You work at that Crown place, don't you?'

'Yes,' said Joanna. 'I've just finished.'

Lumsden skilfully weaved his car through the traffic, and turned up a road towards the Parkside housing estate. After half a mile, snaking through the estate, Lumsden pulled up outside a semi-detached house.

'There you go, sweetheart,' said Lumsden. 'Remember me to your mum, won't you?'

'Yes, Mr. Lumsden,' said Joanna. 'Thanks ever so for the lift.'

She was just about to get out of the car when she hesitated. She looked up at Lumsden.

'What's up, love?' he said.

'Oh,' she said, 'I was meant to drop these off at the Post Office.'

She retrieved the two envelopes from her bag.

'Give 'em 'ere,' said Bob Lumsden. 'I'll stick 'em in the box at the bottom of the hill.'

As he took the envelopes from the young girl, he could see her hesitate further. She eventually spoke.

'They're very important apparently,' she said in a plaintive little voice, 'especially this one from Miss Smith. I was told they had to be posted from the main Post Office to make sure they arrived on time.'

'Oh,' said Lumsden, now holding the envelopes and realising he'd effectively already volunteered himself for the extra errand. *Still*, he thought, *it won't be too far out of my way to call at the Post Office on the way back to the taxi rank.*

'No problem,' he said. 'I'll stick 'em in the main Post Office then.'

Suitably assured, Joanna again thanked Lumsden for the lift, and got out of the car. Lumsden, conscientious as ever, duly drove around to the main Post Office. He pulled up on the double yellow lines outside, turned on his hazard warning lights, or "permission to park anywhere lights" as he called them, and was about to get out when he looked again at the ever so important envelopes with which he had been entrusted. One was white, the other, the one Joanna had specifically referred to, was pale blue. Lumsden could make out a pleasant smell coming from somewhere, and he lifted the pale blue envelope to his nose to confirm the source. He looked at the address on the front, and smiled to himself, before braving the rain.

Chapter Sixteen

'Ah, so this is where the skivers hang out,' said Bradley King as he sneaked up behind Didier Merle.

'I am 'aving a smoke,' said the chef.

'Smoke?' said Bradley. 'Is that what you call setting fire to those disgusting rolls of dried camel droppings and old bus tickets?'

Didier wanted to ignore the jibe, but he felt he had to stand his corner for France.

'Our cigarettes are far superior to your English rubbish. And any 'ow, 'ow do you know? You don't smoke yourself.'

'Too true,' said Bradley. 'One of the few vices in life that's never really appealed to me.'

It was Sunday evening. It was quiet in the dining room, with only three tables filled at the time. Although still early in the dinner sitting, the sky outside was quite dark. Didier's cigarette smoke drifted away in a cool breeze. The two men stood side by side contemplating the view. From their vantage point outside the back door of the kitchen at The Oakland, they had a grand vista encompassing three large-scale waste bins, two empty beer barrels, and half a dozen assorted empty crates. The whole area was almost completely screened from the outside world by some wooden fence panels. Through a narrow access gap, they could glimpse the greater world of the hotel car park beyond.

'Not many in tonight, chef,' said Bradley, conversationally.

'No,' agreed Didier. 'So you can leave early I think.'

'Hmm, maybe,' said Bradley. 'I'd like to be away, but Gillman's landed me with this Hotel Association Meeting.'

'When is that?'

'Half seven,' said Bradley, 'in the number two function room.'

'Your timing, Monsieur King,' said Didier, pulling hard on his cigarette, 'is impeccable.' He pronounced the last word as in French.

'How do you make that out?' asked Bradley.

Didier raised an eyebrow quizzically. 'Because you only come to the smoker's place when there is something to see.'

'What's that then?' said Bradley, still puzzled.

Didier didn't speak but merely nodded towards the car park. Bradley followed his gaze.

Within their limited view of the car park, the two watched as a small hatchback car reversed into a parking space.

'If I am not making a mistake,' said Didier, 'that is the woman Brian and me was telling you about. Now you see 'er for yourself.'

A waiter stuck his head around the kitchen door and shouted, 'Table six away, chef!'

Didier briefly turned to look contemptuously in the direction of the voice before looking back at the newly arrived car. This glance at the waiter was the only acknowledgement the man was going to get from the chef. Didier had all the main meal for table six prepared to absolute perfection, but he didn't want to be seen jumping into action at the call of a mere waiter. He and Bradley watched as the woman glanced at herself in the driving mirror of her car. She had the car door slightly ajar, and in the dull glow of the courtesy light the two men looked on as the woman preened herself. Bradley could make out the long dark hair and the fresh-looking face, and was suitably impressed by what he saw.

'Haven't you got to get the meal ready for table six?' Bradley said quietly and slowly out of the corner of his mouth.

Didier, still at his side, murmured, 'Yes,' but never moved. Both men continued to stare at the woman.

She got out of the car. Even though she was wearing a coat, Bradley immediately appreciated the woman's shapely figure. In the dim neon lighting of the car park, his hormone-charged brain instinctively gauged the dimensions of what he saw, assessed the proportions, assimilated the curves. He and Didier watched the woman lean back into the car and retrieve her handbag.

'Like now,' said Bradley, his eyes still fixed on the new arrival.

'Yes,' said Didier, inching almost imperceptibly back towards the kitchen door, his eyes in the same direction as Bradley's. He squeezed the end of his cigarette between his fingers, and casually flicked it towards the waste bins.

The woman closed the door of the car and locked it. Trousers, Bradley noted.

Still, he thought, *can't have everything, and it is a bit on the cool side tonight.*

The woman, obviously heading towards the front door of the hotel, disappeared from their view. Bradley looked around to see that his chef had finally made it back into the kitchen. He looked back at the now empty car. Recent though his bereavement still was, some things never really changed. The previous weeks of wallowing in largely private grief had only temporarily suppressed his true nature. Standing, hands in pockets, outside the kitchen door, amidst the waste bins, beer crates and other hotel detritus, Bradley King once again felt his mind stirring. His thoughts, totally incongruous given his immediate surroundings, made him smile.

★★★

'What time's the chippy open then, Rose?' asked Joshua. It was the same Sunday evening and, as ever at The Crown, there was no dinner served at such a time. Joshua had arrived only ten minutes before, hopefully to stay for longer than on any of his previous visits to The Crown. Tomorrow he would recommence as a consultant to Walklate and Co.

'Seven o'clock, so he'll be open now,' replied Rose, wiping her hands on her apron. They were standing in the hall of The Crown.

As he'd driven north, he'd vaguely harboured thoughts of asking Tara if she'd like to join him on his search for a Sunday night meal, but he'd been disappointed. She'd gone out for the evening.

'Where did you say Tara's gone?' he asked.

'The Oakland,' said Rose. 'Some meeting or other for hotel

people in Bramton. She said she'd be a couple of hours. How long are you staying for this time, Mr. Latham?'

'Joshua, please,' he said. 'Hopefully the rest of the week, and then Monday to Friday for another five or six weeks.'

'Oh,' cooed Rose, 'that's very good. ''Cause you've only been what I call a "one-nighter" before now, haven't you, Joshua?'

Joshua noted the distinct pause before Rose had said his first name. He thought that the modern trend for overt familiarity was as strange to Rose as it was to some of the supervision at Walklate and Co.

'Yes,' said Joshua dryly. 'For one reason or another, it's only ever been for one night before now.'

'You know,' said Rose, advancing towards Joshua and putting a hand on his arm, 'if it's just a bit of a snack you're after, I'm sure I can rustle you up a sandwich or something. Now, you're a bit of a regular, like.'

Joshua was slightly curious at this newfound generosity. Whilst he'd never found Rose exactly obstructive before, he'd never found her particularly affable either. To him, in his modern management speak, she never really exuded "customer focus". The change in her demeanour now was noticeable, and it made him curious.

'We had some cold beef,' continued Rose, her initial offer not having been taken up in the split second she took between breaths, 'but I think that's all gone now. There'll be some ham, and cheese of course.'

Joshua didn't particularly feel like going out. He would have done in Tara's company, no doubt, but not really on his own. He was tempted by the offer of the sandwich but felt he needed something more substantial.

'Thanks very much,' said Joshua, 'but I think I'll just pop up to the chip shop.'

'Very good, Joshua,' said Rose, still the pause evident. It made Joshua smile.

'I'll be back in twenty minutes,' he said as he went out through the front door of the hotel. In a short while he was standing on the pavement outside the chip shop, tucking into a polystyrene tray full of greasy chips and a piece of battered haddock. The evening was cloudy but thankfully dry, and a cool breeze gently wafted the chip shop smells down the street.

'Welcome to the glamorous world of being self-employed, Josh, me old mate,' he muttered to himself between mouthfuls of chips.

★★★

The number two function room of The Oakland was filling up. About twenty or so people, comprising a few smartly dressed women, but mainly men in suits, milled about drinking coffee and making polite conversation. Bradley entered the room. To his satisfaction he saw that the dark-haired woman in the trouser suit was part of the gathering. He made a beeline for her. 'Hi,' he said, holding out his hand. 'My name's Bradley King. I'm from The Oakland, here. Call me Bradley.'

'Hi, I'm Tara Beaumont-Smith. I'm from The Crown.'

They shook hands. She noted his deep brown, limpid eyes, and the fact that they lingered on her for a split second longer than ordinarily might be the case. His broad smile displayed white, even teeth.

'Welcome to The Oakland, Tara,' he said. As he continued to take her in, he thought she looked simply gorgeous. He couldn't help himself.

'Do I know you from someplace?' he said. *It was an old line, but it would do for now*, he thought.

'Er, I don't think so,' said Tara. 'I've only been here once before, to a party. I take it, you're running things tonight.'

He loved the way she spoke. *Class*, he thought.

'No, not at all really,' he said. 'It's my hotel, sure, but it's just a venue. Some other guy's running the show. So, how's business? You been in the trade long?'

Tara explained the present quiet spell that they were having at The Crown, along with some of her plans and ambitions for her relatively humble enterprise. In the present gathering, Tara was conscious of her very limited experience in running a hotel. She was also conscious of talking to someone who represented the biggest hotel in town. When she said as much, and that this was the first time she'd ever attended a meeting of the august local hoteliers, Bradley became gallantly effusive.

'Don't worry about a thing,' he said, neglecting to mention that this was also the first time that he'd attended this function as well.

'Just sit next to me,' he continued. 'There's nothing to it. Half of 'em here wouldn't know a hotel from their elbow, let alone how to run one.'

He gently took her arm and guided her towards two adjacent spare seats. Almost on cue, one of the more distinguished-looking delegates banged a gavel and, when silence prevailed, asked them all to sit down. The seating was arranged theatre style, with a centre aisle. At the front, there was a long table. Behind this sat the gavel man and three other delegates, one woman and two men.

The man with the gavel turned out to be the chairman of the Association. Over the course of the next twenty minutes, he intoned wearily about the difficulties facing the hotel and guest house trade in Bramton and district, before he moved on to introduce the other guests at the top table. Each of these in turn presented their particular area of expertise. First was the woman, who turned out to be from the local tourist office. She spoke eloquently and with great enthusiasm about a new computerised booking service available to them all. She explained how much better it was than the old system, and laboriously detailed each of the improvements. She sat down sometime later, disappointed that her enthusiasm didn't appear to be shared by the rest of the assembly. Only gavel man asked a question, and there was more than a hint that this was only as a polite token. The next speaker was a distinguished-looking older gentleman who introduced himself as the chairman of the local Arts Festival organisation. With a monotonous voice he delivered a humourless homily on this year's up and coming events.

After an hour, Bradley leant towards Tara, and with his hand partly over his mouth, whispered, 'I don't know about you, but I'm losing the will to live!'

Tara immediately put her hand to her mouth and struggled to stifle a giggle. A stern-looking woman in the row in front of them turned and momentarily stared at them.

Proceedings livened marginally for the third guest speaker, who was from the local council. Although no better than any of the others at presenting his case, his subject matter was more emotive. Recent years had seen large increases in business rates, and hotel owners, not least amongst the local employers, wanted to know where the extra money was going. Part way through, Bradley again leaned over to Tara.

'Excuse me a few minutes,' he whispered. 'I'll be back in a tick.'

He got up and quietly slipped out of the room. Tara continued to give the man from the council her best attention. Given the subject matter, questions from the floor were more forthcoming, and the speaker did his best to defend policy over which he'd clearly had absolutely no say. Within ten minutes Bradley sneaked quietly back into the room and resumed his seat next to Tara. He was just in time to hear the chairman wrap up proceedings. He thanked The Oakland for their hospitality, which Bradley acknowledged with a nod of his head. Gavel man then set the date for the next meeting in six months' time and thanked everybody for coming.

'Well,' said Bradley to Tara as the meeting broke up, 'I bet you're glad you came!'

'Hmm,' Tara smiled at his sarcasm. 'Well, I didn't know what to expect. But at least I've had chance to meet one or two of my colleagues in the business.'

'Competitors,' said Bradley, 'not colleagues. Competitors. Don't forget that. These people are your competitors. Don't be taken in by all the friendly banter from this shower. They'd sooner see you go out of business, shut your hotel down, and get it converted to flats. That'd give them a greater slice of the business, and even the chance to put up prices. Tread carefully.'

'Does that include you? Are you my competitor too?' said Tara.

'No. Ironically, I'm probably the only person in the room who isn't really your competitor. Sure, we're both in the hotel trade, but we're on a big scale here, not like your place. We're offering a different standard of service, in a different price range to you, and for the most part, to a different section of the market.'

Tara could actually see that behind Bradley's slick self-confidence, there was a sharp mind. She could follow his logic.

'I see,' she said, scanning the room with a newfound wariness.

'Stick with me,' said Bradley, 'and you'll learn more than you would from these fossils.'

Again, Tara couldn't suppress a smile at Bradley's irreverence.

He went on, 'Seriously, I've been around. I've worked in lots of hotels. I could help you. From what you told me earlier, I'm sure your place has got lots of potential. I'd like to stop by sometime and have a look. What do you say?'

'Sure,' said Tara. 'That would be super. Call in. I'm there most of the time.'

'OK,' he said, looking at his watch. 'Look, I've got to go.'

This was true. He needed to be in Manchester before eleven o'clock. It was already nearly ten, and he still had some things to attend to first.

'It's been really nice to meet you, Bradley, and thanks for the advice,' said Tara.

'And it's been really good to meet you too,' said Bradley. 'You've brightened up an otherwise tedious meeting.'

His eyes lingered on her again, and his smile broadened as he spoke. With some evident reluctance he turned and left the room.

★★★

'Do you mind if I join you?' said Joshua, tentatively opening the door to the bar. 'I thought it might be a shade warmer in here than in my room.'

'No, no,' said Rose. 'Come on in and sit yourself down. Do you want anything to drink from the bar?'

She'd been sitting in a reclining chair next to Fraser Haxton. She got up without waiting for his answer.

'Hello, Fraser,' said Joshua. 'I didn't see you sitting there.'

Joshua put down a laptop case that he'd carried into the bar and offered drinks to the others.

'You brought your luggage with you, I see,' said Fraser in his slow, lilting accent.

'Oh, that!' said Joshua as he ordered the drinks. 'No, that's just my new laptop. My last one had to go back to my old employer. I just bought it down here. I've got to load some new software onto it. I've got a new mobile phone too, and I just need to configure a few things properly.'

'Oh,' said Rose, putting two pints on the bar, and helping herself to a gin and tonic. 'It all sounds terribly complicated to me. I don't know anything about these electronic things. Do you, Fraser?'

'Not a right lot, it has to be said,' he replied.

As the only occupants of the bar, the three of them sat down at a table together.

After initial small talk, Joshua, took out his new laptop and said, 'You don't normally come in on a Sunday evening, do you Fraser?'

'No,' said Fraser, 'but I just thought I'd do a little unpaid overtime. We've been decorating of late.'

He looked at Rose. Rose looked Fraser. Joshua looked at his laptop.

'Yes,' said Joshua slowly, absorbed in the startup sequence of his new machine. 'I had noticed,' he continued without looking up from the computer screen. 'Looks good.'

The evening wore on. Another round of drinks was procured. When Joshua offered to put the cost on his room account again, Fraser insisted that he pay instead. Joshua continued to tap away at his laptop keyboard. At a convenient interval between software installations, he looked up. Fraser and Rose, sitting close together, had been chatting quietly to each other, but had now fallen silent. They were both looking at him.

Joshua became aware of the ensuing silence, unusual in any room containing Rose Whitworth, but on this occasion, even more so. Joshua couldn't quite fathom the reason. He felt the need to say something.

'I understand you're a Celtic supporter, Fraser,' he said.

Rose sighed quietly, and looked up to the heavens, both gestures missed by the two men.

'Aye,' said Fraser. 'For twenty-seven years, man and boy.'

'You don't look old enough,' said Joshua.

'Well, I was only a wee lad when I started.'

'What made you choose Celtic, the old religious thing?' asked Joshua.

'No, no,' said Fraser emphatically. 'We used to live near Milngavie, and my grandfather, several of my uncles, in fact the whole family, used to support Partick Thistle. If you don't know a lot about Scottish football, I'd guess you'd say that Partick are the third side in Glasgow after Rangers and Celtic. It's kind of funny, really, Partick have generally been a bit of a crappy side over the years, if you know what I mean, but their fans! Their fans sort of look down on those frae Rangers and Celtic. I think it's a class thing. Anyhow, Old Firm fans kind of treat Partick fans with an amusing sorta indifference, as if somehow, they're kinda irrelevant in the grand scheme o' Scottish football.'

Joshua was entranced by the man's accent. The slow delivery and the rolled "R's", made for relaxing listening, and Fraser's normally taciturn nature clearly disappeared when discussing football, or "footba" as it sounded to an outsider. Rose got up and heaved another sigh.

'Well, if you two are going to talk football,' she said, 'I'm off to walk the dog.'

'I'm sorry,' said Joshua. 'I didn't mean to drive you away.'

'Oh, don't worry about it,' she said. 'You carry on. I won't be more than ten minutes.'

'I didn't realise you had a dog,' said Joshua.

'Well, let's just say she's a recent addition to the hotel staff,' said Rose with a smile on her face.

'I'll be back soon,' she said as she left the bar.

'Anyhow,' said Fraser, 'there was a League Cup Final in the early seventies. My grandfather and most of the family went to the match. It was the first match my dad had ever been to. He was only a nipper at the time. Let me see now. It would have been either '71 or maybe '72. '71 it was…' Joshua sat enthralled as the Scotsman regaled him with how a mighty Celtic side, in a freak result, were beaten by humble Partick Thistle.

'After the match,' continued Fraser, 'they were all walking home. There was this bunch of Celtic supporters, mainly old men so I'm told. Any case, this old boy, he sees my dad, and comes right up to him. He throws his scarf to him, and says, wi' a kinda disgust, "There ya go, son. I'm through wi' 'em." Well, my dad was made up. I don't think he even understood what he'd seen really, you know, not really appreciated the significance of the result. And this guy gives him his scarf. And well, much to the old man's disgust, my dad then started following "The Hoops" e'er since. I got on well with ma dad, and over the years he started taking me to games. It's been Celtic for me ever since, although I don't get to many games these days.'

'That's a fantastic story, Fraser,' said Joshua.

They continued to exchange football generalities until they could hear the back door of the kitchen slam, followed by a voice and the sound of footsteps. The door to the bar opened, and in came Rose with a small black Labrador.

'I thought Tara had told you not ta bring her in here,' said Fraser.

'I know,' said Rose, 'but I just had to show her to Joshua here. This is Bess.'

Rose patted and stroked the dog, and generally fussed over the animal. Joshua stroked the dog too. Bess busily sniffed everything in sight and wagged her tail furiously.

'She's a grand dog, Rose,' said Joshua, 'and a nice temperament, too.'

'Oh, she is too,' said the proud owner. 'She's ever so good. I've hardly ever heard her bark. Come on girl, outside, before Miss Tara finds out you've been in here. Come on.'

Rose took Bess out to her basket in the laundry room. When Rose came back into the bar, Joshua finished his pint and scanned the bar expectantly.

'Can I have a whisky, please, Rose?' he said, and again offered drinks to the others. 'Just as a nightcap,' he added.

Rose refused the offer of another drink. Fraser had another pint. Rose again sat down very close to Fraser, their shoulders almost touching. The three sat in silence, save the sound of Joshua tapping away at his keyboard. Shortly, Joshua glanced up from his computer screen, and momentarily noticed Rose extend her fingers and gently touch the back of Fraser's hand. Fraser looked at Rose. Rose looked at Fraser. Joshua now looked at them both, then quickly back to his computer screen. Slow on the uptake maybe, but eventually Joshua made the intellectual leap. Staring blankly now at the screen of his laptop, he cursed himself for his lack of awareness. He realised now why Rose was in such good humour, and it wasn't entirely due to now having a much longed for dog. Joshua no longer wondered why Fraser would do unpaid overtime on a Sunday evening. It dawned on him too, why, instead of doing any decorating, Fraser had sat there in the bar, in his best shirt, jumper and cords. All of a sudden Joshua felt flustered, self-conscious, and above all, unwanted. He slammed the lid of the laptop closed and stood up.

'Look,' he said, 'I'm nearly through with this. I'll finish it off in my room, then I'll go to bed.'

'Oh,' said Rose, standing. 'You can stop here and finish it, if you like.'

'No, no,' said Joshua. 'I'm pretty well tired, and I've an early start in the morning.'

He quickly put his laptop in its case, and picking up his whisky, bade the two lovers goodnight.

★★★

Still that same evening, Bradley slipped off his tie and the jacket of his suit. He looked anxiously at his watch, then, holding the blind of the first-floor office window aside, he scanned the car park outside. He had to hurry, or he would be late for his Manchester rendezvous. He quickly slipped into his motorcycle leathers.

Meanwhile outside, Tara thumped the steering wheel of her car. She turned the ignition key again. The starter motor whined uselessly, the engine failing to fire.

'Damn,' she said under her breath. She leant under the dashboard and pulled the bonnet release. With a clunk the bonnet lifted an inch from its fully closed position. As soon as she'd done it, she wondered why she'd bothered. She only knew where the internal release knob was because a man at the garage had shown her. What was the point of opening the bonnet fully when what was underneath was a total mystery to her? However, feeling the need to at least do something, Tara got out of the car, and fumbled under the partially lifted bonnet for the retaining catch. All she succeeded in doing was chipping a fingernail. She stamped her foot with impatience.

'Got a problem?' said a voice behind her.

She turned to see a slightly sinister-looking figure, clad from neck to foot in black motorcycle leathers. The man carried his crash helmet. As the figure emerged from the shadows, she was relieved to see the face of Bradley King.

'Hi,' said Tara. 'I seem to have a bit of a problem with my car.'

'What's up with it?' asked Bradley.

'It won't start. Well, it started then stopped, and now it won't go at all.'

'Let's have a look. Hop in and turn the engine over.'

Tara did as she was bid. Bradley carefully placed his crash helmet on the ground, lifted the bonnet, and peered at the engine. After several more abortive attempts to start the car, he stepped aside.

'It's difficult to tell, but I reckon it could be a fuel problem. Maybe dirt in the fuel.'

'Is that a big problem?'

'Not especially, but there's not a lot that can be done tonight.'

'I could call a breakdown service.'

'Are you in the AA or something?' said Bradley quickly.

'No.'

'Well, I would leave it here then. It'll cost you a fortune to get someone out to it at this time on a Sunday evening. It'll be OK in the hotel car park overnight.'

'Are you sure?'

'Yeah. We've got a night porter who looks around the car park. It'll be as safe here as anywhere.'

Tara could see the logic.

'But I'll still have to arrange for a taxi.'

'I'll give you a lift.'

'But…' Tara contemplated his bike leathers and the crash helmet lying on the floor.

'It's OK,' he said. 'I've got a spare helmet. It's not far to The Crown. You shouldn't get too cold.'

'Well, I'm not…' Her words tailed off.

'Come on. You'll be home in five minutes.'

She hesitated, but the convenience of being home so quickly swung her. 'OK,' she said, still unsure. She got out of her car and locked it whilst Bradley slammed the bonnet shut.

'Follow me,' said Bradley, leading Tara around the side of the hotel.

'I've never ridden on a motorcycle before.'

'So I guessed. You'll be fine.'

When they reached the motorcycle, Bradley again put his helmet on the ground. He undid the disc lock securing the rear wheel, picking up a spare helmet that was conveniently next to the motorcycle.

'It's my old one,' said Bradley, momentarily remembering how he used to lend it to Sally. 'I keep it as a spare.'

He offered it to Tara and helped her put it on.

'Oh,' she said in a voice muffled by the helmet. It was a full-face type. Bradley lifted the visor, and gently brushed a few strands of hair from in front of Tara's face.

'I'm not too sure about this,' the muffled voice said again.

Bradley pretended not to hear, and quickly dropped the visor down. He put on his own helmet, put the key in the ignition. He dug out some gloves from his pockets and put them on. He flung a leg over the machine, stood astride it, and eased it off the stand.

'Get on,' he said.

He held out his arm, and helped Tara balance as she warily flung her leg over. He told her where to put her feet.

He felt Tara's thighs lie either side of his legs, and her knees project down to his thighs. 'Beautiful,' muttered Bradley to his crash helmet.

'What do I hold on to?' Tara said plaintively.

Honda had designed this high-performance machine with a suitable grab strap for the pillion rider, but Bradley was damned if he was going to tell Tara about it.

'Put your arms around my waist,' he said.

As she did as he instructed, she said with distinct nervousness, 'I'm really not sure about this.'

'You'll be fine. Hold on tight, and remember, lean with the bike.'

Bradley turned the ignition. He twisted the throttle. The engine roared. He put it in gear and slipped the clutch. Tara screamed.

Tara would remember her first ride on a motorcycle for the rest of her life. She found the experience of being on a motorcycle truly exhilarating. For a price not much more than Tara had paid for her small-engined hatchback, she could have bought a motorcycle with a performance to rival genuine top flight sports cars. The power to weight ratio of even a modest motorcycle gives acceleration to leave most cars for dead. For Bradley's sports superbike, there were few rivals on the road, irrespective of two wheels or four. For Tara, riding pillion, the excitement was multiplied. She was acutely aware of not being in control of her own destiny. With the obvious power, speed, noise, and acceleration of the big motorcycle, this abdication now became downright trepidation. And Bradley milked the moment for all he was worth.

The conditions were dry. He got the motorcycle up to thirty miles an hour and back to stationary before the end of The Oakland driveway. This feat brought a more prolonged squeal from his passenger. He paused at the junction with the main road. A car drove past, heading into town. Bradley let out the clutch, and again opened the throttle. He turned to follow the car. As the motorcycle turned, it leaned. Tara let out a more muted squeal, and instinctively tried to sit up straight. Bradley could hear the muffled noises from behind him and smiled to himself. He soon pulled up behind the car that had passed the end of the hotel driveway. Tara looked forward over Bradley's shoulder. She saw the car they were following, and also another one, headlights ablaze, coming towards them on the other side of the road. Bradley positioned the motorcycle towards the middle of the road a few feet behind the rear of the car that they were following.

No, she thought. *No, he is not going to overtake here.*

They had less than three hundred yards to run to the thirty mile per hour speed limit signs at the edge of town. The car on the opposite side of the road closed on them quickly. To a car driver like Tara, overtaking the vehicle in front of them under the present circumstances was simply impossible. It just could not be done.

He will not overtake, she thought.

Bradley flicked the clutch, kicked down a gear, and twisted the throttle.

Oh no! Tara closed her eyes.

The motorcycle effortlessly swerved out and shot forward with breathtaking acceleration. Tara instinctively squeezed Bradley's waist. He swung the motorcycle back into the left-hand side of the road, changed up a gear, and eased back on the throttle. The car coming towards them flashed past, as did the speed limit signs, Bradley giving them but token attention. Bradley had promised five minutes for the journey. With over two minutes to spare, he pulled up in front of The Crown.

He turned off the engine and put the motorcycle on its stand. Tara staggered off the machine, her legs having turned to jelly. Bradley got off, took his helmet off and helped Tara divest herself of hers.

As the cold air struck her face again she said, 'Oh my God! I have never been so scared in all my life.'

'What?' said Bradley, feigning puzzlement. 'You didn't enjoy that?'

'Oh Bradley,' Tara said laughing breathlessly, 'it was unbelievable. I just thought I was going to die! Especially when you overtook that car.'

'Nah problem,' he said dismissively. 'Bags of time. This is a performance machine, don't forget. You can do things on it you wouldn't dream of in a car.'

'So I noticed,' said Tara, still recovering.

'We'll have to do it again sometime. Show you what it can really do.'

'Oh, now, I'm not too sure about that. Phew!'

Tara ran her hands through her now tangled hair.

'Do you want to come in for a cup of coffee and see what a humble little hotel looks like?' she asked, after recovering her composure some more.

Bradley removed a glove and looked at his watch.

'No,' he said, 'I've really got to be going, thanks. Look, I'm on lates this week. I'll pop round one morning sometime, have a look around.'

It was a statement more than a suggestion.

'OK,' said Tara.

Bradley strapped the spare helmet to the rear seat, and watched as Tara made her way through the front door of The Crown. As he got back on his motorcycle, she smiled and waved, and he waved back. When she'd disappeared from view, he looked at his watch again. He was going to be late. Women, he thought, would be the death of him. He thought of a way to save himself a few minutes. He removed his other glove and pulled out his mobile phone from his jacket pocket. He dialled. When he got through to The Oakland, he asked for Didier. Was he still going to be there? After a long minute, the Frenchman came on the phone.

'Didier?'

'Bradley! 'Ow are you? What is this? You have an 'orse, a tip?'

He pronounced the word more like "teep".

'No. Look, I need a favour. Listen carefully. There's a car in the car park. The small Ford hatchback, dark red, it's the one that girl turned up in this evening.'

'I know it.'

'Go to that car and have a look at the exhaust pipe. You know the exhaust pipe, at the back?'

'Of course.'

'Well, you'll find a potato stuck over the end of it.'

'What!'

'There's a potato blocking the exhaust pipe.'

'But why? What is this for?'

'It doesn't matter now. I'll tell you tomorrow. Now listen. Take the potato off the exhaust pipe. OK? It's very important. Someone will come for the car tomorrow morning, and they mustn't see the potato. I shan't be in until later. You must do this for me tonight. Do you understand?'

'I understand. What do I do with the potato?'

Bradley was momentarily lost for words.

'I don't know! Throw it away. Make chips with it. I don't care. Just get it off the damn car!'

'OK.'

The phone system couldn't transmit the image of the chef's raised eyebrows and Gallic shrug of the shoulders, but it didn't need to. Bradley pictured the actions as if he were there.

'Good man. I owe you one. Gotta go. See you tomorrow.'

He hung up and put his phone away. He quickly put on his gloves, and helmet and started the motorcycle up again. With a parting glance across to the front door of The Crown, he put the motorcycle into gear. He roared off at speed, taking the road to Manchester.

★★★

Meanwhile in The Crown, Tara effusively regaled Rose and Fraser with news of her first ride on a motorcycle. She was so enthusiastic that it took her two minutes to question, in her own mind, why Fraser was still at the hotel at this time in the evening. Using her innate intuition, common to most women, she came to the correct conclusion far quicker than Joshua had. Admittedly she knew of Rose's Valentine card, and she could guess that Rose, unable to contain herself, would have carelessly asked Fraser if he'd received any mail lately.

Couldn't keep a secret to save her life, thought Tara to herself.

Smiling knowingly at Rose, Tara made an excuse about going to bed early, and discreetly left her two employees alone.

In an upstairs bedroom, Joshua had gently shut the lid of his laptop. He'd drained his whisky, and leaning across the bed, had turned off the bedside light. He'd lain back and closed his eyes. Oblivious to the traffic noise outside, particularly the obvious throbbing of a motorcycle engine somewhere nearby, he'd soon fallen asleep.

Chapter Seventeen

'Morning Mr. Walklate,' said Shirley Hays as she walked into Theodore's office. It was Monday morning. Theodore, as usual, had been in early, and had completed his tour of the works.

'Morning,' he said, only glancing up from the computer screen on his desk.

'There's your mail,' said Shirley, plonking down a small pile of letters and magazines on his desk.

'I'm sorry I opened that one in error,' said Shirley primly, pointing to the top of the pile.

'The envelope wasn't marked "Private & Confidential",' she added. Once opened, envelopes would normally be thrown away, but in this case, Shirley having seen the contents, felt duty bound to save it, lest Mr. Walklate think her presumptuous. She held the pale blue envelope up for Theodore to look at.

'See?' she said.

'Hmm,' said Theodore unconcerned. 'What is it?'

'Er, it appears to be a Valentine card, Mr. Walklate. It must have arrived on Saturday.'

Theodore looked across his desk at the card. He saw the water colour depicting the vase of red roses.

'Pah!' he said. 'Probably the bloody toolroom having a laugh.'

He picked the card up, opened it and read the verse inside. He turned in his swivel chair and was about to throw the card in the waste bin. He hesitated. He looked again at the verse by John Donne. Something struck him. He looked at the signature, such that it was. "From a secret admirer". He looked back at the front cover of the card. He glanced at the envelope in Shirley's hand. He had to admit, this wasn't the normal toolroom style. Not being well up on English poets, Theodore had only a vague recollection as to who John Donne was, but he sounded serious and above all, legitimate.

'The toolroom? Do you think so?' said Shirley.

'Probably,' said Theodore.

'I could ask around,' said Shirley. 'Ask a few questions.'

'As you like,' said Theodore putting the card back on his desk, still seemingly unconcerned. 'Don't waste time on it if I were you. We've enough on our plate as it is.'

'Very good, Mr. Walklate,' she said, and with the envelope in her hand, she turned and left the office.

Theodore Walklate returned to his computer, slowly dabbing the keys with his two index fingers.

Infinitely more curious than her boss, Shirley's detective work proved far simpler and swifter than she could ever have imagined, albeit at the cost of some nervous energy. After her coffee break, she was walking by reception when she saw, in the smoking hut, the solitary figure of Norman Crabtree. Distasteful though she found the sordid cubicle designated for the smokers, she couldn't afford to miss the opportunity to speak to the toolroom foreman whilst he was on his own. Like Theodore, she knew of Norman's encyclopaedic knowledge of the people of Bramton, both within and without the firm. More importantly she could trust to his discretion. She was probably more curious to know the identity of Mr. Walklate's secret admirer than Mr. Walklate himself, but she knew, above all else, that she must not embarrass her boss by shouting her enquiries from the rooftops.

She entered the Perspex shelter and after greeting each other, Norman said in his usual loud voice, 'And to what do we owe this unexpected pleasure? You've not taken to the dreaded weed, have you?'

'Oh no, Norman, not me. I just wondered,' said Shirley, lowering her voice in a conspiratorial manner, 'if you'd help me out with this.'

She reached into a folder that she was carrying and pulled out the pale blue envelope.

'I'd be interested in who sent this. Have you any ideas?'

'Oh,' he said. 'What's this then?'

'Well,' said Shirley. 'Someone's sent a Valentine card to Mr. Walklate. He reckons it's from one of your men, you know, having a bit of a joke. I'm not so sure. What do you reckon?'

Norman studied the envelope, and Shirley studied Norman. Neither saw the ubiquitous Bob Lumsden drive into the yard in his taxi. After depositing a parcel in reception, Lumsden walked over to the smoking shed.

'Morning all!' he said breezily. 'And how are we all this fine morning?'

Shirley and Norman both acknowledged the interloper.

'Fag, anyone?' said Lumsden, offering his packet around, firstly to Shirley.

'No thank you,' said Shirley haughtily, giving Lumsden a look of absolute horror.

'No thanks, Bob,' said Norman, still with his own on the go.

Shirley had not warned Norman about the confidentiality of the matter under discussion. She had intended to advise him of this as a parting comment. She had not bargained for the brash taxi driver barging into the discussion, and she felt a sense of rising anxiety as the conversation threatened to get out of hand.

'What's this then?' asked Lumsden, looking at the other two studying the pale blue envelope.

'Oh, just something someone's sent to Mr. Walklate. We're trying to work out who it's from,' said Norman. 'You know, it's a Val—'

'It's just some correspondence,' interrupted Shirley, quickly.

She made to take the envelope back, but before she could Lumsden had got a hand on it.

'Hah!' he said. 'That's easy. I'll tell you who that's from!'

Norman and Shirley both looked at Bob Lumsden. The taxi driver beamed in triumph. He was certain he recognised the envelope and the writing. Closer inspection of the post-mark confirmed the date of posting as the previous Friday. He held the envelope and put it to his nose for final conviction. He had held this very envelope before. He leaned forward, savouring the moment. Norman and Shirley instinctively leaned forward too.

'It's that woman at The Crown Hotel,' he said lowering his

voice only marginally. 'You know, Tara Beaumont-Smith. It's 'er! She's sent your old boss a bloody Valentine.'

Lumsden let out a yelp of unconfined glee. Norman Crabtree looked on bemused. He didn't know whether to feel sceptical or simply puzzled, as if he'd just watched a conjuror perform an outstanding trick. How on earth had Lumsden solved the mystery identity that quickly?

Shirley grabbed the envelope from the gloating taxi driver and, bidding him a curt thank-you went quickly back to her office. She felt flustered. She'd been indiscreet in allowing the uncouth taxi driver to become involved. It was only over a trivial matter for sure, she tried to convince herself, not some big corporate commercial secret. But even so, she felt that if word of the Valentine spread, Mr. Walklate would hold her responsible for the leak, and that would reflect badly on her professionalism. And what of the card itself? Like Norman, Shirley Hays could not really imagine Mr. Walklate receiving a Valentine, other than of course, in the joking manner that her boss already assumed to be the case. She toyed with the idea of just telling Mr. Walklate that he'd been right. It had been the toolroom all along, and she could destroy the envelope, denying all other stories to the contrary. Alternatively, could she just forget all about it, and tell Mr. Walklate that she hadn't found the sender of the card at all. She quickly dispelled these ideas. She couldn't now rely on the whole episode remaining confidential, and she couldn't tell lies.

Was Lumsden's assertion correct even? He had sounded certain, but how did he know? Shirley Hays spent the rest of the day distracted. She found herself unable to concentrate on her work. Then, shortly before she was due to leave, she had an inspiration, an idea of how she might verify Lumsden's assertion.

Later still, she went into Mr. Walklate's office. Theodore was sitting behind his desk, reading some papers.

'You still here, Shirley?' he said. 'I thought you'd gone.'

'Not yet, Mr. Walklate.'

She stepped forward and hesitated.

'Yes, Shirley?' said Theodore, clearly recognising that his PA wanted to say something.

'It's just the Valentine card that you received this morning…' she said.

'Oh, that! Good God, I hope you've not spent a lot of time on that!' said Theodore letting out a great guffaw.

'No,' she lied. 'It was a bit of a long shot, but I think I've found out who sent it.'

'Well?' said Theodore, smiling.

'Tara Beaumont-Smith. The woman from The Crown Hotel.'

The smile froze on Theodore's face. His whole look became more serious. Shirley could see that her news was having an effect on her boss.

'How do you know?' he said.

'Well, I still have the replies to the Christmas party invitations on file. I keep them until I have time to go through them and make a list of proposed guests for the next year.'

Theodore eyed his PA carefully.

'It was a bit of a long shot, like I said, but I got her reply out of the file.'

Shirley waved the letter in front of Theodore along with the envelope from the Valentine card.

'You see,' continued Shirley, 'it's the same pen. Same colour ink, and quite a broad nib. She's written the hotel's address in capitals, like the envelope, but you can see, the letters look the same.'

Theodore looked at the two items of correspondence. He had to concede that no matter how hard he looked, the handwriting did indeed appear similar. *No*, he thought, *it's bloody identical!* He looked up at Shirley. He sniffed.

'Very astute, Shirley,' he said. 'Who knows about this?'

Shirley looked at the floor.

'I can't be sure, Mr. Walklate,' was the best that she could manage.

'Leave those with me,' said Theodore, indicating the pale blue envelope and Tara's reply to the Christmas party invitation.

'And just forget about all this, OK? We've got better things to do with our time than mess about with these sorts of distractions.'

'Yes, Mr. Walklate,' said Shirley contritely, before leaving the room.

After Shirley had left and the cleaners had vacuumed the offices and emptied the waste-paper bins, Theodore was quite alone in the now silent building. Not even the hum and bustle of the factory could be heard in the hallowed quarters of his office. He sat down. He got up. He paced around the room. He was a man in utter turmoil. Tara Beaumont-Smith, the young, attractive proprietor of The Crown Hotel in Bramton, had sent him a Valentine card.

The receipt of the card and the identification of the sender marked the culmination of an unlikely series of events. Rose had bought two cards. It had not been her intention, as Tara had so playfully accused her, to be a serial romantic. Rose had intended only a card for Fraser, but in her haste and indecision, she'd bought two. For Rose, with her unwillingness to remain anonymous for long, the choice between the two cards mattered not a jot. Either would probably have secured Fraser's attention. To Tara, the act of sending the spare card had been unpremeditated, impulsive, meaningless, inconsequential, trivial, flippant and even immature; a throwaway gesture, in a throwaway society. Within an hour of sending it, she had put it from her mind.

Had the cards been selected the other way, and Theodore Walklate received the joke card, he would have despatched it to the waste bin with great speed, stopping only to curse the toolroom employees. But he'd received the more seriously romantic one. The design of the card, and the verse inside, had made him hesitate. He'd known subconsciously that even the more exuberant of his employees, out to have a laugh at his expense, would surely not have chosen such a card.

And then there was the discovery of the sender. How Shirley had made the connection between the card and the reply to the Christmas party invitation seemed implausible to Theodore, but that was a separate, and now largely irrelevant question. The evidence of the handwriting made him 95% sure. Tara Beaumont-Smith had sent the card. Was she serious? He barely knew the woman, or she him. What on earth would possess her to send such a card if she didn't mean what it said? It had to be genuine, he reasoned, and the sentiments heartfelt.

What did she mean by the card? If it were genuine, as he supposed, she clearly felt affection for him. He picked up the card and read the verse again.

"Come live with me, and be my love,
And we will some new pleasures prove,
Of golden sands, and crystal brooks,
With silken lines, and silver hooks."
                              (John Donne)

"Be my love." It was pretty obvious. "Come live with me." The message seemed crystal clear to Theodore Walklate. His imagination ran on.

Theodore wiped his hand over his face and stared out of his office window. It was now completely dark outside. What should he do? He recalled Tara's image. He felt flustered. He felt a rising sense of embarrassment. What a woman! The woman who'd sent him a Valentine card wasn't some ageing, matronly dowager. She was a young and very attractive woman. What had happened to his view of beauty as an abstract? Tara Beaumont-Smith was beautiful. He knew this instinctively, but she wasn't the remote intangible that he'd assumed her to be. She had declared her feelings for him, and this made him want to reciprocate. She was as pertinent and palpable to him now as his house, his car, his job, his company. She was attracted to him. It couldn't be! Why should she be so taken with him? He thought for a moment. He was not so old. He still retained some looks. People had described him as distinguished even. He had money, power, position. No, he convinced himself, he had plenty of attractive qualities. He'd read of far more unlikely matches in the media.

No matter how flippant Tara had been in sending the card, to Theodore Walklate it represented a fundamental event in his life, a turning point. His emotions finally stirred. Following their youthful formation, such feelings had lain buried for many decades. Interred so deeply for so long, Theodore could not at first recognise their upheaval as they at last broke the surface.

This latest event was the culmination of several changes in his life. In the last twelve months his company had begun to struggle. His life's work, his all-absorbing job, had started to go wrong, and for reasons he couldn't apparently fathom, let alone control. He'd had to swallow his pride in asking for consultants to be brought in. He now remembered the dinner he'd had with Marjorie and Andrew the week or so before the exercise had started. He recalled how, in the face of his first ever serious professional crisis, he'd envied Marjorie and Andrew their home lives, their partners, and the support they would receive throughout the difficult period that lay ahead. Unbeknown to him at the time but becoming clearer now, as he paced up and down his office on this dark February evening, that dinner had been the first time in his life when he had begun to question his adult life values. Had he been right to pursue his career so single-mindedly? Had he been right to follow so unquestioningly in his father's footsteps? Should he have chosen a different career? Above all, should he have made more effort to find a partner, a wife? He remembered staring into the fire in the dining room of Fallowfield Grange that evening, and his first feelings of regret. From that moment on, he now recognised that he'd never been truly content. Staring into the flames he had felt the first rumblings of an emotional insurgence. Still he had suppressed his feelings. He had thrown himself even more into his work, dismissing his feelings as some sort of mid-life crisis.

Then he remembered the graffiti in the factory toilets. Instead of passing it off as the inane scribbling of a moron, he'd let it bother him. He'd felt deeply insulted, more by the implication of the message, than the words themselves. He'd boiled away inside. He'd seethed at the ingratitude of his employees, a feeling reinforced throughout the Christmas period. Again he had suppressed his feelings. He'd desperately kept the lid on the volcano that his emotional state had become. Over the previous few months, all his adult life choices were seemingly being undermined. Was it too late for him to start again?

Theodore Walklate's personality, fashioned by his upbringing, appeared to all that knew him, as absolutely stable. He was a rock of dependability, an anchor for all those around him. In reality, his character was not stable but, in the true scientific sense of the word, metastable. To all intents and purposes, he appeared in happy equilibrium. But closer inspection of metastable conditions reveals the underlying inherent precariousness of the stability. In the absence of any outside influences, the apparent stability continues unchanged. But as the external factors alter, as they did now for Theodore Walklate, the system risks sudden and spontaneous collapse. Theodore's months of growing emotional unease finally became unsustainable. Carelessly, Tara had unwittingly supplied the ultimate catalyst. Her Valentine card, sent with such flippancy, seemingly so inconsequential in itself, was the final straw. Even this was only just sufficient, relying as it did, on the subtle nuances of the card's design and message, to bring about the reaction within the recipient. After many years, and a huge, remorseless build-up of pressure within the volcano, the Valentine card had cracked the surface of the crater. The eruption to follow would threaten all around it.

Part Three

Chapter Eighteen

Never one to dither over a course of action, particularly one involving an attractive woman, Bradley waited no longer than the Tuesday following the hoteliers' meeting, before visiting The Crown. He stood in the reception hallway of The Crown and pressed the bell push. Within a minute Rose Whitworth came to meet the visitor. Suitably charged with his details she returned to the kitchen, and announced to Tara that there was "some bloke from The Oakland Hotel here to see you." Tara excitedly told Rose that this "bloke" would be none other than her knight in black leather. This would be the man who'd so gallantly helped her the previous Sunday evening with a lift home on his motorcycle, albeit scaring her half to death in the process. Tara quickly went to reception to meet him again.

'Hi,' she said. Bradley stood in his black bike leathers, clutching his helmet.

'Hi,' he replied. 'Have bike, will travel. I'm a man of my word. I just called round to say hello.'

'Great!' said Tara. 'Come on through to the lounge.'

Tara offered her guest a drink. She consequently went off to make some coffee, leaving Bradley to slip off his jacket. When she returned with the two steaming mugs of coffee, he said, 'Did you get your car fixed OK?'

'Yes, thanks,' she said. 'Well, I say "yes", but honestly, I felt such a fool! I called this chap at a garage. Someone that Rose knows of. Rose is the woman you met when you came in.'

Tara was suddenly aware of how she was beginning to babble, delivering a nervous, rapid-fire series of non-sequiturs. For some reason Bradley King made her nervous. She paused, and her self-control returned.

'Anyway,' she said, 'this man from the garage called for me and we went up to The Oakland. Damn me if the car didn't start first time! I felt a proper Charlie!'

She'd actually felt quite cross. The mechanic had been smugly condescending towards her as a "woman" knowing nothing about complicated things like cars. She could have happily slapped him, but instead she'd used the situation to her advantage. With all her self-restraint and feminine wiles, she'd given him her most disarming smile, and got away without being charged.

'Well, it can happen,' said Bradley. 'Like I said, it could have been dirt in the fuel. It may just have worked its way through. Still, it gave you an introduction to riding motorcycles.'

Over their coffee Tara once again related how she'd felt during the ride home, although she now moderated the description. She no longer described herself as being "terrified", instead rather more "exhilarated".

When they'd finished their drinks, she showed Bradley around the hotel. The tour included the bar, the dining room, the kitchen, and the laundry room (where she was pleased to see Rose, as Tara had instructed, had taken the opportunity to take Bess out for a walk). Tara introduced Joanna, who was busy carrying sheets upstairs. Tara and Bradley talked about the business, the staff at the hotel, and Bradley made helpful comments and suggestions. Tara mentioned how she'd come to own the hotel, and again outlined her ideas for improvements, all the time bemoaning the costs involved. After an hour or so they returned to the lounge.

'What about the bedrooms?' asked Bradley.

'Sorry?' said Tara.

'I was just wondering about the bedrooms,' he said, smiling warmly to offset the hint of sarcasm to follow. 'They're obviously rather important to a hotel. I'd just like to have a quick shufty at one, if I may.'

'Oh, of course,' said Tara, innocently cursing herself for the obvious omission.

They went upstairs. Tara showed him an empty twin room, one that had recently been decorated by Fraser.

'Hmm, not bad,' he mused. 'Like you said, better if all the rooms had an ensuite like this one. Got any doubles?'

'Sure,' said Tara, guiding him to an adjoining bedroom. Bradley again commented encouragingly. He walked over to the window and, holding aside the net curtain, looked out at the view.

'Is that the Hexagon centre you can see in the distance?' he asked, knowing full well that it was.

Tara came over and stood next to him and looked out of the window. He moved to within a few inches of her. She confirmed that what he saw was indeed the local conference centre. They continued to gaze at the view.

'Beautiful view,' he said.

She looked at Bradley and blushed faintly as she saw him now looking at her rather than the outside view.

'Yes, yes, it is, isn't it?' she stammered, moving away a step, her nervousness returning.

He reached out and gently held her arm. Her heart raced.

'You know,' he said, 'in all my time in the hotel trade, I don't think I've ever come across anyone quite as striking as you.'

'Oh,' she said coquettishly, hovering between delight at the compliment and being nervous of the conversation going too quickly for her.

'I'm sure you must have,' she said.

'I don't think so,' he said, smiling. 'You are quite simply the one.'

As he spoke, he gently pulled her closer to him. She felt his breath warmly on her cheek.

'Er, no!' she said suddenly, stepping back. She felt a mixture of relief and disappointment at reasserting control of their meeting.

The contrast now between the effect of this rebuff on Bradley, and the effect of the similar one given to Joshua several months before, could not be more marked. All through their dinner at La Scala, Joshua had slowly plucked up courage and consumed not a little alcohol, in order to make his move. His nervousness had been transparent. Bradley, in contrast, had been at The Crown for less than an hour and had exuded confidence in all he'd said and done. Joshua's approach had been gauche and clumsy. Bradley was self-assured and smooth. When Tara had exclaimed her refusal, Joshua's fragile confidence had collapsed, and he'd transformed immediately into a shy embarrassed wreck. Bradley, by contrast, just smiled.

Still gently holding Tara's arm, his mouth actually broadened into a grin. There was no slinking away to lick wounds and hurt pride here. He relished the challenge before him. This was going to be fun! And the prize all the sweeter for the obstacles in the race.

'Tell me,' he said, dropping his hand from her arm, 'you must be free one evening this week?'

She'd already told him that Rose lived in at the hotel, so cover was not a problem. Tara could choose any evening to be free. Even so, Bradley's question was phrased to counter any evasiveness, even if she'd wanted to be excused. She plumped for Thursday.

'Well,' she said, 'I could be free on Thursday.'

'Good!' he said. 'That's my day off!'

Unlike Jeremy Gillman, Bradley didn't have a regular day off during the week. He would frequently leave things to the last moment before discussing time off with his manager. Gillman liked his Sundays off, but otherwise was pretty flexible regarding Bradley's days off. Tara could have chosen more or less any day of the week, and it would have become, as if by some happy coincidence, Bradley's day off too.

'What I think this calls for,' he said, lowering his voice in mock seriousness, 'is lesson number two in motorcycling for beginners.'

He broke into a smile, and she couldn't help but do the same.

He spoke rapidly, 'The lesson involves a ride of sheer terror through the winding lanes of darkest Derbyshire, defying death at every turn. Candidates are advised to wear something "appropriate", noting that the performance of the motorcycle has been known to render the particularly nervous in a state of shock. The lesson includes a quiet meal for two at a country pub of your choice. Return will be before midnight or whatever time the motorcycle turns into a pumpkin. The owners take no responsibility, blah, blah, blah. Shall we say seven-thirty?'

She grinned and looked into his eyes.

'Seven-thirty, then,' she said.

Later that day, some hours after Bradley had departed, Rose and Tara were in the kitchen, sitting together at the main table. Tara was repairing some pillowcases, whilst Rose prepared some Brussel sprouts for the evening meal.

'You know who he is, don't you?' said Rose.

'Who?' said Tara.

'That bloke who came this morning, Bradley King. You know who he is, don't you?'

'Yes,' said Tara slightly perplexed. 'He's the Manager of The Oakland Hotel.'

'Hmm,' said Rose thoughtfully. 'Assistant Manager, I thought it said. He was the one in the Chronicle a month or so back. His fiancée or something got killed in that car accident up on the Congreave road. All over the front page it was. You must have read about it. Terrible business.'

'Yes,' said Tara pensively, slowly making the connection. 'Now you come to mention it, I do remember reading about it. How sad. Only a young girl too, wasn't she?'

'Nineteen, I think.'

'Did you know her?'

'Nah. Heard of her, like. But when you've been in Bramton as long as me, you know of half the town in that way.'

Tara thought of Bradley and the obvious hurt he must still feel, and how well he seemed to mask it. Her reverie was interrupted by the sound of the bell in the hall.

'I'll go,' said Rose, getting up in an instant.

In a moment, she came back into the kitchen, clearly excited, and whispered, 'It's 'im! That frosty bloke. You know, Walklate. The one you sent the Valentine to.'

'What?' said Tara, a chill thought crossing her mind. She'd quite forgotten about the card.

'Mr. Walklate. He's in reception, now. He wants to see you.'

All of a sudden Tara felt anxious. Could he have come about the Valentine? No! That was preposterous. He couldn't possibly know it was she who'd sent it.

'Do you think he's come about the card?' said Rose.

'Don't be silly, Rose,' snapped Tara. 'He's just come for a look around. That's all. When he came the other week for Joshua's address, I asked him if he'd like to look around. He said some other time maybe. He could put some business our way. It's nothing to do with that silly card at all.'

Although she couldn't quite crystallise the thought, Rose had a feeling that Tara was trying to convince herself as much as her. Tara got up and, with some trepidation, went out to the hall.

Theodore Walklate stood in the reception exactly as he had done before. His tall, distinguished frame seemed to fill the room. He turned to greet her.

'Ah! Miss Beaumont-Smith! We meet again.'

'Hello, Mr. Walklate,' she said only just managing to keep the nervousness from her voice. 'It's nice to see you again.'

'Theodore, please,' he said reddening slightly. 'Call me Theodore.'

'Well, Theodore, what can I do for you today?'

He contemplated her. She was as beautiful as he'd remembered. And she'd sent him a Valentine! He felt like a schoolboy. For twenty-four hours he'd agonised over what to do and say. He'd not dared to discuss his delightful predicament with anyone. He'd been quite distracted at work. She had dominated his thoughts. And now she stood before him. He felt nervous – more so than at any time he could remember. This whole scenario before him now was so unfamiliar, and yet, in its novelty, quite exquisite.

He took a deep breath and promptly forgot his oft-rehearsed words.

'The hotel! Your hotel, I mean,' he blurted out. 'I was just wondering if I might have a look around. Er, like you said.'

This jumbled spiel, delivered so tentatively, was so uncharacteristic of the man. Tara nonetheless was almost consumed in a wave of relief, and she failed to notice the somewhat wayward delivery. She was thankful that Theodore's opening salvo had not contained the word "Valentine" at all. Whilst she silently cursed her foolishness in sending the card, and the momentary worry that it had just caused her, she felt relieved that it had apparently passed off undetected. Walklate had only come to view the hotel! She visibly brightened.

'Of course, Theodore,' she said. 'No problem.'

And for the second time that day, Tara found herself giving a guided tour of her establishment. Now better practised, her narrative, combined with her now well-established sense of relief, flowed with more confidence. Unbeknown to her, this belief was being admired by her guest more than her words. *Such confidence!* thought Theodore to himself. *She's as bright as a button! Beauty with brains!*

Theodore asked only polite, practical questions throughout the brief tour. Frankly, he probably knew less about running a hotel than Tara. He only knew about staying at hotels, not how to run one. Right on cue, Rose again appeared to have gone for a walk with Bess. After seeing the ground-floor rooms, Tara suggested going upstairs to one of the bedrooms.

Theodore mentally flapped, initially uncertain of the innocence or otherwise of Tara's suggestion. At his hesitation she said, mimicking the words Bradley had used to her earlier in the day, 'You must be wondering about the bedrooms. They're obviously rather important to a hotel. I'd thought you'd like to see one.'

These words did little to reduce Theodore's rising sense of unease. Was she being particularly forward? What did she intend? He swallowed hard and went upstairs with Tara. After a cursory but very satisfactory examination of the sleeping accommodation, they returned to the lounge, and Theodore berated himself for naively having questioned the virtue of his hostess's intentions.

Once in the lounge, Tara offered, and Theodore accepted, a pot of tea. Rose, having now returned, did the honours, bringing the tea in on a tray along with a plate of biscuits. In contrast to the mugs of coffee that Tara had served to Bradley in the morning, Rose served the tea to Mr. Walklate using the hotel's very best china. There was even a lace doily on the tray, that Tara had never seen before. With a mischievous grin, Rose enquired, looking directly at Tara, 'Everything alright, Miss Smith?'

'Yes, Rose. Thank you,' replied Tara curtly.

Once the impish Rose had departed, Tara started to explain, again for the second time that day, her hopes and ambitions for her hotel business. Theodore was only half listening. The time for him to make his move was fast approaching. He was plucking up the courage to broach the subject of the Valentine. He kept sipping his tea to stop his throat drying. As this totally alien situation unfolded before him, nervous energy drained from him almost visibly. Bradley King's seemingly effortless approach to Tara that morning had shown Joshua's earlier attempts in an amateurish light. Now, in turn, Joshua's tentative overtures put Theodore's efforts in an even more hesitant light. So poor was his approach that Tara wasn't even consciously aware of the fact. In the end, Theodore Walklate's courage failed him. He resolved to put off the Valentine topic to another occasion. What, after all, was the hurry? Once so resolved, his confidence returned. It was reinforced still further as he turned the conversation firmly onto the financial and commercial aspects of business.

'So,' he said, 'do you actually have a business plan?'

'Well,' said Tara, 'I've obviously got certain things I want to do with the place.'

'No, no, I mean, have you got a clearly defined, financially quantified, written business plan, covering say the next three to five years?'

Tara paused. 'Well, no, actually, I haven't.'

'You need one,' he said. 'Listen. You've got ideas for this place. You've told me about improvements you want to make to the hotel. Good ones too, like installing more ensuite facilities in the bedrooms, extending the central heating to the top floor, and so forth.'

'Oh, I could probably only afford to fit one room with ensuite at a time. And to extend the central heating will need a new boiler.'

'Whatever. That doesn't really matter. In any case, you're going to need money. Have you got a mortgage on the place?'

'No.'

'Get one.'

'Get a mortgage?'

'Yes. It's relatively cheap money. A good accountant should ensure that the interest is tax deductible. It could easily be raised against the value of the property, and you could fund all the improvements early in your plan. Put your prices up straight away to cover the repayments. I'm sure it could be made to work. But you need a plan, a financial projection.'

'Are you sure?'

'Positive,' he said. He'd spoken with more conviction than he'd actually felt. What he'd said was sound as a general business proposition, he just didn't know the hotel trade well enough. The principles were right though, and he felt a renewed confidence as the discussion stayed on this safe ground. Although the meeting was not going the way he'd intended, and certainly without any romantic overtones, he felt very satisfied, nonetheless. Another thought occurred to him.

'I could help you,' he said. 'I could help you develop a plan. Establish quotations for the work, quantify the costs, and then…'

He hesitated. This was potentially a committing step, but he rather liked the way it would underpin what he thought of as their developing relationship.

'And then,' he continued, 'I would be prepared to lend you the money. We'd need to discuss it further of course, but I'd be prepared to lend to you at say, half a percent less than the best rate you'd get from the bank. We could fix it to the variable base rate or have some form of fixed rate agreement. Pay it back over an agreed term.'

To Tara, not particularly familiar with bank loans, rates, terms and the like, it sounded impressive, although she hadn't a clue what such an offer meant in terms of hard cash. Theodore had guessed the total likely expenditure of Tara's hotel improvements, and felt the sum easily fell within his significant private funding. Whilst he didn't have a lot of ready cash, Theodore had substantial private wealth tied up in stocks and shares, and some small properties. An instruction to his broker to liquidate even a small portion of his current portfolio would easily give him funds enough for Tara's projects. And what of his reduced return on investment that this small hotel might represent? A small price to pay, he convinced himself, to help him secure what he hoped would be the love of his life.

'That's a very generous offer, Theodore,' Tara said. Theodore basked in self-satisfaction as she said his name. He congratulated himself on a brilliant strategy.

'But what would you get out of the deal?' she asked.

'Oh, that's easy. I'd get a steady income stream, and I'm sure we could come to some arrangement over some sort of discounted room rate for any guests that my company might put up here.'

This argument, made up on the hoof, would not stand thorough commercial examination, but Theodore was now past caring.

'Do you think you'd ever put any custom our way?' asked Tara, now seeing tangible attractions of the scheme.

'You'd be surprised,' he said. 'We do a lot of export business these days and have frequent foreign visitors. It's astonishing how many prefer a smaller, more quaint and typically English hotel. Certainly compared to some of these flash, expensive places like The Oakland's become. Now there's a place! Used to have bags of character. Then it got taken over by some national chain. It's just like a great sanitised warehouse now. Awful! No, I'd certainly prefer to stay at a place like this.'

Their conversation duly ran its course, and all too soon Theodore realised he ought to be going. As he approached the front door, he turned to Tara.

'Well, Tara. You don't mind me calling you Tara, do you?' He held out his hand to shake hers, and summoning up all his courage he looked her in the eye.

'No, Theodore, not at all,' she said, shaking his hand.

'Well, Tara,' he continued, retaining her hand, 'you have a think about what I've said. You've a super little place here, and I'd be more than happy to give you some financial backing.'

'I will, Theodore, I will,' she said, conscious that he was still holding her hand. He brought his other hand up and enclosed her hand in both of his.

'I'll be honest,' he said, 'I've got more money than I really need. It'd give me tremendous pleasure to put some of it to good use. Think about it. No rush. I'll pop back later in the week to take it further if you like.'

'Sure,' said Tara. 'Anytime.'

After he'd gone, Tara returned to the lounge to collect the tea tray. Rose, having heard the front door close, came in with the same intention.

'Everything all right, Miss Smith?' she enquired again with a big grin.

Tara looked from the tray of best china up to her mischievous assistant.

'You did that on purpose, you minx!' exclaimed Tara, laughing. The two dissolved into a fit of the giggles.

'Everything was fine, actually,' said Tara.

'Mr. Frosty didn't mention any Valentines then?'

'None at all, so stop stirring it, you!' said Tara.

'You were worried for a while though, weren't you?' said Rose.

'No, not really,' said Tara unconvincingly. 'I wasn't. And he's not Mr. Frosty. He's actually a very nice man when you get to know him.'

'Is he now?' said Rose sceptically, smiling. 'How nice.'

'Not like that,' countered Tara. 'He's just a kindly old man with more money than he knows what to do with, and guess what?'

'What?'

'He wants to put money in the hotel. I'd have to look into it a bit further, but it sounded a very good deal to me. Isn't that a hoot? We could pay for all the improvements, ensuite bathrooms, the lot, all in one go.'

'Hmm, sounds interesting,' said Rose picking up the tea tray, and smirking. 'So, Tara,' she said, 'he could be your sugar daddy, after all.'

'Rose!'

Chapter Nineteen

Bill Hunter approached Theodore Walklate's office door. Seeing it slightly ajar, he knocked and put his head around it.

'Evening, Theodore,' he said. 'Joshua back in tomorrow?'

Theodore, sitting behind his desk, appeared to be holding a pale blue envelope to his nose.

'Should be,' said Theodore, looking up and quickly putting the envelope in the top drawer of his desk. He slammed the drawer shut.

'Just wondering, that's all,' said Bill. 'I need to talk to him about the production scheduling system.'

'You could phone him.'

'It's OK. It can wait until tomorrow. Where's he been today?'

'He's out with Andrew. Andrew had appointments at Pradit Electronics (UK) Ltd and Nemeth Advanced Electrical. Joshua took the opportunity to tag along.'

'I see,' said Bill, entering the room. 'So this could be the moment?'

'Could be,' said Theodore distractedly. 'After our talk the other evening, I said I'd leave it with him. I'd trust Joshua to pick his timing. Today may give him the opportunity.'

'You still think this is the best approach?'

'Yes, I do,' said Theodore, standing up. He glanced at the darkness beyond his office window. It had been another long day. He felt tired. He'd not slept well these past few nights. He turned and looked around his office, the papers scattered on his desk testament to another fruitless day full of distractions, mostly work related, but one rather personal. He faced his Production Director.

'This is no time to debate the decision. You know as well as I do, Bill,' he said, 'if I deal with Andrew directly, he'll likely go bleating to his mother. From Joshua, it'll have more credibility. Be a bit more independent. It won't seem so much like I'm getting at the lad.'

'And what about Marjorie?'

'Oh, she'll fly off the handle, either way. We just have to accept that. But if we lay the ground right, put our ducks all in line, we'll swing it. She'll get used to the idea eventually.'

'Yeah,' said Bill, turning to leave. 'You're probably right.'

'You still happy with your role in it?' asked Theodore.

'Sure,' said Bill.

Just as Bill was about to leave, he noticed Theodore again staring blankly out of the window.

'Theo,' he said. 'Are you OK?'

'Hmm? Oh, yes. Fine, fine.'

Bill paused on the threshold of the office door. Amongst Theodore's tumultuous thoughts and burgeoning emotions, he now considered his Production Director. He'd known Bill for fifteen years or more. Amongst his business and limited social circles, he considered Bill Hunter his closest friend and ally. He could trust Bill. They thought alike on many issues. He was discreet. He was a married man. Theodore needed to talk to somebody. He had to relieve some of the turmoil that had so suddenly taken over his whole life.

'Bill?' said Theodore.

'Yes.'

Silence.

'Something the matter, Theo?'

'Come in, Bill. Shut the door and have a seat.'

Bill knew that the office cleaners had long gone, and that the two of them were probably the only occupants of the building. They were not about to be overheard, but Theodore clearly wanted a confidential discussion. Bill shut the door and sat down in front of Theodore's desk. The Managing Director of Walklate and Co. paced the room.

'I don't really know what to say,' Theodore started hesitantly. 'It's just…'

His words tailed off. Bill could see the man struggling to form his words in a manner that he'd never quite known before.

'There's this woman,' said Theodore.

A woman! Bill was there in an instant. If Bill hadn't been sitting down, he'd probably have fallen down, but in his shock and amazement, he somehow managed to maintain his customary coolness. He kept silent. Theodore Walklate and a woman!

'And,' continued Theodore, 'well, it's just that she… I think she feels something for me.'

'And you feel the same about her?'

'Oh, yes,' said Theodore, emphatically. 'Yes, I do.'

There! He'd said it. A relief swept over Theodore Walklate at this small but ultimately significant unburdening.

'That's good,' said Bill, and then more light-heartedly, 'do I know the lucky girl? Who is she?'

'Erm, I'd rather not say, just at the moment.'

'Oh,' said Bill. 'She married or something?'

'No, no, no! Nothing like that,' said Theodore. 'No, she's single. There's nobody else as far as I know. I'm sure.'

'Well, I'm very pleased for you. This is good news.'

'Yes, well, it is, of course.'

Bill could tell from this hesitant response that Theodore still hadn't completely related the nub of whatever difficulty he faced.

'So what's the problem?' asked Bill.

'Well, it's just that I don't know what to say. I don't know how to tell her what I feel.'

'And you said she feels something for you? How do you know?'

'She gave me a sign.'

Theodore immediately thought how silly that sounded, as if it was some sort of bloody séance! He may as well tell the whole story.

'She actually sent me a Valentine. I thought it was some bloody joke at first from one of the Herberts in Norman's area, but I checked. I'm positive. It's from her, and it's genuine.'

'You're sure?'

'Yes. I went to see her. We talked. Not about the card, just other things in general. I could tell. I've never felt like this before, Bill, but I could tell. I could see it in her eyes.'

'Well, this all sounds good news to me, Theo. I can't say I'm not surprised, because I am, but I'm very pleased for you. It's good.'

'Yes, yes, it is,' said Theodore, continuing to feel progressively more confident the more he told Bill of his turmoil.

'She's young, you know.'

'So?'

'I'll be fifty in December, Bill. People are going to say I'm just a silly old sod.'

'Since when has the great Theodore Walklate given a stuff what people say?' said Bill with a smile. 'Fifty's the new forty these days.'

Theodore smiled too. Once again, one of Bill's pithy pronouncements had hit the bullseye.

'It's just that I don't know what to say to her, what to do. You're a man of the world, Bill. What the bloody hell do I say to her?'

Bill thought for a while. He'd been rocked by the whole conversation so far, genuinely pleased for his boss, but still coming to terms with this totally new and uncharacteristic aspect of Theodore Walklate. He momentarily struggled to find the words, the advice that Theodore so desperately sought. Bill felt it was like a having a conversation with an adolescent, albeit a grey-haired one.

'You're probably best not rushing into it. Ask her out. Dinner, perhaps.'

'I could invite her to dinner at Fallowfield.'

'No!' said Bill. Then realising that he may have been just a shade hurtful in the speed and vehemence of his response, quickly followed up with, 'No, no. Don't do that. I'm sure Janice could knock up a nice meal, but you might feel a bit under pressure, as the host, as it were. If you see what I mean.'

Bill had conjured up an impression of some delicate, shy, reserved, English flower being totally overawed by dining alone at Fallowfield with Theodore Walklate. He imagined the two of them, Walklate and this mystery young woman, in the draughty old dining room at Fallowfield, stilted conversation echoing around the room, interrupted only by the clink of silver cutlery on bone china.

'No,' said Bill more calmly. 'Book a table at some restaurant somewhere. Let someone else worry about the food and stuff. Out of town. Good food, warm, nice ambience.'

'Good idea!' said Theodore. 'I'll do just that!'

'Take it slowly. Just talk about general things. Let the conversation flow. Anything you really need to say'll come out at the right moment. Be yourself. Be natural.'

Theodore sat behind his desk, arms folded, a picture of contentment. Bill, recognising his counselling had been completed, stood up and made for the door.

'Good luck,' said Bill with a smile. 'Let me know how you get on.'

'Bill?' said Theodore just before the Production Director went out of the door. 'Not a word to anyone else just now.'

'Of course.'

'And Bill?'

'Yes?'

'Thanks.'

'No problem.'

As Bill Hunter walked the short distance down the corridor back to his own office, he shook his head. Wonders would never cease!

★★★

As Theodore was unloading his emotional troubles on his Production Director, Joshua Latham and Andrew Forsythe were, for the second time that day, sitting in a traffic jam. Thanks to a lapse of concentration by a driver several miles ahead of them, their return home on the motorway had been reduced to a snail's pace.

'Bugger!' said Andrew.

'How much further until we get off the motorway?' asked Joshua.

'It'll be at least another three junctions, and then we've got thirty-five miles to reach Bramton. After our early start, it looks like we're in for a bit of a late finish too.'

The two sat in silence. They were in Andrew's car. They had

shared some of the driving, there being so much in an itinerary that involved visiting two of Walklate's more prestigious UK customers. Pradit Electronics (UK) Ltd, a wholly owned subsidiary of a major multi-national company, operated from a large industrial estate just off the M25 in Surrey. Nemeth Advanced Electrical plc, a medium-sized, publicly owned company, were based in Northamptonshire.

'I suppose I've failed the test, then?' said Andrew.

'Sorry?' said Joshua.

'Today, I mean. It was a bit of test really, wasn't it?'

'What do you mean?'

'Well, you consultants have never been near sales before now, certainly not before Uncle gave Holroyd the heave-ho. This was like your first foray into this side of the business, wasn't it? Your chance to examine what's going wrong with sales.'

'Yes,' admitted Joshua. 'That's true. We'd always intended to look right across the company. We'd just never got around to sales before now. With your itinerary today, it just seemed like a good thing. Meet some customers and have a chance to chat while we drove.'

'I don't mind, you know. Not at all really,' said Andrew. 'Even if I have made a frightful balls of it.'

'Oh, I wouldn't say that,' said Joshua, knowing full well that he was being disingenuous.

'Come off it, Joshua,' said Andrew, 'the whole trip's been a complete waste of time. Five-hundred-mile round trip for a cup of bloody coffee, and a chuffing sandwich.'

Andrew was right. The day had been an unmitigated disaster. Having agreed to pick Joshua up from the car park at Walklate's at six-thirty that morning, Andrew had been nearly twenty-five minutes late. By the time they'd reached the motorway, the rush hour was in full swing. The roads had been wet, and rain and spray had made driving difficult. There'd been an accident. As now, it had been some miles ahead at the front of a long snake of traffic. They'd eventually got through it, but they'd then been seriously late. They'd phoned ahead. The man they were to meet, the Chief Buyer, had expressed some displeasure at the disruption of his day. He was a busy guy, he'd said, and couldn't promise to see them if they were really late. They'd pressed on. They'd had to stop for fuel and grab a sandwich. Joshua had taken over the driving. Although he'd driven purposefully, the conditions were against them, and they'd arrived at the Pradit Electronics site an hour and half late. The Buyer had refused to see them. He'd been on a tight timetable. They'd missed their "window" and would have to reschedule for some other time.

Unable to meet the Chief Buyer, Andrew and Joshua had then been palmed off with a Purchasing Clerk. A young woman, obviously not long out of college, she clearly held few executive powers beyond perhaps ordering the stationery. After ten minutes of polite banter and a cup of disgusting coffee out of a vending machine, the two had said goodbye. They'd headed back north, with all speed, in order not to be late for their next appointment.

Joshua had driven this leg of their journey too, and although only ten minutes late when they pulled into Nemeth Advanced Electrical's site, both felt suitably fatigued and stressed. The disaster had continued unabated. The purpose of the trip had been partly to clear up a minor quality issue, but mainly to tender for some new orders. Andrew had clutched his laptop on which had recently been installed some new costing software. Theoretically, quotations could now be prepared in front of the customer. Fast, dynamic, accurate and reliable, this was clearly the way of the future. Or so the Sales Office Manager had said at the end of the training session. Andrew had not, in fact, paid sufficient attention during his training, and had scarcely looked at the program in the weeks since. Consequently, in front of the Buyer and the Design Engineer of Nemeth's, he'd managed to produce, not a nice, neat, accurate quotation complete with company logo, but six pages of complete gobbledegook rounded off by a succinct error message.

'Oh dear,' Andrew had said. 'Appears to be a bit of bother with the old electronic brain here.'

As the Nemeth personnel had looked on politely and made small talk with Joshua, Andrew had tried again but with the same result. Joshua had then politely but firmly suggested that they return to Bramton and send Nemeth Advanced Electrical their quotations by email. Andrew had agreed with this return to the mature, safer technology, and with embarrassed laughs all around, the two had slunk off site to do battle, once again, with the national motorway network.

'I'm not an idiot, you know,' Andrew said disarmingly as the car now inched forwards. 'It's been a disastrous day. There's nothing else you can say about it. You'll doubtless have to report to Theodore about it all.'

'You know,' said Joshua, 'he's actually got a lot of time for you.'

'Oh, I know he has. Blood's thicker than water and all that. But it's not thicker than cash! I know he doesn't mean me any ill will, but at the end of the day, both he and I, and you too now probably, realise that I have my job, not because of whether I'm any bloody good at it, but because of who I am. I'm jolly crap at it, actually, and everybody seems to know it. I'm just not cut out for it, I reckon. But I'm in the family, so everybody agrees to put up with it. Well, how far can we let this go? Don't forget, I'm a shareholder. I too have a vested interest in the sound financial performance of the company.'

Joshua was taken aback by Andrew's frankness, and the objectivity with which he clearly viewed himself. He looked at the Sales and Marketing man in a new light. Like Joshua, he'd got his shirt collar undone and his tie loose. Looking tired and flustered, with his hair characteristically askew, Andrew's slightly portly frame, wedged behind the steering wheel, strained at the shirt buttons. Joshua thought the man next to him had the sort of physique that never looks elegantly dressed, no matter how expensive the clothes. Andrew's suit was hand made for sure, but sitting there, driving up the motorway, Joshua could understand why some of the wittier shop floor employees at Walklate's referred to Andrew as "Bin Bag" or simply "BB" for short. He didn't look the part of company director, and now the man himself seemed to admit the problem was more than just image.

'It's only Mother who thinks I'm any bloody good at it. But she obviously has a rather rose-tinted view of things.'

'I think you're being unduly hard on yourself,' said Joshua. 'Your product knowledge is certainly excellent. With some help on time management and stuff, I'm sure you could do a really good job. I can help you.'

There was a silence as the car nosed further along the road.

'So what's the big plan, then?' said Andrew.

Joshua feigned surprise.

'Don't look like that,' Andrew laughed. 'I have my contacts too, you know. I know you and Theodore and Bill have had your heads together. I really don't mind, I tell you. I'm just intrigued. What's the master plan, that's all?'

'Well,' said Joshua, 'we've obviously considered the sales set up, and there has been a suggestion regarding your position. We can talk about that now, if you like.'

'Look!' said Andrew. 'It's half a mile to the next junction. We could get off there. I'm sure I can remember a really good pub about two miles from here, on the road to Butterbourne. We could stop for a spot of eats and chat there. We can then take the road to Bramton from there, instead of coming back to the motorway. What do you say?'

'Sounds good to me,' said Joshua, relieved that the most difficult job of his day seemed to be resolving itself. 'The sooner we bail out of this traffic the better.'

And so Andrew and Joshua soon found themselves tucking into scampi and chips and with a pint of bitter each, Joshua prepared to divulge the "master plan".

★★★

Meanwhile, at around the same time, Bradley and Tara pulled up outside another pub, The Staging Post, nearly forty miles to the north of the returning businessmen. Parking and securing the trusty motorcycle, the couple went inside.

Having taken a deliberately circuitous route to the pub, mainly to demonstrate the handling qualities of the motorcycle, Tara was frozen stiff, and gratefully accepted a seat at a table by the roaring log fire in the lounge bar. Bradley bought the drinks, a solitary pint of bitter that was all he allowed himself when on two wheels, and a glass of red wine for Tara, and brought them over to their table.

'Enjoy the ride?' said Bradley.

'Yes,' said Tara. 'Very exhilarating. I'm sure it would be even better in the summer.'

'Yeah. Biking in the winter months can be a chilly occupation. What do you want to eat? My treat,' he said, handing Tara a menu.

When they'd made their selection and ordered, Tara said, 'Tell me, are you the Manager or the Assistant Manager up at The Oakland?'

Bradley calmly took a swig of his pint.

'Well,' he said, 'I joined as the Assistant Manager, but, and this isn't public knowledge yet, but Gillman, the Manager there now, will be retiring in a couple of months, and I'll be taking over.'

'Promotion for you.'

'Yeah.'

'Well done.'

Their evening passed in relaxed conversation. As they ate their meal, Bradley spoke of his background, schooling and experience of the hotel trade since joining the Travelite Group, and of course, motorcycling. Tara talked similarly of her background and family and how she'd come to be the proud owner of The Crown Hotel in Bramton.

'And you'll never guess,' she said.

'What?'

'I could have a financial backer too! Someone to help fund the improvements I spoke about.'

'Oh, yes,' said Bradley sceptically. 'Who's that then?'

'Theodore Walklate. The owner of Walklate and Co. in the town.'

'What's the deal?'

Tara explained all about Theodore's visit to The Crown that had occurred not long after Bradley's. She related the offer of financial support as well as she could remember. Bradley looked unimpressed.

'Tara, I don't want to sound like a party pooper, but tread very carefully, won't you?'

Already slightly crestfallen at this view, she asked why.

'Theodore Walklate, and although I've never actually met the man, I know of him, his reputation like, he is, no question, a very hard-headed businessman. He is not Father Christmas, and he is not going to bestow riches on your hotel without exacting some considerable payback. He'll have an angle.'

Other than Rose, Bradley was the first person that Tara had told of her potential benefactor, and she was visibly disturbed to have cold water poured on the possible scheme so soon.

'Do you think so?'

'Tara, trust me. It stands to reason. Why else should he put money in your business?'

Tara, still blissfully unaware of Theodore's true state of mind, thought long over Bradley's words.

Bradley leaned forward, and seeing Tara looking disappointed, took one of her hands in his.

'Look,' he said, 'read the small print, that's all I'm saying. Don't do anything hasty. I'll have a look at any contract before you sign, if you like. You're a really lucky girl, Tara. You're fabulously good-looking, and with that hotel, you've got a fantastic opportunity in life. I don't want you to be naïve and get suckered into some deal you later regret.'

She withdrew her hand, looked up and smiled.

'Another drink?' she said.

Bradley opted for a soft drink and Tara had another glass of red wine. As Tara sat back down with the drinks, she looked into Bradley's face.

'Bradley?' she said tentatively.

'Yes.'

'There's something I just wanted to say.'

'Oh, yeah?'

'I obviously read in the papers the other month, about your fiancée. That was your fiancée, wasn't it, the one in the accident? I just wanted to say sorry. It must be awful for you.'

It was Bradley's turn to look suitably despondent.

'I'm sorry,' said Tara. 'I shouldn't have mentioned it.'

'No, no,' he said. 'It's OK, really. It's surprising how quickly you get over these things. I'm a strong character, I guess. I don't stay down for long. I get up again. You have to face the future.'

'You're very brave,' said Tara with genuine admiration, as she clearly saw Bradley's hurt.

'When were you going to get married?' she asked.

'We hadn't actually set a date,' he said. 'I wanted to, but Sally, that was her name, she kept putting it off. To be honest, and I've never told this to a soul before, but well, we hadn't been getting on too well for a few weeks before, what with the wedding plans constantly being put off. Then, on the day, you know, the day she died, we'd had a row. She actually broke off the engagement. I was devastated. I was pleading with her to get back together, but she wouldn't listen. And when I heard she'd been killed, well, that really was the end. No chance of us ever making it up.'

During this magnificent inversion of events, Bradley's eyes had actually started to fill with tears. Tara was so moved that she reached out and put one of her hands over his.

'Still,' he said brightening, 'like I said, I'm a strong guy. You gotta move on, and as each day goes by, I get better and stronger about it all.'

★★★

Andrew and Joshua, having eaten their meal, were back on the road and, having avoided the motorway, were at last within a few miles of Bramton.

'Nearly half past bloody ten,' said Andrew.

'Yeah,' said Joshua. 'Long day, eh?'

'You can say that again,' said Andrew. 'Now then, so I've got this straight, the plan is to split my department. I take Marketing, and we offer a Sales Director's position to Scott Sanders.'

'That's it,' said Joshua. 'Both Theodore and Bill confirmed that Scott had quite a bit of sales experience in the past.'

'It's true,' said Andrew. 'I can vouch for that. He's a bright lad. He'll pick it up no problem. And you reckon that Bill will cover Scott's old job without replacing him directly?'

'That's about the long and the short of it – Bill, along with some of the existing foremen. We'd cut out a layer from the management structure. So there's no increase in manning overall.'

'Sounds good.'

With Andrew at the wheel, they descended the long steep road into the outskirts of Bramton.

'You stopping at The Crown?'

'Yeah. Just drop me outside,' said Joshua. He then returned to their earlier topic.

'It'll be tough, but Bill reckons, with some of the new systems that I've installed, he can handle it.'

They pulled up opposite The Crown, and with the engine running, continued to talk.

'Bill's jolly good, isn't he?' said Andrew thoughtfully. 'We'd really be in the soup without him. Absolute brick.'

'Yeah,' said Joshua, as he watched a motorcycle pull up on the other side of the road immediately outside The Crown.

'So how do you feel about it all?' asked Joshua.

'Great!' said Andrew. 'Complete relief, really.'

'Yeah?' said Joshua, as he watched the rider and the pillion passenger dismount from the motorcycle. Even before the passenger had taken off their helmet, he could tell from their body shape that it was a woman. Joshua guessed at the identity of the pillion rider even before the helmet came off and confirmed his notion.

'Sure,' said Andrew. 'As I said, I've long since recognised that I've been out of my depth. I appreciate your help with training and stuff, but concentrating just on the marketing, I'll be much happier. It's probably more of a chance than I deserve.'

'Good,' said Joshua slowly, all the time looking at Tara. She passed the helmet back to the man and shook her hair back from her face. She smiled.

'I'm glad you're taking it this way,' said Joshua slowly, 'and I know that Theodore and Bill will be too.'

The motorcycle rider had now removed his helmet and, barely able to contain a groan, Joshua recognised Bradley King. Tara and Bradley both briefly looked across the street to Andrew's car, but not recognising the vehicle, they quickly looked back at each other. Andrew had parked more or less directly under a street lamp and the interior of the car was cast in the shade of the car roof. With no lights on inside the vehicle,

Joshua and Andrew remained unseen by Bradley and Tara. Joshua could see the couple engaged excitedly in conversation, Tara laughing in the way he had come to recognise.

'What about your mother?' said Joshua, distractedly.

'What about her?' said Andrew.

Well,' said Joshua. He watched as Bradley demonstrably looked at his watch, and the couple continued to talk. 'It's just that I know Theodore was somewhat anxious about her reaction to the proposal.'

Joshua could see Bradley and Tara standing facing each other, less than a step apart. They'd stopped talking now. They were looking at each other.

Andrew, oblivious to Joshua's distraction, said, 'Don't worry about her. I'll tell her. She'll doubtless think Uncle's put me up to it, but as soon as I say I'm in full agreement, that'll be the end of it.'

Tara reached up and flung her arms around Bradley's neck. She pulled his head gently down to hers and kissed him full on the lips.

Joshua groaned and wiped his hands over his face.

'Are you OK?' asked Andrew.

'I've felt better,' said Joshua still covering his face. 'I'm just a bit tired, that's all.'

He looked up to see that Bradley and Tara had finished their kiss. Bradley was putting his helmet back on.

'Well, goodnight then,' said Andrew, 'and thanks for today. Help with the driving and all that. Sorry about the screw-ups. Let's say it all got better as the day went on!'

'Sure,' said Joshua. Bradley, now astride his motorcycle, revved the engine. With Tara waving, Bradley powered away. For the town centre, Joshua thought the acceleration and speed employed to be absolutely ridiculous. Joshua waited until Tara had gone inside before he got out of Andrew's car.

'See you tomorrow,' he said as he slammed the door closed.

Andrew drove off, leaving Joshua standing alone under the street lamp. He'd thought he'd got over Tara. His initial feelings for her he'd put down to a temporary infatuation. Since Christmas, he'd felt their relationship had developed nicely as good friends, pure and simple, no more, no less. Earlier she'd even asked him if he fancied stopping on in Bramton over one weekend, and perhaps going for a walk in the hills. Joshua had certainly been tempted. The offer had been made as a friend, and he had been inclined to accept it in the same light. So now, supposedly as friends, seeing Tara in the arms of another man, should not have been such a shocking prospect for him. But it was. He was mortified. He felt a rude awakening of his old feelings, only this time it was accompanied by helplessness. Not only did he suddenly recognise that he still loved her, but he knew now that she'd obviously moved on. Her feelings for him, if she'd ever really had any, were now in the past. She didn't feel anything for him. She loved another. He instantly recognised his jealousy. And it was over Bradley King! Joshua thought of the man he knew from his time staying at The Oakland. What was it that Lumsden, the taxi driver, had told him? King's fiancée had been killed in a car accident. *Christ!* thought Joshua. *That can't be more than four or five weeks ago! He's sure got over her bloody quick!* Joshua then thought of Lumsden's other words. Joshua was not disposed to listen to gossip, but in his mounting jealousy over Bradley King, he wanted to believe Lumsden's version now. Yes, he convinced himself, he is just the type to desert his pregnant fiancée, and then, when the poor girl is dead, forget all about her within a month!

He slowly, absent-mindedly crossed the road, his brain wrestling with his previously latent, but now rediscovered, and above all, unrequited love for Tara. He wallowed in his jealousy and the hopelessness of the situation. *It's her choice*, he thought. *I can't, I won't interfere!* He quickened his pace as he entered the hotel and grabbed his key from the board in reception. He bounded up the stairs three at a time before Rose, or anyone else, could come out to see who'd just arrived. He didn't feel like talking to anybody. He got into his room, shut the door, and leant back against it as if to prevent an army of followers.

He almost shouted. 'Bastard!'

Chapter Twenty

'So, where's this nice Mr. Walklate taking you?' said Rose, with a cheeky glint in her eye.

'Rose!' said Tara with a hint of resigned irritation. She still managed to smile but was becoming ever so slightly weary at Rose's teasing over the matter of Theodore's interest.

'I don't know. He just said on the phone he wanted a chat over a bite to eat, that's all,' said Tara. 'He just wants to run through this loan thing. We'll just go to a pub, somewhere local, I expect.'

'Is that his car pulling up now?' said Rose, craning her neck to see out of the kitchen window. Some car headlights swept the car park at the rear of The Crown Hotel. 'I'll leave you to go round to the front to meet him. Have a nice time.'

Without a word, Tara went through the hall to the front door to await Theodore. In his phone call that afternoon, he'd sounded relaxed and breezy as he'd told her more of his financial proposal. He'd then casually suggested that they might be better off discussing the matter further over a meal. Nothing too special, he'd said, just somewhere nearby. Theodore's apparent casualness allayed any lingering suspicions over the Valentine card that may have remained in Tara's mind. He couldn't possibly know who'd sent the card, she assured herself again. And surely, if he did know who'd sent it, he would have said something before now? Tara had readily agreed to the meeting with a clear conscience.

'Hello, my dear,' said Theodore in a slightly paternalistic manner, as he came through the front door. 'It's so nice to see you. How are you?'

They shook hands, Theodore only releasing Tara's hand with some reluctance.

'I'm fine, thank you,' she said. 'Are you parked around the back?'

'Yes,' said Theodore. 'Shall we go straight away?'

When Tara agreed, the couple made their way back to the car park. She couldn't help but notice his immaculately cut, dark grey suit, crisp white shirt with gold cuff links and his maroon silk tie. She thought he looked rather smartly dressed for a quick bite at a local pub. Perhaps he'd just come from work, she thought, and this was how he always dressed. Theodore gently held Tara's arm as he guided her towards his car. This action and his sartorial elegance sounded a quiet but distinct alarm deep in Tara's mind.

She was not too up on cars, but instantly recognised Theodore's large, dark blue vehicle as a Jaguar. He opened the passenger door for her. As she got in, she immediately sank into the cream leather seats. The smell of the fine upholstery was unmistakable. She noted the walnut fascia and marvelled at the dashboard with its instruments, buttons and switches, thinking the array would do credit to a small aircraft.

Theodore got in beside her, started the engine and put the automatic gear selector into drive. With an effortless, whispering glide, the car swept out of the car park.

'I thought we'd go to The Copper Beech,' said Theodore. 'It's not too far, and they do excellent food.'

'I can't say I've heard of it,' said Tara. 'Whereabouts is it?'

'Oh, it's out on the Manchester road a few miles. It'll not take us long to get there.'

Tara luxuriated in the opulence of the car. She could not remember ever having sat in such a vehicle before. The ride was exceptionally smooth, and so quiet, she sometimes struggled to tell that the engine was still running.

'It's a nice car you have,' she said.

'Yes,' said Theodore casually. 'Not bad. Not so good in the snow, but I've got a Range Rover when it gets a bit iffy underfoot.'

After twenty minutes' driving, interspersed only by stilted conversation, Tara again asked about their destination.

'Not much further,' Theodore assured her. 'Hungry?'

'Just a bit,' said Tara.

Still they drove on. Tara saw signs to Manchester at ever more frequent intervals. Beside her, Theodore caught a slight trace of

Tara's perfume, and knew instantly where he had come across it before. Any residual doubts he may have had were safely dispelled. He beamed smugly at the prospect of the evening.

'It's not quite what I'd have termed "local",' said Tara with a nervous laugh.

'Soon be there,' said Theodore. 'And it'll be well worth the ride, I promise you.'

Eventually, shortly after entering the suburbs of the city, Theodore turned down a side street. After a few more miles and a couple of junctions, they finally arrived at their destination. Some fifty minutes after leaving Bramton, they pulled into a car park in front of a large, imposing, stone fronted building. A big, brightly lit sign announced, "The Copper Beech Restaurant".

'Oh,' said Tara with a slight sinking feeling. 'With a name like Copper Beech, I was expecting a pub.'

'Good Lord, no,' said Theodore. 'This is one of the premier restaurants in the north of England. Michelin star job. Absolutely top quality. You'll love it.'

Again he took her arm as he escorted her into the building.

'We use this place quite a lot,' he effused. 'It's quite handy for the airport. Any international visitors we get to the company, if time is a bit tight and they're just on a quick stopover, we can arrange to meet them here instead of going all the way over to Bramton. It really is first rate.'

Tara immediately noted the décor of the restaurant to be on a par with Theodore's car. On seeing them arrive, a short, dark-haired waiter in a black jacket immediately rushed into the reception area.

'Mr. Walklate, sir! How wonderful to see you again,' the man said.

'Hello, Philippe,' said Theodore.

Another waiter materialised and took Tara's coat from her. Having been led to expect little more than a bar snack, she suddenly felt herself unprepared and more importantly, underdressed for the elegant surroundings she now found herself in. Whilst she was certainly smart – some would argue that Tara never looked otherwise – she felt her plain knee-length, red skirt and cream roll neck sweater were far too casual for the sumptuous surroundings of The Copper Beech restaurant. Never one for a lot of make-up at the best of times, Tara now felt desperately ill-prepared for the occasion, and keenly wished that she'd done something more with her hair. *God, what must I look like?* she thought. *Why didn't he warn me?*

'We 'ave reserved your usual table, Mr. Walklate, by the window,' said Philippe. 'Or p'rhaps you would prefer something a little more "private"?'

'Oh, the small round table in the far corner would be super, if it's free,' said Theodore.

'Certainly, sir,' said Philippe ingratiatingly. 'Would you like a drink first or would you like to come through straight away?'

Theodore looked at Tara for the answer. She sighed inwardly. This was not the evening she'd been expecting. She was not prepared. Her confidence knocked, she now longed for the meal to be over quickly. She elected to go straight through to the restaurant. Philippe showed them to their table. They strode through the restaurant, with its hushed tones and deep pile carpet. Tara noted how the tables were set well apart, and tastefully partitioned from each other by strategically placed screens and potted plants. Tara sat down quickly, thankful for the relative seclusion.

Philippe offered menus to them, saying, 'I can particularly recommend the Paupiettes de Boeuf à la Paysanne or, if you prefer some fish, the Maquereau en Concombre Vinaigrette p'rhaps. They are fresh today. May I get you an aperitif?'

Tara refused. Theodore did likewise, in a clear attempt she felt, to conform with her and make her feel more comfortable.

'Very good,' said Philippe, standing heels together, leaning forwards, wringing his hands with practised ease. 'Maurice will be your waiter tonight. I shall return shortly to take your wine order. If there is anything that you require, please let me know. I am at your service.'

As Philippe, clearly the head waiter of the establishment, walked away, Tara looked at the menu. She noted two things immediately. One, her copy had no prices, and secondly, it was all in French. Having spent some time touring Europe, Tara was not a beginner at French by any means. However, her French was far from the best. With little experience of dining out in top-class French restaurants, the ability to translate the names of fine foods, sauces and cooking methods, as used by the best restaurants, was a little beyond her. She now struggled to decipher the haute cuisine on offer. She felt overawed by the whole place, the atmosphere and, she conceded to herself, the company she was in. Her normal self-confidence ebbed, and she felt unable to ask Theodore or the waiter for help in understanding the menu. Tara ordered a fairly plain Boeuf à la Bourguignonne, this being one of the few dishes she felt sure of. Theodore ordered the Maquereau.

'Anything to start, Tara?' he said.

'No thank you,' she replied.

'I thought you were hungry?'

Tara laughed nervously at this contradiction of her earlier claim. 'Saving room for dessert,' she said, smiling weakly.

Theodore laughed, looked at the waiter who'd come to take their order, and said, 'These women, eh? Always thinking about their figures, what?'

Tara sighed inwardly. The waiter just smiled. Philippe returned for their wine order.

'Any preferences?' asked Theodore of Tara.

'Er, no,' she said. 'Red perhaps, but if you're driving, we could probably make do with a half a bottle.'

Theodore wouldn't hear of such an economy and dismissed the concern over driving.

'A bottle of the Fleurie, the 2014, please Philippe,' said Theodore.

'An excellent choice, if I may say so,' said Philippe, taking the wine menu back, and silently backing away from the table.

Theodore and Tara ate their meal largely in silence. Only polite exchanges accompanied what, Tara had to admit, was truly excellent food. With a fuller stomach and two glasses of fine Beaujolais, Tara began to feel a little more relaxed. They ordered dessert, Tara being confident of what to expect with a Tarte aux Pommes et Amandes. Theodore ordered the same. Their discussion moved to the question of the proposed deal. Theodore was effusive. He said that he knew an architect in the town who would draw up plans for any room alterations required. He could put her in touch with a firm of plumbers and heating engineers. They would be most suitable to install a new boiler and extend the central heating in The Crown to the top floor, and, tapping the side of his nose, said that they "owed him a few favours". Tara could get the most competitive quotation for a loan to cover the work, he said, and he would beat it by a clear one per cent. He got a pen and a calculator from his jacket pocket and, scribbling on some paper, gave Tara some worked examples of the repayments required. Tara had to concede that the deal looked unbelievably attractive, but Bradley's cautious words echoed in her mind.

'I'm still not sure,' she said.

Theodore took this prevarication to be mere bargaining. The waiter took away their empty dessert dishes and served them coffee.

'Tell you what,' he said, leaning forwards across the table. 'I'll make the loan interest free for the first six months. How about that?'

Again she thought of Bradley. This latest extra encouragement did not sound at all like the actions of a hard-headed businessman, and Tara's unease returned. Theodore, still leaning forward, caught a hint of her perfume.

'Well,' she said, 'it's certainly very generous, and I am ever so grateful, but… I can't see what you'd get out of it all. You've explained about the small discount on room rates for anybody you recommend to us, but, well, the figures don't add up. It'll cost you far more than you'd ever get back.'

'Hmm,' said Theodore. He'd really rather have had the deal sewn up before moving the discussion on to the question of the Valentine. But Tara, for all her apparent lack of business acumen, had seen the flaw in the economics of the offer. He played for more time.

The makers of "Lovely" clearly had delightfully confused conversations in mind when they so named their latest perfume.

'Your perfume,' said Theodore, 'it's lovely.'

Tara's heart skipped a beat at the ambiguity. Her anxiety ratcheted up a notch. For the umpteenth time she regretted having sent the Valentine and particularly, now, the impulse to put perfume on the envelope.

'You're well informed,' she said.

'Sorry?' said Theodore.

'You're well informed. About perfumes.'

'I am? Well, not really.'

She saw his confusion.

'It's actually called "Lovely". That's the name of the perfume.'

'Oh, I see! I'll remember that.'

'So,' said Tara, anxious to bring the conversation back to business. 'Back to your offer. What's your... angle?'

Theodore looked down at the scribbled calculations on the scrap of paper before him. There was no formula for what he was about to say. He tried to imagine how Bill Hunter would say it. He couldn't prevaricate any longer.

'Tara,' he said, 'I... I'm sorry it's taken me so long to say this. It must have been an awful time for you, wondering what I felt. I'm sorry. I'm just not used to this sort of thing.'

Tara looked on, puzzled. Theodore looked up at Tara's eyes and reached across the table and put a hand on hers.

'I know you sent me the Valentine card.'

Tara froze.

'It was very sweet of you,' he continued, once again casting his eyes to the table. 'I understand what you must feel, and I just wanted you to know... I just wanted to say that I feel the same way about you.'

There! He'd said it! He let out a long and deep breath and looked back at Tara.

She was dumbstruck. She withdrew her hand quickly from his.

'Oh!' she said. He knew! He'd known for a while. He thought she was serious. She was embarrassed. She cursed herself. She cursed Rose. This was a disaster! What could she do? Could she deny it?

'How, how do you know?' she stammered.

'Oh, a little detective work. It wasn't hard. I'm sure you made it easy on purpose. The handwriting, particularly on the envelope. The perfume clinched it.'

She couldn't deny it. She felt trapped.

'I can tell you're shocked, but don't be,' he said. 'I really didn't mind. In fact, I was damn flattered, to be honest. I really could never have imagined, you know, having a relationship. Not with someone as attractive as you, at any rate.'

'Stop!' she said, her voiced raised in almost a shout. One or two diners at adjacent tables looked across at them.

'I'm sorry,' she said, lowering her voice. 'I really am sorry, but there's been a dreadful misunderstanding here.'

'What?' he said. 'You did send the card, didn't you?'

'Well, yes, but…'

'So? There's nothing to be embarrassed about. It was a very sweet gesture.'

'No! You don't understand. I wasn't serious. I only meant it as a joke.'

'A joke!'

'Yes, a joke. I—'

'But it wasn't funny. The verse inside was very romantic, I thought.'

'Well, yes it was, but I didn't mean anything by it.'

'Oh, Tara, dearest,' he said reaching back to take her hand again. 'I can tell you're overawed. It's this place, isn't it? You've been a little nervous ever since we arrived. I can tell. I should have broached this subject somewhere a little more private. I'm sorry. Let's go. We can talk some more in the car.'

'Oh God!' Tara murmured. Theodore ignored the comment and signalled to Philippe, who immediately rushed to Theodore's side.

'The bill please, Philippe.'

'On the Walklate account, sir?' said Philippe in a hushed tone.

'No, no. I'll settle this one.'

'Very good, sir.'

Tara sat in silence. When the bill arrived on a small silver salver, Theodore discreetly placed a credit card next to it. Philippe collected it and returned within a minute. Theodore tapped in his PIN. Despite Theodore's efforts to be covert, Tara could just make out the initial figure "3" in the bill. The meal had cost over three hundred pounds!

'Thank you for the meal,' said Tara sheepishly.

'Entirely my pleasure,' said Theodore, unperturbed. 'Shall we go?'

They collected Tara's coat, and with Philippe's pleas for them to return ringing in their ears, they stepped outside. Tara shivered in the cold as they headed for Theodore's car. Tara felt resigned at the prospect of the fifty-minute drive back. During the journey, strained silences were interrupted mainly by Theodore's attempts at conversation. No matter how Tara phrased her replies, Theodore didn't appear to listen. He was not to be put off.

'Just think about the deal,' he said. 'I'll even increase the discount if you like.'

Tara, now completely uninterested in "the deal", felt unable, certainly unwilling, to even consider it.

'I don't think it would be a good idea,' she said.

'Now don't be too hasty,' he said. 'You have a think about it. We could just kick it off maybe with a few smaller projects first. Just to cement our relationship, as it were, and then just see how things develop.'

'Things will not develop!' said Tara in frustration. 'Will you please stop implying that there's something romantic going on between us, because there isn't.'

'Tara, listen to me. I know I'm a bit old for this sort of thing, and I don't pretend to know how you women think. I can tell it's all come as a bit of a shock to you. The way I feel about you, I mean. You obviously must feel something for me, or else you'd never have sent that card.'

Tara groaned. She wanted to die with embarrassment. The rest of the drive was spent in silence. As they pulled into the car park of The Crown, Tara had the door open barely before the car stopped. Theodore had been thinking of Bill Hunter's advice. He thought the restaurant had been OK, certainly up to The Copper Beech's normal standards. And he thought he'd let the conversation flow quite well. He'd been "himself". Tara was confused, he convinced himself, that was all. She'd come round. Theodore got out of the car and came around to Tara's side. She was determined not to invite him in for a coffee but couldn't storm off inside without a word.

'I'll say goodnight, then,' she said.

Theodore moved closer. Tara stepped back and held out her hand for him to shake. It felt a ludicrously formal end to the evening. Theodore accepted her hand.

'Think about the loan,' he said. 'It's a good deal for you, irrespective of anything else.'

Tara felt appalled and resigned at the "anything else" and said nothing.

'I'll be in touch,' he said, as Tara turned to go inside.

As soon as she got in the front door, Rose, doubtless on the lookout for the returning car, stepped into the hall.

'Have a nice time? You've been gone absolutely ages. Go somewhere nice?'

Tara stood at the foot of the hall stairs, flustered, lost for words.

'Candlelit dinner for two, then, eh?'

'Rose, please!' Tara shouted. 'Shut up!'

Tara bounded up the stairs two at a time.

'I'm going to bed.'

Chapter Twenty-one

Joshua's summing up presentation to the Walklate's board had gone well. This was partly due to Joshua's innate presentational skills, but mainly due to the content. With one week remaining of the original time span for the project, there were, at last, encouraging signs regarding the financial performance of the company. Appropriately for the time of year, better monthly financial figures had recently begun to show. To the palpable relief of the assembled board of directors, recovery from a long winter of underperformance seemed to have arrived at last. How much of this improvement was directly due to Joshua's contribution could never be calculated with certainty, but in the time-honoured tradition of corporate politics, those with a high profile get the credit, or blame, whenever there is a significant change, up or down, in a company's fortunes. Joshua's profile over the previous six weeks, plus the earlier period under his former employer, certainly qualified him on this occasion as "high profile".

'Thank you, Joshua,' said Theodore Walklate, as Joshua resumed his seat. 'I appreciate that you've not had long to collate your results and make your presentation, but I think we're all agreed. The results speak for themselves.'

Theodore stood up to make his summation. He looked around the room.

'There are many people, particularly those in this room today, who deserve credit for bringing about the turnaround in performance, and our return to what I expect will be consistent profitability. We've all seen Jas's figures, and the projection for the next three months. Scott and Andrew have together produced a very promising-looking forecast. Things are looking decidedly better. Not to decry the efforts of all of you, I would like to single out a few individuals whose contributions have been, and continue to be, very important. A number of us have had to swallow our pride during the recent difficult months, and seriously question our ways of working, even our very abilities. I know I have. Chief amongst these, and worthy of special mention, is Andrew Forsythe.'

There was a murmuring of approval as everyone looked at Andrew.

'Andrew very magnanimously agreed to relinquish the Sales side of his department, leaving him concentrating solely on Marketing. This, along with Scott Sanders taking over the Sales function has, without question, made a substantial difference to us as a company.

'Which brings me onto Scott himself. Somewhat belatedly Scott, I'd like to welcome you formally to the board of Walklate's. In the, what is it, five weeks or so since your appointment, you have certainly… I think the modern phrase is "hit the ground running". Well done, particularly for the new business at Nemeth Advanced Electrical. Early days yet, I know, but I also think your new export drive shows huge promise.

'Now, in order for Scott to take up his new position, there is of course, the small matter of the hole he leaves behind in the Production department. As you know, we are all run by the bean counters…'

Everyone chuckled politely at this reference to the accountants.

'And obviously Jas expressly forbade me from recruiting a direct replacement for Scott.'

There was more polite laughing before Theodore continued, smiling.

'And so it's really fallen to Bill Hunter and his team to pull out all the stops. Not only has the production department made huge strides forward in both quality and productivity, they have done so with a completely new, and smaller, management team. Well done!

'Finally, and I know Bill wishes to endorse these comments, I have had a lot of conversations with employees throughout the company over the last few months. These have been with many people in the organisation, both in this room now, out in the field, and on the shop floor, and there is one man who I think must take much of the credit for the company turnaround. And that man is Joshua Latham.'

Joshua looked at the floor.

'Never in an easy position,' Theodore continued, 'Joshua has combined honesty and integrity with a lot of sound business knowledge and skills. So much so, that he's earned the respect of all of us. Even the toolroom!'

One or two sitting around the boardroom table muttered, 'Hear, hear!' and politely laughed at Theodore's little joke.

'I thought I worked long hours, but over the past month or so, the time that you've put in, Joshua, has been astounding. All I can say is, I'm glad we've had you on a fixed fee contract!'

It was true. Joshua had put in a prestigious number of hours to bring the consultancy exercise to a close. He'd worked single-handedly and covered almost all the tasks that he'd previously set for both him and Martin Meredith. The benefit to the project was unquestionable. But if Theodore Walklate had known the true reason why Joshua had thrown himself so wholeheartedly into the exercise, he would have been even more concerned. Having rediscovered his love for Tara Beaumont-Smith and knowing that his feelings were never likely to be reciprocated, Joshua had found his stay at The Crown uncomfortable. The proximity to the proprietor, attractive as he found her, had become an agony for him, a delicious but forbidden fruit. He knew from Rose of Tara's developing relationship with Bradley King. He understood that they went out together several times per week. Joshua found Tara's close physical presence, combined with her remote emotional one, too much. Consequently, he had devoted himself to Walklate's. His days had frequently stretched well into the evenings. Whenever he had decided to call it a day, normally at the point of exhaustion, he would return to The Crown, often via the chip shop, only to go straight to bed. By prior arrangement with Rose, he was always up early for breakfast, and was away before any of the other hotel staff or guests were about. Without specifically declining Tara's offer of a walk one weekend, Joshua had avoided having to give her an answer. At the end of each week, he had always made a point of leaving for home on Fridays, straight from work, returning to Bramton and The Crown Hotel late on Sunday evenings.

'I have been particularly impressed,' Theodore continued, 'by the improvements in the production planning systems, the productivity gains, the reduced reject levels and the reduction in lead times. And all the time he was doing this, Joshua even managed to change employers! The most important contribution that you've made however, Joshua, is belief. You have made us believe in ourselves once again. Thank you.

'I'm sorry this meeting has dragged on so long. I know it's Friday and you particularly, Joshua, have a long way to go, but I think you'll all agree that it's been most worthwhile as a wrap up to the consultancy exercise. I know officially that you've got one more week to go but, with Scott going on his travels next week, this was our last chance for a while to get us all together. I understand also, Bill, that arrangements have been made for Joshua to return in about six months, just to check on progress, as it were.'

'That's right,' said Bill. 'September, in fact. We've already fixed the dates.'

With no more comment forthcoming Theodore formally closed the meeting. He picked up his files from the table in front of him when Marjorie Forsythe spoke.

'Theodore, may I have a word with you, please?' she said. 'In private,' she added pointedly.

Brother and sister thus made their way the short distance from the boardroom to Theodore's office. Marjorie shut the door behind them.

'Very well spoken,' said Marjorie.

Theodore couldn't be sure whether his sister was speaking sarcastically or not. Either way, he ignored the comment, knowing full well that her "private word", whatever its subject, was unlikely to be so generous.

'What is it?' he said in a perfunctory manner.

'I still don't know what you said to Andrew, but—'

'Oh, for pity's sake, Marjorie, drop it!' Theodore snapped. 'It's been a bloody month now. We've been over this before. The lad's happy.'

'There's no need to shout!' said Marjorie, raising her own voice. 'If you'd let me finish instead of biting my head off, I was about to say that.'

Marjorie paused for a moment, before regaining her composure.

'I've spoken to Andrew at some length,' she said, 'and he assures me that he's quite happy with his reduced role.'

Marjorie accentuated the word "reduced" making it quite clear that she both understood and resented the move involving her son.

'As such,' she went on, 'I have to accept the situation. I'm sure, should further opportunities develop for him to regain his former responsibilities, you would not hold it against—'

'Oh, stop being so bloody pompous, Marjorie! Andrew's happy just running the marketing. He was making a balls of the sales side of it, and you know it! He's a nice enough lad, don't get me wrong, but he's just not up to anything more than the marketing role.'

Theodore drew a deep breath to try to restore his self-control.

'And I'm not going around making commitments to promote him again at some stage in the future, just because he's your son. If he's good enough, fine; if not, tough! We owe it to ourselves as shareholders to make sure we have the best people for each job. Don't ever forget that, Marjorie.'

'Theodore!' said Marjorie. 'Will you stop talking me down and putting words in my mouth! Goodness, I don't know what on earth's got into you lately. We just don't seem able to have a civilised discussion these days.'

There was a pause in their verbal hostilities.

'I really don't understand you lately, Theo,' said Marjorie more calmly. 'Your behaviour lately has been quite extraordinary.'

'What's that supposed to mean?' said Theodore bitterly.

'Well, first and foremost, there's this girl you've been running around after for the last month or more.'

'I have not been "running around" after her, as you put it,' said Theodore with a look of concern. 'Besides, what do you know of that?'

'I know what everybody else knows,' said Marjorie with a derisory laugh. 'It's all round the company, especially, I understand, the shop floor. In fact, the stories are halfway round the damn town!'

'It's none of your business!' shouted Theodore. 'And you shouldn't pay any attention to bloody gossip.'

'It is my business when it affects the company's reputation. You may not realise it, Theodore Walklate, but you've become a ruddy laughing stock in this town.'

Marjorie rarely ever swore, so when she did, the impact was all the more dramatic. Theodore registered the comment.

'As far as I can see,' said Theodore in more measured tones, 'our "reputation" isn't doing too badly from our customers' perspective, and that's what counts. Look at the bloody sales forecasts, for God's sake!'

'It's only a matter of time, Theo. Word'll spread soon enough, don't you worry. Soon, all sorts of people will know what a fool you've been making of yourself. Honestly! A man of your age! You ought to know better than to chase some girl like that.'

'She's not a girl!'

'She's half your age! She could be your bloody daughter, for goodness' sake!'

Theodore had had enough. He put on his jacket and his coat. He took a small packet out of his desk drawer.

'I haven't finished what I came in to say,' said Marjorie, indignantly.

'Well, I've finished listening,' said Theodore, opening his office door.

'Where are you going?' asked Marjorie.

'I'm going to run around after a girl!'

He slammed the door behind him.

Theodore enjoyed his walk in the fresh, spring air. The sky was clear, and in the late afternoon sunshine, the temperature warm enough for him to unbutton his coat. In a few minutes he arrived at The Crown. As he approached, he saw a figure that he recognised walking with a black Labrador. The woman, with coat and scarf, walked around to the rear of the building, heading for the gate to the rear yard of the hotel. Theodore followed.

'Miss Whitworth!' shouted Theodore, as he caught up with Rose. 'Is Tara in by any chance?' he asked.

'Er, I think so,' said Rose, opening the gate to the rear yard.

'I didn't realise you had a dog,' said Theodore, bending down to stroke the animal.

'Oh, yes, for a few months now.'

'What's her name?' asked Theodore.

'Bess,' replied Rose.

'Oh, she's a beauty,' he said, continuing to stroke Rose's docile pet.

At that moment, Tara stuck her head out of the rear kitchen door and spoke. 'Rose? Do you know where the—'

She stopped mid-sentence at the sight of Theodore Walklate stroking the dog. Theodore looked up.

'Ah! There you are,' he said, smiling. 'I hope you don't mind me using the tradesmen's entrance.'

Tara stared blankly. Rose looked on, clearly embarrassed.

'Er, no,' said Tara. 'Of course not.'

'May I come in?' he asked.

'I'll just pop up to the market for some more veg,' said Rose tactfully.

Tara had eventually explained to Rose the full embarrassment of her evening at The Copper Beech. Rose had listened intently, siding with Tara at every notion. 'Fancy that!' she'd said. 'How far?' and 'Well, I never!' all sprang to Rose's lips as Tara unveiled the full story. Rose had apologised for her part in persuading Tara to send the fateful Valentine. Tara had in turn, apologised to Rose for shouting at her. The relationship between the two women had resumed its former equanimity.

The contrast, with Rose's altogether more successful card, had been an embarrassment for The Crown's number two. As Rose's relationship with Fraser had blossomed, she was very self-conscious of Tara having to endure completely unwanted attention. Theodore Walklate had sent Tara bunches of flowers and boxes of chocolates on a weekly basis. He'd phoned regularly, sometimes to talk more about the financial backing he'd offered, sometimes to ask just to see her. She'd refused, claiming to be busy with the hotel, an excuse Theodore saw through immediately. He'd even taken to calling on spec. The first few times Tara had seen him, their resultant conversations had merely perpetuated the impasse. Latterly, Tara had sent Rose out to say that she was out. Theodore clearly suspected on these occasions that he was being palmed off, but he was not to be deterred so easily. To Tara's exasperation, he would simply return a few hours later.

Theodore waited patiently for her answer.

'I suppose so,' said Tara.

As Rose disappeared back the way she'd come, Theodore and Tara went into the kitchen.

'I've bought you something,' said Theodore triumphantly.

'Oh, Theodore, please. I really wish you wouldn't.'

Tara sounded resigned, almost desperate.

'Oh, it's nothing really,' he said, producing a packet from his pocket, and giving it to her.

'Go on,' he said. 'Open it.'

With heavy heart, she unwrapped the package to reveal a small bottle of perfume. It was Lovely.

'See? I remembered.'

'Theodore, you shouldn't buy me these things. I don't want them.'

'Rubbish!' said Theodore, jovially. 'It's your favourite. Of course, you want it.'

'It's not the present,' said Tara, exasperated. 'It's the gesture. I don't want gifts from you!'

Even Theodore, in spite of his now blind love for the woman who stood before him, could see that Tara was upset.

'But, Tara, what else can I do to show you what I feel?'

'Please! Don't! Find somebody else. Leave me alone!'

'But I love you!'

'But I don't feel the same about you.'

'You might, in time.'

'I shan't,' she said, stamping her foot. 'I've found somebody else.'

Theodore fell silent. Tara instantly wished that there had been a different way in which she could have imparted this news. Theodore was clearly hurt. But nonetheless, she saw the effect of her words, and realised, at last, that she'd made him stop and listen. Perhaps now he would believe her.

'I see,' said Theodore slowly. 'Who... Do I know the man?'

'I don't know. He's the Assistant Manager up at The Oakland Hotel.'

'What's his name?'

'Bradley. Bradley King.'

'And do you love him?'

'That's a very personal question.'

'I know. I'm sorry, but... I'd just like to know where I stand.'

'We've been seeing each other for a few weeks now.'

'You're... serious? About him, I mean.'

'Yes, I think so.'

'I see.'

Theodore was silent for some minutes as he struggled to come to terms with this new development. He knew Tara well enough. She wouldn't tell lies. She must be serious about the man. He desperately sought a way around the obstacle.

'What about the loan? It's still a first-class deal.'

'I don't think it would be a good idea.'

'Could I still call and see you? Once in a while. It would mean a lot to me.'

'If you feel you must,' she said, reluctantly. 'But you must promise not to send me any more flowers or presents. If you do, I shall refuse to see you.'

Theodore stared disconsolately at the floor.

'I shall say goodbye, then,' he said.

As he turned to go, Tara said, 'Theodore... I'm sorry. I never meant for it to turn out like this.'

'I understand,' he said, in a tone barely above a whisper.

He left the hotel and walked aimlessly for perhaps half an hour. He found himself wandering the paths between the blooming flowerbeds of the nearby ornamental gardens. Where had he gone wrong? He analysed all he'd done over the previous six weeks or so. He'd followed Bill's advice. After the dinner at The Copper Beech, which Theodore had described to his confidante in rather more optimistic terms than were strictly justified, Bill had suggested he send flowers. He'd done that. He'd bought her presents. He mentally replayed his conversations with Tara, trying to put a positive spin on them, but all the time reluctantly recognising the same inevitable conclusion. She didn't love him! Now it appeared she'd never loved him. How could he have got it so wrong? She loved someone else. He conjured up a view of Bradley King. Who was he? What did he look like? How old was he? What had he got that Theodore hadn't? Theodore, unable to fully accept the inevitable, resolved to find out about this Assistant Manager of The Oakland Hotel.

He sat a while on a bench and stared blankly at some daffodils blooming nearby. As the light faded, he began to feel cold. He got up and made his way back to his company. He thought of what Marjorie had said to him that afternoon. He was the laughing stock of both his company and, apparently, half the town. What had caused him to behave this way? He reflected upon the previous twelve months. He considered his whole life, as he had done on numerous occasions recently, struggling to identify the key factors that had brought him to this low personal point.

He arrived back at Walklate and Co. and, it now being well after the working day, found most offices in darkness. He passed Bill's office. He looked at the frosted panel in the door and saw that there was a light on inside. He was about to knock and confide further in Bill when he heard voices from within. He moved on to his own office. He turned on a small desk lamp and slumped in his chair. He opened the top drawer of his desk and pondered the Valentine card that lay within it. He slammed the drawer shut. Never having been truly in love before, he'd also never experienced heartbreak either. Age didn't make it any easier to bear. He put his head on his arms on top of the desk and wept. He cried in a way he'd not done for nearly forty years, great chest-heaving sobs racking his body.

Some minutes later, alerted by the noise, there was a tentative knock at his office door. The door opened, and in walked Bill Hunter and Joshua Latham.

'Theo?' said Bill. 'Are you OK?'

Theodore looked up and managed to control his weeping for just long enough to utter, 'Oh, God!'

Bill walked behind Theodore and put a consoling arm on his shoulder. Joshua looked aghast at the man who, only a few hours earlier, had spoken so eloquently and assuredly. Joshua found it hard to believe that the formerly confident gentleman had been reduced to this tear-stained wreck. After some more minutes, and further questioning from Bill, they learned the full cause of Theodore's despair. Joshua was stunned. He'd heard the rumours along with everyone else. Never one to pay much attention to gossip though, he'd initially dismissed the stories. But credence had been added with each telling. The latest version Joshua had heard still hadn't revealed the identity of Theodore's love, merely referring to the woman as "some girl half his age, with plenty going for her". As Theodore detailed his anguish and now, without inhibition, seemed not to care who knew the object of his desire, Joshua could barely contain his disbelief. He knew he'd lost Tara to Bradley King, but Theodore's confession made him realise that he was not alone in this plight. In spite of learning of this new, but also ultimately unsuccessful rival for Tara's love, Joshua felt nothing but sympathy for the man. Over the preceding months, Joshua had learned to like Theodore Walklate. He thought him a shrewd businessman, and someone who commanded a lot of respect from those with whom he came into contact. Seeing Walklate now Joshua found truly disturbing. Hard though Joshua had found his own disappointment, he'd come to terms with it, largely thanks to sheer hard work. By his own standards, Joshua could only look on askance at Theodore's graphic suffering. He felt it a pain that no man should have to endure.

What on earth had possessed Tara to do such a thing? Joshua tried to think rationally. He knew Tara well enough. She could be impulsive, she admitted that herself. She could be flippant even, but Joshua couldn't believe her vindictive. She must have made a mistake, he thought. Her Valentine card must have been some sort of joke, no matter how misguided. Whatever reason Tara had had, she could not possibly know the true depth of anguish that she'd caused. She could not possibly appreciate the transformation she'd caused, turning this once distinguished, some would say austere, figure, into such a pitiful, broken man.

'I'm sorry,' said Theodore eventually. 'Please excuse my behaviour.'

'It's quite OK, Theo,' said Bill. 'You've nothing to be ashamed of.'

'Do you know this Bradley King?' asked Theodore, recovering his composure.

Bill looked blank and shook his head.

'I do,' said Joshua, 'from when I used to stay at The Oakland.'

'What's he like?' asked Theodore.

'What difference does it make?' said Joshua, trying to be tactful.

'I want to know!' Theodore Walklate, even in his despair, could be a forbidding man to cross.

'He's young,' said Joshua. 'Maybe late twenties, dark hair, clean-shaven, good-looking, I suppose. He's the Assistant Manager at the hotel. Rides a motorcycle.'

'But what's he like?' repeated Theodore. 'Is he a good man? I couldn't bear to think of Tara with anyone… unworthy.'

'I'm not sure what you mean,' said Joshua genuinely. He struggled with Theodore's expression of traditional gallantry. 'I believe he is now,' he said.

'What do you mean he is now?'

Joshua instantly realised his earlier answer had been less than judicious. In Theodore's present state of mind, anything less than a full and wholesome answer was instantly seized upon.

'I believe he was once engaged to another,' said Joshua.

'And he's not now? What happened?' asked Theodore.

'Well,' said Joshua, 'there was a tragedy. His fiancée was killed in car accident.'

'I know the one you mean now,' said Bill. 'That accident up on the Congreave road, early on in the New Year. It was in the news.'

Perhaps out of sympathy over his young rival's bereavement, Theodore initially seemed satisfied with this knowledge. But after a short pause, he commented, 'I remember reading about it too. So within a few weeks of the death of his fiancée, he starts going out with… another woman. I wonder if Tara knows of this?'

Joshua wondered too. Tara must know, he thought. More particularly he thought again of the rumours he'd heard about Bradley King. He'd been more than a little disturbed to discover some of his less savoury characteristics. Tara had made her choice, he'd concluded, and the consequences were up to her. He knew now that Theodore still had this hurdle to surmount. But now was not the time, and Joshua kept his counsel.

'I would have thought so,' said Bill. 'Besides, Theo, what difference would it make?'

Theodore was silent for a good few minutes.

'Come on, Theo,' said Bill. 'Let's go and have a pint and a bite to eat.'

'I think I'd rather just go home,' said Theodore weakly.

'You don't get a choice,' said Bill. 'You and I are going to the pub.'

Slowly, reluctantly, Theodore got to his feet.

'You're welcome to come too, Joshua,' said Bill, 'but I know you've got a long way to drive.'

Joshua was certainly tempted but ultimately he declined.

'Thanks,' he said, 'but I think I'd better be going. I'll see you both next week.'

After Joshua had said goodnight, Bill and Theodore walked to the nearest pub. Once out in the fresh air, Theodore again began to question where he'd gone wrong.

'I followed your advice, Bill, I really did,' he said.

'I'm sure you did, Theo, I'm sure you did. Maybe it was just not meant to be. You're not the first bloke ever to be mystified by the actions of a woman.'

'I really was myself, just like you said. I was as natural as I could be. I said what I felt.'

'Sure.'

'They say there's no fool like an old fool, eh?'

Maybe Bill was right, thought Theodore. Maybe, no matter what he'd have said or done, Tara was simply not destined for him. Theodore honestly believed what he'd just said. In his emotional confusion, though, there had been one glaring omission, something he'd thought all along but neglected to say. As Tara had emerged, with all her attendant good looks, from the abstract into the reality of his everyday life, he'd failed to grasp something of significance. It may ultimately have made no difference, of course, but in all his conversations with Tara, he'd never once told her outright just how beautiful she was.

Chapter Twenty-two

The following Friday was Joshua's final day in Bramton. 'It's going to seem quite strange without you, Joshua,' said Rose, 'and you must see Tara before you go. Just to say goodbye, like.'

'Yeah,' said Joshua. 'But she'll have to hurry up. I'll just have one more whisky and then I'm going off to bed.'

'Oh, I'm sure she won't be long now,' said Rose, climbing off a barstool and going behind the counter.

'Do you get to go out much these days, Rose?' said Joshua. He glanced aside to Fraser, who sat on a stool beside him, making sure Rose understood his meaning.

'Oh, yes, as much as we want to, don't we Fraser?'

'Aye. Don't give him anymore of that awful stuff!' said Fraser with alarm, as he saw Rose about to pour a measure of spirit into Joshua's glass. 'I'll stand you this one, Joshua. Since you're leaving in the morning, this calls for a special. Get out the bottle under the side there.'

'Oh, you are honoured,' said Rose. 'He doesn't normally let anybody even know we've got this stuff. If there was anybody else in the bar, this'd stay under the counter, I'm telling you!'

Rose produced a bottle from under the bar and passed it to Fraser.

'No, as I've said before, there's obviously always got to be somebody "in" as it were, looking after the hotel. So if Tara's out, we stay in. And if Fraser and I go out, it means Tara has to stay in. We take it in turns, sort of, but we don't mind stopping in, do we, dear?'

Fraser ignored the question, concentrating.

'He won't even let me pour it, will you?' added Rose, with a laugh.

'I feel really honoured,' said Joshua, as he watched Fraser decant a generous measure of the pale straw-coloured liquid into a fresh glass.

'Nothing innit, mind,' instructed Fraser. 'It's no' allowed. You have to drink it as it comes.'

'Cheers! Thank you.' Joshua sipped his drink.

'Well,' he said, 'I'm not a connoisseur, but that is beautiful! What is it?'

Fraser showed him the bottle. Joshua recognised the malt as a common enough name. Seeing Joshua's slightly blank look, Fraser pointed to the label and said, 'Have a look at the age. It's no' your normal ten-year-old.'

Joshua saw that the liquor had been aged for thirty years.

'Wow!' he said. 'Where did you get this stuff?'

'Och, it's not for sale. Ye canna buy it. We was given it by someone from the distillery. Must have been afore Christmas. It's pure nectar!'

As they spoke, they heard the front door of the hotel open, then close.

'That'll be Tara, now,' said Rose.

True enough, the door to the bar opened and in walked Tara. Joshua's jaw dropped. Carrying a crash helmet under one arm, she was dressed in tight-fitting, two-piece, black motorcycle leathers.

'Ah!' said Rose, returning from her bar duties to sit next to Fraser. 'Here's the biker girl.'

'Hi,' said Tara. 'Everything under control?'

'Fine,' said Rose. 'We've had a quiet evening here, just the three of us. Number twelve are in their room. The couple in number eight went out earlier and aren't back yet.'

'You're taking this bike riding pretty seriously, aren't you?' said Joshua, as he continued to gape at Tara's figure-hugging attire.

'Sure am,' said Tara with a smile. 'Do you like it?'

She ostentatiously did a twirl in the middle of the bar room.

'Very nice,' said Joshua self-consciously.

'It was a birthday present from Bradley,' said Tara.

'Your birthday!' said Joshua. 'I never knew it was your birthday.'

'Oh, it was a couple of weeks ago,' said Tara.

'I'm sorry I missed it.'

'That's all right,' said Tara. 'You weren't to know. After the first week or so, I've not seen much of you.'

'No,' said Joshua. 'I've been doing some pretty long hours. Your birthday. I should have guessed from all the flowers around the place.'

'Oh, no,' said Rose. 'They were all from Mr. Walklate.'

Fraser gave Rose a nudge. It was meant as a covert gesture, but Joshua saw it out of the corner of his eye. He was sure Tara wouldn't have seen it, but the atmosphere in the small bar room seemed to change in an instant. There was a brief, slightly awkward silence. Inevitably, it was Rose who somewhat nervously stepped into the breach.

'Time to walk that dog,' she said, grabbing Fraser by the arm. 'Come on you. It's time you were off, too.'

'Aye,' said Fraser, draining his drink, and then addressing Joshua. 'Well, if I don't see you again afore you go, I wish you all the best with your business. It'll be tough to get it going, but I'm sure you'll be fine.'

Fraser shook hands with Joshua.

'Don't forget I'll be back in September,' said Joshua. 'You've got me down in the book, haven't you, Rose?'

'Oh, yes,' said Rose. 'You're down in the book alright.'

'And thanks for the "special", Fraser,' said Joshua, as the Scotsman was being bundled out of the door by Rose.

'You're honoured,' said Tara, as she looked at Joshua's drink, and helped herself to a glass of wine from behind the bar. She then took off her leather jacket and came round the bar to sit on a stool next to Joshua.

'There's not a lot of room in those leathers by the look of things,' said Joshua.

'Made to measure.'

'Spray on?'

Tara smiled knowingly and raised an eyebrow. 'So,' she said, 'you'll be off tomorrow?'

'Yeah,' said Joshua.

There was a further, slightly awkward silence. There was a lot that Joshua wanted to say, but he couldn't find the words. He wanted to know how serious Tara's relationship was with Bradley King. He wanted to know how much Tara knew of Bradley King's background. These questions, though, arose from simple curiosity. Far more than this, he wanted to know why she'd treated Theodore Walklate the way she had. He started with the easier topic.

'You and Bradley are pretty serious, then.'

'We get on fine, if that's what you mean. He's good fun to be with.'

'I'm sure he is,' said Joshua, unwilling or unable to hide some of the bitterness that he felt.

'You must know him from your time up at The Oakland. You don't like him, do you?'

Joshua shrugged. 'What I think is irrelevant,' he said petulantly, taking a mouthful of his whisky.

Tara broke the silence that followed. 'I'm sorry, Joshua.'

'What about?'

'I know it's been a bit difficult for you these last few weeks. We've not really had much chance for a chat or go for that walk we talked about. It's almost as if you've been avoiding me, but—'

'I've been working! It's taken a hell of a lot of effort to finish the job at Walklate's on my own.'

'Of course, I'm sure it has. But I just wanted you to know that I understand how you've felt about—'

'Well, whatever,' he interrupted. 'So long as you're happy. That's all that matters. I'm sure you know Bradley King better than I do.'

'What's that meant to mean?'

Joshua thought momentarily. He considered his bitterness uncharitable – as if it somehow diminished him. He drew back from saying anything further about his rival.

'Nothing,' he said. 'Simply, you must know Bradley King better than me. I'm sure he's a great bloke, and you'll be really happy with him.'

Joshua finished his whisky and got off the barstool. Tara resigned herself to the subject being closed.

'Can I get you another drink?' she asked.

'No thanks,' he said. 'I'll be going off to bed now.'

'I probably won't see you in the morning,' said Tara. 'So I'll say cheerio. I hope you get some more work soon.'

'Thanks,' he said.

He partially turned to the door, then stopped. He had to know.

'Just tell me one thing, Tara,' he said, looking straight at her. 'Why did you do that to Theodore Walklate?'

'What?'

'You know perfectly well. Stringing him along like a bloody dog, and when you'd finished with him, dropping him like a damn stone.'

'What? I did no such thing!' said Tara, eyes blazing indignantly. 'It wasn't like that at all!'

'You sent him a bloody Valentine! What was he meant to think?'

'That was nothing. It was joke, that's all.'

'Bloody hilarious.' He almost spat the words out. 'Do you know?' said Joshua, stepping closer. 'Can you honestly say you know the man? Have you any idea what you did to that guy? I worked with him. I've seen him.' Joshua was almost shouting now.

'He thought it so bloody funny that I've seen him weeping over it all, literally, a grown man, nearly bloody fifty, crying like a baby, and all because of you!'

Joshua pointed a finger accusingly at Tara. He could see Tara's eyes, angry, but filling with tears.

'That's not fair!' she blazed. 'You don't know half of it. I can't help it if the man's deluded, if he lives in some sort of fantasy world.'

'The man may have problems relating to women,' said Joshua, calmer. 'He wouldn't be the first. I just don't think that gives you the right to trample all over him.'

'I did not "trample all over him", thank you. You need to get your facts straight.'

Tara was nearly crying now but managed to contain her tears. 'And frankly, Joshua Latham, I couldn't care less what you think. My relationship with Theodore Walklate, or Bradley King for that matter, is none of your business.' Tara was shouting now. 'It doesn't concern you.'

'Fair enough,' said Joshua with a shrug.

'Like you said,' she said, her voice still raised, 'it's irrelevant what you think.'

Joshua turned to go.

'You're just jealous, that's all!' she threw at him bitterly.

Joshua hesitated. He'd not wanted to part like this. He regretted getting sucked into an argument but the way he felt at the moment, he couldn't trust himself to be civil.

'Goodnight!' he shouted over his shoulder, slamming the door on his way out.

★★★

Some weeks after Joshua had left The Crown in these rather acrimonious circumstances he felt compelled to send an email to Tara. He needed to get over all he wanted to say and felt he couldn't be sure of doing so on the phone. He compiled the email over several days on his laptop, choosing his words carefully. Eventually, satisfied, he clicked send.

Dear Tara,

I write to apologise for what I said on my last night at your hotel. I had intended to part on good terms and wish you all the best for the future. Perhaps Fraser's whisky was stronger than I thought! Anyway, I'm sorry for any upset caused.

Having worked with Theodore Walklate I can honestly say that he is a very genuine man and shrewd business operator, but, like you said, he does have a slightly detached view, particularly when it comes to women. I also know you well enough by now and know that you haven't an ounce of vindictiveness in you. I fully accept that your initial intention was meant as a joke. I'm only sorry, as I'm sure you are, that it didn't work. If I were you, I wouldn't blame yourself though. There was, I feel, an air of inevitability about the whole situation. If it hadn't been you who sent Walklate off into the deep end, then somebody else would have done. I'm sure, like all men, he'll get over it in time. And it's important too, that you and he re-establish a better understanding. As I've said before, he's an important local businessman, and could be important to your hotel as a source of business.

Rose told me of the offer of finance that Walklate had proposed. I hope this wasn't meant to be confidential. Did you ever take him up on this? Personal feelings aside, it did seem like a good deal, and there's still plenty to do at the hotel. (Sorry, that's not meant as a dig! I mean things like the ensuite bathrooms and the new boiler.)

Finally, I'm sorry if I was at all rude about Bradley King. I think, as you were trying to say during our last meeting, you know how I felt about you, (and still do, in fact!), and that I was finding your relationship with Bradley a bit hard to come to terms with. Perhaps I am jealous. If so, I'm sure that it's the same for half the population of Bramton! Anyway, no hard feelings. I wish you all the best for the future.

Finally (really!), I look forward to coming back to stay in September (if you'll have me back!). The way things are going here, it'll probably be my next pay cheque! Seriously, there are one or two bits and pieces in the pipeline, but, as I expected, starting off on one's own is tough. There's a lot of sitting around waiting for the phone to ring. It's all about advertising, marketing and networking – just like drumming up business for the hotel! Anyway, I'll see how it goes – I'm sure I won't starve!

Best wishes and regards to all of you at The Crown. Sorry again for any offence caused.

Joshua

PS: Tell Fraser to keep up with the painting and keep some of that whisky aside for me!

Tara was delighted to receive the email. Although she also took time over a considered reply, the result was rather more rambling. She emailed:

Dear Joshua,

Thank you for your email, and I'm sorry it's taken me some time to reply. I can't say how relieved I felt when I read your email. I thought during your stay in Bramton that we'd become good friends. Like you, I didn't want to part on bad terms. Of course I forgive you, and you'll be more than welcome to stay at The Crown when you come back in September!

I can't tell you how much I bitterly regret sending the Valentine card to Theodore Walklate. It's kind of you to say he'd probably have "gone off into the deep end" anyway, and I suspect you're right, but why did it have to be me that caused the problem? I know I can be impulsive at times, but I can't think what possessed me to do it. He still occasionally phones, and when I speak to him, he seems calmer. Hopefully he's getting over it all. As you say, he's potentially an influential person around the town.

We haven't taken up his offer of finance. Let's just say, I didn't feel comfortable with the idea. Bradley has some savings and, along with a modest loan from the bank, we should be able to start work soon. Bradley says we should wait until business drops off for the winter, when there'll be less disruption to the guests, but I can't wait that long! I'd at least like to get a couple of the bedrooms upgraded within the next two or three months. We'll see! They might even be ready for when you return!

Bradley is getting on well at The Oakland. Gillman, the Manager there, whom I'm sure you must remember, has retired now, and Bradley has been promoted to Manager. I know it's been on the cards for a while now, but I'm ever so proud of him now that it's actually happened.

(I've just reread the last few paragraphs. I didn't mean to go on about Bradley quite so much. I know how you feel on that subject! Sorry.)

Rose sends her love, and Fraser says he'll save some of the whisky for you. Rose also says that Bess sends her love too! (She's mad! Rose, I mean. The dog's the only sane one amongst us!) They've just gone out for a walk. The weather here is beautiful, really warm and sunny. It's a pity you've never seen Bramton in the summer. I bet you think it rains here all the time! Hopefully, it'll still be warm in September. The thought just occurred to me. I've been taking the dog for some long walks in the hills recently. Rose only takes Bess around the park or down the road, and really she needs more exercise than that. (The dog I mean this time, not Rose!) Rose would take her, but as you know, she doesn't drive, and one of us has to be at the hotel. (Fraser doesn't drive either, incidentally. What a pair! Well suited.) Anyway, Muggins here, ends up going walkies to the back of beyond! The dog seems all right in the car so long as I don't go too far or take the corners too quickly. Anyway, what I was going to suggest is do you fancy that walk we promised ourselves, next time you visit? Bring your boots with you in any case, and we can decide at the time. It would be nice to have some company besides the dog, and Bradley won't go anywhere that he can't ride to! I know you'll probably say you'll be too busy, but the offer's there if you want to.

I'm sorry to hear that your management consultancy is a bit slow to start. I'm sure that given time, you'll be fine. I think you're very good at it anyway! Just follow all the advice you gave me!

Must close now. I think I've rambled on enough. Stay in touch. Look forward to seeing you in the autumn.

Love,

Tara

PS: Because I know you are going to be too busy for a walk next time you come to Bramton, you must stay over the weekend. I'm sure we could give you a discount on the room rate. Gosh! I can't believe I just wrote that. And I'm meant to be a businesswoman?!

Chapter Twenty-three

Theodore Walklate walked purposefully through the ornamental gardens, the scene of his emotional nadir a few months before. He was on his way from Walklate's to The Crown Hotel. His route through the gardens was not strictly the most direct, but it being such a fine, sunny, summer's day, he couldn't resist the short detour. It would give him additional time to think, he reasoned, away from the hustle and bustle of the office, and the constantly ringing telephone. The company surely couldn't begrudge him the indulgence. The corporate performance continued to improve, the profits steady now, and the sales outlook remaining sound.

Theodore had, to all appearances, recovered his composure following his earlier heartbreak. However, the restoration of the shrewd, dignified, hard-nosed businessman was but a veneer. The man underneath still brooded. He was calmer and more calculated now, stoical on the subject of his love life, even when in discussion with Bill Hunter. But deep down he still refused to accept the finality of Tara's rejection of him. He harboured the hope that she would tire of Bradley King, and he would once again be able to press his case, unrivalled. Irrespective of any emotional ties, he continued to believe that Tara would see the compelling commercial sense of his loan offer. Surely she must see the attractiveness of the deal? If she accepted, he would need no better excuse to keep in touch with her. She could hardly avoid him!

Theodore Walklate had heeded Tara's advice. He'd stopped sending her flowers and had brought her no more presents. He'd called at the hotel a few times, on spec, and when Tara had been in, their conversations had been civil but perfunctory, covering mainly only the state of their respective businesses. He'd mentioned the loan once, but again Tara had declined. He had then dropped the subject, but leaving Tara in no doubt as to the open-ended nature of the offer. Theodore had phoned a few times too, but was conscious of not making himself a nuisance. Each time he had spoken to Tara, he'd asked oblique questions of her plans and intentions, particularly with respect to Bradley King. Each time he'd learned that she and Bradley were still "an item".

However, he refused to give up completely. Summoning all his usual tenacity and combining it with the fire that still burned within him, he now planned another attempt. He walked up to the front door of The Crown. He entered the reception and pressed the bell. In a short time, Tara emerged from the kitchen. Theodore's heart quickened.

'Hello,' said Tara, warily.

'Hello,' he said. 'I was just passing and thought I might call.'

'You've walked?'

'Yes. Lovely day, and everything's shipshape at work, so I thought I'd come out for a breath of fresh air.'

'Good for you,' said Tara. 'We do seem to be having a nice summer so far, don't we?'

Tara offered him a cup of tea, which, after initially showing surprise, he readily accepted. This was the first genuine hospitality Tara had really shown him since their dramatic fallout in March. Tara seemed more confident, too, in a way that he couldn't quite define.

As they drank their tea, they continued with small talk, until finally Theodore plucked up sufficient courage.

'Tara,' he said, slowly.

'Yes,' said Tara, matching his delivery.

'The offer of a loan, you know. It still stands.'

'I thought it might, but I'm—'

'Now, I know we've not always seen eye to eye over the issue, and that you think there'll be some strings attached, but there aren't, I assure you. And eventually you must see what a good deal it is.'

'No, Theodore. It's—'

'Please. Don't be so offhand about it. I know my approach to you has been all wrong, but it's all been with the best of intentions.'

'I'm sorry, Theodore, but I don't need the loan.'

'You don't need it?'

'No.'

'Why ever not? Are you not doing any of the improvements?'

'Yes, we are. It's just that I've got the funds for it from elsewhere.'

'What? Surely not at the same terms?'

Tara didn't answer immediately.

'I know you don't have to tell me, but... where are you getting the money from?'

'Theodore,' said Tara, quietly, 'I'm afraid there's no easy way to break this to you.'

Theodore stared at her expectantly.

'We'll need a small bank loan to cover all the work, it's true, but... most of the money's coming from my husband.'

'Your... husband!'

Theodore was floored. Once again, he found himself speechless at the hands of the one he loved. He fought for self-control. Under the table on which their teacups stood, he clenched his fists. He let out a huge sigh and brought his hands up to his face. Slowly, wearily, he let them drop into his lap.

'You're married? To whom?'

'To Bradley.'

'When was this?'

'Just last week. We've been thinking of it for a while now. We just went off to a place I know in the Lake District. Only a registry office, nothing spectacular. I'm sorry, it's clearly a bit of a shock to you.'

'Well, yes, you can say that again. It's all so sudden.'

Tara tried to explain that long-term engagements weren't always the way things were nowadays but ultimately, she felt that he wasn't really listening.

'Well, that's it for me then!' he said eventually.

Theodore stood up and made to leave.

'I wish you both all the best for the future,' he said, stony-faced.

Tara stood too, and for the first time, Theodore noticed the plain gold band on Tara's wedding ring finger.

'You both live here, I suppose, at the hotel?'

'Yes. He only had a rented flat in Chapel Harrington. We've had to move into one of the bigger rooms here, but…'

She could see that Theodore didn't really want to hear this extra embellishment.

'He still work up at The Oakland?' said Theodore.

'Yes,' said Tara. 'He's the Manager now.'

'Gillman's retired then?'

'Yes. Did you know him?'

'Yes,' he said. 'It's been a while since I've seen him, but yes, I know him. We have our Christmas functions up at The Oakland. Of course, I forgot, you came to the last one, didn't you?' Theodore paused as he remembered the occasion. 'And I've dined there on numerous occasions. Well, good show for your husband, then.'

'Theodore?' said Tara softly.

Theodore, suddenly feeling very old, looked up at her.

'Please believe me,' she said, 'when I say that I'm truly sorry for the upset I've caused you. I've been foolish. I never meant you any harm.'

He reached out and took her hand.

'I know,' he said. 'I know. I suppose I shouldn't be so surprised at the way it's all worked out.'

He continued to hold her hand. He looked her in the eye. He still loved her, even though he knew now that he'd lost her for good. During the course of his infatuation with Tara, his research about the man who'd now become her husband, had uncovered a few facts about Bradley King that he'd found difficult to stomach. Only this love for Tara, along with his traditional sense of chivalry, prevented him now from telling her what he'd discovered. Perhaps she already knew all about his background, he thought, and maybe it didn't bother her. He spoke with honesty.

'Tara, I'm still very fond of you. You know that. Your happiness is my happiness. I accept now that you'll never be mine, and that fact is… breaking my heart.' He swallowed hard and continued. 'But I sincerely hope that we can remain friends. And, above all, I wish both you and your husband all the very best in the future. If there's anything that I can do for you, anything, you must let me know.'

'That's very kind of you, Theodore,' she said. 'I'm sure we can remain friends.'

'And, you mark my words,' said Theodore, still retaining hold of Tara's hand, 'that husband of yours had better be good to you. He'd better look after you, or else… or else he'll be answerable to me!'

Theodore looked stern as he spoke these words, but there was a slight glint in his eye. Tara couldn't be sure whether he was being serious or jocular.

'He will,' she said, with a faint smile. 'I'll be fine.'

He released her hand and turned to go.

'Theodore?' she said.

He turned back to face her. She smiled. 'Thank you.'

He nodded, almost imperceptibly, turned and left.

★★★

In the days that followed the meeting between Theodore Walklate and the now married Tara King, each were involved in further difficult conversations, not with each other this time, but equally vexatious, all the same.

The Crown had been full the previous night, and Tara had spent the morning upstairs helping Joanna Pierce make beds. She now returned to the kitchen. Normally she would have done this via the shortest route, that of the rear stairs, but on a whim, on this occasion, she chose the front way. The rear stairs, leading directly to the kitchen, being narrow, wooden and prone to creaking, always clearly telegraphed any approach to anyone within the kitchen. By using the hotel's main stairs, which were fully carpeted, Tara's approach to the kitchen went unheard. The door separating the main reception from the kitchen was a fire door, and according to regulations, was suitably fitted with an automatic closing device. Due to the hot weather, however, and with scant regard to the regulations, Rose had that morning wedged this door slightly ajar. A similar action on the rear kitchen door thus gave a through draught to alleviate some of the worst of the heat in the kitchen.

These contrivances, Tara's use of the front stairs, and Rose wedging open the inner kitchen door, enabled Tara to approach the kitchen with a quite unplanned stealth. As she neared the kitchen, she heard the unmistakable voices of Rose and Fraser, deep in conversation. There was nothing unusual in this, but something occurred that made Tara instinctively pull up short of the partially open door. Rose's voice was uncharacteristically low and conspiratorial, and Tara clearly heard her mention her husband's name. Out of curiosity, she stood stock still, and listened.

'Well,' Rose was saying, 'that's not what I heard.'

'Aye?' said Fraser.

'No. I heard it was him that chucked her!'

'Yeah? How do you know?'

'Well, apparently, when Bradley and this girl were arguing, it was in The Red Lion, I think. Well, they were going at it hammer 'n' tongs. They were overheard. Well, it couldn't be helped. They were shouting at each other so loud, this bloke reckoned you could hear 'em outside! But it was definitely 'im that chucked 'er, no matter what Bradley King says!'

There was a definitive, almost triumphal tone to Rose's statement.

'It was Lumsden that told me, and he got it from one of the other drivers, a chap who'd given a lift to one of them that were at The Red Lion at the time, like, so I don't doubt it's true. Tells lies he does, that Bradley, I don't like him.'

'No,' said Fraser quietly. 'It's not quite the same since he's come to live here.'

Tara, indignant at this previously unseen, seemingly malicious aspect to Rose's character, prepared to enter the kitchen and explain a few "facts" to her. But she hesitated, and Rose started up again.

'And that's not all. Not only did he dump this girl, she was pregnant, too!'

Tara, silent outside the kitchen door, put her hand to her mouth.

'No!' said Fraser.

'She was. That's what they were arguing about, apparently. She wanted to settle down, get married and stuff, and have the baby, but he wasn't having it. Poor cow. Left all alone like that, got herself killed. Wouldn't be surprised if she hadn't crashed on purpose, but you don't like to say these things, eh? Guess we'll never know. And now he's come here! I only hope Tara married him with her eyes open, that's all I can say.'

'Aye,' said Fraser. 'He'll doubtless bring all his fancy big hotel ideas here as well.'

'Always going on about how he's now the Manager up there,' said Rose. 'Gets right on my nerves, that does. Treats us as though we know nothing. As I said, I only hope Tara's gone into it with her eyes open. She's too good for him, if you ask me. He's just treating her like a bloomin' meal ticket.'

Tara could stand no more of this gossip. She quietly opened the door fully and went into the kitchen. Rose, in the process of making cakes, had her flour-covered hands in a mixing bowl. Fraser, standing next to her, saw Tara in an instant, and looked suitably shocked and embarrassed. Rose, concentrating on her cake mix, was still speaking. 'Meal ticket, I tell you.'

Fraser gave her a nudge. Rose looked up and froze.

'Rose Whitworth! How dare you!' Tara's eyes were round with fury, her fists clenched. 'Bradley King did not marry me as a "meal ticket" as you put it. He has his own career, thank you very much.'

Tara moved closer to Rose, fixing her all the time with a piercing stare.

'He happens to know more about the hotel trade than you and I put together, and if he chooses to bring any of that expertise to The Crown, then we should be grateful.'

Tara struggled to control her temper. Rose looked at the floor, her face as white as her hands.

'Fraser!' shouted Tara. 'What are you doing here anyway?'

'Er, I was washing the glasses.'

'Well,' said Tara icily, 'you normally do that in the sink in the bar, and the bar's that way.'

Fraser mumbled an acknowledgement and sheepishly slunk off in the direction that Tara was pointing.

'Well,' said Tara, once the two women were alone in the kitchen. 'A fine and loyal employee you turn out to be!'

'I'm sorry, Tara,' said Rose quietly, her eyes filling with tears. 'I didn't know you were there.'

'Rose! Whether I was standing there or not, it doesn't alter the fact that you were spreading malicious gossip, and—'

'It was only to Fraser.'

'I don't care! It's still malicious. What you said is not true. Do you hear me? It's simply not true. I've heard the rumours.'

Tara hadn't heard the rumours at all. Almost all that she'd overheard Rose say was, in fact, news to Tara. But with the blind faith in her husband that stemmed from being so recently married, she was prepared to defend Bradley King against almost anything. She simply would not countenance any criticism of her husband.

'I know the man,' she said, moving closer, still furious. 'I know about the break-up with his fiancée. It wasn't at all like you said. The rumours are completely untrue. I'm sorry, but you just don't know what you're talking about.'

Rose struggled to hold back her tears. Tara drew a deep breath. She was calmer now but resolved not to soften her tone on account of Rose's obvious upset.

'Not only will Bradley bring his expertise to The Crown, he'll also be investing in the business too. He's going to put his own money into this hotel. Do you understand? His own money! And you, Rose Whitworth, should be grateful. Your continued employment here may depend on that! Just remember that. And don't let me hear you speaking like that about him again. Do you hear?'

'Yes Tara.'

'Ever!'

Tara left, slamming the kitchen door so hard that a calendar hanging on the adjacent wall fell to the floor.

★★★

Later that same day, Bradley, in the first-floor office of The Oakland, leant back in his chair with his feet up on his desk. His desk! He looked around the office with a sense of satisfaction. He was now master of the place. Answerable only to Head

Office, he basked in the sole responsibility for the site that he now enjoyed. The phone rang. He picked it up.

'Yep!'

'Bradley,' said Jane Hope. 'There's a Mr. Walklate here. Says he would like a private word with you.'

Bradley took his feet off the desk and sat forward in the chair.

'Bradley?' said Jane.

'Yes, yes,' he said. 'Tell him I'll be down in a minute.'

Bradley purposely waited a few minutes, thinking quietly, before slowly making his way to reception.

'Mr. Walklate?' said Bradley, introducing himself.

'How do you do?' said Theodore Walklate, shaking hands. 'Is there somewhere private where we could have a quiet word?'

'Well,' said Bradley, suddenly conscious that his office upstairs was unlikely to be as grand as that of the businessman who now stood before him, and that fact somehow bothered him. 'It's a nice evening. Why don't we step outside?'

Theodore agreed and the two men made their way out through the hotel's automatic doors. They stood on the broad front steps of the hotel.

Theodore cleared his throat. 'I'll come straight to the point,' he said.

Bradley remained silent, curious.

'I understand,' the older man said, 'that congratulations are in order. On two counts in fact, as I understand it.'

Still Bradley kept his counsel, merely raising an eyebrow.

'Firstly,' continued Theodore, 'I understand that you have been promoted to Manager here at the hotel.'

'That's right,' said Bradley, finally.

'I knew Jeremy Gillman, of course. I had a good working relationship with him, and this hotel. I congratulate you on your promotion, and hope that we can carry on with that good working relationship.'

'Certainly,' said Bradley, with just a slight air of wariness.

'And secondly,' said Theodore, pausing to clear his throat again, 'I understand that congratulations are in order over your...'

He hesitated. Bradley looked at Theodore silently, quietly enjoying the anticipation of what was coming up.

'… your recent marriage.'

'Thanks,' said Bradley smugly.

'I'll make no bones about it, King, the woman you married, I was… Well, I still am, very fond of her.'

'Are you now?' said Bradley knowingly.

'Yes. I'd been to see her on numerous occasions.'

'So I'd heard,' said Bradley quietly. Incorrigible as ever, he couldn't resist livening the conversation up a shade.

'Pardon?' said Theodore.

'I said I'd heard you'd been sniffing around her.'

Theodore looked at Bradley with an ill-concealed expression of distaste. 'Anyway,' he continued, 'she's made her choice, and I accept that. I wish it could have been otherwise, but there you go.'

'What?' said Bradley with a sneer. 'You mean, you reckon there was actually a chance she might have chosen you before me?'

'That was my hope, yes.'

'You're bloody delusional, you are!'

'What!' Theodore spluttered. He reddened visibly but managed to contain his growing outrage at Bradley's impertinence. Bradley noticed a small blood vessel visible in Theodore Walklate's neck, just above his collar. He could see it pulsing.

Bradley spoke. 'Listen, sunshine, if Tara had wanted an old fossil like you, she'd have gone to a bloody museum.'

'Look, King,' said Theodore, 'I didn't come here to trade insults. I just wanted you to know that Tara…' He said the name almost reverentially. 'That Tara,' he continued, 'means a lot to me.'

Bradley shook his head. Theodore was determined to finish what he'd come to say.

'Her happiness is important to me.'

Bradley laughed contemptuously.

'You may have present custody of her heart, but—'

'"Present custody of her heart?"' Bradley repeated sarcastically. 'What sort of talk's that? What fucking planet are you on, Granddad?'

Bradley noted with sadistic satisfaction that the blood vessel in Theodore's neck pulsed even harder now.

'Look, King!' Theodore was shouting now. 'I know you. I know how you treat women.'

'Oh, yeah?'

'Yes!' said Theodore, noting for the first time that he'd dented Bradley's cockiness, albeit only momentarily. 'I know about your fiancée, the one you discarded so disgracefully. I've done some investigating. She was pregnant too, wasn't she?'

'You know nothing.'

The two men were now standing almost toe-to-toe. Theodore, the taller, spoke through gritted teeth.

'All I'm saying, King, is you'd better look after Tara. Treat her properly, or else…'

'Or else what, Granddad? What are you going to do about it, eh?'

'Or else you'll be answerable to me!'

'Listen, old man, I've heard enough of this pompous shit. I've more important things to do than listen to you.'

Theodore Walklate fumed impotently. 'Don't you dare speak to me like that!'

Bradley turned to go back into the hotel, but before doing so sneered, 'Why don't you just fuck off and die.'

Chapter Twenty-four

Theodore stabbed the button of the intercom on his desk. 'Shirley. A minute, please.'

Within seconds Shirley stood in front of him. Seated behind his desk, Theodore, without looking up, said, 'Shirley, the Christmas party, I know it's only June, but is it booked yet?'

'Oh yes, Mr. Walklate. We have to book at least twelve months in advance. There's only The Oakland with a room big enough for us, and it gets snapped up ever so quickly.'

'Cancel it.'

'Pardon?'

'I said, cancel it.'

'But Mr. Walklate! It'll be too late to get in anywhere else.'

'I know,' said Theodore with a slight sigh of exasperation.

'Oh,' said Shirley. 'So we're not having a party this year…'

'No, we're not.'

'I'm sure there'll be a lot of disappointed people, especially on the—'

'Well, tough!' said Theodore abruptly, as he stood up. 'They do nothing but bloody moan about it anyway. Well, this year we're not having one. See how they like that!'

'Is this a board decision, Mr. Walklate?'

'It's my decision! Are you questioning that?'

'Oh, no, Mr. Walklate, not at all. That's fine. I'll get it cancelled straightaway.'

She turned to go, but Theodore stopped her.

'And another thing,' he said, 'we don't put anyone up at The Oakland ever again. No visitors, guests, no functions, nobody goes there on business for lunch, dinner, for anything. Understand?'

'Yes, Mr. Walklate. I take it… I take it we've fallen out with the people at The Oakland.'

'That doesn't matter. I have my reasons. Just put the word around. Nobody goes there. Put up a works notice about the Christmas party. OK?'

'Yes, Mr. Walklate.' Shirley hesitated. 'Mr. Walklate?' she said, tentatively. 'At the Christmas party… What about guests, you know, people from outside the company? It normally goes down well with them. I just wondered…'

Theodore thought a moment, calmer now.

'Oh, we'll work something out for them,' he said.

After further reflection, he looked at Shirley who still hovered nervously, and said, 'Look. I'll be fifty in December. I was thinking of having a bit of a party up at Fallowfield. Nothing too grand. I was thinking of inviting the other directors, one or two of the senior management, their partners, a few friends, and so forth. I could invite a few guests who otherwise would have gone to the Christmas do. Yes, that's what we'll do. OK?'

'Very good, Mr. Walklate.'

'I'll see you about the arrangements a bit nearer the time.'

Intuitively knowing the interview had now finished, Shirley Hays left the room.

★★★

Over the following few months Tara struggled with married life. She brooded over the gossip that she'd overheard from Rose. Following her inadvertent eavesdropping and subsequent argument with Rose, Tara felt her relationship with Rose somehow permanently damaged. Regretfully, she found herself unable to speak to Rose with quite the same intimacy as before, and she recognised that Rose appeared to be equally at odds with her. The two women were no longer confidantes, and Tara, in particular, missed this. Rose's relationship with Fraser appeared to be deepening, albeit slowly, and Tara knew that Rose now confided solely in Fraser over matters that she would previously have discussed with her. Tara concluded that her rebuke of Rose and Fraser had actually served to bond the two employees together more strongly than before. This allegiance to each other appeared to be at the expense of their respective allegiances to

Tara. The two were never actually disloyal to her, and always seemed to work conscientiously, but an atmosphere now prevailed whenever they were all in the same room together. At such times, this atmosphere could never really be described as strained, but it was never as carefree and happy as it had been before.

Tara, for her part, hadn't been able to build up a similar rapport with Bradley, as Rose had with Fraser. Whilst they hadn't argued over anything, Bradley had displayed a strong sense of independence that Tara found frustrating. She certainly didn't begrudge Bradley any freedom, far from it. But in marriage she felt that there were certain responsibilities that fell to the partners. To her, these included at least informing each other of where they were at any particular time. Tara thought it only a common courtesy that Bradley should let her know where he was going to be during the day. She didn't ask for a blow-by-blow account of every minute, but just in general terms, she wanted to know what he was doing or intended to do on a given day. Was that so much to ask? Bradley treated this type of questioning more as an inquisition, an infringement on his freedom. He would go for a motorcycle ride, for example, when he chose, and would return when he wanted. He felt having to advise when and where he was going as almost akin to asking for permission, which he resented. Similarly, he went to work at times to suit himself. Now, as the Manager of The Oakland, he enjoyed ultimate job flexibility, arriving and leaving, and taking his days off, almost entirely at his own choosing. As in Gillman's time, Bradley often chose his time off at the last minute. Typically, Tara would only discover that he'd taken the day off when she would return mid-morning from a shopping trip, to find him still in bed. Bradley dismissed any discussion on the subject. Tara, he felt, should expect him home when she saw him.

As a consequence of both Rose and Fraser's burgeoning alliance, and Bradley's continuing independence, Tara actually felt quite isolated. Her sense of isolation was made worse by Bradley's often direct methods of cultivating a rapport with the employees of The Crown. No matter that Fraser, and particularly Rose, were at best distrustful of Bradley, they were too meek and humble to make these feelings obvious. Bradley would make great efforts to be sociable, even friendly towards them, and they, not wishing to appear churlish, would reciprocate, all of them getting bowled along in a tide of apparent bonhomie. Bradley, with his enthusiasm and wit, even managed to coax the odd smile and word out of the shy Joanna Pierce. There had been a couple of occasions when Bradley had led Fraser and Rose in quite late-night drinking sessions in the bar of The Crown. On one of these, Bradley had been perfecting his somewhat drunken interpretation of a Scottish accent, much to the hilarity of the others, when Tara had gone off to bed. Somebody she felt, had to be up early to prepare breakfast.

In her developing sense of mental isolation, Tara would often find herself physically alone too. Sometimes she would find herself making beds alongside Joanna Pierce. With Joanna not being a big conversationalist, this was tantamount to solitude too. Tara would take Bess for long walks in the surrounding countryside, again on her own. All this time on her own gave rise to introspection, and this, in turn, started doubts in Tara's mind. Had she been hasty in marrying Bradley? She certainly didn't feel unhappy about the decision, but with Bradley maintaining his independent lifestyle, she found mutual trust, so important in any marriage, difficult to build.

She thought about the gossip that she'd heard Rose repeat, which had so distanced the two. Bradley had never spoken of his relationship with his former fiancée since his first real date with Tara. Tara recognised that Bradley had clearly loved the girl, and perhaps still missed her, but she felt it a subject best left for time to heal. The circumstances of Bradley's relationship with this other girl at the time of her death shouldn't matter to Tara now. Nor indeed should it matter whether the unfortunate girl was pregnant or not. Tara assured herself, it didn't matter. 'Don't let it bother you,' she would say to herself. But it did bother her. It was during one of her longer sojourns with Bess that Tara realised that it actually didn't matter either way, whether it was Sally or Bradley who had finished the relationship, if indeed the relationship had been finished at all. Likewise, it didn't matter whether or not Sally was pregnant at the time. What really mattered now, was what Bradley had actually said and not said on the subject. He had told Tara one thing, and the gossip mongers, for no apparent reason otherwise, had said another. Similarly, there appeared strong conviction in all the stories, that Sally had been pregnant, but Bradley had somehow never mentioned this to Tara. Did Bradley tell lies as Rose had so vehemently opined? Trust could never develop without a strong rebuttal to this question. But at the same time, it was a difficult subject for Tara to broach, especially as it concerned a subject upon which her husband, for ostensibly very understandable reasons, didn't want to be drawn. Tara shrugged to herself and concluded that given time, the matter would resolve itself.

To compound her sense of isolation still further, Tara also felt frustrated at the slow progress with the improvements to the hotel. It was true that they now had flat screen TVs and satellite in all of the guestrooms, but the really serious work, ensuite bathrooms and the heating project, remained on the drawing board. Bradley had said that he had almost all the money needed to proceed, but he continued to stall. Tara would have been more than happy to get a small bank loan to top up their finances and get the project underway immediately. Bradley, on the other hand, said that they should wait another few months. This, he argued, would bring them to a quieter time of year, and there would be less disruption to the business. He also claimed that the extra wait would enable the amount he'd saved to grow sufficiently to obviate the need for a loan from the bank at all. In the end it was, as he constantly pointed out, his money, and therefore the project would move forward at his pace. In her frustration, Tara had even thought again of borrowing the money from Theodore Walklate, but she quickly dismissed the idea. Bradley, she knew, didn't like Walklate for whatever reason, and she knew that such a move would be very provocative. She bottled her frustration.

She thought of Joshua. She'd sent him a card some while earlier to announce her marriage to Bradley. Joshua had then phoned to congratulate her and followed it up with a card addressed to the happy couple. On the phone he'd sounded pleased for her. She'd been touched by his magnanimity. He'd been effusive and generous in his compliments, and it rekindled within her a reciprocal feeling. During her walks with the dog, she could bring a smile to her face simply by remembering their conversations together, and particularly their dinner at the La Scala. *The poor man!* she thought. She remembered the feeling of surprise she had felt at the time, and acknowledged a twinge of regret at the strength of her rebuttal.

She'd always found Joshua easy to talk to, and generally good company to be in. It was a few weeks after her phone call from him that she'd realised that there were now probably only two beings in whom she felt able to confide her present frustrations and anxieties. Joshua was one, and Bess was the other!

Tara's anxieties came to a head on a Thursday in the middle of August. The early summer sunshine had not lasted, and the season had seen more than an average amount of rain. Not to be put off by the damp conditions on the Thursday in question, Tara had driven up to The Staging Post with Bess, straight after breakfasts had finished at The Crown. Her intention had been to park up near the pub and do a four-mile circular walk with the dog. As she'd left The Crown, Bradley had still been in bed. As was his habit of late, he often now went to The Oakland as late as nine-thirty in the morning, so Tara was not immediately concerned at his sleeping in. On returning from her walk, however, shortly after eleven o'clock that morning, she noticed as she pulled up at the back of the hotel that Bradley's motorcycle was still parked up. It was in the same place that she'd seen it earlier. She knew he wasn't due another day off as he'd taken two already earlier in the week. Bradley had been out late the previous evening, and Tara's first thought was that Bradley had overslept. She went via the back gate and yard into the kitchen where she found Rose busy unloading the dishwasher.

'My, you were quick,' said Rose.

'Where's Bradley?' said Tara, ignoring the comment.

'He's upstairs, in bed,' said Rose.

'Asleep?'

'Oh, no,' said Rose. 'He came down about an hour ago for a bacon sandwich. He took the paper and a cup of tea back to bed with him. Something up?' said Rose, but her question went unanswered.

Tara quickly stamped purposefully up the back stairs, and along the landing to the bedroom she shared with Bradley. On entering the room, she immediately saw Bradley still in bed. He was sitting up, his torso naked, the newspaper he was reading laid out on the quilt in front of him. As Tara came in, he casually looked up.

'Hello darling,' he said casually. 'Been out?'

'What are you doing here?'

Bradley smiled and couldn't resist the temptation for a spot of fun. Looking around the room with a puzzled expression, he said, 'Er, I think I'm sitting in bed, reading the paper.'

'Very funny,' said Tara with a straight face. 'I mean, why aren't you at work?'

'Ah, yes!' he said, still smiling. 'That big ugly building on the outskirts of town.'

'Bradley! Cut it out. It's not funny. Why aren't you at work? And you weren't there yesterday evening either.'

'Oh, quite the little detective, aren't we?'

'I phoned the hotel as you never seem to answer your mobile. I wanted to talk to you. The girl there said you'd gone into Manchester.'

'Yes, she would.'

'Bradley!' said Tara, her voice rising with frustration. 'It was embarrassing. She sounded so surprised that, as your wife, I hadn't a clue where you were. Why don't you just tell me these things?'

'Oh, darling,' he said, leaping out of bed. He was wearing only a pair of boxer shorts. 'There's no need to be so sensitive,' he said. As he did so, he gripped her by her shoulders and pulled her towards him. He kissed her firmly on the lips. Tara was unresponsive and struggled to back away. But Bradley's grip, his arms now encircling her, was too strong. She moaned and wriggled, and eventually pulled her mouth away.

'Bradley! Stop it!'

'Come on, darling, come back to bed.'

'No!'

'We've got time, and Rose'll answer the phone.'

'Bradley, I said no!' shouted Tara, finally breaking from his grip. 'We need to talk, Bradley,' she said, pouting.

Bradley put his hand up and stroked her cheek. Looking suitably doe-eyed, he said, 'We can talk, darling,' he said, 'anytime.'

'Right,' said Tara, walking over to the bedroom window and opening the curtains. 'How about now?'

Bradley eyed her silently, still projecting an expression of caring concern.

'Where were you last night?' asked Tara.

'I went into Manchester to meet some business colleagues,' said Bradley.

'What time did you get in?'

'It was late. You were asleep.'

'I know,' said Tara. 'I must have gone to bed at midnight, and you weren't in then. It's a bit late to be having a business meeting.'

'You should know, darling,' said Bradley benignly. 'The hotel trade never sleeps.'

'Who are these so called "colleagues". How come you've never introduced them to me?'

'They're just people I know. People in the hotel business. Contacts I've built up over the years. One day they could come in real handy.'

'Why aren't you in work today?' said Tara still quite unconvinced. 'You've had two days off this week already.'

Bradley was silent for a moment.

'Darling,' he said, 'perhaps, I should have discussed this with you before, but I shan't actually be going into The Oakland again.'

'What?'

'No,' he said. 'You see, I've resigned.'

'Resigned!' Tara shouted the word. She stared at Bradley, open-mouthed. It took her almost a full minute to regain her composure. 'Resigned,' she repeated. 'But why? Gosh! Bradley, whyever have you done that? I thought you enjoyed it there. You've only just been made the Manager, for goodness' sake!'

'Well,' he said casually, 'I've been thinking. Having made it to the manager's job, I felt like a new challenge. I reckoned that Travelite had probably taught me all they were going to, and that if I am to progress I'd do better on my own.'

'On your own? What do you mean?'

'Well,' he said, 'consider this place. Now we're married, we can run this place. As a team, we can certainly make it pay more than it does. Giving up my job at The Oakland will enable me to concentrate my efforts more on this place. Make it generate more income.'

'Like now, I suppose,' said Tara sarcastically, 'concentrating on testing the beds all morning. Just what we need right now!'

'Darling, darling, darling. I'm sorry. Like I said, I can see I ought to have talked to you earlier about this, but really, it wouldn't have made any difference. I'd really made up my mind anyway.'

'Bloody hell,' said Tara. Swearing was pretty uncharacteristic of Tara, and its effectiveness was enhanced by its rarity. Bradley took a step closer to Tara, but with a cold stare she defied him to come any closer.

'If we're supposed to be a "team" then how come you didn't discuss this at all with me first? Don't I get any say in the matter?' said Tara. 'What about your salary? We needed that to repay any loan we might get to cover the work to the hotel. Oh, Bradley, this is hopeless!'

'Don't fret, darling,' he said, once again advancing towards her. 'We've probably got just about enough to make a start now anyway, if we still want to.'

'If we still want to!' Tara repeated incredulously. 'What do you mean, "If we still want to"?' She could not believe the conversation as it twisted and turned yet again.

'Well,' said Bradley calmly, 'I've been thinking about that too. You see, it could be as well to spend a bit of money on this place. Just to get the turnover up a bit. Make it more saleable.'

'More saleable?' said Tara, now beginning to panic. 'Bradley, what are you talking about? What do you mean "saleable"? We're not going to sell it!'

'Calm down, calm down!' he said. 'Trust me. Who's the hotel expert around here? Listen. If we sold this place, we—'

'But I don't want to sell this place!'

'Hear me out, please.'

'I like it here.'

'Yeah,' said Bradley, 'but you'd like it here, rotting away until your dying day! Where's your ambition? Where's the daring, adventurous, go-get-'em girl I married?'

Bradley paused as if to let his words sink in. Tara just shook her head.

'If we sell this place,' he continued, 'along with the money I've got put by, and a smallish loan from a bank, we could trade up to a serious hotel. Something easily as big as The Oakland, and it would ours! Now doesn't that sound good?'

Tara put a hand across her forehead.

'Bradley, I can't take all this in. It's so sudden. What are you thinking about? Why sell it? We can't sell it. It's my hotel.'

'Tara, it's *our* hotel. Come on, you can't pretend you've developed some great sentimental attachment to the place, Hell! You've been here less than a year. We should be ready to move on. Get somewhere bigger, better. You'll never make serious money out of a place like this. We simply have to trade up.'

Bradley's words sent a chill through Tara. For the first time, in her short married life, her initial inklings of doubt began to crystallise. Hearing Bradley talk of The Crown as "our" hotel gave her a real feeling of losing control, and not just of possessions, but of the whole situation. She no longer felt in charge. It felt like being a pillion passenger again, only this time, the ride was rather less enjoyable.

Tara felt overwhelmed, and she turned to the dressing table to hide her rising emotions.

'Darling,' said Bradley, 'trust me. I can see that you're struggling with the concept of business at this level. But you're bright. You'll soon get the hang of it and see the sense of it all. It's for the best, I assure you. I won't let you down.'

'But where would we go? How much would it cost?' she said mechanically, still not at all convinced that she wanted to sell The Crown, still wondering how they would manage the improvements to it without Bradley's income.

'Well, that's what I've been researching, if you like, in

Manchester. I thought we could go for a place out towards the airport. There's a few out there. Forty to fifty room jobs, just ripe for development.'

'But Bradley, how on earth would we afford it?'

'We'd get a loan. That's what businesses do, you know.'

'But it would cost a fortune! Certainly a lot more than this place. The loan would have to be huge!'

'Tara, you have to think of the loan in terms of your income. What we'd get for this place would just be a deposit. The loan repayments would be covered by the income of the hotel. Big repayments sure, but big hotel and therefore big income. It'll work, I know it will.'

'Well, I'm not convinced,' said Tara, swallowing hard. 'Not at all.'

'You will be in time.'

'But your job, Bradley! You've committed us. Oh, why couldn't you have talked to me about it first?'

'I'm sorry, darling.'

'Bradley, please, promise me you'll not take any more steps like this until we've talked them over first. Please!'

'OK, I will. Promise,' he said, then after a pause, 'Give us a kiss.'

'No,' she said, turning and storming out of the room.

Tara went through the kitchen and out to the laundry. To Rose's amazement, Tara collected Bess and proceeded to take the dog on her second walk of the day. As Tara walked through the local park, the dog listened patiently whilst Tara explained her latest woes.

Chapter Twenty-five

Following Bradley's sudden resignation from The Oakland, Tara's problems continued. Bradley's "efforts" around The Crown appeared confined to the occasional stint behind the bar in the evenings, and what he called "planning for their future". This in turn seemed to consist of more evenings, and sometimes days, visiting his so-called colleagues in Manchester. Whether genuine or simply to assure Tara of some sort of progress, Bradley did occasionally show her some brochures, or send her some links to various websites. These purported to be from various trade agencies specialising in the sale of hotels. To Tara they seemed to simply describe hotels of debatable attractiveness, for sale in equally debatable locations. The only common themes she could ascertain were their size, all being considerably bigger than The Crown, and their price, which seemed to go in proportion. The prices scared Tara. Other than this, she felt a complete detachment, both from these new business prospects, and increasingly, from her own hotel.

To relieve her frustrations and sense of isolation she phoned Joshua on several occasions. Ostensibly each call was just for a chat, to bring each other up to date on their respective latest developments, but for Tara she felt an additional need. She wanted someone to talk to about her concerns in a way that she seemed incapable of doing even with her husband or lately, her hotel employees. But, easy as she felt it to talk to Joshua in person, she found conversation over the phone more difficult. Each time, after exchanging pleasantries and small talk, Tara drew up short of broaching the real nub of her concerns. Discussion of The Crown was fairly perfunctory. Tara told Joshua of Bradley's departure from The Oakland, news that was greeted with the appropriate surprise and disbelief. Tara's in-built loyalty to her husband prevented her from explaining her true feelings about Bradley's resignation. Much as she wanted to confide otherwise, she merely repeated to Joshua all of Bradley's platitudes about his commitment to developing The Crown, "in due course". Tara declined to mention that Bradley's "business plan" even stretched to selling The Crown. A further phone call to Joshua, primarily to confirm the dates of his next visit, left Tara unexpectedly happier. She inwardly resolved, when she next met Joshua face-to-face, that she would unburden herself of her worries. Thus fortified, she anticipated his September visit all the more keenly.

Joshua duly arrived in Bramton on a Friday. Having set out before dawn, he'd arrived shortly after nine-thirty in the morning. By prior arrangement he went straight to Walklate's, where he spent a very long day reviewing progress, considering reports and financial figures, sales forecasts and the like, and inspecting the systems that he'd put in place earlier in the year. After dinner in the evening with Theodore Walklate and Bill Hunter, Joshua finally turned up at The Crown at around ten-thirty in the evening. Suitably exhausted, he went to bed, having first confirmed with Tara that he'd brought his walking boots and other outdoor clothing with him, and that, providing she didn't intend to set off too early, he'd be delighted to go on a walk with her.

On the Saturday morning after breakfasts had been served, Tara found herself alone in the bedroom she shared with Bradley. As had become almost a habit over recent months, she stood gazing out of the window, reflecting on her present circumstances. She ruminated on the state of The Crown and its still undeveloped potential. She thought of Bradley's grand designs, also equally unfulfilled. More fundamentally, she thought of her marriage. Short though it had been so far, she had been shocked at the speed at which it had apparently soured. She despaired at how quickly their carefree, loving exchanges had turned to a frosty impasse.

Tara turned from the window and looked at the dresser in the room. On top of it was a small jewellery box. Impulsively she picked it up. She knew it well as the one containing some cufflinks that she'd bought Bradley as a wedding present. She opened the box to view the gold, engraved items within. They were there, but her attention was immediately drawn to an additional piece of jewellery in the box. It was a ring. It was gold and contained a single small stone of a type Tara couldn't be certain of. It looked like an engagement ring, and she immediately knew to whom it had once belonged.

Tara held the ring and thought, not so much of its physical worth, which she suspected was not considerable, but of its sentimental value. She thought of Sally Jones. She immediately pitied the girl her untimely death. She then wondered what she'd been like as a person. Bradley, she quite understood, had never wanted to talk much about Sally, and Tara had only the vaguest ideas of her husband's former fiancée. From the sketchiest details that were all she knew, Tara tried to imagine the girl, what she'd looked like, what her personality had been like. Had Sally been pregnant when she'd died, Tara wondered? Whatever the truth, and Tara had some while ago resigned herself to never knowing for sure, she felt an almost overwhelming sympathy for the girl. Had she gone through what Tara was now experiencing? Had she also seen a joyous, happy relationship with Bradley turn sour? So deep was Tara's reverie that she failed to hear the footsteps approach the door to the room. It was only when the door opened that she looked up. She saw Bradley standing on the threshold.

'Hello,' she said distractedly, trying to hide her surprise. 'I thought you'd gone out.'

'What are you doing?' said Bradley looking at the ring in Tara's hand.

'Oh, sorry,' said Tara. 'I was just look—'

As Tara made to put the ring back, Bradley stepped forward and snatched it from her.

'Give that here!' he barked. 'It's not yours!'

'I was just looking at it.'

'I don't care. It's nothing to do with you.'

'Oh, Bradley please, I know how you must feel about—'

'You!' he shouted. 'You! You know fuck all about how I feel!'

Tara looked at Bradley's round, staring eyes, and instinctively stepped back from him. She had never seen him so angry, and certainly never been the subject of such anger herself. She felt genuinely scared. After half a minute of stunned silence, she tentatively spoke.

'Bradley, I'm sorry. What I meant was I appreciate how much you felt about her.'

Bradley put the ring back in the cufflink box. He snapped the lid shut and put the box in the top drawer of the dresser. He slammed this shut, all the time maintaining a stony silence.

'Bradley,' Tara ventured again, 'You don't have to bottle it up. You can talk to me about it, if you want. I don't mind. If it'll help. I understand that you must have loved her.'

'So I loved her,' he shouted. 'So what? She's dead now. Gone! What can you do about that?'

'Well,' said Tara hesitatingly.

'Exactly!' said Bradley with a tone of sneering satisfaction. 'You can do fuck all about it.'

'Bradley, please don't talk like that.'

'Like what? Saying I loved her?'

'No, I meant, there's no need to swear at me. I'm only trying to—'

'So I loved her?' he shouted, ignoring Tara's plea. 'And I suppose you're wondering whether I loved her more than I love you, eh? Is that it?'

'No.'

'Well let me tell you, Mrs. King, Sally Jones wouldn't have stood in the way of my plans like you do!'

'What?' said Tara, shocked.

'She would have known a good thing when she saw it. Oh, she may not have had your money and your la-de-da bloody education, but she had spirit. She had guts.'

Bradley advanced towards Tara. Tara felt the wall behind her and could back off no further. Bradley came within inches of her. She could smell his breath, faintly stale, on her cheek. He grabbed a fistful of her blouse and bodily hauled her towards him. She screamed. With his face almost touching hers, he snarled, 'She may have been more humble than you, but she was a better woman. Do you hear that? A better woman! I said, do you hear that?'

Bradley shook Tara, who said in weak voice, 'Yes.'

'Don't ever forget it,' said Bradley. 'Bitch!'

With that he released his grip on Tara's blouse and pushed her back to the wall. Tara stood there, transfixed. She watched Bradley pick up his bike leathers and crash helmet from a heap of clothes on the bedroom floor. He took it all and stormed out of the room. As Tara's fear gradually subsided, her legs felt weak. She staggered forwards and supported herself on the edge of the dresser. She now found her fear only replaced by an almost overwhelming sense of utter bewilderment and self-pity. She blinked back silent tears, still refusing to cry.

★★★

Later that day, Tara and Joshua sat together by the banks of a stream. The spot, known locally as Three Counties Head, was where the political boundaries of three counties joined, and perhaps more importantly, two streams converged. The two youthful streams, each tumbling down waterfalls before they ran into one another, cut deep channels in the bedrock. The confluence, just downstream of an ancient packhorse bridge over one of the streams, provided an area of unique beauty. It was a natural amphitheatre, sheltered on three sides from the wind, and for most of the day, providing a trap for whatever sunshine fell upon it.

In weak autumnal sunshine, Bess frolicked in the shallow waters of the stream, and Tara and Joshua unpacked their picnic and flask of coffee.

'What's the matter, Tara?' asked Joshua after they'd silently munched their way through lunch.

'Sorry?'

'I said, what's the matter? You've hardly said a word all morning.'

'I'm sorry,' she said.

'Are you not well?'

'Oh, no, I'm fine really, I suppose,' she said making the effort of conversation. 'How long did you say you were stopping until?'

'I'll have to see how it goes. Tuesday probably. Wednesday maybe.'

'Have you got any other work lined up?'

'No,' said Joshua slowly. 'I've done one or two other bits and pieces, but frankly it's pretty dire. I've been applying for other jobs too, employed work, rather than just concentrating on consultancy stuff.'

'What sort of work?'

'Oh, management, production stuff, manufacturing operations mainly.'

'And no luck so far, then?'

'Nah. One interview. Didn't get it. That's all so far.'

Tara smiled encouragingly at him.

'You'll be all right, I'm sure,' she said.

'We'll see.'

Joshua looked thoughtful as he watched Bess scamper off downstream.

'Has Bradley gone out this morning?' he said.

'Yes,' she said, quietly sipping her coffee.

'Where's he gone?'

'I don't know,' she said, in a matter of fact way.

'You know,' he said, 'I couldn't believe it when you rang to tell me he'd resigned from The Oakland.'

Tara remained silent. She picked up a pebble and tossed it into the stream.

'Beautiful here, isn't it?' he said. 'I never knew this place existed.'

'Yes, it is nice, isn't it? I often come here. You're often not alone for long, though. It's quite a popular spot. But I like it. There's some peace and quiet, and I can just sit and think.'

'Why did he leave The Oakland so suddenly?'

'Well, like I said really, he's got these "big plans" apparently. Thinks he can get on better if he's on his own.'

'So what's the real reason?' said Joshua.

Tara and Joshua looked at each other for a moment, then Tara looked again at the stream.

'You don't have to tell me, if you don't want to,' he said, 'but I can tell you don't believe that's the reason he left any more than I do.'

Tara remained silent for another few minutes, wrestling with her conscience. Having earlier resolved to confide in Joshua, at least giving him some broad outline of her present worries, she now found the moment more difficult than she'd anticipated. In spite of Bradley's assault on her only that morning, she felt talking about her marital difficulties with a third party implied a certain disloyalty to her husband.

'So what does he want to do? What's the grand design? By the looks of The Crown still, more ensuite facilities don't feature high in his priorities.'

'No,' said Tara quietly. 'Actually, he wants to sell up.'

'What!'

'Yes. He wants to sell up and buy a bigger hotel, somewhere near the airport.'

'And you don't?'

'No. I'm happy doing what we're doing. It'll never make me a millionaire, but that's not what drives me. It does him, it seems.'

'How much bigger a place is he talking about?'

'Oh, three times the size. And three times the price.'

'Can you afford it?'

'He says so, but I'm not so sure. I don't think he's got as much money as he led me to believe. I really don't know. He keeps his finances very much to himself. Either way, it would mean a huge loan. More importantly, I don't really want to move. I like it in Bramton. I know I've not been here long, but it feels like my place. And now he wants to sell it, irrespective of what I think.'

'It's still not a reason for leaving The Oakland,' said Joshua. 'I mean, if he'd got these plans, surely he'd wait until it was a done deal before severing his links with Travelite? No, I'm sorry, there's something else.'

Tara put her hand up to her eyes as if to shade them from the sun. Behind her hand, unseen by Joshua, she silently blinked away her tears.

'You're not happy, are you?' said Joshua quietly.

Tara merely shook her head, all the time keeping her hand over her eyes. Joshua moved to sit closer to her. He put his arm around her shoulder and gently pulled her towards him. He put his other arm around her and slowly, almost imperceptibly, rocked her back and forth. As he did so, Tara let out a plaintive sob, and at last, her tears flowed unabated.

After perhaps five minutes, Tara stopped crying and regained some composure. Joshua slowly released her from his arms.

Wiping her eyes with her hands, she looked up at Joshua, and blinked. 'I'm sorry.'

'It's OK,' he said tenderly.

'The problem is,' she said, 'we just don't talk. It's like we're strangers. He never tells me where he's going, when he'll be back, what he's doing, nothing. It's so frustrating. It's as though he's just completely independent of me, as though we weren't married at all.'

Now she'd started, she felt able to carry on.

'I suppose I don't trust him, if I'm honest. If you're in a relationship where you don't talk, it's difficult to develop trust. I know he still hurts over Sally. That was his fiancée, you know, the one—'

'I know.'

'I'm sure it would help if he could just talk about the way he feels about her, about anything, but he doesn't. He did once, when we first went out together, but not since. Whenever I approach the subject, he just rants and raves. I get quite scared at times.'

'He doesn't… hurt you, does he?'

'No, not as such,' she said, 'but, well, let's just say he sometimes gets quite threatening. Oh, Joshua, promise you won't say a word of this to anyone.'

'Christ, Tara! What do you take me for?' he said with a gentle firmness, putting his hand on hers. 'Of course I won't say anything. I'm just happy to listen, if you find it helps.'

'Yes, I'm sorry. It does help. I'm sorry. I know I can trust you. It's been such a strain lately. I've had no one to talk to really. Only the dog.'

She gave a little laugh at that, then wiping her face again with her hands, carried on.

'I just think sometimes, what did his fiancée go through?'

'How much do you know about her?'

'Not much. Like I said, Bradley only talked about her the once. But it's as though she's with us all the time. It's… It's just that you hear so many stories. I try not to listen, but sometimes I just can't help it. Rose once said something too, and I'm afraid

I rather shouted at her. We've never been the same since. We used to be such good friends really, Rose and me. We'd talk about anything. But not anymore. That's why I've never had anyone to talk to about… about all this. Not until now.'

She looked up, and through still watery eyes, smiled weakly at Joshua.

'Rose and Fraser are still going strong, I take it?' he said.

'Oh yes,' confirmed Tara. 'They're pretty steady, I guess, in more ways than one. They're hardly a dynamic couple. They seem quite happy to sit and hold hands all evening, for hours on end. Rose just talks and talks and Fraser just listens. It's quite funny really. At the rate they're going they'll probably get married in another ten years.'

Again, Tara gave a short, slightly ironic laugh at her little joke.

'Nothing impulsive about our Rose,' she continued. 'No rushing off to marry the wrong man for her.'

'Is that what you think? You've married the wrong man, I mean.'

'Oh, God, Joshua, I don't know.' Another tear ran down her cheek. 'I guess you always think you haven't, and that everything will be fine. You turn a blind eye to all the evidence, but it slowly mounts up. Eventually, you have to face the facts. Perhaps I have made a mistake. God, it's not taken that long to go wrong either, has it? Maybe I should never have married him. Why did I marry him?'

At this last utterance, she threw her head back and looked up at the blue sky.

'But I have married him now, so what difference does it make? There's no point in crying over it.'

Tara once more broke down, sobbing, and Joshua comforted her. She buried her head in his shoulder, and he gently stroked her hair. Bess came running up to them and crouched on the ground facing them, looking both puzzled and expectant.

'Oh Tara,' whispered Joshua, as he held her tightly, 'I wish I knew what to say. It breaks my heart to see you like this, so upset. It's so… different. I've only ever seen you strong before, always in control. And I'm sure you will be again. You're made of stern stuff. Something'll work out.'

He knew even as he said the words, that they were meaningless. No matter how much sympathy he could dispense, he was actually devoid of practical suggestions. He saw no merit in further discussion of Bradley King, his sudden departure from The Oakland, Bradley's former fiancée and all the speculation and rumours, The Crown Hotel, and Bradley's plans for the future. Joshua simply took what satisfaction he could in holding in his arms, for the first time ever, the woman he loved. Even so, under the current circumstances, he couldn't deny the utter helplessness and frustration that he also felt. What else could he do?

'Well,' said Tara between sobs, 'I must admit before now, I've always felt as though I could handle anything, be really strong. But not now. And now I've shown how weak I can be, it's almost worse than if I'd never been strong in the first place.'

'Don't be silly,' he said. He brushed his thumb over her cheek, wiping her tears away. 'You are strong.'

As he gently held her, she put her arms around him. With their faces within inches of each other, they looked, impassioned, into each other's eyes. In that moment, without a further word passing between them, they suddenly knew what each meant to the other.

With a start they heard footfalls approaching. They released each other and the moment was gone.

'Afternoon!'

The voice was that of a short, portly red-faced elderly man crossing a nearby stile.

'Afternoon,' said Joshua politely.

The man stopped and helped his equally dimensioned, equally elderly, woman companion to climb over the stile.

'Grand spot for yer snap!' said the man.

'Yes,' said Joshua, resigned. 'Super.'

The elderly couple then sat on a patch of grass not five yards from Joshua and Tara and proceeded to unpack and eat their picnic.

Tara looked at her watch.

'Come on,' she said. 'We'd better go. I promised Rose I wouldn't be too long.'

They stood. They spied Bess some fifty yards downstream, and at Tara's call, the dog came bounding back to them.

★★★

That night, in spite of a further sample of Fraser's "special" whisky, Joshua found it difficult to sleep. With the hotel full, he'd been put in a small bedroom over the kitchen, overlooking the back of the hotel. The room was warm, very probably because of its position over the kitchen. He lay awake, restless, constantly turning over in his mind the events of the day. With the project at Walklate's seemingly going so well, he felt a curious detachment from his work. Instead, his mind was preoccupied with Tara and her problems. He and Tara had arrived back at the hotel from their walk to discover that Bradley had returned to the hotel, and then, after changing, packing a bag, and having something to eat, had gone straight back out again. Typically, he hadn't said where he was going or when he'd be back. When everybody else had retired to bed, sometime after eleven-thirty, Bradley had still not returned.

After a fitful hour in bed, Joshua got up and lifted the sash window in his room by a few inches. The cool night air immediately refreshed the room. Joshua returned to his bed, and soon began to slumber. As sleep slowly suppressed his thoughts, he was vaguely aware of a slightly curious, slightly acrid smell drifting in from outside. Additionally, his semiconscious brain registered, somewhere to the rear of the hotel, the muffled barking of a dog.

Chapter Twenty-six

Fire! Joshua immediately sat up in bed. He was fully awake in a second. The smell was smoke, he was sure. He leapt out of bed and ran to the window. Opening it fully, he looked out. The laundry outbuilding was below his bedroom window. He could see black smoke pouring from an extractor vent. He heard Bess barking frantically within.

He hastily put his walking boots on his bare feet. He'd no time to lace them. Quickly putting on his coat and grabbing his mobile phone, he dashed out of the room. On the landing there was a fire extinguisher. He grabbed it and sped through a fire door and down the main stairs. A table lamp on the reception desk illuminated the hall. It was dim but still sufficient for him to see a break glass fire alarm point. He swung the heavy extinguisher. The base of the unit smashed against the alarm point. The break glass unit shattered and came clean off the wall. An insistent, penetrating ringing noise then flooded the hotel.

The connecting door from the hall to the kitchen appeared locked. The fire extinguisher was once more put to effective use, or more correctly, abuse: he hit the door with it. There was a sharp splintering sound. A small bolt flew across the floor. The door swung open, and Joshua charged through. The kitchen was largely in darkness. The only light was that coming through the windows from some outside lights. In the gloom Joshua found the back door. As he expected, it was locked. He fumbled around the handle. The key was in the lock. He turned it and yanked the door open.

Once in the back yard, he tried the door of the laundry room. It opened. Bess let out a yelp and shot out past Joshua's legs. As the door swung open, a cloud of dense black fumes billowed from the laundry room. Temporarily blinded, Joshua crouched near the floor. He pulled the pin on the extinguisher, and aiming it just inside the door, he squeezed the trigger. White powder whooshed into the laundry room for perhaps twenty seconds. The extinguisher ran out. Smoke continued unabated. Throwing the extinguisher to the floor, Joshua made his way to the back gate. With Bess at his heels, he slid back the bolts on the gate, opened it, and stumbled out into the car park.

The car park was deserted. The fire alarm could still be heard. 'Come on,' said Joshua under his breath, 'shift your bloody selves!' He took his mobile phone from his coat pocket and dialled 999. As he barked his details into the phone, the first few, ill-clad hotel guests started to spill out of the front of the hotel. As they slowly moved around the side of the hotel to the car park, Joshua recognised Tara.

'Tara!' he shouted.

Complete with dressing gown and slippers, she ran towards him. 'Joshua! Oh my God! What's happening?'

Tara looked pale, her eyes wide with fear.

'It's the laundry room! It's on fire!'

'Oh no! Bess is in there!'

'She's not. I got her out. Listen! Go back to reception and get the visitors' book.'

'What?' she said, looking puzzled. 'Has anybody called the fire brigade?'

'Yes. Now get the visitors' book!'

'The visitors' book?'

'Yes, the book the guests sign when they arrive.'

At that moment Rose ran up to them. With Tara still transfixed to the spot, staring at the billowing smoke, Joshua shouted at Rose.

'Rose! Listen to me! Go back to reception and bring me the visitors' book.'

'Oh!' said Rose.

'Now!' yelled Joshua.

Without a further word, Rose spun around and went back to reception.

'Fraser!' yelled Joshua, suddenly seeing the Scotsman standing nearby in the shadows. He wore a dressing gown over a set of paisley pyjamas.

'The fire's in the laundry room. Go back in the front of the hotel and bring me out as many fire extinguishers as you can carry.'

'Aye,' said Fraser, dashing off.

'Fraser!' exclaimed Tara. 'What on earth are you doing here?'

The question made Fraser stop.

'Fraser!' shouted Joshua. 'Now, man! Now!'

The Scotsman once again turned and ran back to the front of the hotel. Joshua looked at Tara's face. She looked utterly bewildered. Rose then came running back with the visitors' book.

'Well done,' said Joshua. 'Now take the book and go and get the guests together. Check them off in the book. OK? I need to know that they're all accounted for. Understand?'

'Yes,' said Rose.

'And Rose?'

'Yes.'

'When you've done that, report back to me. Clear?'

'Yes, Joshua.'

Rose set about her task.

'Right, Tara,' said Joshua with unabated urgency, 'your job. Go to the front of the hotel and as soon you see the blue lights of a fire engine coming, you get the driver's attention. OK?'

'OK,' said Tara mechanically. 'Like what do I do?'

'Anything. Wave your arms around, jump up and down, anything. Just make sure they see you. Then point him in this direction.'

Joshua indicated the car park at the rear of the hotel. Tara now understood and quickly ran to the front of the hotel. Within seconds, Fraser staggered up, carrying two fire extinguishers.

'Good man!' said Joshua. 'Follow me.'

The two men went back to the laundry room with the extinguishers. Black smoke, thicker than ever, continued to pour from the door, and the occasional flame could be seen within. Almost lying flat, the two men let off the extinguishers one after the other into the dark interior of the outbuilding. They seemed to make little difference to the volume of smoke. As the last was exhausted, Joshua slammed the door shut. He then heard a short blast of a siren, and seconds later a fire engine pulled into the car park.

As soon as it stopped, a well-organised crew disgorged from the vehicle, and with calm assurance, immediately started to deploy their equipment. Tara and Rose ran up and stood beside Joshua to watch. Impulsively, Tara grabbed Joshua's arm.

'Everybody out?' asked Joshua.

'Yes,' said Rose. 'There's just Bradley I'm not sure of.'

Tara looked disconsolate. 'He's not come back yet,' she said.

'But it's bloody one o'clock!' said Joshua.

As they spoke, the first fire hose snaked into life. With a powerful surge, a huge jet of water smashed clean through the side window of the laundry room.

The fire officer in charge sidled up to Joshua and said, 'You the boss here, mate?'

'Not exactly,' said Joshua, 'but I called you out.'

'Everybody out?' he said.

'Yes,' said Joshua.

'Good, oh,' said the fire officer in a somewhat relaxed manner. 'Any electrics on in there?'

'Yes,' said Joshua, and turning to Tara said, 'What's in there exactly?'

'A washing machine, a tumble drier and two freezers.'

'Does the power come from the main building?' asked the fire officer.

'Aye,' said Fraser joining the group. 'There's a consumer unit in the hall. That outbuilding's on the same circuit as the kitchen, mind.'

'Cut the power,' said the fire officer. 'Turn it all off if you have to. And if you know how to cut the alarm, do that too, will you?'

With a brief acknowledgement, Fraser again went back to the main building to set about his new tasks.

Before a second hose could be brought to bear on the flames, the fire was extinguished. Two fire fighters entered the now smouldering building, and after a cursory inspection of the blackened interior of the laundry room, the fire officer in charge had a chat with his crew and walked back over to Tara, Joshua and Rose.

'OK, folks,' he said breezily, 'that seems sorted now. Not too much damage. It was just the washing machine that had caught fire. It didn't catch anything else. Never got that hot. The rest is just a touch of smoke damage. Lick of paint and a new window, and it'll be as a good as new. You'll need to dry things off, but if you can safely get power onto them freezers again sharpish, you'll probably save the contents too.'

'What made it catch fire?' asked Tara.

'Can't be absolutely certain, but it was probably the wiring. One of the biggest causes of domestic fires, you know, washing machines. Funny, isn't it? The building looks sound. No smoke alarms out there like there are in the main building, I suppose? You were lucky. You caught it early. Could have been nasty otherwise.'

The fire chief wished them all goodnight, turned on his heels and bellowed to one of his crew, 'Right. Tell John to give the stop message, and then let's be having you.'

The fire crew quickly put their hoses and other equipment away, and the desultory band of hotel guests were told that it was safe to return indoors. Fraser once again returned, and Joshua said, 'Have you got a cable reel, or any spare electric cable lying about?'

'Aye, we've a cable reel with my tools.'

'Go and fetch it then, and your tools, and then show me this consumer unit.'

'Can I do anything?' asked Tara, still looking pale and clearly overawed.

Joshua gave her a kindly smile, and gently held her arm.

'For now,' he said, 'I'd settle for a nice cup of tea. You'll have to take the kettle into the bar, mind.'

Half an hour later, with the hotel guests back in their rooms, Tara, Rose, Fraser and Joshua were in the bar enjoying a cup of tea. All of them were still in their incongruous mix of nightwear and overcoats. Joshua, with Fraser's help, had managed to put on a temporary electricity supply to the freezers in the outbuilding, and was explaining how, in spite of there being no electricity in the kitchen, a makeshift breakfast service could be offered to the guests for later.

'What damage is there outside?' asked Tara, sitting at a table with her chin resting on her hands. She'd been too fearful yet, to look for herself.

'Well,' said Joshua, 'the washing machine's had it, but the tumble drier and the freezers look fine. The whole place wants mopping out. And obviously you need a new bit of glass in the window. All in all, I think you got off lightly.'

'Joshua,' said Tara, 'how can I ever thank you? You were fantastic. Thank you. I'm afraid I just panicked. I couldn't think straight at all. I just froze.'

'Oh, yes,' chimed in Rose, 'and you saved poor Bess's life.'

Rose bent down and stroked the dog.

'I think,' said Joshua, 'it's Bess that deserves the credit. Without her barking, I'd have probably gone right off to sleep. Is she OK?'

'Yes, Joshua, she looks fine,' said Rose.

'And Fraser, you were terrific too,' said Joshua.

All eyes then fixed on the Scotsman, who suddenly stared at the floor, seemingly more self-conscious than ever. Rose then started to look suitably guilty, too. There was a short, awkward silence before Joshua said, in a mock, high-pitched, polite voice, clearly in imitation of Tara, 'Fraser! What on earth are you doing here!'

Tara kept tight-lipped, but her eyes, looking up at Joshua, belied her struggle to keep a straight face. Joshua looked sideways across at Tara. She smirked, then broke out into a laugh.

'Well,' she said, smiling. Rose and Fraser then joined everybody else in laughing.

'That,' said Joshua in his normal voice, 'had to be the daftest question of the lot! I'll give you, "What's he doing here?" It was pretty damn obvious to me.'

'Oh, Tara,' said Rose, 'I'm ever so sorry. I didn't mean to embarrass you. He's not stopped overnight before, have you Fraser? Well, perhaps just once before. I am sorry. We won't do it again.'

'Rose!' said Tara. 'It doesn't matter. This is the twenty-first century. I'm not a prude, for goodness' sake. I'm just a bit, well, shocked, I suppose.'

Joshua piped up, addressing Rose and Fraser, 'The lady of the house here, she had you pair down as not reaching this stage for ten years!'

There was more laughter from the group, slightly embarrassed giggling to start, followed by less inhibited hilarity. Tara then said, 'I can't believe this! It's two o'clock in the morning, and we're having a party. If we don't hurry up and go to bed, it won't be worth it.'

'Funnily enough,' said Joshua, 'I don't actually feel that tired anymore.'

The group agreed, then fell silent for a minute before Tara sighed and said, 'Well, I suppose it's not every day you nearly lose your home, your livelihood, and your husband walks out on you.'

There was a stunned silence as the three others looked at Tara.

'Tara!' said Rose. 'Whatever do you mean?'

'Bradley's gone,' she said, 'and I don't think he's coming back.'

'How do you know?' said Joshua.

'Well,' she said, glancing up at the group and then back at the floor. 'Rose, you said he came back later this morning, I mean yesterday morning now, whilst Joshua and I were out. And he packed a bag before leaving again. I checked some of his stuff. He's taken his wallet with all his cards in, mobile, some clothes and toiletries, and… some jewellery.'

'Jewellery?' said Joshua. 'What sort of jewellery? Your jewellery?'

'Oh, no. Just… just a ring. But it was one I know he rather treasured.'

'Oh, don't be so silly,' said Rose. 'He'll be back.'

'He won't,' said Tara very definitively. 'I know it. He's gone.'

She put her hand up to cover her face and stifled a cry. Rose rushed across the room and kneeling, put her arms around Tara.

'Don't cry, Tara, don't cry,' Rose implored, as she too started to cry.

'Oh, Rose,' said Tara between sobs, 'I'm ever so sorry. But I'm glad he's gone!'

'Don't say that!'

'But it's true. It's what I feel. You were right all along. I feel so used by him! I'm sorry I ever shouted at you.'

'Oh, that's alright.'

'No, I am. I really mean it, Rose. Please say you forgive me!'

'I forgive you, Tara, of course I do! We're good friends, aren't we?'

'Oh, yes… Rose, oh, I've missed being able to talk to you.'

'And I've missed talking to you, Tara.'

Both women, continuing to embrace each other, dissolved into further tears. Joshua and Fraser, somewhat embarrassed, looked at each other slightly awkwardly. Joshua twiddled his empty teacup and placed it on the bar. Fraser looked from the two women to Joshua.

'Time for a "special"?'

'Why not?'

★★★

The next few days saw electricity safely restored to the kitchen and the now dried outbuilding. All the repair work was carried out and a new washing machine purchased. Joshua also made a point of fitting a smoke detector in the laundry room.

As Tara had predicted, Bradley didn't return. With this and Tara and Rose's demonstrable reconciliation, there was an instant improvement in the working atmosphere at the hotel. Everybody was keenly aware of how sensitive a subject Tara's husband represented, and little conversation passed on the issue. But with everybody sharing a common view of the matter, sympathy and understanding, much of it unspoken, replaced the earlier discord. Out of largely humanitarian concern, Tara reported Bradley's disappearance to the police late on the Sunday evening. Whilst she still felt an almost overwhelming sense of relief at Bradley's departure, she felt that she wouldn't be able to forgive herself if he and his motorcycle were lying in some ditch somewhere across the moors. The police officer she telephoned took the details, and promised they would keep a record. He seemed quite disinterested and suggested that Tara check with the local hospitals if she had any concerns over the man's safety. He made it quite apparent, though, that it was still a free country. He patiently explained that fit and healthy adults were free to leave home, walk out on their spouses or whatever, as they pleased, and that a simple defection was not, as such, a police matter.

In this state the matter rested. Joshua spent the Monday and Tuesday at Walklate's, making further review of the company performance. Confirming his findings from the previous Friday, he was gratified to find that things were going well. Systems that he'd put in place were being maintained, and improvements in performance duly noted. Andrew Forsythe received further training from Joshua on time management, and seemed genuinely pleased with his new, diminished role. Scott Sanders was blazing a trail across Europe on a sales drive. His enthusiasm and his profound product knowledge more than made up for any limited sales experience, and new orders had started to flow. Joshua left Walklate and Co. late on the Tuesday afternoon amidst promises that he would stay in touch with Walklate's, and they would stay in touch with him. He had intended to drive back home on the Tuesday afternoon, but since it was late, and he'd got little specific to rush home for, he decided to stay one more night. The Crown was not full, and Tara, partly in recognition of Joshua's heroics on the Saturday night, and part in tacit acknowledgement of their enduring friendship, waived any charges.

On the Wednesday morning, just as Joshua was about to carry his bags out to his car, he saw a vehicle pull into the hotel car park. Having loaded his luggage, Joshua returned to the hotel with the intention of saying goodbye to Tara. As he re-entered the building, he saw Tara shaking hands with a stocky, fair-haired man with a moustache. Tara appeared concerned. She looked at Joshua and said, 'Joshua, may I introduce you to DC Knowles. Mr. Knowles, this is Joshua Latham. He's a very good friend of mine. Anything you have to say, I'd appreciate it if he could hear it too.'

'Sure,' said the police officer warily, looking at Joshua. 'Whatever. Is there somewhere we can talk?'

Tara showed them into the front lounge, where they pulled up three chairs.

'Mrs. King,' said Knowles, 'have you any idea where your husband is at the moment?'

'No. He left on Saturday, before lunchtime. I've not seen him since.'

'And he didn't say where he was going?'

'No. What's this all about? Have you found him?'

'He's not phoned up at all?' asked Knowles, pointedly ignoring Tara's question and rising anxiety.

'No!' said Tara. 'He took his mobile with him, but it seems to be turned off. Please! Have you found him?'

'No, Mrs. King. Not yet. Do you have any idea,' continued the detective, looking across at Joshua, 'why your husband would suddenly up sticks, and run off?'

'Not really,' said Tara. 'And it's no use your looking at Joshua like that.' She looked disdainfully at Knowles and spoke rather haughtily. 'My husband and I may not have been getting on well lately, but it was not because of anything that I'd been doing.'

'No, no, no,' said Knowles, suddenly adopting a more conciliatory approach. 'I didn't mean to imply anything shall we say, untoward, on your part. So, your husband was not too happy just lately. Any reason for that? Anything suddenly change in his life? Any problems he may have been facing that perhaps he shared with you?'

'Well,' said Tara with a deep sigh, 'he resigned from his job quite recently. A few weeks ago, in fact. It was quite sudden, but it was his decision.'

'He worked up at The Oakland, didn't he? Assistant Manager or something.'

'Yes. He was the Manager.'

'And why did he pack it in, Mrs. King?'

'I... I don't know for sure. We didn't talk that much. He just said he felt he wasn't going much further with Travelite. That's the hotel group that owns The Oakland. He wanted to branch out on his own.'

'And you believed him?'

'Look, Mr. Knowles,' said Joshua, 'where's this all leading? You've said you've not found him, and your officer on Sunday night said that missing people like this wasn't a police matter. Yet here you are, asking all these questions.'

'Yes, well Mr… er, Latham, normally missing persons aren't automatically police matters, but this case might not be quite so straightforward. Mrs. King, did you suspect your husband had any other reason for leaving his job so suddenly?'

Tara swallowed hard. 'Not really. But he resigned. He wasn't sacked or anything like that.'

'So, no suspicions?'

'One sometimes gets suspicious, I suppose.'

'Suspicious of what? Was he having an affair with anyone, for instance?'

'No!'

'Sure?'

'Well…'

'It's OK, Mrs. King. I'll level with you. When you reported your husband missing at the weekend, we weren't initially too bothered. However, when we started going through our records, we discovered that we actually wanted to interview Mr. King.'

'What about?' asked Tara with alarm.

'The investigation's actually being carried out in Manchester. One of my colleagues there alerted me to their interest in your husband.'

'But what's it all about?' asked Tara.

'Well, investigations are still in their early stages at the moment. Let's just say that there may have been some problems in one or two business activities that your husband may be able to help us with.'

'What! What do you mean help you with?'

'Mrs. King, did your husband have any savings accounts? I mean any accounts other than his cheque account.'

'I think he had a building society account with the Nantwich.'

'How much was in it?'

'I don't know. We kept our finances pretty separate. A few thousand, I expect. We were saving up to do some improvement work on the hotel.'

Knowles looked around the room as if trying to gauge what improvements he would do to the place. 'So a few thousand quid then?'

'Yes.'

'Ten thousand?'

'No, I don't think it was that much.'

Knowles reached into his pocket and pulled out a piece of paper. It was statement for the Stretford and Provincial Building Society. Knowles held it part unfolded so that Tara could see the name and address, but not the current balance. She saw that the account was in Bradley's name and the address given was that of his old flat in Chapel Harrington. Knowles looked at Tara intently. 'Recognise this?' he said.

'No,' she said softly.

Knowles opened the statement fully so that Tara could see the present account balance. He continued to study her face. He needed to see her reaction.

'Not a hundred and fifty thousand quid then?'

Tara stared wide-eyed at the statement, and immediately put her hand to her mouth. She was quite unable to speak for several seconds.

'I… I never knew he had anything like that much!' Tara stammered.

Knowles folded the statement up and put it back in his pocket, satisfied.

'I know you didn't, Mrs. King. Thank you for your time,' he said. 'You've been most helpful. I'm sorry to have troubled you.'

As the detective stood and made to leave, Joshua said, 'But officer, what's this all about? What's he supposed to have done?'

'Well, like I said, it's still under investigation. My colleagues in Manchester have been watching this account for a few weeks now, but after a few fairly hefty withdrawals, we've actually had it frozen for the time being. One of the branches in Manchester confiscated the card that goes with it when Mr. King tried to make another withdrawal. Any more than that, I can't say at the moment. Oh, and should he contact you at all, Mrs. King, be sure to let me know.' Knowles smiled and handed her a card with his phone number on it.

'I'll see myself out,' he said cheerily.

When they were alone, Tara collapsed back in one of the lounge chairs.

'My God!' she said. 'It just gets worse.'

'Are you going to be OK?' said Joshua, as he put an arm around her.

'Yes, yes,' she said, putting her hand over his. 'I'll be fine. It's just such a shock. What on earth has he been up to? Where did he get that kind of money?'

'Not on an Assistant Manager's salary, that's for sure.'

After further inconclusive discussion, and more assurances from Tara that she would be all right, Joshua got up to go. Having earlier said goodbye to Rose and Fraser, he now did the same with Tara. She stood and held his hand.

'You'll keep in touch, won't you?' said Tara pleading.

'Sure,' said Joshua. 'But you've got Rose for support again, now.'

She looked forlornly into his eyes. 'Yes, I know,' she said, 'but... Now you've finished at Walklate's, you'll probably not come back to Bramton again. I might not... I need you.'

'I'll phone. And I'll come and stay again before Christmas. We can have another walk.'

'Promise?'

'I promise.'

Tara swallowed hard and could feel her emotions welling up again. 'I think I've cried more in the last few days than I have in the last ten years,' she said, putting her hands up to her face. She took a deep breath, and said, 'You'd better go.'

They looked into each other's eyes for a few seconds, as if reading each other's thoughts. Simultaneously they seemed to conclude that life was complicated enough as it was, and with a superhuman effort, Tara said quietly, 'Just go!'

She turned and ran from the room.

Chapter Twenty-seven

In early November, Theodore Walklate issued invitations to his fiftieth birthday party, to be held early in December up at Fallowfield Grange. As originally intended, he invited all the board of Walklate's and their spouses. He also invited some of the other senior management of the company and some of the key local suppliers. He invited Joshua Latham. Joshua readily accepted, and not only because of the prospect of sherry and mince pies in the draughty old country house. Amongst other local dignitaries invited were representatives of the hotel trade. Following the news of Bradley King's departure, a delegate from The Oakland was once more deemed acceptable to Theodore. Far too late to reinstate the company Christmas party there, Theodore felt disposed to invite some representative from the largest hotel in the area almost as some form of penance. Personally, knowing no one else connected with the current Travelite management, he invited the retired Jeremy Gillman and his wife. First on his list of local hoteliers was, of course, Tara King. He delivered her invitation personally. He did so on the pretext of not knowing whether or not to extend the invitation to include Tara's husband. In this he was disingenuous. His sources of information, as reliable and unimpeachable as ever, had indicated not even the remotest possibility of Bradley King being in residence at The Crown. If he had been, Theodore would have asked neither her nor her husband. Confident that Bradley was still mysteriously out of circulation, he wrote the invitation to Tara alone, and delivered it, with a suitable accompanying note, by hand.

When he'd first heard of Bradley's disappearance, Theodore had been both hopeful and incensed. Over the succeeding weeks, as the rumours and details filtered out, he'd grown even more livid. Gossip over Bradley's affairs, in more senses of the word than one, true or not, believable or not, only served to vindicate Theodore's view of the man. He thought Bradley King a completely unscrupulous lowlife, the total antithesis of all he, Theodore Walklate, believed in. Ironically, part of Theodore actually keenly anticipated the time when Bradley King would return, as surely one day he thought he must. He relished the prospect of Bradley getting the most well-deserved comeuppance. However, whatever King had done in his business affairs, whether illegal or merely immoral, Theodore knew King's punishment would be nothing compared to what he deserved for his treatment of Tara. Theodore Walklate still yearned for Tara. Bradley's exploitation of her he saw as nothing short of gross abuse, a complete betrayal. Theodore, having lost the woman of his dreams, the first real love of his life, he felt was bad enough, but seeing Bradley's humiliation of her had heaped utter misery on top of the original disillusionment.

Theodore's old-fashioned chivalry had placed him, he felt, in an invidious position. Tara, although notionally free of her husband, was still a married woman. In his view, any attempt by him to rekindle his previous, more amorous approach to Tara, would be clearly adulterous. His conscience wouldn't let him do this. His respect for Tara was too deep. He wouldn't dare cheapen his feelings for her with any coarse overtures. But still he wanted to be near her, talk to her, assure her of his support during her "difficult times". The party invitation, and the party itself were ideal opportunities, he thought, to let Tara know how he felt still, to let her know that she could avail herself of any help she needed, within the scope of his not inconsiderable power and influence.

He called at The Crown one cold, rainy afternoon in the second week of November to deliver the invitation. After an awkward start, their conversation flowed quite freely. Tara found Theodore very sincere and well meaning. He was entirely gentlemanly, as ever, in his approach, and very reassuring towards her. If there was anything, simply anything, that he could do to help her, she had only to call him. As she confirmed that Bradley was still missing and had not been in contact, Theodore fought to control his rising anger. He thought Tara looked pale and drawn, her vivaciousness crushed, her smile far less ready than he remembered. He burned inside at the thought of how Bradley had brought her to this state. He so desperately wanted to comfort her, to hold her in his arms, but instead, with great effort, he had to content himself with simple words.

Theodore pressed her for an affirmative response to the party invitation there and then. He told her that there would be people attending that she would know. There would be people from Walklate's whom she would have met before, and of course there would be "that Joshua Latham chap", whom he understood had stopped at The Crown before now. Tara smiled at this, and assured Theodore that she would reply to his kind invitation within days. She duly wrote him a letter of acceptance, having first phoned Joshua for a chat and to confirm that he, too, would be attending the party.

The day of the party, a Saturday, arrived. Joshua had travelled up to Bramton late on the Friday afternoon and had spent a convivial evening with his friends at The Crown. During the day he and Tara had once again taken Bess up to Three Counties Head, although this time the weather precluded a picnic. In the evening, Joshua and Tara stepped into Bob Lumsden's taxi for their ride up to Fallowfield Grange. With a mere three other guests in The Crown, they left Fraser and Rose to another quiet evening together in the bar.

Joshua and Tara sat in the back seat of the taxi. Out of Lumsden's view in the driving mirror, Joshua discreetly held Tara's hand and gave her some whispered assurance about the evening ahead. As per the invitations, Joshua wore a dark lounge suit, and Tara an evening dress. Looking at the pale blue, silk-finished dress, Joshua couldn't help but smile as he remembered the previous time he'd seen it. Before they'd left The Crown, he'd told Tara how beautiful he thought she looked. He'd then tempered this by saying that if his memory of Fallowfield served him, she would likely freeze to death in the thin, backless creation. She'd smiled and fetched herself a shawl to wear over the top.

They arrived at Fallowfield. As Joshua paid off the ever-smiling taxi driver, Lumsden gave him a conspiratorial wink. The interior of the house was as vast, and almost as cold, as Joshua remembered. But Theodore Walklate had made great efforts. All the downstairs rooms were heavily decked out in Christmas decorations, and a huge illuminated and tinsel-covered tree sat in the hall. Outside caterers had worked under Janice Hartle's direction to prepare, set out and serve a wonderful buffet in the dining room, fit for the fifty or so guests. A rear study had been converted to a makeshift bar, and the front lounge, largely stripped of its furniture, had been given over to music and dance. This alternated between a string quartet playing live, and a hired DJ playing music more suited to "the younger ones".

Tara circulated between the lounge, where she enjoyed listening to the music, and the dining room, where she could pick at the food and warm herself by the roaring log fire. With Tara elsewhere, Joshua was standing in the dining room talking to Jeremy Gillman when Theodore Walklate came up to join them in conversation.

★★★

As the party at Fallowfield was in full swing, Fraser and Rose had their quiet evening at The Crown interrupted. Sitting alone together in the bar, they heard the front door open. Rose got up to see who the visitor was, but even before she could get out of the bar, the door burst open. Standing before them was Bradley King.

Dressed in jeans, trainers, an old jumper and a donkey jacket, he looked tired, thin and gaunt.

'Bradley!' said Rose.

'Where is she?' he barked before Rose could formulate any questions.

'Tara, you mean?'

'Yes, of course!' Bradley snapped. He looked agitatedly around the room.

'She's gone out.'

'Where?'

'She's gone to Mr. Walklate's birthday party.'

'Him!' exclaimed Bradley.

'He's fifty today. It's up at Fallowfield Grange,' volunteered Rose. 'Oh, Bradley, where have you been? Tara's been worried about you.'

'I bet she has,' he said scornfully.

'We all have.'

'Don't give me that shit. I bet you were all glad to see the back of me. When's she due back?'

'Probably not until midnight or so.'

'Too late.'

He quickly turned and made to go out of the bar. Before he reached the door, he turned back to face both Rose and Fraser.

'Listen! Neither of you have seen me here tonight. Got that?'

'Yes,' said Rose meekly.

Bradley turned again and went back to the hall. Instead of going out of the front door though, he bounded up the stairs. Rose and Fraser looked uncertainly at each other. Hearing the noise of banging doors upstairs, they gingerly made their way out to the hall. Within minutes, Bradley came back down the stairs carrying a small holdall. At the bottom of the stairs he paused, and again told them not to tell anyone that he'd been back.

'What about Tara?' said Rose to Bradley as he opened the front door. 'We must tell her.'

'Oh, she'll find out soon enough!' he said, closing the door behind him. Rose and Fraser rushed to the front door only to see Bradley getting into an old estate car. It was parked half on the pavement in front of the hotel with its hazard warning lights flashing. Bradley got into the driver's seat, started the engine, and soon sped off.

***

'So, how's retirement suiting you, Jeremy?' asked Theodore heartily.

'Not bad at all, really, although I did go back for a few weeks back in September.'

'Really?' said Joshua. 'I thought you couldn't wait to get out of the place. Ready for retirement and all that.'

'Well,' said Gillman slowly, 'it was only a relief stint for a few weeks, just to tide 'em over before the chaps from Head Office could make a more permanent arrangement. There'd been a spot of bother over my successor, you see. You must know him, Joshua. He was my Assistant Manager at the time. Bradley King. Did you recall him?'

'Yes,' said Joshua dryly. 'I remember him. What sort of bother?'

Theodore merely stared at the former manager of The Oakland Hotel. Gillman, oblivious to the unnaturally rapt attention he had now generated, blundered on.

'Well,' he said, 'it was all pretty embarrassing really, but it transpired that our Mr. King was on the take. To be honest, his little scam must have started in my time, but there you go.' Gillman looked suitably contrite at this point. 'But anyway, it only came to light when the head housekeeper, a woman called Anne Barrowclough – you must have seen her about the place too – she uncovered a few, shall we say, discrepancies in the laundry returns. Super woman, Anne, one of the old school, very reliable. She had a thing about Bradley King. Not like that, I mean. She really didn't like the man. I never knew why. Most of the other women were falling over themselves to get their hands on him. One of Anne's girls was even engaged to King at one time. Tragically she got killed...'

'Yes, yes,' said Theodore somewhat impatiently. 'So what was it exactly that King was up to?'

'Oh, yes,' resumed Gillman. 'Anyway, Anne couldn't really stand the sight of our young Bradley, and, well, I don't know how she managed it, but one day she came across some of the laundry returns. This was not long after I'd left.'

'What do you mean, "laundry returns"?' asked Joshua.

'Well, at a place like The Oakland, we have a contractor who does all our laundry. You know, washes all the sheets, tablecloths, that sort of stuff. They collect and deliver three or four times a week. They're a company called Summer Park. It's a national contract that Travelite has with them, but we deal with their Manchester office. Anyway, every time they deliver and collect stuff, Anne signs a return. It just itemises the amount of stuff to launder. That then forms the basis of Summer Park's charges to us. So one day, Anne Barrowclough comes across copies of some these returns, and…' Gillman now leaned forward and lowered his voice, 'they were all signed by Bradley King, and Anne didn't recognise any of 'em! King was obviously filing false returns. Effectively making it seem as though we were asking Summer Park to launder more stuff than they really were. Well! Anne agonised over what to do for a week or more.'

Gillman smiled smugly. 'I'm sure she would have confided in me if I'd still been there. In the end, she tipped off some chap at Head Office, and they obviously did some snooping around. On receipt of the false returns, Summer Park then sent out invoices for all this stuff they hadn't laundered. And who was it authorising all the invoices for payment on behalf of Travelite? None other than Bradley King! I always wondered why he was so keen to do that little administrative chore. He was obviously in with some bent employee within Summer Park. I don't know how they managed it after that, but apparently when Travelite paid the invoices, the money for the "extras" somehow got diverted into the private bank account of this Summer Park employee. He then split the proceeds with King. All very crafty, but they hadn't banked on the eagle-eyed Anne Barrowclough.'

'Very cunning,' said Joshua.

'A few days later, bang! The balloon goes up. The chaps came from HO, mob handed, to see King. They'd got plenty of evidence, but it was all really a bit circumstantial. All payments to King apparently were strictly cash. Difficult to prove anything with certainty.'

'So they made him resign?' said Joshua.

'Yes,' said Gillman. 'As I say, it was difficult to prove anything for sure, and Travelite never wanted to get the police involved – bad publicity and all that. So they just gave him the chance to resign, and he did.'

'How much did he get away with?' asked Theodore.

'Oh, I suppose we'll never know for sure, but several tens of thousands of pounds.'

'What!' exclaimed Theodore. 'That much! The absolute rogue!'

As he'd listened to the whole sorry tale unfold, he'd progressively become more and more incensed. He was now quite red-faced, and he shook his head in disbelief.

'Yes,' said Gillman. 'You'd be surprised – big hotel like The Oakland. You cream off an extra ten or fifteen per cent of the laundry bill, and it soon mounts up. And we'd no idea really how long it'd all been going on for. And the best bit is, they now think there were other suppliers too, like the brewery company, who were supposedly in on a similar scam. Huh! The sky's the limit! Who knows how much money he salted away?'

'Bloody amazing,' said Joshua.

'So there's Bradley,' continued Gillman, 'having lost his job, thinking that everything had blown over…'

Gillman was now positively gleeful. Still he didn't query why he commanded as much of Theodore and Joshua's attention as he did. At that moment, the three men were aware of raised voices and what sounded like a woman's scream coming from the hall. Thinking simply that the party was getting slightly high-spirited, they concentrated on Gillman's continuing monologue. Theodore looked up impatiently in the direction of the hall, but recognising that Gillman hadn't quite finished, turned back to the former hotel manager.

'Travelite may not have wanted to involve the police, but Summer Park, once they discovered that they'd got a crooked employee, certainly did. They called in the Old Bill.'

Gillman chuckled. 'Oh dear,' he sighed with a smile. 'Young Bradley obviously got wind of their investigations, and decided to scarper, lie low for a bit. Ha!'

'So that's why he suddenly decided to run off,' said Joshua thoughtfully.

'Yes, but I'm sure he'll get caught eventually.'

Again, raised voices were heard, and this time, one was clearly that of a woman screaming.

'Excuse me,' said Theodore, as he dashed off towards the hall.

★★★

Bradley pulled up in front of Fallowfield Grange. He got out of the car and rang the front doorbell. It was soon opened by a member of the catering staff. Bradley pushed past the young girl.

'I'm sorry sir,' she said. 'Have you got an—'

'Shut it!' snarled Bradley. 'I've come for my wife.'

At precisely that moment, Tara came out of the lounge and into the hall. As soon as she saw Bradley she froze.

'There you are!' he said. 'God, it didn't take this old sod long to start sniffing around you again.'

'Bradley!' she said. 'What are you doing here? Where have you been?'

Her voice was shaky. She continued to stare at him. He advanced towards her, and she took a step backwards.

'Have you got your handbag with you?'

She looked puzzled, and he repeated the question, almost shouting, insistent.

'It's in the cloakroom. But Bradley, what is it? What do you want?'

'Go and get it!' he shouted. Some of the other guests, alerted by the raised voices, looked in his direction.

'Why? What do you want?' said Tara.

He could hear the fear in her voice. He advanced towards her, threateningly. He grabbed her arm. Tara screamed. She had a glass of wine in one hand. As Bradley shook her to add urgency to his words, she dropped the glass. It shattered as it hit the floor.

'We're leaving. Now, just go and get your bloody handbag!'

She quickly turned and ran to the downstairs cloakroom, designated that evening for the use of the ladies. Bradley paced around the hall, waiting for her. Other guests began to stare at the ill-dressed intruder and murmured amongst themselves. Bradley could see their expressions of distaste. Tara collected her bag and shawl. She cowered in the cloakroom for a minute, wondering if she should stay there. But she knew he'd soon come for her. She emerged from the cloakroom, her shawl draped over her arm. She came within a few feet of Bradley, and stopped, overcome with fear.

'Where are we going?' she said.

'The bank. I need money.'

'But… I don't want to go.'

A member of the catering staff now appeared with a dustpan and brush and proceeded to sweep up the broken glass, all the time glancing up at the arguing couple. Other partygoers started to drift into the hall to see what the commotion was all about.

'Come on!' he said, 'I've got a car outside.'

'A car?'

'Yes,' he said, sighing. 'A fucking car! You can't sleep in a motorcycle. Now come on!'

Bill Hunter, who had come in from the lounge, stepped up.

'Excuse me,' he said, addressing Tara. 'Is this man bothering you?'

'Keep out of this, you!' shouted Bradley. He lunged forward and grabbed Tara by the wrist. She screamed and tried to wriggle free.

'King!'

The word was bellowed at a volume easily heard above the music that filtered in from the lounge nearby. Bradley stopped and looked up as soon as he heard the shout. Tara pulled her arm free.

'How dare you!' shouted Theodore Walklate, advancing into the hall. 'How dare you show your face in this house!'

Theodore's face assumed a hideous, almost purple, hue. His fists by his side were tightly clenched.

'I will not stand by and see you abuse that woman anymore! You will leave her alone immediately!'

Theodore almost screamed the words. Bradley noticed, as he had once before, the engorged blood vessel in Theodore's neck. Bradley thought the man about to explode.

It was Bradley's turn to shout. 'You don't tell me what to do with my wife.'

'Get out of my house this minute, or…' raged Theodore.

'Or what, old man?'

'Theodore!' Unseen, Marjorie Forsythe had joined the crowd now gathered in the hall. 'Don't let him antagonise you. Don't let him spoil your—'

'Shut up!' bellowed Theodore.

'Come on, Theo,' said Bill Hunter, pulling at Theodore's arm. Joshua now advanced through the crowd. Across the hall his eyes met Tara's. She stood helpless, almost pleading.

Theodore, impotent, turned in disgust and left the room, shouting over his shoulder, 'Just get that damn man out of here!'

An awkward silence prevailed, before Joshua said, 'Bradley! Please. Leave Tara alone. She's frightened. She doesn't want to go with you.'

'My!' said Bradley sarcastically. 'How touching! Well, Tara my dear, you don't seem short of gallant gentlemen here, do you? Too bad, none of 'em are man enough to do anything about it. Come on. We're leaving. We've wasted enough time with these bastards.'

Bradley, reaching forward, retook Tara's arm. She protested. Joshua was about to intervene when he felt himself pushed aside from behind. There was a deafening report from over his shoulder. A shot had been fired. Bradley's body jerked backwards. A look of absolute amazement spread over his face. As he clutched his hands on an ever-increasing red patch over his stomach, he staggered backwards. He reached an arm out and grabbed Tara's shoulder. She let out a piercing scream. Apart from Bradley, everybody stood stock still. Theodore Walklate advanced further through the crowd, and again put his shotgun to his shoulder. Before anyone could grasp the reality, a further shot sounded. Bradley recoiled again. He brought his other arm up and fell against Tara. The pair staggered backwards and collapsed together in a bloodied heap on the floor.

'No!' screamed Tara. Willing hands quickly rushed to her and tried to haul her to her feet.

'No!' she shouted again, shaking them off. She remained slumped on the floor, kneeling by the prostrate figure of her husband. Theodore Walklate lowered his weapon, and glowered through the clearing smoke at the prone body on the floor of his home. He turned and quietly walked away. As he passed a stunned Bill Hunter he said, in a very calm, quiet voice, 'Bill, I'm just going to lock my gun away, then I'll phone the police. I'll wait for them in the kitchen. Would you see to the guests, please.'

Bill stared at Theodore in disbelief as the man walked out of the hall. In spite of the ringing everyone now heard in their ears, the hall was actually in complete, stunned silence save for the sound of Tara gently weeping as she cradled her husband's head in her lap.

Joshua knelt beside Tara and put his arm around her. She stroked Bradley's cheek, her pale blue dress now liberally spattered with blood and gore. Bradley's eyes still looked at her imploringly. He made to speak. Tara lowered her head to his face. She heard a gurgle in the back of his throat. She hugged his head to her breast. After a minute she slowly raised her head and looked again at Bradley's face. His eyes still looked at her, his expression unchanged. She let out a wail and hugged him tightly to her body once more. She continued to weep, but quietly now, silent tears running down her cheeks.

Epilogue

In early April, some four months after the death of Bradley King, Joshua Latham and Tara were, once again, sampling the Italian cuisine of La Scala in Bramton.

'So,' said Tara, 'tell me all about it. How did it go today?'

'It's difficult to be sure really. I wasn't the only one interviewed. There was one other external candidate and one from within Walklate's.'

'Who did the interviewing?'

'Bill Hunter. He's in charge there now. They made him acting Managing Director within days of Theodore's arrest. Theodore in fact, resigned more or less straight away, although I think he still retains some shares. It was only after the court case that they confirmed Bill as the permanent MD. Obviously they now want to appoint a new Production Director, and that's what I applied for. To be honest, the self-employed consultancy crack just isn't working. As I've said before, I've been applying for jobs back in corporate employment. I think it suits me better. This job at Walklate's isn't quite the way you think of job opportunities arising, but it's a good one, and I'm sure I can do it, so why not?'

'I'm sure you can, and I bet you did really well today, too. They'll give the job to you.' She reached across the table and patted the back of his hand.

'I'd give it fifty-fifty, myself. We'll see. Anyway, I should know within a week, and I've obviously also got the advantage of being able to start more or less immediately.'

'You'd have to move.'

'Yes, but there's a relocation package. They'd help me sell my place down south, legal stuff and help to buy a place around here. They'd even pay for temporary accommodation for a short time while I looked around too.' He grinned. 'Like modest hotel charges.'

Tara smiled. 'Well, you'd better find somewhere cheap then, hadn't you? Our prices have gone up now.'

'Yeah, so I'd noticed.'

'Don't worry,' she said teasingly. 'You qualify for special discount!'

The Crown now boasted central heating to the top floor and all but two of the bedrooms were now ensuite.

'How did you finance the work in the end?' asked Joshua.

'The bank,' said Tara. 'The rates weren't bad, and to be honest there was no other way. All of Bradley's money, if indeed it is his money, is still frozen. The police are still investigating it all. It could go on for absolutely years. And I couldn't very well ask Theodore Walklate, even though I suspect he'd still be prepared to lend me money, poor man.' She looked momentarily downcast. 'I often think about him.'

'I'm sure you do,' said Joshua. 'We all do. But it was just one of those things. He was just a time bomb ticking away. You shouldn't blame yourself because you happened to be closest when he went off.'

'I was more than just the closest. I was really the cause of it all.'

'Don't be so hard on yourself. You didn't pull the trigger.'

Tara shuddered. 'How long will he be in prison for, do you think?'

'Well, for life imprisonment these days, they reckon on about ten to twelve years for good behaviour. And if there's one thing we can be sure of, Theodore Walklate'll be an absolutely model prisoner.'

The couple were silent for a while, finishing their coffee.

'Are you OK?' asked Joshua.

'Yes. It's just when I stop and think about the last eighteen months or so; I feel I've learnt an awful lot about myself. I've made mistakes, particularly in the way I've behaved to people around me.' She looked pointedly at Joshua. 'But I'd like to think I've learnt my lessons.'

'I'm sure you have,' said Joshua, as he requested the bill from a passing waiter.

The two argued over who should pay for the meal this time. Tara won, partly on the grounds that Joshua had paid previously, but mainly because she pinched the bill as soon as the waiter had put it down.

Afterwards, they walked slowly, via a slightly circuitous route through the park, back to The Crown.

'How are Rose and Fraser?' asked Joshua.

'They're fine,' said Tara. She surreptitiously linked her arm through Joshua's. 'Same as always. Fraser still lives with his mum, but I think he and Rose are saving up for a house. They may even get married one day. And, would you believe, he's started having driving lessons.'

They were now in sight of The Crown.

'Do you fancy a sitting for a while,' suggested Tara, pointing to a park bench, 'as it's fairly mild out this evening?'

Joshua agreed and they sat on the bench. Their conversation continued distractedly for some minutes, before Joshua shivered.

'It's not that mild,' he said, arising from the bench. 'Shall we go in? Rose and Fraser'll be wanting to walk the dog as well.'

Tara reluctantly stood up too. Joshua looked up at the sky. 'Clouds are breaking up, you see. That's why it's cooling off so quickly.'

As he continued to stare skywards, Tara moved closer. She could feel his breath on her face.

'You can see quite a few stars now,' he said. 'I wonder if you can see—'

'Joshua.'

He looked down at Tara. He was surprised to see her quite so close. She was looking intently into his eyes.

'Yes,' he said slowly.

'Can we just skip the Brian Cox bit…'

'Sure,' he said warily.

'And just kiss me.'

He lowered his head to hers. Their lips met. It was a short kiss. They continued to look at each other. She smiled. He looked dumbfounded. She reached up and put her arms around his neck. He slipped his arms around her waist. Their next kiss was gentle, long and passionate.

★★★

Within a week, Joshua Latham was confirmed as the new Production Director of Walklate and Co., starting work the following Monday. He travelled up to Bramton on the Sunday before, driving a heavily laden estate car, hired specifically for the purpose of transporting a lot of his personal effects. As he approached The Crown Hotel, he noticed Tara in her car, just ahead of him. He was about to flash his headlights to attract her attention when his mobile phone rang. On the display he saw that it was his new boss, Bill Hunter, calling. He watched Tara swing into the drive of The Crown a short way ahead of him. As he followed, he reached for the phone, nestling in its cradle, in order to accept the call. At the same time he swung his car around to park next to Tara's. Distracted by his phone, he misjudged the situation. He stamped on the brakes but was a little late in doing so. There was a slight crunch as the front bumper of his car clipped the taillight of Tara's.

'Damn!' he said.

He stopped, got out and walked around the car to inspect the damage. Tara slowly got out of her car. Both stared at the small collection of broken glass on the floor near the rear of Tara's car.

'Oh, Tara,' he said, 'I'm ever so sorry. I got distracted by my phone. I'll pay for the damage. Bloody hell! Sorry. God, what a fine start!'

He stopped his ramble and looked up from the broken glass to Tara. He was taken aback to see her smirking at him. 'What?' he said.

Tara now laughed out loud. Slowly the symmetry dawned on him too, and he shook his head. He slowly walked up to her. They put their arms around each other and kissed.

'Welcome to The Crown, Mr. Latham,' said Tara. 'How long is Sir intending to stay?'

'Forever.'

THE END

Acknowledgements

I acknowledge the impetus given me to write this novel in the first place by my good friend, Andrew Nichols. I'd been prevaricating for years, wanting to write a novel but failing to think of an original storyline. It was Andrew who told me to stop trying to think of a new story, just pick a favourite one and retell it. John Hill for giving me advice on paramedics' radio chit-chat. Similarly, Nic Davies for her insight into how the fire service deals with domestic callouts. And not least, my wife, Helen, who has stoically put up with conversing with the back of my head as I tapped away at a keyboard!